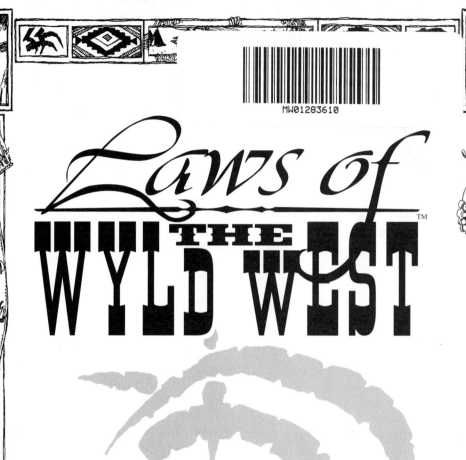

# Laws of the Wyld West™

**Written by Peter Woodworth**

# Credits

**Written by:** Peter Woodworth

**Development by:** Jess Heinig

**Editing by:** Cynthia Summers

Previously published material has appeared in: Laws of the Wild and Werewolf: The Wild West

**Art Direction by:** Lawrence Snelly

**Photography by:** Laura Robler

**Front and back Cover:** Ron Thompson

**Layout and typesetting by:** Ron Thompson

# Special Thanks to:

**Ken** "Twisting" **Cliffe**. Don't get yer knickers… well, you know.

**Justin** "Court Spice" **Achilli**, for the lessons that one learns — and none heed.

**Rich** "Oh, Hell" **Dansky**, for diving into the Hell of Additional Development.

**Ed** "Tire Irons & Machetes" **Hall**, while hunting for something hefty.

**Shane** "Three for One" **DeFreest**, after that brutal attack on the Brujah…

**Charles** "That's 'Mr. Tremere Lord' to you" **Bailey**, for finally turning to the Dark Side. Welcome, my son!

**Author's Dedication:**

For my mother, who taught me to love human nature for all the wonder and wildness that lies within us.

For my father, the last real cowboy and true Western spirit I know.

**Playtesting:** Sarah McIlvaine, Jim Vasquez, Jody Gerst, Alyson Gaul, Julie Miller, Rachel Biren, Tracy Miller.

One World Phoenix: Michael McLaughlin, Krissy Ryan, Christi Lawson, Wendy Walters, Andy Knudsen, Bryan Culp.

Graven Images Playtesters: Marc Spencer, Tori Mauslein, Geoff Hinkle, Mike Metcalf, Shannon Cass, David Blackwell, David Flannery, Mike Chambers, Stacey Flannery.

WHITE WOLF GAME STUDIO

735 PARK NORTH BLVD.
SUITE 128
CLARKSTON, GA 30021
USA

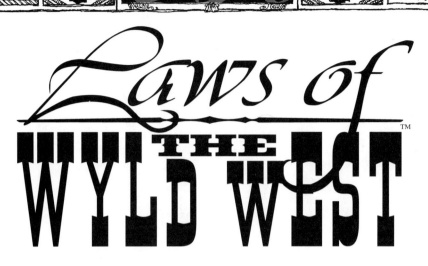

# Laws of the Wyld West™

## TABLE OF CONTENTS

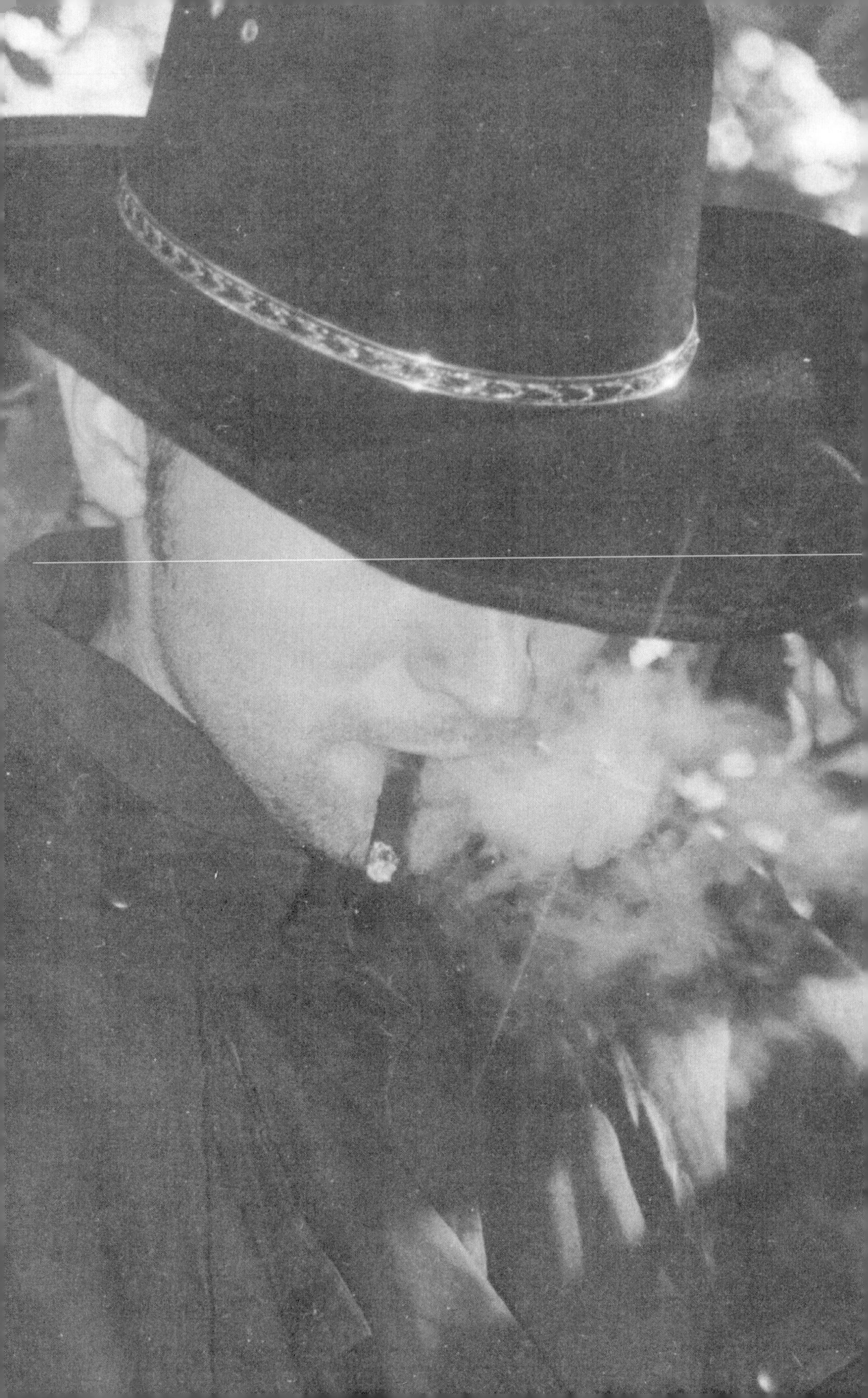

# Injun Magic: A Coyote's Tail

Buzzards shrieked and winged up into the sky overhead as the two riders approached the remnants of the wagon train, the stench of decay wafting on the tiny breeze that stirred above the dusty land. One of them, much older and heavier and with a bright silver star attached to the breast of his beaten brown shirt, dismounted and took in the grisly scene. Five wagons were overturned in the drifting sand, their contents strewn about crazily, but that was not what caught his eye. Remains of a small fire glared blackly at him, the ground around it littered with bodies, some nothing but bleached bones, but others recent enough to be giving off the stink he'd smelled a hundred yards away. No telling what had killed the skeletons, not without taking them back to town, but at first glance it would have been hard to place the origin of any of the seven other corpses as human. Maybe the buzzards had something to do with the gore, the sheriff thought, but he doubted that notion even as it occurred to him. Not even buzzards scattered bodies like this.

He shifted his considerable girth and planted his hands on his hips, ignoring the buzzing flies as best he could. So much for the wagon train he'd heard of coming through from Calder's Point a month or two back. He remembered being in Kat's saloon, that damn Chicano fella Lucas laughing at him and asking why a wagon train would stop by Dragon's Gulch when it could just as easily be gouged by another town with nicer stables. *Can't say I'd blame them, either*, that smirking loudmouth had said, flipping in the air one of those silver dollars that he always carried with him. *It's just your smiling face that keeps me here, Sheriff Burton*. Damn mutt. Probably stole those silver dollars from an honest man. Word about town said that Lucas was into strange Injun magic and other dark things, so Burton gave him and those no-account friends of his a wide berth just to be on the safe side. Still, he'd love to put that grinning face behind bars given just half a chance. He cracked his knuckles, smiling slightly at the picture.

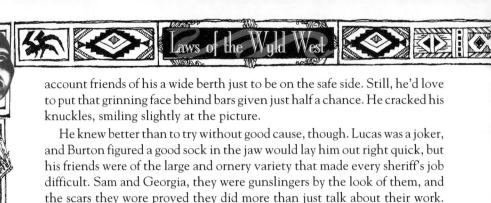

He knew better than to try without good cause, though. Lucas was a joker, and Burton figured a good sock in the jaw would lay him out right quick, but his friends were of the large and ornery variety that made every sheriff's job difficult. Sam and Georgia, they were gunslingers by the look of them, and the scars they wore proved they did more than just talk about their work. Then there was that Irish drifter, Pat what's-her-name — not only could she throw a knife through a dollar from a hundred yards but, what's worse, she had drunk Burton under the table one Friday night in front of half the damn town. She still laughed at him whenever he came in for a restorative after duty was over, her and that skinny little doctor who taken to spending time with her. Even Kat and that nice, rich Miss Lily from back East seemed partial to that damn Chicano, no matter how much Burton tried courting either of them. A damn mutt with a mutt collection of friends, that's what it was! It was enough to set his blood boiling.

Not only that, but Lucas had been right after all, at least about the wagon train. Privately, Sheriff Burton *had* wondered where the wagon train had gotten to, but figured just Devil's Drop or another town on the line. Now this. Good Lord, what a mess.

"Deputy Long," he said at last, chewing thoughtfully on his tobacco. "Come on over an' tell me what you think."

Blanched and sweating to begin with, the younger man got within six steps of the sheriff before he threw his hand over his mouth and turned aside at the gruesome sight. The sheriff stared impassively at him until he had regained his nerves. "Sorry, sir," he said, an embarrassed flush battling the paleness of his cheeks, "I just ain't never seen anythin' quite this bad before."

"No, I reckon not," the sheriff waved dismissively. "Can't say I've seen much in this way either. You fit now, deputy?" The younger man nodded, looking almost absurdly small under his wide ten-gallon hat, and the sheriff walked over to the first of the bodies, whose arms, legs and a good share of his guts were now all keeping house separately. His eyes, though filmy and clouded in death, were still wide enough that there was no question he had died frightened out of his wits. Burton examined the corpse's right hand and the pistol he still clutched in a deathgrip; the fingers were bloody and raw, and the trigger lay in the sand a foot or two away — he had torn it clean out in his panic. A cheap pistol maybe, but still no mean feat. "What d'you make of this one here?"

Deputy Long swallowed hard, his normally high-pitched and youthful voice — it always cracked at the worst of times, much to his chagrin — still an octave too high. "Looks like he an' his... friends came after this group was long dead, sir."

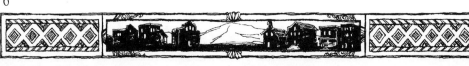

"Maybe. Any notion a' what killed 'em?"

"Looks like… wild animals, sheriff. Wolves, coyotes maybe."

The sheriff grunted. "Naw, a coyote'd never have the nerve to attack a gang this big. Wolves, maybe, though I ain't ever seen wolves take to territory like this, not around here leastaways." He spat, a dark splotch on the pale ground. "Damnation! Well, deputy, you go on an' check those other bodies over there for bullet holes, see if maybe the wolves didn't come after somethin' else already got these poor bastards."

"Yes, sir." The "sir" was so weak the sheriff just rolled his eyes and waved the younger man away with one meaty hand.

"Aw, hell, Long, I'll do it myself! You just check the wagons, see if anythin' of value's left — or if it looks like somethin' real valuable's gone missin'. And keep your eyes open for tracks — horse, man, wolf, whatever."

"Yes, sir." Relief fairly gushed from Long's voice, and he was off faster than a scalded jackrabbit. Sheriff Burton sighed and leaned to the unpleasant task of figuring out just what (*didn't he mean who?* nagged his mind) had killed a whole group of strong men and possibly a wagon train before that — and what had scared armed men so badly before tearing them apart.

Burton had finished looking over all the fresh bodies, and his first hunch had been right — two of the men had bullets punched into them, one damn near full of lead from head to toe, and another had been torn up good by a real large *something* — but not before a knife had been liberally applied to his throat and midsection. The cuts were clean and skilled, almost like a butcher's work, and he thought grimly to himself that's exactly what it had been. Murder, plain murder, and he liked it that way — nasty stuff, but people had been killin' each other since Cain and Abel, and he knew how to handle that.

It was the other bodies that worried him — no bullets, no knives, just huge gashes that were unmistakably claw tracks and worry marks that belonged to sets of fangs too big to think about. Burton had seen a body torn apart by a cougar once, but this… *animal* must make a cougar look like Sarah Ann's little old housecat Patches. "Maybe they were wounded when they were fightin', and then the animals got 'em," he whispered aloud, half-convincing himself. "Yeah, I reckon that was it. A whole pack of wolves, well, it could look like one big wolf if they all fell on a man."

Trouble was two things: one, there were boot tracks among the scattered wolf prints he found near a couple of the bodies. (Wolf prints that measured the length of his boot, that is, but he figured that was because of the way the ground had shifted. *Had* to be.) Now, it was easy enough to think that the boots had been there before or after the wolves, but something in his head told them that wasn't the case. Whoever had left those tracks had been there *with* the wolves, not apart from them. But who kept pet wolves, especially ones as big and vicious as these ones must've been? Hell, who could tame such monsters to begin with?

What's more, there were no wolves around, had never been in his life, just like he said; he knew the signs of wolf attacks from his days on his family's ranch up north, and the last time he had come across a carcass wolves had been at was over 12 years ago. Unwanted, his mind kept turning back to the fear in the dead men's eyes, which had been the same in every single staring crow-picked pair. When Deputy Long called out, a shrill cry in the windy silence, Sheriff Burton thought he would jump out of skin. His heart raced in his ample chest, and it took a deep breath to quiet it before he answered. "What is it, deputy?"

"I — I think I found something big, sheriff!"

Sheriff Burton came around the back of a wagon rolled on its side, and saw Deputy Long sitting by a heavy wooden chest. It was battered and the iron bindings that held it closed had been twisted nearly off, and Deputy Long was rubbing his eyes. "Why'dja holler like that? What is it? What'd you find?"

The deputy pointed out across the flat land. "I found tracks, sheriff, leading away from the train. Couple of horses and a pair of boots, looks like." He gulped and gestured to the box. "I found this half-under the wagon, lid still on, but when I went to open it, well, I guess I just had a little flash a' heatstroke, an' I thought I saw somethin' spring out at me, that's all." He stood shakily. "It does look a bit like a strongbox, but somebody's got at it already." He turned the box back upright and almost yelped again at something carved into the top of the box. "Sheriff, look at this!"

Some kind of symbol had been scratched deep into the heavy wood with rough strokes, a spiral shape with three big gashes cut through it. Below that were three words carved in the same crude hand, slashed into the heavy wood with an angry slant:

*DIE WYRM SPAWN*

"What the hell do you think that means, sheriff?"

"Damned if I know," Sheriff Burton said, feeling irritated and somehow small, as if he was seeing part of a larger picture and didn't understand what that could be. "Probably some outlaw warning or some such nonsense, so's to scare people away from followin' them." He ignored the deputy's politely unconvinced shrug and peered inside the box. "Now let's see what they everyone got killed for." He caught sight of something, licked one finger and fished around the bottom of the box. He brought his finger back up, coated in an unmistakable yellow substance. Deputy Long gaped as Burton whistled. "Gold dust," the sheriff breathed. "Box's coated with it. Damn thing must've been full a' gold before it was gotten into."

"How much would it be worth, you think?"

"More 'n enough to kill for, that's certain," Burton answered, his mind turning this information over. Wiping his finger carefully on his denim pants, he stood, his voice keeping pace with his thoughts. "Tell me what'cha think of this, deputy," he began, wanting no such response. "The wagon train's carrying this here gold, I dunno what for, but we can telegraph Big John in Calder's Point to find out."

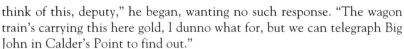

"Sure, sheriff."

"This gang gets word of the gold on the train," he kicked at one of the fresh bodies, "and they set up an ambush, I dunno how. They're carryin' enough powder to take out a whole train, though, if they've got the drop on 'em. So they kill the settlers, and they get to settin' up camp so they can divvy up the loot. Only somethin' goes wrong — somebody's holdin' out, two men find out they've been courtin' the same girl, anything — and they pull lead on each other. Big gunfight, some knives, and pretty soon most of 'em are dead and anyone who can still ride hauls out." He waved his hand vaguely at the tracks, which were neatly preserved in the soft, dry land. "Then out come the wolves," — he made a ghastly chopping gesture across his throat — "and that's the end of it for those who were still alive back here." And there it was, nice and simple and true to what he knew of most bandits, who'd kill each other for a nickel no matter what you heard about "outlaw loyalty."

Deputy Long gulped. "Then… then how come there're skeletons of some, and fresh bodies of others?"

Sheriff Burton's brow furrowed. "I dunno. Maybe some savages led 'em, maybe they left 'em out for the vultures early, who knows? They've been here a while as sure as I'm standin' here, and even these fresh ones here ain't smellin' like roses."

"Sorry, sheriff, I —"

"Don't worry 'bout it. Just take the chest and see if you can't find a way to get it back to town. Oh, and make sure there's nothing else like it lyin' around — I don't want any scavengers layin' claim to it." Burton was already walking over to the tracks in the dirt, ready to make a count so he knew how many survivors he'd be looking for before setting out for town again. Two, three, four sets of hooves, and the same pair of boot tracks from before, that looked like they ran alongside.…

Tobacco drooled unnoticed from Burton's mouth as it fell open. Just ahead of him, stretched out in the sand, the boot prints turned into coyote tracks. No question of being faked, erased or even followed — one minute they were regular footprints, the next four paws had run off. He could even see where the runner had planted his feet for a leap and where he had come back down with paws. He felt himself sitting hard in the dirt, half-speaking nonsense in his disbelief, when suddenly a glimmer next to the first coyote tracks startled him back to his senses. Reaching out with slightly trembling fingers, he plucked the object from the ground and examined it on his palm.

It was a shiny new silver dollar.

Far away, the high sound of a coyote's laughing howl carried on the wind.

# Chapter One: Introduction

## What This Book Is

You hold in your hands **Laws of the Wyld West**, a historical setting of live-action **Werewolf** rules for **Mind's Eye Theatre**. In essence, this book puts **Laws of the Wild** in a time machine, and transports the grim World of Darkness to the untamed wilds of the Savage West. New rules, powers and setting information add to the transformation, blending actual history with best of the classic westerns and the tragic fury of the Garou.

The game is still **Laws of the Wild** in many ways. It's just with six-guns now.

### Warning! Buy Our Stuff!

Due to space considerations, not every Gift and power can be reprinted from **Laws of the Wild**. If you don't already have a copy of that book, you'll need to purchase one before play. This book covers the special differences and setting of the Savage West, and some material was updated to cover minor changes in function or mood. However, **Laws of the Wild** is referenced heavily, and a copy of that book is necessary to play **Wyld West**.

Hey, we hate it as much as you — but we can only cram so much into one book.

## The Rules of Safety

Behave yourself so that everyone can enjoy this game. **Wyld West** is to be played in the home, at conventions or at other safe locations. At all times, you should remember that it is a game, only a game, and nothing but a game. If you feel yourself getting too wrapped up in what's going on, take a timeout and step back from gameplay for a moment. It's for your own good.

# The Only Rules That Matter

Here are the rules of **Mind's Eye Theatre (MET)**, the only rules that absolutely must always be obeyed. These are common sense rules to keep everyone — other players, yourself, strangers in the area and the police — safe and happy with your game.

These rules are designed to limit the opportunities anyone has to destroy the fun of your game. They're not intended to interfere with gameplay or your enjoyment; they're here to make sure that you play sensibly and safely.

## #1– It's Only a Game

This is by far the most important rule. If a character is killed, if a plot falls apart, if a rival wins the day — it's still only a game. Don't take things too seriously, as that will spoil not only your fun but also the fun of everyone around you.

Leave the game behind when it ends. Playing **Wyld West** is a lot of fun; spending time talking about the game is great. However, calling the person who plays the sept alpha at 4:13 a.m. on Sunday to discuss an idea your character has for a new rite is another matter entirely. Make sure to keep a little perspective.

## #2 – No Touching

Never actually have physical contact with other players, no matter how careful you are. Accidents happen, and someone will get hurt. Rely on the rules to cover physical logistics.

## #3 – No Stunts

Never climb, jump, run, leap or swing from anything during a game. Keep the "action" in your action low-key. If you can imagine you're a nine-foot-tall gunslinging werewolf, you can imagine that you're leaping across a ravine as well. Avoid attracting the attention of people who aren't playing, and use your imagination to its fullest.

## #4 – No Weapons

Fake or real weapons of any sort are absolutely forbidden. Even obviously silly toy weapons are not allowed. Such props give other people the wrong impression as to what you are doing, and in the dark they could conceivably be mistaken for the real thing. Use item cards to represent weapons instead, no matter how cool you think it would be to wear toy six-guns on your belt.

## #5 — No Drugs or Drinking

This one is a real no-brainer. Drugs and alcohol do not create peak performance. They reduce your ability to think and react, meaning that, among other things, your roleplaying ability will be impaired. Players impaired by drugs or alcohol are a danger to other players, and to the game as a whole. There's nothing wrong with *playing* a character who's drunk or stoned, but actually bringing such stuff to a game is in bad taste at best and illegal at worst. Don't do it.

## #6 — Be Mindful of Others

Remember, not everyone you see, or who sees you, is playing the game. A game can be unnerving or even frightening to passers-by. Be considerate of nonplayers in your vicinity, and make sure that if you are in a public area, your gameplay actions are not going to alarm anyone. Trying to explain that you didn't really kill your friend, your Get of Fenris just "throated" him, to a policeman at 3 a.m. is often an exercise in futility.

## #7 — The Rules are Flexible

Feel free to ignore or adjust any of the rules in this book if it will make your game better. We at White Wolf call this "The Golden Rule." If some rule included in this book (beyond the ones listed here) doesn't work for your troupe, change it. Just be consistent and fair. Nobody likes rules that change every week or "no-win" scenarios. If your troupe finds a new way to handle, say, the Storm Umbra, that works better for you than the one in this book, go for it. The idea is to have fun.

Another important point to express, especially with a historical setting, is the emphasis of fun over detail. If you troupe likes playing with period costumes, vocabularies and equipment, by all means enjoy yourselves -that's what a historical setting is all about. On the other hand, few things are as annoying as other people nitpicking your costume or your speech for "anachronisms" or spurning your character for being "too Hollywood." Many of us know this type of person from Renaissance faires or **Long Night** games, and they're just as irritating in the Savage West. It's one thing for a player to try to bring an Uzi to Dodge City, it's quite another for someone to miss when a style of clothing was invented by a year or two. Let the story dictate what's appropriate if any doubt exists, but most of all — relax.

## #8 — Have Fun

Not "Win." Not "Go out and kill everyone else." Just "Have fun." The object of **Wyld West** is not to win. In fact, there are no rules for "winning." The goal is to tell great stories, not to achieve superiority over the other players. In the Savage West it's not about how the game ends, it's about the journey and what happens along the way.

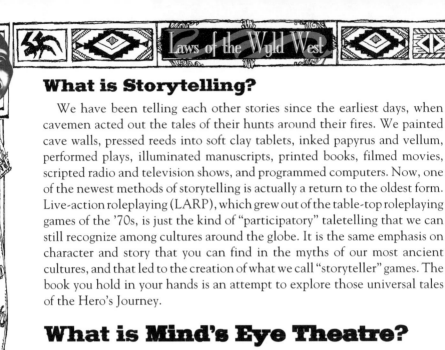

## What is Storytelling?

We have been telling each other stories since the earliest days, when cavemen acted out the tales of their hunts around their fires. We painted cave walls, pressed reeds into soft clay tablets, inked papyrus and vellum, performed plays, illuminated manuscripts, printed books, filmed movies, scripted radio and television shows, and programmed computers. Now, one of the newest methods of storytelling is actually a return to the oldest form. Live-action roleplaying (LARP), which grew out of the table-top roleplaying games of the '70s, is just the kind of "participatory" taletelling that we can still recognize among cultures around the globe. It is the same emphasis on character and story that you can find in the myths of our most ancient cultures, and that led to the creation of what we call "storyteller" games. The book you hold in your hands is an attempt to explore those universal tales of the Hero's Journey.

# What is Mind's Eye Theatre?

This game is probably different from any game you have played before. In many ways, this is really not a game at all. **Wyld West** is more concerned with stories than winning, rules, game boards or dice. You will find that this game has more in common with childhood games of adventure than with card games or *Monopoly*-type board games. This book contains all the information necessary to catapult you into worlds of imagination. You create the action, and you choose your own paths. We have a name for this style of game. We call it **Mind's Eye Theatre**.

Playing **Mind's Eye Theatre** is like being in a movie. You and your friends portray the main characters, but the script follows your decisions. The director of this improvisational movie is called the Storyteller; he, along with his assistants, called Narrators, creates the stage and the minor characters with whom you interact during your adventure. Most scenes are played out in real-time, and always in character. You should only break character when there is a rules dispute or a change of scene which requires adjudication from the Storyteller or Narrators.

In **Mind's Eye Theatre**, there are no limits to the worlds you can explore. In the Savage West, you will discover the breathtaking beauty of a pristine continent, as well as face one of the greatest threats to Gaia ever seen, a malevolent spirit known as the Storm Eater. You assume the persona of one of her guardians, and learn what it is to be a werewolf, one of the people called the Garou.

### The Character

When you play **Wyld West**, you take on the persona of a Garou, a defender of the world's natural places against the ravages of those who would corrupt, defile and destroy those few that remain. Your character can be anyone from any walk of life. The only limit on your character concept (besides the rules) is your imagination. You create a character, then roleplay her over the course of a story and perhaps a chronicle (a series of connected stories). You decide what your character does and says. You decide what risks to accept or to decline.

During the game, you speak as your character. Unless you're talking to a Narrator or Storyteller, whatever you say is what your character says. Because most of what a **Mind's Eye Theatre** player perceives depends on the characters around him, players must be vivid and expressive. The characters direct the plot, but at the same time the events of the game guide and develop the characters, helping them to achieve the story's goals. To an extent, as a player in a storytelling game, you have a responsibility beyond simply portraying your character. You need to consider the story as a whole and your role in making sure that other players enjoy the game.

Creating a character for **Wyld West** is easy and only takes a few minutes. Only a few things are necessary to define a basic character, and once you've done that, you can play the game. There's another phase to creating a character, though, one that makes playing **Mind's Eye Theatre** all the more rewarding. Your character should be more than just a series of Traits and numbers. Rather, she should be a living, breathing personality with a past, motives, drives, likes, dislikes — everything you want to see from a character in a movie or a novel. So it's probably a good idea to take time to figure out *who* your character is as well as what she is *before* you start playing. While certain details and personality traits will come out while you're playing her, you'll want to have the basics in place before you start playing. It's just like an actor asking his director for his character's motivation.

Characters are the heart and soul of a story. Without them, all the patient efforts of the Storyteller would be for naught. Appreciate the Storyteller's efforts by following the rules and taking an active part in the game.

## Narrators

In **Wyld West**, Narrators are the people who help the Storyteller present adventures. Narrators are the impartial judges who describe scenes and events that cannot be staged, adjudicate rules, and occasionally play the roles of antagonists. Generally, enlisting the aid of one Narrator for every 10 players makes for a good ratio. The best number of Narrators for your game usually depends on the gaming experience of the players; the more experienced your players, in all probability the fewer Narrators they'll need. Narrators usually play characters of their own as well as helping out certain situations. That way they can be a part of the action instead of just trying to correct it from the outside.

## Storyteller

Every game must have a Storyteller, who serves as the ultimate authority and final judge in any game of the **Wyld West** that you play. The Storyteller creates the basic elements of the plot, and makes sure that the story unfolds well — in addition to doing everything the Narrators do. Storytelling is a demanding job, but it is also a very rewarding one, for it is the Storyteller who creates the framework upon which the players build their experiences.

The Storyteller makes certain the story has content, interesting hooks and a narrative flow. This does not mean that a Storyteller should just sit back and dictate the plot — characters who don't have free will are no fun to play. Instead, a Storyteller creates the "framework" elements of the plot, then turns players loose in order see what happens.

During the game the Storyteller must be watchful and ready to create new elements to make sure that the story works out well. He is also responsible for safety, ensuring that all of the players have something to do, and that everyone is abiding by the rules. Although performing all of these tasks simultaneously can be exhausting, the sense of accomplishment gained from creating a successful story makes the whole process worthwhile.

In the end, the goal of **Wyld West** is for everyone to have fun.

## Props

Props can be anything that the Storyteller approves of that helps to define your character, including costumes, makeup and jewelry. Have fun and employ any props that you feel are necessary to enhance your character. However, if you have any doubts as to whether a prop (such as anything remotely resembling a weapon) will be allowed in-game, consult your Storyteller and abide by her decision.

## Elegantly Simple

This game was designed to be easy to learn and easier to play. **Wyld West** is a storytelling game. The rules are aimed at resolving conflicts quickly so that players can stay with the story without ever stepping outside their characters in order to figure out what happens. We have made every effort to create rules that maintain the integrity of the story and the background in which the story is set.

## Werewolf: The Apocalypse

The basic premise of **Wyld West** is derived from the table-top roleplaying game **Werewolf: The Wild West,** which is in turn derived from **Werewolf: The Apocalypse**. It is not necessary to own or know **Werewolf** in order to play **Wyld West**, but the world of **Werewolf** has many useful source materials which can be adapted easily for games based on **Wyld West**.

With this book as your guide, you will be able to tell stories about the secret defenders of the Earth. In the Savage West, you take the part of a Garou, a werewolf. Together with your shapeshifter brethren, you must heed Gaia's cry for help and try to defend the remaining wild places of the world in an era of expansion and turmoil. Welcome to **Mind's Eye Theater: The Wyld West**.

# The Savage West

The fictional time of **Wyld West** is based on the time we "know" all classic Westerns take place in, when settler families traveled west in search of a new land and a new life, while the natives who had lived there for centuries tried to adapt to the arrival of these strange people. However, it is still a time much like today: Children are born, grow up, work hard, grow old and die. The sun rises and sets day after day. However, this is not the Wild West of history texts or even Hollywood scripts. The land is harsher, the people harder, the world as merciless as the heat of the sun it burns beneath. This difference is expressed in the land itself: desolate wastelands, burning deserts, frozen woods and endless grasslands, most as yet unspoiled by civilization. Nature is more vibrant and alive than it ever was in reality, and it seems to carry a mighty grudge against those who would interfere with it — it is Savage in the classic sense. Society, too, has a touch of this darkness, its people more suspicious and cynical than was actually true to the times; to borrow the best of a classic phrase, lives are nasty, brutish and often far too short. And yet it is still the time of cowboys, quick-draws, bandits, boom towns, native pride and nights of coyotes howling that is familiar to us from countless movies and stories — the West in its biggest, boldest sense. That's why this time is called the Savage West, as it is the combination of these two elements that define the overall mood and setting of the game.

## Guardians of Dying Ways

It is not easy to understand the ways of the werewolves, or the Garou, as they call themselves, even when one bears the full heritage of their blood. They are not the mindless killers of Eastern European legend, nor are they the skin-changing medicine men of the native tribes, but the best and worst of both along with a whole lot in between. Garou are also not wholly wolves or humans, but rather a mystical sublimation of both into something as desperately natural as it is alien; in short, the Garou are a paradox even they themselves are hard-pressed to understand. It is simpler to simply be Garou than to explain Garou, as the eldest of them say, but that does not mean a werewolf is simple by any length. As protectors of ancient ways and keepers of legends from distant times, even the most urbane Garou born of European stock feels a tie to the earth far beyond the ken of most mortals. Surrounded by a world whose customs are rapidly growing foreign to them, Garou defend

Gaia the Earth Mother not from some modern notions of political or societal urgency, but simply because it is their way and always has been. They are genuinely confounded by those who would seek to use the earth without sustaining it, and their attachment to ways society finds increasingly outdated and unwise ostracizes them from those they seek to teach and protect. Even those born and raised among wolf stock find themselves isolated from the rest of their pack, made whole only once their true heritage has become known to them.

This game is about playing an individual on a quest to understand herself after a powerful revelation about her true nature, a change that makes her no longer merely a human or a wolf but something far greater, a shapeshifter. At the same time she comes to accept her place in this high and ancient culture, however, she must also come to terms with the growing darkness all around her and the terrible enemies who seek to lay waste to all she now holds dear.

Garou in the Savage West, whether born to European settlers or a native tribe, must balance their sacred duty to restore and protect a wounded earth with their responsibilities in the earthly realm as members of their respective cultures. Some choose to abandon their mortal ties altogether, so that they might serve Gaia more directly; this is a noble but taxing road, with only the company of one's packmates and sept companions to ease the trials of life. However, to the shame of all Garou, an increasing number choose instead to turn their backs on the great struggle and live their lives out as "normal" folk. Enemies of the Garou claim many of these deserters, but madness and despair still more, for while the fury of Gaia's fire seems a curse to many Garou, they are not and can never again be "normal," and only fellow shapeshifters truly understand the heavy burden they bear.

Garou are heroic, fearless, arrogant, compassionate, mysterious, predatory, angry, passionate, stubborn, rugged, wise, alien and noble. All Garou battle on behalf of Gaia, although a European and a native are likely to have very different notions of what exactly Gaia is. (Indeed, many werewolves and their kin have died over lesser matters in these antagonistic times.) It is important to note, however, that over all conflicts between tribes as to the specifics of Gaia's nature, no Garou dismisses the importance of the battle against the forces of decay and corruption embodied in the entity the Garou call the Wyrm. Agents of the Wyrm take advantage of the wide open spaces and worst parts of human nature in ever-increasing numbers, taking the timeless war between themselves and the Garou to all new fronts at a pace many Garou are at a loss to compete with. It's the reaping time of the age-old "adapt or die" the Garou themselves once fostered.

Now come close to the fire and listen as Lucas Laughs-At-Life, Nuwisha wanderer, relates the history of the Garou and the tragic times that have overtaken the nation.

## Legends of Loss, Struggle and Triumph: The First Times

I can see in your eyes that you're wondering why a Nuwisha, one who turns not into a wolf but a coyote, and who is one of Luna's forsaken, now stands before you ready to speak to you about the Garou. Some of the more perceptive folk among you are probably also wondering why a dusty Chicano such as myself speaks more like an Eastern university professor. Well, my life is a story for another time, but the first question underscores an important lesson about the West: few things are ever as they seem here, even the land itself. Do you really think a desert lies motionless? It swirls into storms, flows like the ocean and hardens like granite over time. And if such an easily noticed thing as a desert is never truly as it seems, how easy can it be to understand an ancient race like the Garou? I have spent my life watching their strange ways, sometimes walking among them under Coyote's veil, even claiming those who would have me as brothers, and while there is yet much that remains a mystery to me, I have been able to uncover many truths that I suspect even Garou are unable to, and that is why I speak to you now.

Yes, young ones, even such great beings as the Garou are often blind to their own failings, or unable to see past the limits and fences they crowd themselves with. That is, after all, why the Nuwisha were created, to show the Garou what lies beyond these fences, but that too is a tale for another time. Content yourselves in the meantime knowing that the Garou were not always this blind, nor must they be even now, as the greatest of them realize, and great is the fear of the Wyrm when it sees such a hero. What's that? What is the Wyrm? Oh, children, I envy your innocence! But patience- the tree must be felled before the bow may be carved, as my people say, and young arrows such as yourselves certainly must know the wood they are formed of before they can seek the hearts of their enemies. This tree has been passed down from the First Times in the form of ancient myths and legends, which the Garou call the Silver Record, and which I have had the good fortune to study at different times in my life.

The Silver Record is the memory of the Garou, and it records the greatest triumphs and darkest tragedies without mercy or fault. Each tribe knows it in different ways, as suits their own beliefs and prejudices, but at the heart it remains the same — an oral tradition that preserves the deeds of legendary Garou far beyond their own lifetimes. I can see that gleam in your eyes, the hope that you and your pack will someday be immortalized in the Silver Record. Well, take that to heart, young ones — such dreams are the stuff that heroes are made of, and such heroes are the stuff that dreams are made of. Speaking in riddles, you say? *Tsk tsk*, cubs — the Silver Record is seldom as direct as you would like to think. A legend about a powerful warrior conceals many other truths about honor, courage, duty and nobility within its folds, just as the tale of a tragic downfall cautions hot-blooded young folk to mind the risks of excessive pride and rage. Those who think myths are simply children's stories are doomed to remain children in their minds long after they have gone old and toothless. However, they *are* still wonderful stories, and that must not be forgotten. Quiet your restless selves and I'll tell you how the world began — and how it will end. The tale begins far beyond this smoky campfire and the glorious splash of stars, with the three great forces of the universe: the Wyld, the Weaver and the Wyrm.

## Three Eternal Forces Doomed to Battle

Before there was Gaia — what you call the Earth — there was nothing, a Void. This Void was colder than a creek bed at midnight and as empty as a saloon on Sunday morning, but that could not be for long. Nothingness, as my people say, is boring, and creation is nothing if not interesting. (I see by your smiles that you agree. Good. *Now hush!*) And so into creation came the three forces I spoke of: the Wyld, which embodied unceasing creation and chaos; the Weaver, which took the things of the Wyld and gave them stability and form; and the Wyrm, which broke down the constructs of the Weaver and allowed the Wyld to re-use the pieces. It was a perfect cycle, which ensured that none of the three forces would ever become unbalanced, and for a time all was balanced in the universe. This is the time that Gaia, her sister Luna, and the spirit worlds that surround Her came into being, and it seemed that Gaia would be the greatest design the three forces had ever created. Wyld energies surged across Her face, creating great beasts and natural places; the Weaver gave these creations stability and permanence, and the Wyrm maintained the natural order, killing the old and weak and eroding great mountains to make way for new forests and deserts. This was a great time, when the Garou were not even needed, for all was in harmony and it seemed the Triat — for such would they come to be known — had perfected their alliance.

However, all was not well, in fact. During this great time of bounty, the Wyrm became jealous, feeling that the Wyld and the Weaver were receiving too much praise for their work. Because even though all creatures understood the role of the Wyrm, they had come to dread his coming, as all things fear their undoing. And the Wyrm was a cowardly creature, and could not bear the loathing and rejection offered to him by the creation he was a natural part of sustaining. So his heart swelled with hate and jealousy for his fairer siblings, and he plotted a way to exact revenge on them. Listen well to these words, cubs, for this lesson rings true to this day — the Wyrm is still a lonely child, full of hate for himself, and if you are sly you can know his followers by their inner sorrow and their longing to end their own lives. It is by no means an easy way, but it is seldom wrong, and this splinter of doubt the Wyrm's children have for themselves can be used against them in a pinch.

Ah, but these were the times before the others knew of the evil boiling in the Wyrm's heart, and so they were unprepared when he sprang his trap. The Wyrm knew of the pride of the Weaver and used it to his advantage, convincing her to create a race of creatures that would enforce their own will on the world and advance new Weaver ideas all the time. Naturally she agreed, but she didn't see the seeds of hate and self-loathing the Wyrm planted within these new creatures, seeds that would lead this new species — mankind — to one day spurn his old ties to the wild and seek destruction, even against his own kind. So was humanity created, and before long Gaia began to groan beneath Man's terrible weapons and foolish ways, and the Wyrm laughed. But it was to be bitter laughter, for the Wyrm had bound himself within the Weaver's web with his meddling, and the more he struggled the more entangled he became, until he went mad with rage. This is why to this day the Wyrm is often wrapped in the guise of the Weaver, as a look into the hungry eyes of the railroad men or army soldiers will show you. It is also why the Wyrm has overstepped his role in the natural cycle and seeks to destroy the world instead of helping to maintain it, for it is the only way he can think of to end his pain. But this is only part of why I tell this story to you tonight.

When Gaia was in pain, Her sister Luna took pity on Her and asked what she might do to bring Her comfort. In a fury of agony, Gaia screamed that She needed warriors to cut the human sickness from Her flesh, as a surgeon cuts away an infected limb to save the patient. So Luna called on the bravest of Gaia's Children to come and save their Mother, and of them all none surpassed Wolf for ferocity and courage. But then the fever of Gaia's illness passed, and She took pity on the humans for being duped by the Wyrm's scheme, and desired to save them from complete destruction. So She told Luna to gather the wisest and most spiritual of the humans and teach them the ways of the spirit world, that they could counsel their kind to respect their Mother. And, having charged Luna with bringing both wisdom and death on the human race, Gaia passed into a deep, feverish sleep, from which She has yet to awaken. Oh, She comes to us all in dreams sometimes, and at other times She is nearly awake with some purpose or another, but most of the time She sleeps and dreams of better times. If She will wake from Her sickness refreshed or wither away, well, that is our duty and our destiny to determine.

But enough. We left poor Luna with the impossible task of combining warriors and shamans into one force that would cull the worst of the humans and teach the others the proper way of living, as well as battle the excesses of the Wyrm, and Luna could not bear the weight of this responsibility. Who could? She went mad, but in her madness she saw the answer, and thus the Garou — a mystical combination of wolves and men — were born. She showered these new guardians with gifts: the ability to walk the spirit world, the power to change their forms, and many friendships with spirits, who taught the Garou many different powers. Coyote, for example, taught — no, another time. There are too many spirits to tell of, but all Garou know at least a little of their power, and honor the spirits whenever they can. However, the madness that created them left its mark on the Garou, and they are possessed of terrible tempers, forever unable to truly live among anyone but themselves for fear of harming those they love in their fury.

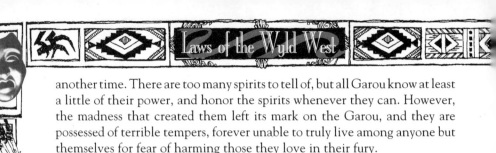

Thus even the mightiest Garou knows the echo of the Wyrm's cries within his heart, for not only is he capable of great violence and destruction, but he is also very lonely deep inside. Both wolves and humans die quickly without the company of their fellows, and even the most lowdown gunslinger has a gang that rides beside him or a favorite madam he chews the fat with. That is also why Garou run in packs, to this very day, and why most Garou would gladly bleed the last of their heart's blood dry if it meant saving their pack, for they are so very alone inside.

Pah! Enough sorrow for now. Far too much of this life is happy to focus on just the sadness, as my kind know, and I can see you want to know exactly what it is Luna did when she created the Garou, magnificent folk as they are Yes, young ones, even though dark clouds loom on the horizon I still have faith in the Garou, and as I look at such strong and brave young faces, it makes my heart swell with joy. So sit a while longer, let the fire burn down a bit, and I will teach you what it is to be Garou.

## Born with Power, Destined for Battle

When Luna melded the fierce wolves and wise humans, she gave the Garou the ability to control the shapes they wear, so that they might understand and transcend both worlds. Sliding between forms may seem tough at first, but with practice any shape from human to wolf becomes easy. Garou may assume the form of a natural wolf (Lupus), a mighty dire wolf form (Hispo), fully human (Homid), bestial human (Glabro) or the most powerful and frightening form (Crinos), the half-wolf/half-man shape. In Crinos, most Garou stand two hands taller than a cactus, weigh more than a Conestoga wagon and can stop a man's heart just by looking at him mean.

But Luna, crafty crazy Luna, knew that muscle isn't enough. Ever see one of those new repeating rifles, or hear the legend of John Henry and the rail-laying machine? Well, if you haven't, just know that sooner or later even the greatest physical strength is surpassed. So Luna remembered the wise humans she had saved, combined their thinking with the natural bond of the wolves, and formed a potent spiritual resource for the Garou, called Gnosis. Gnosis expresses a Garou's bond with the natural world, and fuels many of the powers that spirits teach them; divine currency, in a way. All Garou are beings of two worlds: Gaia and the spirit world, called the Storm Umbra. They can move into this spirit world, where the spiritual is real and our reality is only a shadowy reflection. Entering the Storm Umbra is commonly called "stepping sideways," or "reaching" by more traditional Garou. What's this Storm Umbra like, you ask? Such curious young ones! Well, that I'll get to soon, but this lesson's note quite over yet, so keep your ears up, cubs.

In her madness Luna remembered Gaia's call for warriors and the ferocity of the wolves she had summoned, and imbued the Garou with a vast, deadly anger, called Rage. Now, as anyone who's ever been in a saloon dust-up knows, sometimes anger's a blessed thing — it clears the head, gets the muscles going, and lets you forget your hurts and focus on your goals. And if a Garou's got a good head on his shoulders, he rides his Rage well, using it to let him fight terrible enemies without batting an eye or to act faster than a bullwhip's crack. But there's always a little madness in a Garou's soul, thanks to Luna's touch and the seed of the Wyrm that was planted in the humans long ago, and sometimes even the best Garou loses control of his Rage and commits horrible acts of slaughter and destruction. I've seen a cub not much older than you young'ns come to his senses coated in blood and realize he just tore his best friend's arm clear off, and believe me that's not a pretty sight. So Rage is a mixed bag — use it too little and you'll likely be squashed by some Wyrm bogey, use it too much and you'll wake up surrounded by pieces of your closest friends, *if* you wake up. Remember, no matter how it feels, even Rage doesn't make you invincible. Don't just release it and hope for the best; ride it carefully and rein it in when you have to. A bucking bronco beneath you is still better than one bearing down on you.

I should say that much is made of Luna's madness, but she is not always this way, and it would be unkind to say so. Indeed, Luna still takes the time to know each Garou personally, before they are born. It is a practice said to have started with the very first Garou, whom Luna took to her lodge in the sky and peered into their souls. She looked into each Garou's heart and saw what fire burned within, and what phase the moon was in at the Garou's birth. She saw that most Garou had tempers that were bound by their birth moon, and so she provided the Garou with spirit Gifts to fit each one's personality. She then told them of the role they would play in Garou society, a tale that accounts for what are now called auspices, the places determined by the phase of moon under which a Garou is born. I see some of you bristle at this thought — *No moon told me who I am!* you think — but that is not the way it truly is. Auspice is not a punishment to be served, but a destiny to be lived. Not only does it help determine what other Garou think of a cub's role in society, but it also entitles them to certain secret lore within their auspice, and, to an extent, helps others predict a given Garou's personality as well.

## Family Ties: The Tribes

Forget this talk of auspices for a moment, then, and try to think of what shaped you more than anything when you were a young'n. Your family, right! Remember what they say: blood's thicker 'n water, and Garou are no different. They've all got family trees that run back to the earliest days, and if you give them a moment to talk about it every one of them will talk you blue about how they're descended from this or that great hero. But family's where the heart is, from the home back on the ranch to the pack that ran with a Garou before the First Change (where they transform for the first time and realize what they truly are), and no Garou can ignore the call of his tribe. A tribe is more than just family, though: A tribe is a philosophy, an outlook on humans, and a way of seeing the whole world all rolled into one. Even those rare Garou who forsake their tribe still never forget it.

Once, they say, all Garou were one tribe, but as time passed and the Garou spread out, different tribes based on race and location came about. Now, of course, the main battles are between the native Garou, who call themselves the Pure Ones, and the European newcomers, but old hatreds and alliances still remain between the tribes as a whole. Of the 16 original tribes, 13 remain: the *Black Furies* (she-wolf alphas who watch over women and wild places), the *Bone Gnawers* (lowdown sneaks and scavengers who guard the poor folk of the cities), the *Children of Gaia* (peacetalkers who envision the Garou united and humanity enlightened), the *Fianna* (brave and boastful immigrants of Irish stock), the *Get of Fenris* (hard workers and grim warriors who follow their Teutonic kin), the *Iron Riders* (irreverent city-dwellers and proponents of technology) the *Red Talons* (an all-wolf tribe of hunters and pack alphas), the *Shadow Lords* (schemers and politicians who hail from Slavic lands), the *Silent Striders* (enigmatic scouts and messengers of African ancestry), the *Silver Fangs* (noble warriors and hereditary leaders of the Garou), the *Stargazers* (philosophical and meditative Garou), the *Uktena* (sly Pure One shamans and medicine men), and the *Wendigo* (ferocious and cunning warriors of the Pure Ones).

Now, sometimes you'll run across Garou without a tribe; most call 'em Renegades or Lone Wolves, but whatever their name these Garou are usually bad news. They are those who have renounced everything about their tribes and are now in exile (willingly or otherwise), and that makes them dangerous. Many are just soft-hearted or wounded souls who want no part of the battles going on around them, but others have less noble motives and may even turn to the Wyrm. I call them as I see them, but most Garou consider a Renegade to be at least partially touched by the Wyrm, and unfortunately that's a good rule to follow in most cases.

## Life on the Plains: The Garou in the Savage West

As I told you, since the earliest days the Garou have fought on behalf of Mother Gaia, mostly against the Wyrm, sometimes against the Weaver, and for a long time against humanity in general. This last period, called the Impergium, was a time of bloodshed and terror when Garou culled human populations like ranchers watch their herds. Do not look so astonished — if you have learned nothing yet, you should have learned that the Garou are just as capable of atrocity as their enemies. It was only by a great convocation of all the tribes — led by the Stargazers and the Children of Gaia — that the Impergium was finally ended, and even so voices of dissent (mostly Shadow Lords and Red Talons) grumble to this day. Indeed, many Garou look at the way cities are spreading and humans are fouling the land and say that the Impergium never should have ended, but I tell you they are fools. All that killing the humans did was teach them to hate and kill Garou, and it did nothing to stop their spread anyway. What is the answer, then? All I can say is that the answer lies neither in slaughtering humans nor aiding them, but something in between. Yes, that is a difficult road, but one that anyone with eyes sees must soon be taken if we are to have a Gaia left to defend. And that's where we finally find the American continent, another front in the eternal war against the Wyrm, and where the sky stretches above us even now.

### The Fallen: Lost Tribes

Most Garou don't like to speak of those tribes they've lost, but time and battle have taken their toll, and two tribes are now lost for all time: the *Croatan* (the "Middle Brother" tribe of Pure Ones who sacrificed themselves to defend the Pure Lands from the Wyrm) and the *White Howlers* (Pictish Garou who succumbed to the seduction of the Wyrm, and are now known as the Black Spiral Dancers). Now, keep this hushed, but another tribe's slowly going the way of the buffalo, and it's mostly their fellow Garou who're at fault. They're called the *Bunyip*, and they're from Australia. I've even heard of one or two wandering the trails out this way, but you didn't hear that from me. For all I know, they're nearly all gone, and so they're counted among the lost.

As you know, before any European ever set foot here, the Pure Ones and their Kinfolk came to this land. It was as beautiful as it is today, but it was also full of great Wyrm-spirits, which the tribes battled as they made their settlements and traveled the length of the land. Unable to destroy many of these great spirits, the Pure Ones bound them instead, combining the rituals of their tribes to create potent prisons for the Wyrm-things. The battles were many and fearsome, but in the end the Pure Ones prevailed and the spirits were jailed. A whole society of Uktena shamans came into existence to maintain the wards and ensure that the spirits within slumbered ceaselessly. Thus, while danger remained always in the background, the tribes flourished and enjoyed the land largely without fear of the Wyrm or its minions. That is, until the Europeans arrived.

I see some of you bristling as I say that. Well, let me tell you one thing — I have some Pure One in me, though most would hate to call me brother, and while I know they can be every bit as cruel and petty as the Europeans many of them despise, my heart remains with them. It's very simple: without the arrival of the settlers, the Croatan would still be alive, and the loss of that tribe remains a black mark on all Garou, for it could have been avoided. Perhaps if all Garou had worked together, Eater-of-Souls might have been defeated without the need for the Croatan's sacrifice, but I guess it's not worth talking about now. What's done is done.

All that needs to be known about that period is that it touched off the first violence between the Pure Ones and the Europeans, setting a pattern that continues to this day. Settler battled with native, and despite peace talks and legendary tales of cooperation between the two sides the distrust nestled deeply on both sides. To the Pure Ones, the Europeans brought only arrogance, violence and thievery; to the Europeans, the Pure Ones represented a savage threat to the new life they were trying to establish. And when such primal dreams clash, cubs, rest assured there will never be peace, because deep down both sides believe they are right and that they will triumph in the end. I have seen too many wars in my time to know otherwise.

## The Great Migrations

Numbers and equipment were on the side of the Europeans, though, and in time they could lay claim to the eastern shores of this country. Those first Pure Ones who were "resettled" by the newcomers were to become haunting visions of the future for many other tribes, who watched the eastern skies uneasily and hoped the wide Mississippi would mark the end of European ambitions. The Wendigo and the Uktena licked their wounds, mustered the occasional raiding party or peace conclave to test European resolve, and consulted the spirits as to their course of action. Angered by the violation of the ancient pacts and frightened by the disruption of many of the spirit prisons the Uktena used to tend, the spirits were as uncertain as their allies and gave many contradictory orders to different tribes. Thus, the Pure Ones were unable to present a united front whenever the Europeans advanced, as some tribes abided by a totem's request for peace and understanding while others believed the sacred ways called for taking the warpath. In the end, all it convinced the settlers was that all natives were to be feared and treated as a threat, because one never knew when a "friendly" tribe might suddenly turn on its allies. Oh, Gaia, what fools we all are at times!

Things did not begin to simmer until the turn of this century, though. It was then that the great cities and towns of the East, filled to bursting, began to disgorge the great streams of settlers that have marked this time. Before there had been scouts, explorers, religious groups and the occasional Army patrol, but never have any of the tribes seen anything like the current flood! It is as if the Europeans have their great cities on a string and are dragging them across the plains, covering the grasses and breaking the forests to replace them with towns, churches, forts and railroad stations. Yes, the railroad — a sight that all too often heralds the approach of another city, welcome or not. The determination of railroad men is legendary, but so is their greed, cubs. Never forget that no matter how much money they offer, they seek only to cut another scar into Gaia's face and bring more tools and more settlers to the land. And the suffering of the workers in many of the railroad camps, the conditions they endure in order to further the schemes of a few men back East, is beyond what any being of Gaia should tolerate. Many of the worst of these camps fall victim to "native raids," which is the European newspaper lingo for foremen being torn apart by Garou war parties as the workers are freed to their own destinies. And, though it may seem prideful to you youngn's, quite a few camps suffer humiliating setbacks and dangerous sabotage, as we Children of Coyote do our best to play jokes on the arrogant railroad men. Just because the Pure Ones and the European Garou both call this land theirs doesn't mean we can't have our fun too!

As if the railroads weren't enough, though, these towns also bring the telegraph, which allows the Army to contact the Great White Father back East and settlers to communicate their wishes to each other faster than any rider. Ah, such a puzzle, the telegraph! A man in a saloon once told me that the telegraph was a "wonderful invention for human relations," but I am not so sure. It is certainly a marvel to be able to speak to one's relatives without riding long days and risking great dangers, but in my sight it always seems that the better the Europeans communicate with each other, the more they desire to live closer to each other. What is meant to let them travel farther apart only brings them closer together, like binding the legs of a flock of geese together and bidding them to fly. A man might not ride 30 miles over desert or through snow to see his brother if he was not sure his brother still lived where he last saw him, but he is more than happy to do so if he received a telegraph from him the day before. The more messages he receives, the more he desires to see him, and the closer he is willing to move to do so, or the more he wishes a railroad built between their two towns. Yet the very reason many of them chose to move West was because they were tired of having so many other people living close to them in the first place! Perhaps one of you cubs understands this thinking, but it is beyond what Coyote has given me, and so all I can do is laugh.

Now it seems that the Europeans have two gods, one they call "progress" and the other they call "Manifest Destiny." The first demands that all things be "civilized," no matter how long a society has stood without the toys of the newcomers; the second is a ceaseless call to see more, own more and make more. More of *what* is not always clear, but the hunger remains despite all the gains that are made. Surely, many tribes have seen the hand of the white man's church at work, and many missionaries have made their way across the plains in the last three centuries, but the drives that burn behind the eyes of most settlers are alien to the peaceful god they claim to believe in. There are those who devote themselves to their faith with zeal, but they can be just as violent as their regular cousins when they think they're dealing with "heathen folk" who won't accept the "truth" of their religion. In all the churches I've seen, only one priest had what I'd call True Faith, and he was a humble man with a humble church in a tiny Texas town. The bigger the church, cubs, the bigger the man who runs it usually thinks he is, and the less likely you are to see tolerance and peace practiced by the congregation. It's a sad truth, but a truth nonetheless.

## Peace and Hate Along the Border: Settler and Natives

I see by your faces that you're tired of hearing the works of the Europeans run into the ground, and that a few of you are thinking about seeing if a Chicano coyote really can run like a jackrabbit. Well, I assure you I'm plenty fast, but I have no intention of leaving the fire just yet. And while I will make no excuses for the worst Europeans — evil remains the same behind any mask — I can say two things that might soothe your tempers: first, the great majority of Europeans that I have met have been ordinary people, not much different from the average native tribesman they see themselves as pitted against. They are folk living difficult lives in a difficult land, doing the best that they can to feed their families and prosper within what they believe is the right way to live. Yes, they are often manipulated by other Europeans seeking nothing but personal gain, but perhaps this is little different than the corrupt shamans and arrogant chieftains who sometimes appear in native lands and lead their tribes to ruin. By and large they are decent people who are forced into living lives against Gaia's way by the very standards of the European lifestyle here in the West, a lifestyle established by greedy men. Still, they feel the same fear hearing wolves howling in the night that their ancestors did, laugh at the same jokes from town to town, and desire the same happiness for their children that a she-wolf feels for her cubs. For those reasons, I do not condemn all Europeans, as many Pure Ones do; they are too much like myself to do so. And it wouldn't make sense to shoot myself when I'm having this much fun, now would it?

But there are forces of great evil afoot among the Europeans, cubs, and while not all settlers deserve your wrath, remember that a soul lost to the Wyrm is just that: lost. No matter how innocent they were before or still appear to be, those in the coils of the Wyrm are better off dead than living the mockery their lives become. That is why those fully claimed by the Wyrm are known as "mockeries," because they are but a hollow shell of their former selves, a bitter joke of the spirits. And if Coyote hates one thing above all else, it's humor used to an evil end, which is why many mockeries end their lives peering down the barrel of some Nuwisha prank or another. My people are known for their sense of humor, but do not forget that Coyote has died countless times trying new pranks and battling those who would spoil the beautiful life Gaia offers. We are not afraid to put some meaning in the word "punchline," if it suits our purposes. Oh, and by the way, when you go to refill your canteens tonight, steer clear of the three crossed sticks in the clearing. Oh, it's nothing really, just a surprise for some trapper friends I saw the other day. What's that? Not thirsty now? Just as well, cubs, just as well.

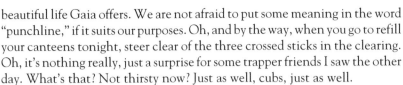

The other reason I cannot condemn the Europeans entirely is that the Pure Ones hold an equal share of the blame, if not the casualties, for the tragedy that is unfolding in the West. Where a respect for the land once dwelled, many tribes now harbor a bitter sense of regret, which leads them to forsake their ways and ignore the spirits. In others, the white man's sense of property has poisoned their old view of a land without boundaries, and while there has always been battle with other tribes over prime herds and the like, now many tribes are as afraid of strangers as the worst shantytown dwellers. Some even sell their services to the whites, trying to save their own skins as they see their tribes dying. They don't realize that when you save your skin, you still have to live within it, and the guilt eats them up inside something awful. Maybe the best way to understand the problems facing the Pure Ones today is to think about it this way: It seems like the tribes are drifting apart like sand through fingers, and no one knows how to stop it. If you make a fist the sand spills out anyway, but open your palm wide and the wind sweeps it away just as fast. And so the Pure Ones must watch their way of life pass away in front of them, and nothing seems to be able to even slow it down.

Now listen here, cubs, and listen good — I'm not asking you to excuse the Pure Ones from anything any more than I'd ask you to feel sorry for the Wyrm mockeries or corrupt railroad barons the Garou put down. What I *am* trying to do is get you to see just what it is that makes the Uktena so sad and the Wendigo so angry, to walk a mile in their moccasins, as the saying goes. This way, before your pack rushes out to burn a native village to the ground for raiding the local fort, maybe you'll stop and think about what it is that made them so angry in the first place. Maybe the cavalry violated a treaty in taking the land, perhaps the railroad built over their burial grounds, or maybe their children are starving because all the buffalo have been slaughtered by white guns. Of course, action of some kind is still necessary, but if they have been controlled by the Wyrm, struck from hatred, or otherwise have acted without reason, at least your conscience will sleep better knowing you tried understanding first. Perhaps, as is usually the case, only a small part of the tribe is responsible, and then your thinking will have stopped another senseless slaughter in favor of real justice against the guilty. Use your heads, cubs! Violence may be the way most Garou think of to solve problems, but you need not heed the call of your anger every time — events may have forced a tribe to think there was no other way to save their people, and if you approach them with empathy, both sides just might be spared adding more blood to the gallons that have painted the West already.

Ah, but I can tell you have heard this coyote speak enough of tolerance for tonight. As Laughing Manyskins, one of Coyote's most blessed children, is fond of saying: "A joke is a joy told once, a pleasure told twice, a smile told thrice, and nothing but annoying after that." Which is a polite way of reminding big-mouthed folks like me that they should get off their soap box once in a while and see things from the crowd, so to speak. The fire's getting low, leastaways, and if we mean to make Dragon's Gulch by noon we'd best get some rest soon. There's a lot left to tell, about how Garou society works and wonderful things like that, but maybe it's better off told to you by a Garou, and not a sly Nuwisha like me, who will never know the ways of sept and caern. What's that? Well, a caern is — no, no, I'll let my friends explain tomorrow. Time for sleep, cubs, and deep at that, so we can make good time at dawn.

## The Storm Umbra

Still awake, eh? It is beautiful out here under the stars, don't you think? Ever wondered what lies beyond them? Well, if you remember what I said earlier, the world doesn't end at Gaia. No, no, not hardly — outside of Gaia there are more worlds than trees in all the forests of the world, and even my people have yet to see them all. But for now a simple explanation will suffice. Right beyond this world lie four worlds Garou know: the Penumbra, the Middle or Near Umbra, the High Umbra, and the Low or Dark Umbra. The Penumbra is like a shadow of the world, identical in a lot of ways, but everything is more, well, spiritual. It's hard to explain, but you'll know what I mean when you get there — true natures become more visible there. The Near Umbra is where most of the spirits Garou see dwell, and where the realms of what the Pure Ones call the Animal Fathers reside, ancient lodges where nature and Gaia are revered. It is not the reflection that the Penumbra is, but it is still familiar most of the time, with many lush landscapes and friendly spirits at hand. Of course, not all realms or spirits are friendly there, so you'd best watch your steps, cubs.

The High Umbra is the realm of ideas, and it's said to be where the gods of the European Old Country dwell. I've never been there, but I've heard there are mazes and puzzles there that stagger the brain, but also wisdom and answers beyond your wildest dreams, so if you feel you need to go just keep your wits about you and remember that the High Umbra is the place to use your mind, not your muscles. As for the Low Umbra, where the dead dwell, I'll let someone who knows more explain it some time, but I do know it's much like the Penumbra: a shadowy reflection of the world, except everything there is dark and decaying. Ugh! I saw it once in a vision Coyote gave me, and that was enough. If you ever have business there, finish it and finish it fast; the place has a way of eating at your hope and your spirit.

At the edge of all three worlds is a great barrier called the Membrane; beyond it lie the Heavens or the Deep Umbra, depending on who you ask.

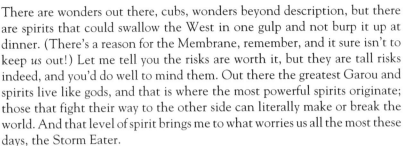

There are wonders out there, cubs, wonders beyond description, but there are spirits that could swallow the West in one gulp and not burp it up at dinner. (There's a reason for the Membrane, remember, and it sure isn't to keep *us* out!) Let me tell you the risks are worth it, but they are tall risks indeed, and you'd do well to mind them. Out there the greatest Garou and spirits live like gods, and that is where the most powerful spirits originate; those that fight their way to the other side can literally make or break the world. And that level of spirit brings me to what worries us all the most these days, the Storm Eater.

## The Storm Eater

Most Garou will tell you the Storm Eater is a myth, nothing more, but that's because they're scared, cubs — they've thrown their best at it, and all it's done is smile back at them. I don't blame them for their fear, but I also think this threat deserves to be taken seriously, not wished away like some serialized romance. Legend has it the Storm Eater was once a powerful Bane that fed on Wyld energy until it was so massive that it took the entire Uktena nation to weaken the spirit until it could be bound, where it remained until the arrival of the Europeans. Freed by the weakening of its bindings due to European attacks on Uktena land, the Bane joined with a powerful Weaver spirit it had tricked into helping it and the Storm Eater was born at last.

Now it rampages across the Umbra, draining Wyld energies where it can and spawning children with the worst mix of Weaver and Wyrm in them to wreak havoc on Gaia. Where it passes in the Umbra, its touch creates areas so wild and chaotic that they are known as the Storm Umbra, and I fear almost all the West bears some taint of this wildness now, however slight it may be. Of course, the Wyld spirits are mad with rage, but given their nature they are as likely to strike at us as they are to lash out at the true villain. This means the Umbra is rapidly dissolving into a mess no Garou or spirit would choose to call home, and the Wyrm laughs even as it watches the destruction caused by its strangest child, since the Storm Eater creates many powerful minions and leaves people and towns it passes over ripe for corruption. These are dark times, cubs, not hopeless by any means — the Storm Eater was bound before, and could be again — but we all must be on our guard for this threat.

The Garou as a whole, however, I fear are not doing much to stop the devastation. The Europeans, when they choose to speak on the Storm Eater, know little about it, and their talent for pretending it is not there means they are learning far too slowly. And those who are wisest in the ways of the Storm Eater, the Pure Ones, have no desire to help the Europeans who brought this menace on with their careless ways, even though they know that now the Storm Eater has grown too big to be defeated alone. And so both sides, who together might come up with some way to contain this beast, sit instead across opposing fires and glare at each other in a pointless staredown while Gaia screams in the night. It is not the first time you will see this out West, cubs, but it is perhaps the most tragic, for it is not only the Garou who suffer for this mistake. The Storm Umbra is a danger now, but do not forget its glory, which could be won again. My people have never forgotten, and while we weep the harder for it, you can also see the gleam of the stars in our eyes because of it.

Dream now, and know that you will awaken to face the beginning of the most glorious days of your lives — your first days as real Garou.

## Traditions of the Garou

I see Lucas dragged yer sorry carcasses to me to finish his lessons for 'im. Well, don't that beat all, a bunch of tenderfoot cubs to wean. Leave it to that tricky coyote to have all the fun and let everyone else pick up his chores. Well, since you aren't goin' nowhere and neither am I, I might as well be polite and introduce myself. I'm Patricia McKinnon, the Garou know me as Fights-For-Truth, but you can start with plain old Pat. What's that? You heard of me? How so? Well, you see, that's a whole other bronco to bust; I could you tell all about my innocence, but that won't do no good now. Lucas tell you 'bout the tribes just yet? Well, that's one good thing he's done 'cause I'm of Fianna blood, and that means I get to tell you about how Garou society works. Why? On account of how the Fianna are the greatest lorekeepers and storytellers of all the tribes, and I've got a nice pair of knives to say you won't disagree to that. All settled? Good. Now belly on up to the bar — Kat's a packmate, so yer on my tab till you all start pulling your own weight — and I'll tell you all about what makes us Garou tick. Lord only knows what that Lucas has told you!

In some ways, Garou're a lot like people; only figures, I suppose, since we've all got a little monkey in us all, even the wolf-borns. But we Garou love laws like any upstandin' member of society, and there are a lot of 'em to know if you really want to get down to it. Yer probably wonderin' how we all get along in the first place, on account of how we're as different as a boxcar full a' broken china and kill each other as much as we scuff up the Wyrm. The real secret is the laws underneath it all, and if you don't take away nothing else from this lesson, you remember them good. They're called the Litany, and if you break them yer up to yer neck in nasty stuff, no matter what company yer in. See, Gaia made us better than most folks, and that's hard enough to live with without gettin' puffed up with pride, but what with our tempers and the tricks the spirits teach us most of us get to feelin' beyond the law sooner or later. And that's what the Litany's for — showing both hot-blooded cubs like yerselves and elders who could lay ya'll out with a wink that they have to answer to somethin' or someone sooner or later. You mind these laws, cubs, and not only will you earn favor in the eyes of yer elders, but you'll come a little bit closer to reining in that blazing stallion that burns in yer heart. It ain't even laws that make men civilized, it's knowin' in yer heart when the laws are right.

First of all, I'm flattered by the attention, but you better mind those looks some of you are givin' me, on account of how one of the oldest laws of our kind is that Garou don't lie with Garou. You cross a horse and a donkey, you get a mule; you cross two Garou, you get, well, if you get a child at all you get one that ain't quite right. They're called metis, though most Garou call 'em nastier things, and each and every one is sterile as the desert itself. Somethin' else is always wrong with 'em, too, from a misshapen limb to a cleft lip to bats in the belfry, if you know what I mean. It boils down to this: wouldja take a tumble in the hay with yer brother or sister? I didn't think so. And all Garou are family under Gaia, so next time you feel like making eyes at a fellow changer you just think to yerself that you might as well be lying with old Jimmy or Jody Lee. Hah! Thought you might need another glass after that one!

The next most important thing to keep in yer head is: Garou don't exist. At least, not to mortals we don't. There's yer pack, yer fellow Garou and maybe some Kinfolk (humans who share our blood but didn't get kissed by Luna and made into Garou); after that, if anyone learns about the Garou they ain't allowed to keep their memory or their head- yer choice. Unless the sept approves of you letting someone in on the whole deal, we're as good a secret as yer ever gonna keep. We call this custom "the Veil," and you best mind it if you wish to keep your own pelt. It'll be tough sometimes, trust me, especially if you lay eyes on some pretty stranger and want to share yer life with them, but remember it's for everybody's good. Humans got real good at huntin' us once, after the Impergium, and we're in no hurry to see those days come again. All it takes is one good Army report or one big story in those damn Eastern papers, and the game's up. We got our hands full with the Wyrm and with our Kinfolk fightin' all over the place, we don't need to fight another bunch a' nuts bent on tracking us down. Lucky for us there's a little trick mad old Luna taught us, called the Delirium, which makes it a little easier to hide most of the time. You see, because we hunted humans fer so long back in the Impergium, they got so scared of us that the fear started being born into 'em. And it still is. Folks who've never heard of Garou, much less seen one, will run away screaming their heads off if they see a Garou in Crinos form, and likely as not they won't recall a damn thing about it come mornin', that's how scared they get. So a lot of the time you won't have to worry too much if a human wanders in on the action, but take care anyway. Some folks are just so tough or so damn stupid the Delirium doesn't work on them too well, and those you gotta watch out for.

There are lots of other little rules, most of 'em the "mind yer elders and yer manners" variety, and they'll come naturally enough in time if you keep yer ears perked. Most of all, though, listen to the legends when the time comes to gather round the fire. My tribe loves 'em more than most anyone, but all Garou like stories, and we use 'em as a way of teaching our heroes, reliving our history and warning those who are starting to walk outside the lines. All this friction between Europeans and Pure Ones (which I think is a load 'a

## You 'n' Me 'n' Some Whiskey Makes Three: Cultural Relations in the Savage West

Cultural relations are a key theme and an incendiary subject in the Savage West; while the differences between settlers and natives will be the most obvious cultural line in many games, there are dozens (if not hundreds) of other cases that can be a ground of rich roleplaying and historical flavor. For example, there are at least as many traditional conflicts between the different native tribes as Europeans know between their homelands, which is a great theme to stress in games with a high number of Pure One characters. (And despite the popular Hollywood image of "one Indian knows all Indians," the differences in languages and customs for a Sioux encountering a Zuni camp are roughly the same as a Frenchman abruptly dropped off in Transylvania.) A little research into the tribes of different characters can lead to excellent background material, as well as provide the Storyteller with possible plot hooks for the future.

Of course, Europeans nurse their own hatreds within their ranks. A true Yankee is unlikely to be very welcome in the house of a good Southerner, especially if a game takes place during or after the Civil War. As far as ethnic populations go, Irish, German, Italian and other immigrant groups are regularly mistreated by the "established" population, who ignore their own history of being abused and use these newcomers for cheap labor in factories and on the rail lines. Prejudice against Catholics (not to mention other Christian groups such as Mormons) in this still largely Protestant country — especially in the East — is another vicious shadow over the population. Many settlers seek the wide spaces of the West as much to escape brutal ghettoes and discrimination as much as to find their own piece of land, and a character from a "minority" can expect some ribbing and stereotyping at the very least, even in the most urban environments.

Other groups — which don't fall so clearly into the standard Western archetypes — abounded in the actual West, and can easily play a part of any **Wyld West** game: blacks, Chinese and Jews, just for starters. Black settlers make up an impressive portion of pioneers, seeking a better life than is offered in the prejudiced East, and roughly a quarter of all cowboys are black. Chinese laborers, who tend to live among their own and settle things away from the eyes of outsiders, present a unique puzzle to the Occidental sensibilities of their fellow pioneers, and because of it they suffer great abuse for their appearances and habits. Jewish settlers — along with Mormons and Jesuits — help bring the first universities to the West, encouraging education and anchoring the cities that grow along the frontier by removing the need to travel East for higher education. Women also fill many more roles than just school marms and frontier mothers, proving that masculinity is by no means a requirement for business owners, ranchers, outlaws, healers and countless other professions.

When it comes to the portrayal of cultural nuances, the real key in **Wyld West** is more to try to look through a different set of eyes than it is to select the right wardrobe or props. It can be a great deal of fun, but it can be also be very difficult. As always, when in doubt, fun should be emphasized over history. If players are willing to go in depth and play out the tensions between different immigrant groups or tribes, wonderful; if some cultural problems need to be ignored in order for the story to work, don't worry. Avoid stereotyping as much as possible, though; not only are cigar-store Indians or caricature Irishmen just plain offensive, they're also broadly inaccurate. Respect people's out-of-game sensitivities; good players know when to draw the line or call it a night, and most of the time it's empty comfort to someone who's upset when you try to explain that you were only acting in character when you insulted a particular nationality or religion.

bull, the whole lot of it), though, means we're losin' old legends right and left as tribes die out and the old ways are massacred. I reckon this is just the way war is, but part of me says that there's more than a little bit of the Wyrm in it all to be just the fortune of war.

## Shadows at Midnight: The Other Beings of the Savage West

You've probably guessed that Garou can be found just about anywhere in this great country, and you'd be right. Heck, right now yer probably thinkin' back on all those people you knew before you Changed, wonderin' if any of them were in on the way the world really is. It's a helluva thing to know, but if you think some of them did, yer likely right. Trouble is, we Garou ain't the only things that walk these trails, so listen good, because you don't get a second chance with most of 'em.

Ever hear of vampires? Bloodsucking old cusses who rise from their graves and get a bug in the bonnet of all the pretty young things in town? Well, that ain't quite right, but it's close enough. Call 'em Leeches, vampires or what have you, they're real, cubs, and they hate us right pretty. I reckon it's because we've been killin' 'em since time long gone, and believe me when I say they're Wyrm-ridden, each and every one. Oh, if you catch one it'll spin you a yarn 'bout how it hates what it is, and it just wants to live in peace, but it's all lies. They feed on blood, just like the legends say, and most of 'em have powers that'll twist yer brain like a little girl's hair ribbon and turn you into their personal slave, so yer own pack has to put you out of yer misery. The damn things even work at building up the Wyrm-ridden cities, helping spread poison all over Gaia! Fortunately, most of 'em have less guts than a sack full a' jackrabbits, so they stay East where they can do all their unnatural acts unnoticed. Even the biggest cities of the West aren't big enough for most vampires, which means we tend to smell 'em right quick out here, and so they're waiting us out fer now. When we meet, like I said, it's usually short and unpleasant, but they have a way with humans that makes 'em hard to pin down. A lot of times there's an uneasy truce of some kind or another, but I'll tell you now I don't know a single Garou who wouldn't gladly cut the throat of even the nicest Leech, so you can imagine how well these peaces usually hold. Watch out for 'em, cubs — they're slippery as snakes in a tub full of oil, and they don't like nothin' better than to make us fight each other if they can.

Sometimes a tribe's shaman has real power, or you see a city magician whose tricks really work, and these folk are a mystery to us. A lot of mystics seem to use spirits, like we do, but others make things happen with sheer force of will. Some European magicians use machines to work their "magic," and these stink so bad of the Weaver it'll make you choke. I once ran across a hellfire-and-brimstone preacher, just north of Happy Jack, Arizona, whose eyes burned with the energy of the Wyrm. He had a whole cult 'a followers, and I barely made out with my skin in one piece before a local pack set on him and tore him up. As a rule, cubs, when it comes to mystics, there is no rule. Most are strongly marked by one of the Triat — Wyld, Weaver, Wyrm — and that's just 'bout the best way to figure out how to deal with 'em. Help the Wyld ones when you can, judge what needs doin' about a Weaver one, and show a Wyrm one the quickest way to his boss is at the end of yer claws. Fortunately, they're mighty rare out here, but take real good care when you meet one — they're as powerful as they are strange.

The legend of the banshee comes from my country, but ghosts don't know no boundaries. Lots of people die unhappy out here, like it or not, and many of 'em can't quite handle the fact they ain't breathin' anymore. These dead folks — we call 'em wraiths, so you don't mix 'em up with the regular spirits — are most often found 'round places that saw a lot of joy or sorrow in life: battlefields, ghost towns, graveyards, love cottages, you know the places. A lot of 'em are too wrapped up in their own ways to notice the livin', but some do, and they always want something. *Always*. Usually it's to help them settle an old score or tell their wife they love her one last time, but they don't take kindly to being refused and they can do all sorts of nasty tricks if you're not careful. Of all the tribes, the Silent Striders are the ones most likely to have truck with the dead, but the Dark Umbra — where the wraiths dwell — ain't a place any other Garou are particularly interested in seein'.

I reckon you remember all sorts of tales that were told to you when you were knee high to a grasshopper- stories of trolls, gnomes, dragons and those kinds of things. Well, at least half of those stories are true, because faeries are as real as you and me. We Fianna have long ties with 'em — they throw great parties, young'ns, never turn one down — but just about all tribes know a little 'bout 'em. Nowadays they call themselves changelings, and they're half-fae and half-human, which means they know all 'bout balancing two lives like we do. Some of 'em are straight out of nightmares (not all stories have happy endings, I guess), but most love a good time and a good joke, and that makes 'em all right with me. An evening with faeries can lighten yer heart when just about nothing else will, so if you spot one, do yer best to strike up a friendship. We see too much fightin' in our lives as it is.

You've already met Lucas, so I guess you've figured there's more changers than just us Garou. And you'd be right 'bout that — there're all kinds of Changing Breeds, though most won't have much to do with us these days. Bad blood from the old days, cubs. There are some you should know about, though, since they share the West with us. There's the Gurahl, the bear-folk- they're rarer than rain in the sunshine, but wiser than anyone we know, and great healers too. Then there's the Pumonca, the cougar-people. They're loners, like the Gurahl, and on account of most of them being of Pure One stock they ain't too fond of us Europeans. Still, they're trackers like you wouldn't believe, and they know more tricks about surviving the wilds than all but the Red Talons know what to do with. Next come the Corax, the Children of Raven; they're great friends of ours, and with their curiosity they make excellent spies and scouts. (Can't hold their tongues or their liquor, though, but don't tell 'em I said that!) Finally, as Lucas proved, there's the Nuwisha, Coyote's brats. They're tricksters, teachers, liars and loafers all around, more like faeries than Garou most of the time. But they have no more love of the Wyrm than we do, and they *do* lighten up the town when they mosey on through, even if they tend to rub yer fur the wrong way after a while.

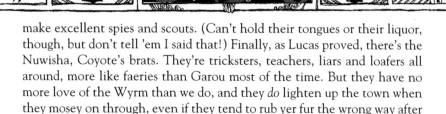

The Wyrm makes a lot of minions, too, and they're some of the trickiest *hombres* to rassle with, mostly 'cause a lot of 'em are hard to pick out of a crowd unless you've got a talent for smellin' out the Wyrm. Mockeries — Lucas taught you about them? Good. — are the worst of these, but they ain't the only ones. Sometimes regular folk turn on the Garou, out of religious fervor, personal revenge or just fer the hell of it. A lot of these hunters get wise to our ways sooner or later, despite the Veil, and that makes 'em dangerous, cubs. They're the ones who'll use silver against us, and let me be the first to tell you nothin'll kill you faster than a dose of silver, no matter how tough you think you are. All the legends got that one right, I'm afraid to say. So you take care 'bout who you talk to, who you anger, and most of all who you kill. Those last ones may not get you themselves, but a lot of folks have unforgiving relatives who're more than willin' to put a silver slug between yer shoulders when you least expect it. Kind of gives you the crawling flesh, eh?

Hah! But that's enough for now. You see, the worst enemy a Garou has all too often is another Garou, especially these days, so it's time you learned a little bit about the society you're coming into. Still awake enough after all those drinks? Good! Yer fine Garou, that's sure enough!

## Garou Society

When it comes to society, Garou mind their wolf ties as much as their human roots. This can be a little confusing to those of us born to human kin, but you get used to it right quick, trust me. More or less it's a series of circles, little "family" groups each Garou belongs to: breeds, auspices, tribes, septs and packs. Every one's a little bit different — an Ahroun meet is different from a Ragabash circle, a Shadow Lord trial doesn't much resemble a Wendigo council, and few things in life come close to just sitting around chewing the fat with yer pack — but the feelings they stir in you are as strong as any you have for the family yer born to: romance, friendships, even rivalries. But when it comes to seeing who's top dog (pardon the pun), human notions like charm and wisdom come up a little lacking. We Garou are a rough bunch, and we favor wolf qualities in our leaders, which means our solutions seem pretty brutal as often as not. Still, it's our way, and has been for too many years to mention.

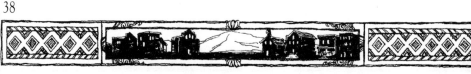

## The Pack

Yer pack is yer real family, period, end a' story. And that means exactly what it does with yer blood family — you can argue with them like a drunken sailor, but when trouble comes down you'd gladly give yer life for any of 'em, and they'd do the same. It also means the pack stands together on all outside matters, no matter what you feel. The Wyrm loves nothin' more than a pack divided; they're a hell of a sight easier to kill, for one, and just plain bad to be around for another.

If you've been with yer pack long enough, you'll know when they need you. Simple as that. It may sound strange, I know, but hell, yer already a werewolf, ain't you? Packs that've been together a real long time, you can tell it when you see 'em, especially in battle. They move like they share thoughts between 'em, one falling back as the other strikes forward, like a dust storm blasting their foes from all sides. Then there's the pack totem, a kind of guardian spirit that watches over the pack and gives 'em a sense of purpose when they're lost. Some packs serve war totems, and make the Wyrm quake in its boots when they pass; others follow the paths of honor or wisdom, which are just as important but a lot harder in most ways for our kind. We're raised on battle, and it never leaves us.

How did you cubs find each other? That's what I thought. Most packs're like you, made up of Garou who did their Rite of Passage together. The Rite's one of the toughest times of yer life, and for good reason — the last thing the Garou need are real tenderfeet in their ranks. So don't you pay no mind to the jokes anyone makes on you — you may not know much 'bout the West just yet, but yer plenty tough as Garou or you wouldn't be here to hear me talkin'. The only time a pack ever makes any kind of real big change in the way it works is if only one or two of you are left, because of battle or some such. In that case, most times you join up with another pack or find some other Garou in the same spot you are and make a new pack, down to a new totem and everything. It's sad, and I've seen Garou who ain't ever been right again after they lose their pack, but you gotta go on. It's that or death, and no Garou worth the name will join the big round-up in the sky without at least taking her pack's killers with her.

Yer pack have a name yet? Not just yet, eh? Well, best think up one right quick, on account of how it starts letting you make a name for yerselves. Ever hear of that lowdown cuss Earl "Dead Cat" Vasquez? Didn't think so! Know why? 'Cause his name ain't worth spit for making a reputation! He killed six men gunslinging last month, good men, but just because one of the town whores once saw him let fly on a stray tomcat, he's stuck with that dumb name. And a pack has to choose its name real careful, unless you want to wind up being laughed at behind yer backs like poor old Earl. A pack's name should tell other Garou what yer mission is at first glance. If yer pack is a bunch a' hard-ass *hombres*, you want a name like Wyrm Stalkers to let everyone know any fools who mess with you are headed out the saloon window face first. If yer pack's into visionquests or solving riddles, I reckon a more mysterious name like Wind Dancers will do you better. You get the idea. (And don't tell Earl I let you in on his name; he likes to say nowadays it's on account of how many pumas he's killed, and tends to be real sore if'n he's corrected.)

I can see just by lookin' at yer pack that ya'll are from different tribes, at least mostly. Easy, cubs, easy, that's all right. More 'n' more packs are turning up multitribal these days, and I think it's a good thing, what with how our kin are mixing and all. All that you really want to try to cover is that you have most, if not all, of the auspices in yer pack — it tends to make sure you got all yer areas covered. I'll tell you this, too — their packs are just about the only place most metis can rest easy, and if anyone stands up for 'em, it'll be their packs. My own pack's got two metis, two of the finest Garou you'd ever have occasion to know, and I'll see my heart bleed dry before I let anyone say different and live to repeat it. Even if a pack starts gettin' older, and its members start livin' farther and farther apart, the bond never really dies. A pack is a pack, to the death and sometimes even beyond. From the Rite of Passage on yer family, like it or not, and if all the cards come down it's the only family most of us will ever have.

Lucas tell you much 'bout Renegades? Lone Wolves? Well, if he did I ain't one to bore you by repeating things, but listen good to this — I knew a Lone Wolf once, out by Lincoln way, and he was the saddest thing I ever saw. Real nice and polite, but *empty* inside, like a lantern with no flame. What was missin' was — you guessed it — a pack. Never had one in his life and said he didn't need it, but I saw his eyes. If ever there was a lonelier soul, I ain't seen it yet, and I'll tell you one more thing — I think he'd turn to the Wyrm in a second if it looked like it would ease his loneliness. Think on that, and you'll know all about how the Wyrm gets so many of our kind these days.

## The Sept

You ever wander through some place and get a feeling in yer gut, a deep down feeling like you belonged there, even if you've never been there before? Might've been at a little clearing in the woods, a cave at the edge of town, even the local saloon, doesn't really matter where, it's the feeling that counts. Well, there are places on Gaia that collect the power of the spirit world, and we call them caerns. We use 'em to gather, lick our wounds and plan our new strategies, because the power that gathers there is as close to pure Gaia as you'll ever see on Earth. Now, the group that gathers around a particular caern to defend it is called a sept, although it's really just a collection of one or more packs and any Kinfolk they've got in the area. If a moot's gonna be called, it'll be at a caern. As you might imagine, there're plenty of chores to be done around the caern, and while a lot of 'em require older and wiser Garou, sometimes you'll see a younger pack filling in. It's really a question of who has the best head on their shoulders more than anythin' else, and if you prove you can do yer job then you might just get it.

## Sept Positions

Way things are these days, you don't always find all these posts full at a sept, but it's a good idea to try if you can, even if it means doublin' up on yer chores. Ignoring 'em is just bad manners, and don't do much good for the Garou at large, either.

### Sept Alpha and Beta

Just like wolf packs have their alphas, so do we. Alpha is head of the sept, and that's that. You got a problem with it, you take yer complaints to him right quick or shut yer yap for good. Not that all alphas are male, mind you; just take a look over at the Black Furies, and you can see being the best and brightest don't have anything to do with *cojones*. If the alpha talks, you listen and you listen good, because the alpha's the most honored and respected Garou in the sept, and didn't get that way by indulging fool cubs who don't mind their elders. Of course, the alpha's always an elder, but her word goes beyond that — she has final say on anything in the sept, even over what the other elders say. Most times this ain't a problem, though, since the alpha's also the wiliest Garou you'll lay yer eyes on and knows what really needs doing. Sept beta is the alpha's right hand man and confidant rolled into one, and acts as sept leader when the alpha ain't around.

### Warder and Guardians

Warders and their Guardians are the toughest gang of fighters the sept can muster, and you can bet yer bullets most have the scars to prove it. The Warder's the Garou in charge of seeing to it the caern is safe from all kind of threats, from Wyrm attacks to human hunters and anything else that wanders in with an itchy trigger finger; the Guardians are his "deputies," and do whatever the Warder says needs doin'. If a matter's got anything to do with the safety of the caern, you can bet the Warden wins the argument. Now, they can't whip up a war party — that's the alpha's job — but if a sept goes on the warpath, the Warder tells who goes and who stays back to keep an eye on the caern. Finally, the Warder can bar anyone from the caern, and if he needs to he can "close the caern" if things get hairy. Most Warders have a real tough job, what with the way the West is these days and all, and tend to have real short tempers for those who don't do their jobs, so it's best to stay on their good side, if you know what I mean.

### Master of the Rite

Garou society's so full of rites and rituals, you sometimes wonder how anything ever gets done. Thank yer lucky stars, then, for the Master of the Rite, because if it wasn't for him, we'd never figure it all out. If yer pack wants to run a rite at the heart of the caern, you go knockin' on the Master of the Rite's cabin first; if you want a good part in a Moot Rite, well, you get to be real friendly with the Master of the Rite and show 'im you've got the right stuff for the role. Of course, if you and yer pack want to run a little personal rite, away from the heart of the caern, that's yer own business; but if you start gettin' noticed by outsiders or bring harm on the rest of the caern, you can bet the Master of the Rite's gonna come callin' right soon. And he's not too likely to be very happy with ya'll, either.

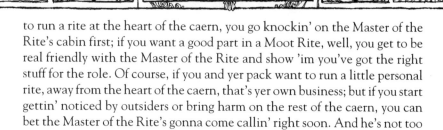

## Master of the Challenge

Ah, there's a title to make hot-blooded young Garou pant like dogs in heat! Master of the Challenge gets to oversee all the ritual challenges that take place at the caern, and the Master of the Challenge had better be real good at everythin' from cussin' and riddlin' to good old barroom brawlin' if she wants to keep her title fer long. Only thing that can reverse the word of the Master of the Challenge is if the whole darn crowd says otherwise, and that's downright rare, on account of how well-liked and trusted you gotta be to earn the title in the first place. If it gets out that a body got by cheatin' on yer watch, though, you better right that wrong mighty fast, or you risk gettin' run out on the same rails the cheater is!

## Gatekeeper

The West is a real big place, and if it weren't for things like Moon Bridges most of the time Garou'd never get anywhere in time to help anybody. The Gatekeeper is the Garou with the sacred trust of opening and closing all Moon Bridges. Like a Garou-styled railroad dispatcher, she keeps an eye on when Moon Bridges travel to and from the caern, and keeps anybody out who don't belong. If the Gatekeeper says a Moon Bridge won't be opened to another caern, for whatever reason, even the alpha listens up, because Moon Bridges ain't no laughing matter, and no caern can afford to tick off the spirits by opening an unwelcome bridge. If you get to be Gatekeeper, you get a little fetish, called a Pathstone, which lets the Gatekeeper get the sept totem's ear whenever she needs to in order to open bridges. You guessed it, cubs — Gatekeeper is another post they don't put anyone in charge of who ain't crackerjack material from the get-go.

## Keeper of the Land

Now, when you first get to the caern, make sure you mind the flower beds around the house, understand? And don't you dare snap a branch off the tree out back to fish for yer dinner in the river or other such nonsense! Why not? Well, you might not think it's a great matter, but the spirits are real particular about the way a caern looks, and if it ain't up to snuff, neither are the spirits who come around. That's the job of the Keeper of the Land, keeping the bawn of the caern all neat and tidy so the spirits get the proper respect. If he needs the help, or if a Garou gets caught doin' somethin' real dumb and the elders feel like humblin' her a bit, the Keeper can recruit other Garou to help in his duties. And if he calls, you do it without the littlest bit of complaint, or you'll wind up muckin' out the caern stables on top of anything else you gotta do, hear me?

## Den Mother or Father

Somebody's got to train all the tenderfoot cubs like you, and while all Garou are supposed to learn you a thing or two if they can, most of that chore falls on the Den Mother or Father. They're the ones who lead you through the worst part of learnin' to be a Garou, sit with you through yer first moots and keep you from embarassin' yerself too badly, and otherwise keep you out of trouble as best they can before you know enough to do it yerselves. Don't look so offended; teachin's done more good for this old world than all the guns and knives ever made, and if you know what's good for you, then you mind yer teachers when they speak. A good Den Mother's right up their with the sept alpha, at least respect-wise, mostly on account of everyone knowin' how much of a pain raising cubs is, but also because she's got more patience and stamina than a wolf in winter. Who knows? You last long enough 'round here, you might even get the nod from her to teach some cub gunfightin' or public speakin' — you usually wind up learning as much as the cub, take my word for it.

## The Sept and Society

Just like a Garou ain't much good without a pack, those packs ain't much good to anyone without a sept. There're a whole mess of good reasons fer it, most of 'em real practical. Callin' yerself king of that tree or that hill doesn't do yerself much good; getting a whole mess of Garou together, on the other hand, not only lets you watch over an impressive chunk of territory, it also lets you put a real good scare into the Wyrm. One pack don't scare most big nasties, even two packs in some cases, but get a whole sept together and most Wyrmies'll go runnin' to Mexico in a hurry. And just like human law, Garou justice don't mean much unless there are plenty of Garou around to make sure it's fair and it's given out when it should be. Sure, there're some real legendary Garou, elder Philodoxes mostly, who travel around like renegade lawmen, helping bring order to lonely septs, but you can't exactly count on 'em to show up just when you need 'em. Most of the time you got to look out for yer own out West, and that goes double with sept business. Hell, putting a lot of Garou in one place is also the only way to keep the Wyrm from ruinin' the stronger caerns, too, and we can afford to lose those like we can afford takin' silver bullets in the eyes.

If you want to be more political 'bout it, septs are the backbone of Garou government, such as it is. The Silver Fangs control the strongest septs (or more of 'em, anyway), and so they hold the reins, though the Shadow Lords'd like to see 'em eat crow soon as they can. If one sept has problems they can call on others for help, and while you'd think that Garou would be honor-bound to help their fellows, a lot of 'em are real picky about who they help and how much. Garou can be even pettier than humans, sometimes, and if someone in one sept has his hackles up about something his neighbor did, he might "forget" to send some packs, or at least hold off until his neighbor's real desperate. Not that that happens real often, mind you (although it'll be a cold day in Hell before the Pure Ones help most Europeans septs and vice versa, but you probably figured that already), but too often for my taste. Justice is one thing, but lettin' other Garou get in danger or worse just because yer in a snit just ain't right. I'm sure the Wyrm loves it, though. About the only thing that *always* brings other Garou is if a caern is about to fall to the Wyrm; no snit's worth losing that, and even the most snot-nosed Silver Fang knows it.

All that aside, though, we Garou need septs like humans need cities, really. I know a lotta Red Talons who'd rip my guts out fer sayin' it, but it's true. Without septs we've got no way of swappin' stories, learnin' news, practicing Gifts and otherwise keeping each other company. And while we tend to fight more than's good for us, we still like our own kind more than any other when it comes to sittin' by the fire. Most rites also require plenty of Garou around, and where else are you gonna get that? Yer saddlebag? If you like, you can look at it this way, young'ns — how you ever think yer gonna rise in rank if other Garou never hear yer name? Shadow Lords love spreadin' rumors and politicking at septs, and the Silver Fangs tend to throw their weight around a bit, true, but all of us love to let our septs know what we've been up to lately. Wolves are a competitive bunch, and we Garou ain't much different, always wresslin', tellin' tall tales and otherwise seein' if we can outdo each other. It's kinda hard to do that all by yer lonesome, so you better head on down to the sept as often as you can if you want to keep from going crazy.

## Gettin' Acquainted

Well, seein' as how it's getting late and the bottle's getting empty, I'll leave you with a few other wee things to know. The first is real important, from tomorrow when you see the sept for the first time to whenever you see a new sept, and that's introducing yerself. Usually it's just a good howl or a polite how-do-you-do, nothin' fancy, but forgetting it is a fine way to make yerself mighty unpopular with the elders. Sometimes ya'll give a howl, not thinkin' too much on it, and all of a sudden you'll get a real urgent howl back — that's the Warder asking for help, and quick. You hear that and you make for the caern just as fast as you can, on account of how you'll never hear it unless there's danger that a sept can't handle on its own. Pray you never hear it, cubs — it's never a pretty sight.

## All the West's a Stage, So Where in Tarnation are the Players?

At first glance it may seem like the Savage West is too big for live games, with its vast landscapes, train rides, horse chases and ghost towns (let alone the Storm Umbra). But a few simple techniques can help keep your game under control and the players firmly in the vivid world of the Savage West. Most of this is discussed in the Storytelling chapter on page 245, but a few essential pointers deserve mention here.

First of all, designate clearly where your game is being played — even if it is an anonymous "dusty old saloon," the players should know where they are, how they got there, and why they're there. This is especially important if the location of the game changes but your actual play area does not. Actual set dressing is a good start, obviously, but above all, players should have an excellent mental picture of their surroundings. If they do, almost any scene can be played, no matter how bizarre the setting. If they don't, they get distracted and it becomes an uphill battle to pull off even a simple setting.

Set aside other rooms or areas to be used by scenes taking place at other locations, and let players know ahead of time. Nothing's more annoying than walking into a room and starting to roleplay only to be told "We're not here, we're on a stagecoach to Dallas."

Give your players good reasons to stay where they are. This doesn't mean posting guards at all exits or using strong-arm plot twists to force the players into staying at a site — there are few ways to anger players faster than hamfistedly tying them down — but giving characters reasons to want to explore the place you've chosen for the game, rather than wander off on their own. If they do wander off, don't get angry, but let Narrators handle the travel and try to smoothly guide them back to the game.

All in all, a sept is a complicated scene, full of action, intrigue, fellowship and danger. Logically enough, this makes the sept an ideal site to center many games of the Savage West around, as it is conducive to the social setting of **Mind's Eye Theatre**. Of course, unless you have a large troupe this may require the creation of Narrator characters to fill in sept positions and the like where needed (unless the story hinges on a position being empty), but the results of a well-done sept setting are immensely rewarding. Given time and imagination, though, nearly any place can be conjured up in the minds of your players.

If you decide yer gonna join a new sept, as ya'll probably will come tomorrow night, the way it goes is you ask the Warder and he gets all the sept together to give you the hairy eyeball. The Ragabash especially come out, as the sept is allowed to pretty much say what they please to you, especially since you're cubs, asking whatever questions they feel like and seein' what you do. If you keep yer heads on yer shoulders, then the Galliards will get together and sing any songs of praise they've heard 'bout you, while the Ragabash make all kinds of jokes and try to drown out the songs. If the Galliards win, the sept decides if you're worthy. Most of the time this is just being formal, especially with cubs like you, but sometimes it gets right heated, and the alpha may even have to step in.

## Moon Bridges

One last thing, and then you better unpack yer bedrolls fer the night. What's that? Staying here? Not bloody likely! If you can't stand just one night under the stars out here, I'll kick you outta the sept myself! Anyway, remember what I told you about Moon Bridges and how important they are. A caern ain't just a sacred place to Gaia, it's also the best way to get around in the world. Forget all that talk of trains and horseless carriages! A Moon Bridge can take you a thousand miles in the blink of an eye, and that's just fer starters. If the Gatekeeper knows enough, and yer pack's got a good Theurge, you can travel all over the world without ever seein' a human toy. I myself want to get back to the Old Country some day, just to see what it's like, but that's a tale for another day and another bottle. We've got our hands full out here, and don't you forget it.

## Partin' Words

The West is a strange and frightening place most a' the time, as wild as it is wide open. You got railroads, gunslingers, boom towns, card sharps, war parties, gold mines, tornadoes, stampedes, thunderstorms- hell, you just name it and if it can kill you, chances are it's already crawled out here someplace to try. But Garou are as tough as Gaia can make 'em, and I can see in yer eyes it's startin' to feel a little bit like home out here. That's good, mighty good. Because this place is home to me in more ways than one, and let me tell you, the bond only gets deeper as you get older.

Welcome to the West, cubs.

Don't forget to tip yer hats.

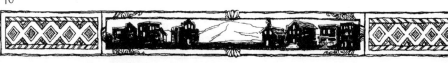

# Lexicon

*Dear cubs,*

*A good friend of mine, the noted if somewhat unlikely "Doc" Heaurt of the Bone Gnawers, recently published the first draft of an interesting work, which I thought I'd pass by you now. So far it is a reservoir of quack Garou remedies, which I have helpfully removed, but more importantly it is a collection of terms and definitions (several of which I've contributed, I must say), and I thought you might appreciate it. There's not much to most of them, but in a pinch this book might just prove handy if you forget what Pat or I taught you in the last few days. I think someday Doc means to turn it into a regular history, but all he's got worth reading are the words so far, which should suit your needs just fine anyway. After all, a new life calls for a new vocabulary, and I'm not just talking about the colorful speech down at the local saloon. Who knows? Maybe someday you'll hand this to a group of cubs yourselves. Just keep this out of the hands of non-Garou, and you should be all right. Now enjoy, and may our howls mix joyfully in the nights to come.*

*Lucas Laughs-At-Life*

## Doctor Heaurt's Miracle Remedies and Book of the Garou, Volume One

**Adren**: A pupil or a student who learns from a mentor. Also used for the title of a Garou who is Third Rank.

**Airts**: The magical paths within the spirit world (e.g., Spirit Tracks, Moon Paths, etc.).

**Aisling**: A journey into the spirit world.

**Anchorhead**: A spirit gate between the Near and Deep Umbra.

**Anruth**: A Garou who travels from caern to caern but is bound to none of them.

**Anthro**: Teacher, mentor; also used for the title of a Garou who is of the Fourth Rank.

**Apocalypse:** The age of destruction, maybe even the end of Gaia Herself — a time that werewolves prophesy will come when the Wyrm tries to swallow Gaia forever. Most Garou feel this will be the final battle, and many look to the ravages of the Storm Umbra as proof that the Apocalypse is coming, if not already here.

**Auspice**: The phase of the moon under which a particular Garou is born; commonly thought to determine personality and tendencies. The auspices are: Ragabash (New Moon; Trickster), Theurge (Crescent Moon; Seer), Philodox (Half Moon; Judge), Galliard (Gibbous Moon; Moon Dancer), Ahroun (Full Moon; Warrior).

**Ape**: A slang term for humans and homid-born Garou. Often but not always derogatory; "monkey" always is, however. Not common to the Pure Ones.

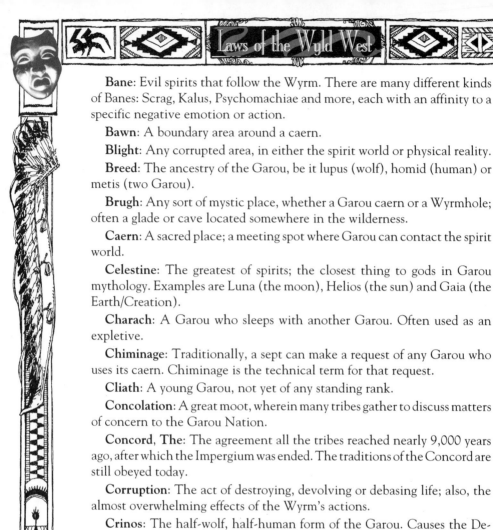

**Bane**: Evil spirits that follow the Wyrm. There are many different kinds of Banes: Scrag, Kalus, Psychomachiae and more, each with an affinity to a specific negative emotion or action.

**Bawn**: A boundary area around a caern.

**Blight**: Any corrupted area, in either the spirit world or physical reality.

**Breed**: The ancestry of the Garou, be it lupus (wolf), homid (human) or metis (two Garou).

**Brugh**: Any sort of mystic place, whether a Garou caern or a Wyrmhole; often a glade or cave located somewhere in the wilderness.

**Caern**: A sacred place; a meeting spot where Garou can contact the spirit world.

**Celestine**: The greatest of spirits; the closest thing to gods in Garou mythology. Examples are Luna (the moon), Helios (the sun) and Gaia (the Earth/Creation).

**Charach**: A Garou who sleeps with another Garou. Often used as an expletive.

**Chiminage**: Traditionally, a sept can make a request of any Garou who uses its caern. Chiminage is the technical term for that request.

**Cliath**: A young Garou, not yet of any standing rank.

**Concolation**: A great moot, wherein many tribes gather to discuss matters of concern to the Garou Nation.

**Concord, The**: The agreement all the tribes reached nearly 9,000 years ago, after which the Impergium was ended. The traditions of the Concord are still obeyed today.

**Corruption**: The act of destroying, devolving or debasing life; also, the almost overwhelming effects of the Wyrm's actions.

**Crinos**: The half-wolf, half-human form of the Garou. Causes the Delirium in humans and is considered a threat to the Veil if witnessed by outsiders.

Deep Umbra: See *Heavens*.

**Delirium**: The madness suffered by humans who see Garou in Crinos form.

**Domain**: A mini-Realm in the Umbra, usually connected to a larger Realm in the Deep Umbra.

**Elder**: A leader of Garou society. The most well-known and renowned members of a sept are called elders. Also used for the title of a Garou who is of the Fifth Rank.

**European:** General term for all Garou not of Pure One stock, regardless of their actual country of origin.

**Feral**: Slang term for lupus.

**Flock, The**: All of humanity, particularly those humans from whom the Garou recruit their Kinfolk.

**Formori**: Humans or animals who have turned to the Wyrm and draw power from it. These tainted things are blood-enemies of the Garou. Also called *Mockeries*.

**Fostern**: A Garou's pack brothers and sisters; those who are family by choice. Also used for the title of a Garou who is of the First Rank.

**Gaffling**: A simple spirit servant of a Jaggling, Incarna or Celestine. Gafflings are rarely sentient.

**Gaia**: The Earth and Her related Realm, in both a physical and spiritual sense. Most often referred to as Mother.

**Garou**: The term werewolves use for themselves.

**Gauntlet**: The barrier between the physical world of Earth and the spirit world of the Umbra. It is strongest around places of technology (Weaver), but weakest around caerns (Wyld places).

**Heavens, the**: The aspects of the Umbra that lie outside the Membrane. Reality becomes more and more fragmentary the farther one travels from the physical Earth. The Deep Umbra is comparable to deep space in reality.

**Hispo**: The near-wolf form of the Garou; does not cause Delirium and does not threaten the Veil.

**Homid**: A Garou of human ancestry. Occasionally used disdainfully by ferals (e.g., "That boy fights like a homid.").

**Gallain**: The Kinfolk of the Garou. Those humans and wolves related to Garou by blood, but not manifesting the recessive gene that creates full Garou. "Breeding true" occurs only 10 percent of the time with humans and 12 percent of the time with wolves. Gallain are not prone to the Delirium.

**Glabro**: The near-man form of the Garou. It does not cause Delirium, nor does it threaten the Veil.

**Harano**: Inexplicable gloom; inexpressible longing for unnamable things; weeping for that which is not yet lost. Some say it is depression caused by contemplation of Gaia's suffering.

**-ikthya**: "Of the Wyrm"; a suffix appended to a name.

**Impergium**: The 3,000 years immediately following the birth of agriculture, during which strict population quotas were maintained on all human villages by Garou "shepherds."

**Incarna**: A class of spirits; weaker than Celestines, but still greater spirits by any measure.

**Jaggling**: A spirit servant of an Incarna or Celestine.

**Kenning**: The empathic calling some Garou perform when howling.

**Kinain**: The relationship among Garou who are related by blood through an ancestor. This term of endearment and pride is never used when referring to metis.

**Leech**: see *Tick*.

**Litany**: The code of laws kept by the Garou.

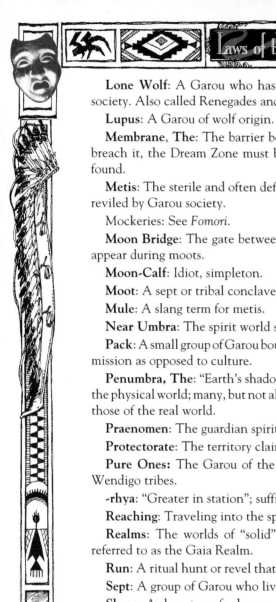

**Lone Wolf**: A Garou who has chosen or been forced to leave Garou society. Also called Renegades and less sociable names.

**Lupus**: A Garou of wolf origin.

**Membrane, The**: The barrier between the Near and Deep Umbras. To breach it, the Dream Zone must be traveled, or an Anchorhead must be found.

**Metis**: The sterile and often deformed offspring of two Garou, generally reviled by Garou society.

Mockeries: See *Fomori*.

**Moon Bridge**: The gate between two caerns. Moon Bridges most often appear during moots.

**Moon-Calf**: Idiot, simpleton.

**Moot**: A sept or tribal conclave that takes place at a caern.

**Mule**: A slang term for metis.

**Near Umbra**: The spirit world surrounding the Gaia Realm.

**Pack**: A small group of Garou bound to each other by ties of friendship and mission as opposed to culture.

**Penumbra, The**: "Earth's shadow"; the spirit world directly surrounding the physical world; many, but not all terrain features in the Penumbra mimic those of the real world.

**Praenomen**: The guardian spirit of a pack.

**Protectorate**: The territory claimed and patrolled by a pack or sept.

**Pure Ones:** The Garou of the Pure Lands; the Uktena, Croatan and Wendigo tribes.

**-rhya**: "Greater in station"; suffix appended to a name.

**Reaching**: Traveling into the spirit world.

**Realms**: The worlds of "solid" reality within the Tellurian. Earth is referred to as the Gaia Realm.

**Run**: A ritual hunt or revel that takes place at the conclusion of a moot.

**Sept**: A group of Garou who live near and tend an individual caern.

**Sheep**: A slang term for humans.

**Stepping Sideways**: Entering the spirit world. Most elders consider this term flippant and disrespectful.

**Storm Eater, The:** A great spirit, part Weaver and part Wyrm, that devours Wyld energy to feed itself. Often seen as sign of the Apocalypse.

**Storm Umbra:** The wild and chaotic Penumbra of the American West; also used to describe the areas in the Middle Lands that have suffered from the Storm Eater's taint.

**Tellurian**: The whole of reality.

**Throat**: To best someone in ritual combat. Used as a verb (e.g., "I throated his worthless carcass!").

**Tick:** One of many derogatory terms for vampires. Other common terms are Leech, Carcass, Cadaver, Corpse and Deadskin.

**Totem**: A spirit joined to a pack or tribe and representative of its inner nature. A tribal totem is an Incarna, while a pack totem is an Incarna avatar (a Jaggling equivalent).

**Triat, The**: The Weaver, the Wyld and the Wyrm. The trinity of primal cosmic forces.

**Tribe**: The larger community of Garou. Tribe members are often bound by similar totems and lifestyles.

**Urrah**: Garou who live in the city; also, the tainted ones.

**Umbra**: The spirit world.

**Veil, The**: The term used to describe the present situation, where the Garou attempt to keep the reality of their existence hidden. Also see *Delirium*.

**Ways, The**: The traditions of the Garou.

**Weaver, The**: The manifestation and symbol of order and pattern. Railroads, science, logic and mathematics are examples of the Weaver's influence on the material plane.

**Wyld, The**: The manifestation and symbol of pure change. The chaos of transmutation and elemental forces.

**Wyrm, The**: The manifestation and symbol of evil, entropy and decay. Vampires are considered manifestations of the Wyrm, as is pollution.

**Wyrmcomer:** Uktena and Wendigo term for Europeans, who natives see as having brought the Wyrm to the Pure Lands.

**Wyrmhole**: A place that has been spiritually defiled by the Wyrm; invariably a location of great corruption.

**yuf**: "Honored equal"; a suffix appended to a name.

## Below is a list of Mind's Eye Theatre specific terms, that is, definitions of words that are used in the rules of the MET system.

**Ability**: Your character's skills, knowledges and talents; the things you know and can do.

**Challenge**: The system by which conflict between two or more characters is resolved through bidding of Traits and the playing of "Rock-Paper-Scissors."

**Rank:** A measure of a character's standing in Garou society. Garou refer to the rank system among themselves as well, but since it is also a game mechanic for measuring the relative power and respect of a character it deserves mention here as well.

**Renown**: The descriptive Traits a character earns from their sept for performing acts of Glory, Wisdom and Honor. Renown is needed at certain minimal levels to secure higher rank in Garou society.

**Traits**: The adjectives used to define your character.

You have come to the place of adventure. Now you need to decide who you are and what part you play in the story that unfolds before you.

Before you can play in the Savage West, you must first create a character. Unlike simple make-believe, in **Mind's Eye Theatre** you don't just make up a character as you go. Instead, you create your character before you start playing, which prevents confusion or arguments down the road.

A character is, quite simply, the person you choose to portray in the game. Your character can continue from one story to the next, or you can play a different character each time. The choice is up to you. One given of the matter, however, is this: The more creative effort you put into your character during the creation stage, the more depth and believability she has when the story begins.

This chapter contains all the information you need to create your Garou character. The process is relatively simple and proceeds in a step-by-step fashion.

## In the Beginning...

You need to decide on your character concept: Who he is at heart, what his upbringing was like, and what motivates him. Next, develop your character's background and history, which in turn helps make up your character's personality. Get a general idea which breed, tribe and auspice would best suit the personality and background you've developed, and you've already got the framework in place to create a fully fleshed-out character.

Generally, it is assumed that a new character is a young Garou who has recently undergone the *Rite of Passage*, and is now an assimilated member of a pack. Beyond that, your character's background is left open for you to decide.

It is possible that the Storyteller may limit your character creation choices for the purposes of the story she wishes to tell. It is also possible that she offers you choices not listed here. Many times, a story has certain roles that need to be filled, and you may be asked to create a character to fill one of those roles.

This game's character creation system is based on a process of selection, allowing you to design a character to your specifications. By choosing Traits (qualities that describe your character) from a series of lists, you build the capabilities of the persona whom you play. It is best to list all the Traits and qualities you would like your character to have and then eliminate the ones that aren't essential to your concept.

## Character Creation Process

**• Step One: Character Concept — Who and what are you?**

Choose Nature and Demeanor
Choose a breed
Choose an auspice
Choose a tribe (the Storyteller has the right to refuse any of your choices)

**• Step Two: Select Attributes — What are your basic capabilities?**

Prioritize Trait Attributes (seven primary, five secondary and three tertiary)
Choose Traits

**• Step Three: Select Advantages — What do you know and what can you do?**

Choose five Abilities
Choose three Basic Gifts (one each from breed, auspice and tribe)
Choose five Backgrounds
Note Renown (by auspice)

**• Step Four: Finishing Touches — Fill in the details.**

Record Rage (determined by auspice)
Record Gnosis (determined by breed)
Record Willpower (determined by tribe)
Choose Negative Traits (if any)
Select Merits and/or Flaws, if desired (see page 188)
Purchase Influences, if desired

**• Step Five: Spark of Life — Narrative descriptions and other details**

## Step One: Character Concept

Before you write anything down on your character sheet, you need to find inspiration for the character you want to play. Are you a gunslinger, a banker, a brave, a madam? These are just a few of the thousands of concepts you can base a character on, but once you have an idea of this basic form, the rest of the character should flow around the structure of that initial inspiration. Work with your Storyteller throughout the character creation process, which should help make your character eminently suitable for the chronicle in which you will be playing. Remember, your choices should be made to develop a character, not to gain a game mechanic advantage.

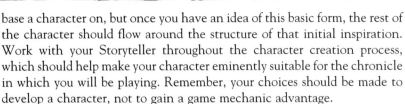

Character development begins with defining her personality. This is where you decide who your character is, what her private innermost self is like, and what sort of face she shows to the world.

## Nature and Demeanor

Your character's Nature and Demeanor define the basic tenets of her personality. Nature and Demeanor are, quite simply, the disposition and image of your character. Once you have defined your basic concept, the next step in character creation is selecting appropriate Archetypes for your character's Nature and Demeanor from the list below.

A character's Nature is her true inner self, while her Demeanor is the mask she most often shows to the world. It is not unheard of for a character to have the same Nature and Demeanor; however, it is unlikely. Few people are that honest with other people, or even with themselves.

### Archetypes

• Alpha — You are a born leader. You pride yourself on knowing what you are doing and what needs to be done next. Getting others to follow you is not a matter of if, it is a matter of when.

• Arbitrator — You seek the truth and reconciliation in everything. You have little time for the games of others, and strive to reach the heart of every matter.

• Architect — You believe in creating something of lasting value. You seek to leave a legacy of some kind for those who will come after you, and want to know that what you do will last.

• Bravo — You're a bully. Fear equals respect in your mind. You reinforce your own self-worth by pumping yourself up and denigrating others, and you take every opportunity to make others respect you. From braves on the warpath to drunks in a saloon, your motives and methods may differ, but in the end only raw domination — yours — matters.

• Caregiver — People need tending, and you have the touch. You are highly concerned about helping others fight the constant pull of frenzy and Harano, and help Garou and kin find common ground. Those who deserve help shall receive whatever aid you can render, and in a place as rough as the Savage West, that's a lot of folks.

• Competitor — Gunslingers have nothing on your ken for a tournament; everything is a contest to you. As far as you're concerned, if you lose you're as good as buried.

• Cub — Still a tenderfoot, you are naive at times and have an air of innocence about you, but you know that you can get what you want if you pout and whine enough.

• Curmudgeon — Sour cuss through and through, you find the wry humor in life's little woes. You are the first to see the bad news coming, for you have always put your faith in the ineptitude of others.

• Deputy — You may never take the lead, but you always pull your share of the work, whether or not anyone else notices. Taking orders is natural to you, as is following them to the best of your ability. Getting recognized for your achievements isn't what you're after; that's someone else's cross to bear. You're just here to make sure it gets done in the first place.

• Deviant — You do not quite fit in, but it's not as if you want to. You are happiest when the trail you take is one you're blazing yourself, but don't expect others to accept or even understand what you're doing.

• Elitist — Nobody ever measures up to the standards of your chosen clique, whether it's race, auspice, wealth or some other quality — if they're different, they're lessers by definition. Note that no one is immune to elitism; some of the poor are as bad as those who pass them in their fancy carriages. Observing the failures of these lessers amuses you and reinforces who you are.

• Enigma — Whoever you are, whatever happened in your past, you're determined to keep such secrets to yourself. Whether you adopt fake identities or hide behind an actual mask is your own choice, but in the end hiding your true face keeps you from being hurt, and that's what really matters.

• Explorer — The Savage West is a huge place, and the joy of finding new people, places and things fills your existence with the greatest excitement imaginable. It's not what you find that's important, it's the discovery itself that matters.

• Gambler — The kind to stake all you have on one toss of the dice, you believe life is about taking chances. You do things, not for the outcome, but for the thrill. Whether you win or lose is not necessarily important; you thrive on the high that comes from risking yourself time and time again, and as the stakes get higher your smile gets wider.

• Jester — You find humor in everything. Life is one big joke, and someone has to look on the bright side, and that someone is you.

• Listener — You have a way for getting people to tell you all kinds of things, but you're always careful not to abuse this trust, considering it a high honor indeed. You strive to earn the respect and confidence of others.

• Lone Wolf — You exist on the periphery. You have your own plans, and they do not include getting bogged down by others. Having to work with others means you have to rely on them; you prefer to rely on yourself.

• Loyalist — You are totally willing to make sacrifices for your beliefs; even unto death. Knowing that someone else is happy makes any misery you put yourself through worthwhile. You do not want any rewards other than recognition for your sacrifices.

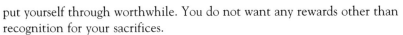

• Omega — You are strong-willed and a real free thinker. If the system needs to come down, you are just the one to start it tumbling. There always seems to be something you are rebelling against, though you do not necessarily have a better solution in mind. You just know that things cannot stay the way they are.

• Penitent — You wish to atone for who or what you are, or to make up for something that you've done. You always feel you should have done better. As far as you're concerned, Gaia is losing because you, personally, are not carrying your own weight. The Storm Eater is coming, and it is all your fault, because you haven't lived up to what you should be.

• Predator — You are the quintessential hunter. Stalking and chasing are all part of your art. The world is full of targets and challengers to be brought down and feasted upon.

• Progressive — You are interested only in what is new or on the cutting edge. You must be the first to discover or create something that people have never seen before. You are interested in seeing everyone live better and fuller lives because of new advances, and while not necessarily arrogant you do believe the best hope for the future lies in casting aside the old ways.

• Reluctant Garou — You long for a normal life. The life of adventure and danger isn't for you. Why can't you just have to face the perils of the Savage West without all these mystical complications? The world survived all these years without you fighting its battles, and you're sure it will continue long after you are gone.

• Reveler — You live to experience life's many pleasures. Your hedonism might draw disapproving looks from the church-going folk, but no matter what, your pursuit of new pleasures is your main concern. If it doesn't hurt innocents, there's nothing wrong with it for you.

• Scoundrel — You have no problem taking from women and children to get what you want, and to hell with anyone else thinks about it. It doesn't matter what it takes to get something you want, you're up to it, and if other people don't have the sense to see such simple solutions, then it's their own fault.

• Show-Off — You get your self-worth from others. Be the brightest dresser, the silliest, the boldest, the brashest — that's what you need to feel good about yourself. If others do not pay attention to you, it's because you have not done anything worthy of their attention.

• Survivor — You always pull through. No matter what happens, you intend to survive. You will never say never, even to the rough life you lead now. No matter what Fate throws at you, you will fight to the bitter end for just one more minute of existence. Sometimes that means sacrificing things (and people), but it's a price you're willing to pay.

• Swindler — Whether you work the marks with your "amazing elixirs" or take money from suckers with loaded dice, you get by in the world by taking advantage of others. As far as you are concerned, the rest of the population consists of pigeons for you to exploit, laws to ignore and sheriffs to avoid. You are always trying to get someone else to do your dirty work for you.

• Traditionalist — The Garou have hundreds of rites, rituals and observances, and if you had your say, every cub around the fires would be able to name them all. More than that, you subscribe to the past standards of society in general; after all, there are tried and true ways of dealing with things, and you follow them because they work. Why take a chance on an "iron horse" when your faithful flesh one is waiting for you at the post?

• True Believer — You are obsessed with a cause. You alone know the truth; any contrary viewpoints are automatically wrong. If others disagree with you, it is because they are against you and must be dealt with, whether through proselytizing or even violence.

• Visionary — You see beyond the boundaries of the conventional. You know there has to be something more to it all, something unimaginably greater than just existence. This is what keeps you going.

## Breed

The Garou are the Changing Race, torn between the two worlds of wolves and men. However, the very nature of their existence prevents them from truly having a home with either race. Indeed, they are doubly cursed, for Garou cannot mate with Garou, and thus, the Changing Breed must dwell within, yet never truly be a part of, the worlds of humans and wolves.

While passions run deep in the changing folk, Garou who choose to mate with each other violate the oldest laws of their kind. The product of a Garou-Garou union is always sterile and usually malformed. Such werewolves are called metis, and are often shunned by their lupus and homid brethren. Therefore, Garou must continually mate (or breed) with those outside their own race.

The Garou keep close track of the offspring of those humans and wolves with whom they breed, watching carefully for signs that the recessive gene that controls changing has been passed on or "bred true." The product of a Garou mating with a human or wolf is not always a Garou. Very few children breed true and pure enough to undergo their First Change, but when they do, it is a cause for all Garou to celebrate.

There are three breeds of Garou to choose from: homid (human), lupus (wolf) and metis (offspring of two Garou). A Garou's breed is determined by the breed of his mother. The three breeds are:

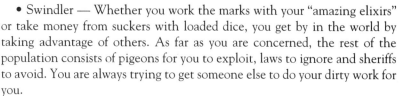

• **Homid**: Born to human parents, you were probably always a bit of a wild one, and were haunted by strange feelings and ominous dreams of the wilderness throughout childhood. However, until adulthood was upon you and the First Change came, you had no idea of your true lineage.

**Nickname**: Monkey

**Initial Gnosis**: One

**Breed Gifts**: (choose one) *Jam Gun, Persuasion, Smell of Man, Staredown*

• **Metis**: The shameful product of the union of two Garou, you are sterile and malformed, and are treated as an outcast by other werewolves. You do, however, understand the inner workings of Garou society better than the other breeds do, having been raised on the short end of it for so long.

**Nickname**: Mule (one of the nicest of the many out there)

**Initial Gnosis**: Two

**Breed Gifts**: (choose one) *Create Element, Curse of Hatred, Sense Wyrm, Wildcat Eyes*

• **Lupus**: Raised as a wild wolf, you did not discover your Garou legacy until you were almost fully grown. The ways of the humans mystify you, as you were raised closer to the heart of Gaia than the other breeds were.

**Nickname**: Feral

**Initial Gnosis**: Three

**Breed Gifts**: (choose one) *Catfeet, Heightened Senses, Scent of Sight, Spook the Herd*

## Auspice

Your auspice is the phase of the moon under which your character was born. This aspect is held in astrological reverence by most Garou. It does more than predetermine certain aspects of your personality, it also helps to define your role in Garou society.

There are five auspices under which a character may be born. Each has its own special strengths and weaknesses. Many commonly held ideas about auspices can be dismissed as superstition, yet there is certainly some truth behind them as well.

Some truly exceptional Garou rebel against their moon-signs. They renounce their born auspices in favor of other ones. These Garou are rare indeed, for one loses everything when one chooses a new auspice. Such a renunciate must start her education over again.

For more on auspices, see pp.109

The auspices of the Garou are:

## Ragabash

New Moon

The Trickster

**Initial Rage**: One

**Auspice Gifts**: (choose one) *Walk Under the New Moon, Spider's Song,*

*Carried on the Wind, Scent of Running Water*

**Beginning Renown**: Three Renown Traits in any combination

### Theurge

Crescent Moon

The Seer

**Initial Rage**: One

**Auspice Gifts**: (choose one) *Mother's Touch, Name the Spirit, Sense Wyrm, Spirit Speech, Sight from Beyond*

**Beginning Renown**: Two Wisdom Traits, One Glory or Honor Trait

### Philodox

Half Moon

The Judge

**Initial Rage**: Two

**Auspice Gifts**: (choose one) *Resist Pain, Scent of the True Form, Strength of Purpose, Truth of Gaia*

**Beginning Renown**: Two Honor Traits, One Wisdom Trait

### Galliard

Gibbous Moon

The Moon Dancer

**Initial Rage**: Two

**Auspice Gifts**: (choose one) *Beast Life, Call of the Wyld, Distractions, Mindspeak*

**Beginning Renown**: One Glory Trait, Two Wisdom or Honor Traits

### Ahroun

Full Moon

The Warrior

**Initial Rage**: Three

**Auspice Gifts**: (choose one) *Inspiration, The Falling Touch, Razor Claws, Spirit of the Fray*

**Beginning Renown**: Two Glory Traits, One Honor Trait

### Tribe

A tribe is a character's family of sorts. It is his lineage and heritage, at once genetic, cultural and social. Your tribe says a great deal about who and what you are. Each tribe has its own beliefs, pursuits, strengths and weaknesses. There is a great variety of tribes; 13 in all still fight the Wyrm.

For more information on the tribes, see pp. 113.

The Garou tribes are:

• **Black Furies**: This tribe, composed almost entirely of women, strikes out in defense of the Wyld and to protect those who cannot defend themselves.

**Initial Willpower**: One

**Backgrounds**: No restrictions.

**Tribe Gifts**: (choose one) *Kneel, Sense of the Prey, Sense Wyrm, Song of the Seasons*

• **Bone Gnawers**: Vagrants, laborers and others on the low end of society, the Gnawers are incredible survivors, but they receive little notice for their efforts.

**Initial Willpower**: Two

**Backgrounds**: May not buy Past Life or Pure Breed, or begin the game with *Finances* Influence; must spend two Traits on Kinfolk.

**Tribe Gifts**: (choose one) *Cornered Rat, Hide in Plain Sight, Odious Aroma, Stone Soup*

• **Children of Gaia**: Proponents of unity between the tribes and healing the rift between the Europeans and the Pure Ones, the Children are mediators of the Garou and defenders of humanity.

**Initial Willpower**: Two

**Backgrounds**: No restrictions.

**Tribe Gifts**: (choose one) *Calm, Luna's Armor, Mother's Touch, Resist Pain*

• **Fianna**: Immigrants from the Emerald Isle and beyond, the clannish Fianna are passionate and fiercely proud of their heritage.

**Initial Willpower**: Two

**Backgrounds**: No restrictions.

**Tribe Gifts**: (chose one) *Family Tree, Glib Tongue, Howl of the Banshee, Resist Toxin*

• **Get of Fenris**: Honorable and relentless warriors, the ferocious Get are also among the tribes in the worst conflict with the Pure Ones.

**Initial Willpower**: One

**Backgrounds**: May not begin the game with more than three Influences.

**Tribe Gifts**: (choose one) *Cry of the Killer, Razor Claws, Resist Pain, Safe Haven*

• **Iron Riders**: Heralds of towns and progress, the Iron Riders claim that cities are only one more step in the evolution of Gaia.

**Initial Willpower**: Two

**Backgrounds**: May not buy Past Life or Pure Breed; also start with an additional Influence.

**Tribe Gifts**: (choose one) *Control Simple Machine, Iron Fur, Persuasion, Sense Weaver*

• **Red Talons**: Fierce opponents of human expansion in all its forms, the all-lupus Talons are highly spiritual and deadly opponents.

**Initial Willpower**: Two

**Backgrounds**: May not begin the game with Influences.

**Tribe Gifts**: (choose one) *Beast Life, Eye of the Hunter, Scent of Running Water, Sense of the Prey*

• **Shadow Lords**: Mysterious intriguers and powerful warriors, the Shadow Lords care only for the strong, and covet the leadership of the tribes.

**Initial Willpower**: Two

**Backgrounds**: May not begin the game with more than three levels of Influences.

**Tribe Gifts**: (choose one) *Aura of Confidence, Clap of Thunder, Fatal Flaw, Mark of Suspicion*

• **Silent Striders**: Trail dust forever on their soles, the enigmatic Striders have wandered far and seen much in both the physical realm and the Umbra.

**Initial Willpower**: Two

**Backgrounds**: May not buy Past Life, or Influences that are not accessible worldwide (Storyteller approval).

**Tribe Gifts**: (choose one) *Dust-Talking, Messenger's Fortitude, Sense Wyrm, Speed of Thought*

• **Silver Fangs**: Noblest of the tribes, the Fangs lead the battle against the Wyrm, strive for recognition among the Pure Ones, and fight against crippling madness and pride within.

**Initial Willpower**: Two

**Backgrounds**: Must spend at least three Background Traits on Pure Breed.

**Tribe Gifts**: (choose one) *Imposing Gaze, Lambent Flame, Luna's Armor, Sense Wyrm*

• **Stargazers**: Exotic and enlightened voices in the Savage West, members of this tribe hail from any known land, and bring a wisdom born of all of them wherever they go.

**Initial Willpower**: Three

**Backgrounds**: May not begin the game with fetishes or Influences.

**Tribe Gifts**: (choose one) *Catfeet, Inner Strength, Measured Step, Sense Wyrm*

• **Uktena**: Crafty keepers of ancient magics and fetishes, the Uktena are one of the two surviving tribes of the Pure Ones.

**Initial Willpower**: Two

**Background**: No restrictions.

**Tribe Gifts**: (choose one) *Flick of the Fish's Tail, Pass as the Shadow, Sense the Tunneler's Passage, Sense Medicine*

• **Wendigo**: Composed entirely of Pure Ones and simmering with rage over the invasion of their lands, the Wendigo take the warpath against all who would encroach upon them.

**Initial Willpower**: Two

**Backgrounds**: May not begin the game with Influences other than *Tribal.*

**Tribe Gifts**: (choose one) *Call the Breeze*, *Camouflage*, *Cutting Wind*, *Song of the Seasons*

## Step Two: Attributes

Attributes are everything a character naturally is. Are you strong? Are you brave? Are you persuasive? Questions such as these are answered by the way you distribute your Attributes.

There are three categories of Attributes: Physical, Social and Mental. You must prioritize the three categories, placing them in order of importance to your character. These choices may well be influenced by your auspice, for most auspices tend toward one Attribute category more than the others. For example, the player of an Ahroun usually sets his Physical Traits primary and his Social Traits tertiary, while a Ragabash's player is likely to make Social Traits most important.

Attribute Traits reflect your character's competence at different kinds of actions. The more Traits you have in one Attribute category, the more skillfully your character performs actions involving that category and the higher you can bid on relevant tests. Those Physical and Mental Traits specifically marked "Gunfighting Traits" are also used to form a special Gunfighting Pool for use with the optional quick-draw showdown rules on page 228.

### Attribute Categories

Physical Attributes describe the capabilities of the body, such as strength, dexterity and endurance.

Social Attributes describe a character's appearance, charisma and capacity to influence others.

Mental Attributes describe a character's mental prowess. They include things such as awareness of one's surroundings, resolve, memory, self-control and concentration.

Traits are adjectives that describe your character's strengths and weaknesses, defining your character just as a character in a novel is defined. In your primary (strongest) Attribute category, choose seven Traits. Choose five Traits in your secondary category. Choose three Traits In your tertiary (weakest) category. You can take the same Trait more than once to illustrate that the character is particularly gifted in a certain area (a character who is a gunfighter might well have the Trait: *Quick* three times).

## Physical Traits

**Athletic**: From steer-roping to pitching stones to kicking open a barroom door, your body is conditioned to respond well, especially in competitive events.

Uses: Sports, duels, running, acrobatics and grappling.

**Brawny**: Able to wrap your arms around a bear and make him feel it, you possess bulky, muscular power.

Uses: Punching, kicking or grappling in combat when your goal is to inflict damage. Power lifting. All feats of strength.

**Brutal**: Tougher than a rattler's heart, there's no action that you're not capable of doing if it means survival.

Uses: Fighting an obviously superior enemy.

**Dexterous**: Your hands are steady and your fingers fly; if any trade takes skill with your hands, chances are you can do it.

Uses: Weapon-oriented combat. Picking pockets. Punching. Gunfighting Trait.

**Enduring**: A mesa in the desert winds, you don't lie down in the face of persistent physical opposition.

Uses: When your survival is at stake, this is a good Trait to risk as a second, or successive, bid.

**Energetic**: Full of get up and go from the day you were born, if anyone's still eager to put in more hours at the end of the day, it'll be you. And even when the trail ahead threatens to really get ornery, you still have a whole well of energy just waiting to be drawn on.

Uses: Combat.

**Ferocious**: You leave your enemies in plenty of pieces when you set out to do harm, and once you have it in for a man your determination to put the hurt on him is nothing shy of amazing.

Uses: Any time that you intend to do serious harm. When in frenzy.

**Graceful**: The envy of county fairs and fancy balls alike, you have an excellent sense of control and balance over the movements and uses of your entire body.

Uses: Combat defense. Whenever you might lose your balance (crossing a river on stepping stones, fighting on four-inch-thick rafters).

**Lithe**: As hard to lay hands on as a greased cottonmouth, you possess excellent flexibility and suppleness.

Uses: Acrobatics, gymnastics, dodging and dancing.

**Nimble**: Jackrabbit toes and the reflexes of a deer mark this talent for light, agile movements.

Uses: Dodging, jumping, rolling and acrobatics. Hand-to-hand combat.

**Quick**: Greased lightning looks slow by comparison; your body tends to react to stress or danger even before your head knows what's what.

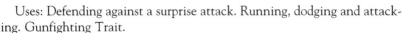

Uses: Defending against a surprise attack. Running, dodging and attacking. Gunfighting Trait.

**Resilient**: You tend to bounce back from illness much faster than most, and folks can count on one hand the number of times you've complained about the weather.

Uses: Resisting adverse environments. Defending against damage in an attack.

**Robust**: Taking punches is no problem for you, nor five days of constant riding.

Uses: Defending against damage in an attack. Endurance-related actions that could take place over a period of time.

**Rugged**: A true product of the Savage West, you know how to take the worst life throws at you; you can light a match with your chin after being shot twice in the arm and still feel up to finishing your day's work.

Uses: When resisting damage. Any challenge that you enter while injured.

**Stalwart**: When it comes time to take your licks, you stand your ground and impress even the most lowdown of bandits with your gumption.

Uses: Resisting damage, or when standing your ground against overwhelming odds or a superior foe.

**Steady**: Folks set their clocks by your actions, and you're always on top of any task you set yourself to. It's as much in the head and in the body, though- you have a firm understanding and control over everything you do, unfaltering and balanced.

Uses: Weapon attacks. Fighting in exotic locations. Piloting clipper ships. Gunfighting Trait.

**Tenacious**: Wolves on the hunt have nothing on your ken for seeing through what you've started, with your sheer stubbornness keeping you going if need be. This isn't always wise, of course- you tend to stay in the ring long after most fighters know to throw in the towel.

Uses: Second or subsequent Physical Challenge.

**Tireless**: After a couple dozen miles of riding, a foot race and a swim across the Rio Grande, you're still not out of breath, and your endurance easily outstrips many people.

Uses: Any endurance-related challenge, second or subsequent Physical Challenge with the same foe or foes.

**Tough**: If harsh, uncompromising attitude alone was enough to tame the Savage West, you'd already be king of all you survey. Folk reckon you'll give in to a challenge around the same time man walks on the moon.

Uses: Whenever you are wounded or winded.

**Vigorous**: No snake oil sells this kind of raw energy and intensity, and you live to prove it.

Uses: Combat and athletic challenges when you are on the defensive.

**Wiry**: Built like a coil of barbed wire and twice as strong, you might not look like you have much meat on you, but you more than make up for it in compact, muscular power.

Uses: Punching, kicking or grappling in combat. Acrobatic movements. Endurance lifting.

## Negative Physical Traits

Note: For more information on Negative Traits, see page 89.

**Clumsy**: Nobody asks you to hold their drink, much less carry anything valuable or latch the barnyard gate. If anyone falls in a mud puddle or a cow pie, it's likely to be you.

**Cowardly**: Yellow bellied to the last, when danger calls you make darn sure you have other plans. Even when you're winning, you sometimes lose your nerve and haul tail anyway, just from habit.

**Decrepit**: Either age or constitution has not treated you kindly, and you move as if you're old and infirm. Recovery from even slight injuries is a long time coming, you tire out fast, and you are unable to apply all your physical strength.

**Delicate**: Perhaps you are slight of build, or maybe you were a true mama's boy after all, but regardless you are easily hurt by physical forces.

**Docile**: When it comes to having your say, you're about as outspoken as wet clay and twice as malleable. The opposite of the *Ferocious* and *Tenacious* Traits; you lack physical persistence and tend to submit rather than fight long battles.

**Flabby**: You're in perfect shape, if man is meant to be built like a damp sack of flour. You have trouble using your strength against opponents, and your muscles are just aching for some kind of exercise.

**Lame**: Maybe a horse rolled over on you, or perhaps you lost an eye in a bar fight, but whatever the cause you're crippled in one or more limbs. This can be as easy to spot as a missing leg or as subtle as an arm that just ain't quite right anymore.

**Lethargic**: A herd of turtles walking uphill through molasses in January is still likely to beat you in a race, and you move like you're about to lie down for a *siesta* any time now. Maybe you had some South American sleeping sickness, or you could be just plain lazy, but whatever it is you have trouble mustering any energy or drive.

**Puny**: A true runt of the litter, you must have been last in line when muscles were handed out. This often, but not always, also means diminutive size.

**Sickly**: It's a wonder if you walk to town on most days, let alone ride a round up or enter a bar fight. Whether you're actually sick or not, your body responds to stress as if it were in the last gasps of a debilitating illness.

## Social Traits

**Alluring**: Setting hearts afire with a wink and a smile is no problem, and you're skilled at using your natural presence to inspire such desire in others.

Uses: Seduction. Convincing others.

**Beguiling**: There's the Devil, there's Daniel Webster, and then there's you. Snake oil salesman study your silver tongue, and spinning a yarn and getting folks to believe it is second nature to you.

Uses: Tricking others. Lying under duress.

**Charismatic**: You have a gift for rousing the hearts of others to your cause, from saloons to council fires, and your bearing carries all the signs of a strong leader.

Uses: In a situation involving leadership or the achievement of leadership.

**Charming**: Most folk are sweet on you from the start, as your words and deeds just seem to strike them in a pleasing fashion.

Uses: Convincing. Persuading.

**Commanding**: Your voice brings cattle back to the herd and snaps soldiers to attention at 30 yards, and when things get chaotic people naturally look to you to sort things out. You just have a knack for bringing people in line and getting them working on what needs to be done.

Uses: When you are seen as a leader. Direct confrontations.

**Compassionate**: Some folk study the lives of the saints for lessons on feeling care or pity for their fellow creatures, but they'd do just as well to watch you from day to day.

Uses: Defending the weak or downtrodden. Defeating major obstacles while pursuing an altruistic end.

**Dignified**: Even covered in trail dust or up to your elbows in grease, you look right ready to walk into the most delicate of situations. You walk tall and inspire trust with your posture and manner, and no matter what people comment on how well you comport yourself.

Uses: Leadership situations. Might be important in impressing some tribes for advancement.

**Diplomatic**: Defusing social situations like a bomb expert with dynamite, your careful speech and thoughtful manner ensure that few walk away from conversations with you with hard feelings.

Uses: Very important in intrigue. Leadership situations.

**Elegant**: High society and a sense of nobility follow at your heels, and while you do not need money to be elegant, you nevertheless give off an air of sophistication and taste.

Uses: High society. At moots with Silver Fangs.

**Eloquent**: Your way with words is well-known, and your ability to put a convincing phrase or moving speech together is quite respectable.

Uses: Convincing others. Swaying emotions. Public speaking. Storytelling.

**Empathetic**: Finding out what makes folks tick is your specialty, and identifying the moods and emotions of others comes naturally to you.

Uses: Sympathy. Gauging the feelings of others.

**Expressive**: No matter what you're actually saying, from selections of the Bard to lines of your own devising, you fascinate audiences with your colorful, meaningful presentation.

Uses: Producing art, acting, performing. Any social situation in which you want someone to understand your meaning.

**Friendly**: Why, you're a regular huckleberry, and even if you've only said three words to someone in your whole life he can't easily bring himself to dislike you.

Uses: Convincing others.

**Genial**: A warm campfire in a night of conversation, you're kindly, polite and easy to be around.

Uses: Mingling at parties. Generally used in a second or later Social Challenge with someone.

**Gorgeous**: There are some God makes more in His divine image than others, and you're one such lucky soul. Your body and face are attractive to most people you meet.

Uses: Modeling, posing and flirting.

**Ingratiating**: Getting into folk's good graces is second nature to you, and you know just how to mind your betters.

Uses: Dealing with elders in a social situation.

**Intimidating**: Most people would rather sleep with an angry rattler than get on your bad side, and you've won more than a few fights before they started with just a cold look, a cocked eyebrow and a sneer. When you choose, you have a talent for making others wish they were elsewhere fast.

Uses: Inspiring common fear. Ordering others.

**Magnetic**: People just naturally seem to want to be around you, and they find your speech and actions interesting.

Uses: Seduction. Intimation. Leadership.

**Persuasive**: You have a way of getting others to accept your side of the story, and win more arguments than you lose. When others sit astride the fence, unsure of what to do, you have a talent for getting them over to your point of view.

Uses: Cajoling or convincing others.

**Seductive**: In a proper town scandals follow you like horseflies on a gelding, but no one can deny the power of your honeyed charms. You can use your body and manner to ensnare others, and once you've got them it's often a simple matter to get what you want.

Uses: Subterfuge and subversion.

**Witty**: You can set the party rolling with your quips, and being perceived as a funny person takes very little effort.

Uses: At parties. Entertaining someone. Goading or insulting someone.

## Negative Social Traits

**Bestial**: Garou or not, there's something about you that is deeply not right to human eyes, and you look decidedly inhuman (or subhuman). Maybe your bones show through your skin, or your eyes glow green like a wolf's, or maybe your smile has a few too many pointed teeth for comfort.

**Callous**: Most figure they have a better chance of tossing snowballs in Hell before they'll get a tear or a kind word from you; your heart is as cool as the deepest river bed in the territories.

**Condescending**: Like it or not, folks see a strut in your walk or a snook of your nose that just telegraphs your contempt for your fellow creatures.

**Dull**: People roll their eyes when they see you coming to talk to them, and joke behind your back about dying of boredom when you're around. You have trouble making yourself seem interesting to others.

**Naive**: Wide-eyed and untouched by the air of worldliness that others carry, you strike them as someone who's seen little and knows less.

**Obnoxious**: You're fingernails on a chalkboard as far as those around you are concerned, whether it's because of the way you act, what you say, or just how you look.

**Repugnant**: When you show your ugly mug, babies cry, men wince, and girls close the kissing booth at county fairs. Someone took the ugly stick and set upon you but good with it.

**Shy**: Deer are less skittish than you when it comes to people, and your timid hesitation has lost you your share of chances in social circles.

**Tactless**: Some people have mouths that they just love to put their feet in, and you possess just such an orifice. What is "proper" for a situation always seems to be the opposite of what you manage to do.

**Untrustworthy**: Perhaps you are rumored to have a shady past, or maybe you just can't keep a secret, but no matter what the cause (or if there's any truth behind it) you are considered unreliable by others.

## Mental Traits

**Alert**: Your mind is as well-oiled as a bear trap, and reacts quickly in the face of danger.

Uses: Preventing surprise attacks. Gunfighting Trait.

**Attentive**: Minding little details in your daily routine is second nature, and if anyone notices the cattle looking nervous just in time to prevent a big stampede, it'll be you.

Uses: Preventing surprise attacks.

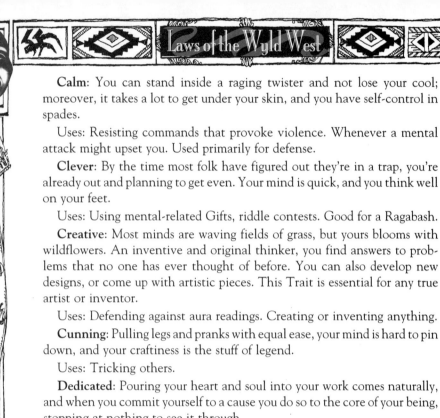

**Calm**: You can stand inside a raging twister and not lose your cool; moreover, it takes a lot to get under your skin, and you have self-control in spades.

Uses: Resisting commands that provoke violence. Whenever a mental attack might upset you. Used primarily for defense.

**Clever**: By the time most folk have figured out they're in a trap, you're already out and planning to get even. Your mind is quick, and you think well on your feet.

Uses: Using mental-related Gifts, riddle contests. Good for a Ragabash.

**Creative**: Most minds are waving fields of grass, but yours blooms with wildflowers. An inventive and original thinker, you find answers to problems that no one has ever thought of before. You can also develop new designs, or come up with artistic pieces. This Trait is essential for any true artist or inventor.

Uses: Defending against aura readings. Creating or inventing anything.

**Cunning**: Pulling legs and pranks with equal ease, your mind is hard to pin down, and your craftiness is the stuff of legend.

Uses: Tricking others.

**Dedicated**: Pouring your heart and soul into your work comes naturally, and when you commit yourself to a cause you do so to the core of your being, stopping at nothing to see it through.

Uses: Useful in any Mental Challenge when your beliefs are at stake.

**Determined**: A train has a better chance of rushing through a mountain than a man has of changing your mind once your course is set.

Uses: Facedowns. Useful in a normal Mental Challenge.

**Discerning**: Fine details, little faults and other things normally overlooked appear clear to your eyes.

Uses: Researching or when perception-based Gifts are being used.

**Disciplined**: Either through formal training or just a ramrod disposition, your mind is tightly controlled, and battles of will are little trouble for you.

Uses: Facedowns. Asserting your will. Concentration. Gunfighting Trait.

**Insightful**: Your have a formidable ken for figuring out the dynamics of a situation at a glance.

Uses: *Investigation* (but not defending against it). Using *Heightened Senses*.

**Intuitive**: You trust your gut feelings more than most, and with good reason: things that come to you that way just seem to have a habit of being true.

Uses: Seeing through Disciplines or Gifts meant to cloud your mind.

**Knowledgeable**: Sometime in your life you spent time in serious, scholarly study, and it shows. You have a lot of detailed information about a wide variety of subjects, reflecting the "book learning" of the time.

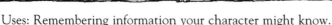

Uses: Remembering information your character might know.

**Observant**: If the sheriff is asking witnesses about a crime, he goes to you first, since your ability to notice important details is well-known.

Uses: *Heightened Senses*. Picking up on subtleties that others might overlook.

**Patient**: Mountains move in less time than it takes for you to lose your temper, and you can wait out the longest dry spells or hard times.

Uses: Facedowns or other mental battles after another Trait has been bid.

**Rational**: Man may be the quintessence of dust, but that doesn't mean he doesn't play by rules, and you have a firm notion that sanity, reason, logic and sobriety are the standards to measure against. Your talent for reducing problems to their barest terms has served you well in your time.

Uses: Defending against emotion-oriented mental attacks. Not used as an initial bid.

**Reflective**: A thoughtful soul and deep thinker, you consider all aspects of a problem before offering a solution.

Uses: *Meditation*. Remembering information. Defending against most mental attacks.

**Shrewd**: You have a considerable talent for settling disputes, escaping jams and otherwise accomplishing mental feats with efficiency and finesse.

Uses: Defending against mental attacks. Plotting tactics or playing politics.

**Vigilant**: You play with your cards close to your vest, and your watchful eye is the bane of pickpockets and other ne'er-do-wells everywhere.

Uses: Defending against *Investigation*. More appropriate for mental defense than for attack. Gunfighting Trait.

**Wily**: Full of trickery and guile, not only can you lead a horse to water, you can get his rider to buy the whole watering hole.

Uses: Tricking others. Lying under duress. Confusing mental situations.

**Wise**: Other hands mind your words when they share the fence with you after a day's ride, and when you speak the others around the council fires respectfully fall silent.

Uses: Giving advice. Recalling ancestral wisdom.

## Negative Mental Traits

**Forgetful**: Wait, I was where when? And did *what*?

**Gullible**: There's a sucker born every minute, and chances are it's in your family. If anyone buys from the man with the wide smile and the wagon full of wonderful elixirs, it's you.

**Ignorant**: You have yet to make the acquaintance of the inside of a schoolhouse, and it shows.

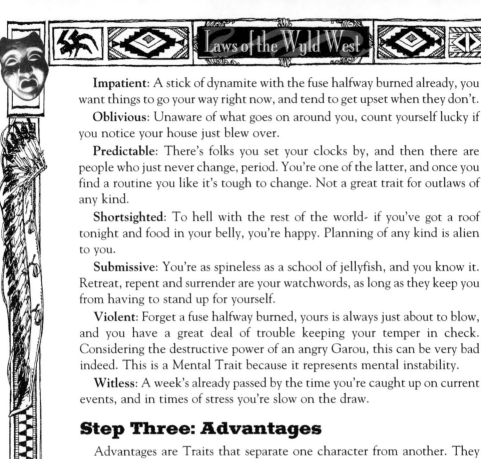

**Impatient**: A stick of dynamite with the fuse halfway burned already, you want things to go your way right now, and tend to get upset when they don't.

**Oblivious**: Unaware of what goes on around you, count yourself lucky if you notice your house just blew over.

**Predictable**: There's folks you set your clocks by, and then there are people who just never change, period. You're one of the latter, and once you find a routine you like it's tough to change. Not a great trait for outlaws of any kind.

**Shortsighted**: To hell with the rest of the world- if you've got a roof tonight and food in your belly, you're happy. Planning of any kind is alien to you.

**Submissive**: You're as spineless as a school of jellyfish, and you know it. Retreat, repent and surrender are your watchwords, as long as they keep you from having to stand up for yourself.

**Violent**: Forget a fuse halfway burned, yours is always just about to blow, and you have a great deal of trouble keeping your temper in check. Considering the destructive power of an angry Garou, this can be very bad indeed. This is a Mental Trait because it represents mental instability.

**Witless**: A week's already passed by the time you're caught up on current events, and in times of stress you're slow on the draw.

## Step Three: Advantages

Advantages are Traits that separate one character from another. They allow a player to take actions that would otherwise be impossible. There are four categories of Advantages: Abilities, Gifts, Backgrounds and Renown.

### Choosing Abilities

Abilities represent the skills you've developed and the training you've had up to this point in your life. They summarize the "mundane" things you know and can do. Many Abilities allow you to perform specific tasks that are only possible through training, while others enhance your performance of every-day tasks and functions. Some specialized tasks are only possible with training: riding horses, solving puzzles or plugging a nickel in the air. Obviously, some Abilities do not translate well or do not apply to the Savage West. Others have been incorporated into the Attributes and can be performed by executing challenges.

If your character is defeated in a challenge, you may choose to sacrifice a level in an appropriate Ability to call for a retest. While any Traits risked are still lost, it is possible to still win the challenge. An Ability lost in this manner is recovered at the beginning of the next session.

Choose five Abilities from the list below. You can take the same Ability more than once to illustrate a higher degree of skill in that particular field. This table gives a rough idea of what multiple levels represent in an Ability (any level beyond this should be considered supernatural talent and is allowed at the Storyteller's discretion only):

1 Competent (Good enough to earn a decent living with this Ability.)

2 True Professional (Licensed, can supervise others at this Ability.)

3 Journeyman (Bachelors degree, can teach others this Ability.)

4 Expert (Masters degree, can experiment into new areas of this Ability.)

5 Master (Doctorate degree, can lead trends in this Ability.)

The use of Abilities is often accompanied by a challenge of one sort or another. Some of these will be performed with a Storyteller who will not only assign the relative difficulty of the challenge (measured by a number of Traits), but will actually perform the test with you. This sort of test is called a Static Challenge.

As a rule, one or no Traits are risked for trivial uses, two to four are at stake in novel, unusual or challenging projects, and five or more are risked by attempting taxing, groundbreaking or unlikely feats. These numbers may be modified to suit the needs of the story and the power level of the characters, of course. More details concerning difficulty and factors that influence it are included with each Ability.

Other Abilities, such as *Subterfuge* or *Melee*, are almost always used directly against another player and rarely need the assistance of a Storyteller to use.

## Abilities

### Animal Ken

From the gentle ways of the horse whisperers to the lion tamers that travel with circus sideshows, this is the ability to understand the actions of animals. As Garou normally spook animals by their very presence, this skill represents a character having carefully re-established the bond between herself and the animals of the world (or perhaps you never lost that talent to begin with). Characters with this Ability can not only live alongside animals and predict their actions, but can also calm or enrage them. Given time you may train an animal to perform simple tasks — fetching, guarding, attacking and so on. When a command is given, the animal must make a Mental Challenge to understand and carry out the order. In order to give a successful command, you must bid between one and three Traits, depending on the difficulty of the task. You may also attempt to calm an injured, attacking or frightened animal by defeating it in a Social Challenge.

### Brawl

Useful when your favorite tavern erupts into a spray of flying glasses and angry bodies, you know how to fight bare-handed. This includes punching, kicking, grappling, throttling, throwing, gouging, clawing and biting. *Brawl* serves as a catchall term for any form of unarmed combat, from exotic martial arts to good old street fighting.

### Bureaucracy

*Bureaucracy*, a.k.a. the System, is theoretically an organization for getting things done more efficiently. *Bureaucracy* can allow you to access to appropriate licenses, use contractual agreements to your advantage, and recover, alter or destroy records. *Bureaucracy* often requires a Static Mental or Social Challenge, depending on the type of roleplaying performed, or as a Storyteller sees fit. In a time enamored with land deeds, water rights, railroad permits and other forms of paper, this is a subtle but powerful Ability to have. Difficulty depends on such factors as security, accessibility, nature and cooperativeness of the target or information.

Lupus characters may not start the game with this Ability.

### Enigmas

This Ability concerns solving mysteries and puzzles. In essence, it is a measurement of your problem-solving skills and how well you combine scattered details into a coherent solution. *Enigmas* comes in handy when solving mazes, answering riddles and the like. This Ability is used with Mental Challenges in order to see if you figure out a problem set before you. The Storyteller may require a variable number of Traits to be risked, depending on the relative difficulty and the character's familiarity with the enigma in question.

### Fast-Draw

Above and beyond normal uses for weapons, you've developed the ability to draw and ready yours with an impressive display of speed. This skill is obviously critical in classic gunfighting showdowns, and can also prove quite handy in other situations where a slower character might be caught unprepared; you may spend a level of this Ability to cancel an opponent attempting to surprise you with a combat challenge, as long as you have your trusty weapon in reach and ready for battle. (In reach and ready for battle is defined as follows: weapons cannot be across the room, guns must be loaded, knives cannot be hidden in an inside thigh sheath that you have to dig for, etc.) As always, use common sense when determining if this skill can be applied; while a character may cancel the surprise of a person trying to pull a weapon on her across a poker table, it is unlikely that this Ability will help if the character is asleep, caught from behind, or the target of a sniper's bullet. Storytellers have every right to suspend this advantage for characters who attempt to use this skill to cancel every Surprise sprung on them.

Although it is especially appropriate for firearms, you may choose to use take this skill in relation to any weapon the Storyteller allows, from throwing knives to rifles to cavalry sabers. You must possess at least two levels of the *Firearms* or *Melee* Ability, whichever is appropriate to your weapon of choice, before you may purchase this Ability. You must also name a *specific* melee weapon or type of firearm when this skill is taken, and this Ability never applies when using any type of weapon but the one chosen. Of course, if you wish, you may take this Ability more than once to represent your ability to fast-draw with a variety of weapons. For information on how this Ability is used in quick-draw showdowns, see the special gunfighting rules on page 228.

Lupus characters may not start the game with this Ability.

**Finance**

You can manage money, and even have some limited resources to draw upon. Many companies employ traveling accountants to check on the state of their various enterprises across the territories, and this Ability allows you to follow money trails, perform and verify accounting, and understand such concepts as investments and bonds. These actions are a function of a Mental Challenge, the difficulty of which depends on any precautions taken by the subject, the amount of money in question and the availability of information. Storytellers should set reasonable totals for monies that can be gained through the use of this Ability each session, although combining this Ability with the *Finance* Influence can make for a wealthy character in no time.

Lupus characters may not start the game with this Ability.

**Firearms**

This Ability covers both how well you can shoot and your skill at maintaining, repairing and possibly making minor alterations to firearms. In the tense, gunslinging world of the Savage West, this skill can be the saving grace for characters with quick reflexes, or big mouths. The most common use of this Ability is in combat, but a Storyteller can also allow you to attempt a Mental Challenge in order to perform other functions (such as hunting). This does not cover quick-draw talent; that is the function of the *Fast-Draw* Ability, above. Those with the *Firearms* Ability may choose to use Mental Traits instead of Physical Traits during a challenge in which a firearm is involved.

Lupus characters may not start the game with this Ability.

**Gambling**

From poker to craps to blackjack, you've seen just about any wager imaginable, and you've developed a talent for games of skill and chance. Over time, you've learned enough to generally come out ahead (or at least break even) by hedging your bets and knowing when to bet it all or leave the table. Of course, you've also learned enough to know how to get fate to help you out a bit if you choose, but being caught cheating is one of the easiest ways a body can wind up in a shallow grave. Gambling, or its illicit alteration, is generally a Mental Challenge, although the Storyteller may rule that certain games are Social or even Physical Challenges. If you choose to actually play cards or roll dice during play, characters with this Ability may — at a Narrator's discretion — expend a level of this Ability to reroll or take a new draw, to better simulate their expertise at handling the game. All levels expended are still lost until next session as usual. Use common sense when determining what falls under the province of this ability: for example, playing most card and dice games does, as does figuring out a good amount to bet on a horse race, but determining the outcome of such wagers as foot races or shooting an apple off someone's head does not.

**Investigation**

While detective methods in the Savage West are a far cry from the precise science of the modern age, you know how to go beyond the basic "He went that way, sheriff!" With a combination of expertise, intuition and experience, you have learned how to conduct a proper criminal investigation, deduce a criminal's *modus operandus* and even reconstruct a crime scene. By succeeding at a Mental Challenge (no Traits are at risk for either party), you can even tell if a person is carrying a concealed weapon or the like. When dealing with plots, you may also request a Static Mental Challenge against a Storyteller to see if any clues have been overlooked, piece together existing clues, or uncover information through formal investigation. Unfortunately, many hunters also employ this Ability to track down Garou.

**Larceny**

You're a lowdown cuss. You have experience in and knowledge of the variety of ways humans have developed to cheat and steal from each other, as well as how to navigate the underbelly of polite society without getting killed. Not only can you counter physical obstacles to your illicit prosperity such as safes and locks, but you can make use of a variety of scams to fleece your fellow creatures, from card sharping to confidence schemes. You also know how to survive on the streets, such as they are at the time, and how to utilize the network of personalities they house, from brothel madams to drifters to saloon owners. Some uses of *Larceny*, such as rumor gathering, require a Social Challenge, the difficulty of which is influenced by such things as composition of the local community (temperate, lawless, Garou), while others such as safecracking or picking a lock require a Static Mental or Physical Challenge.

**Law**

This is the measure of how well you understand the legal system in which you are entangled. In the world of humans, you can use the *Law* Ability to write up binding contracts, defend clients and know the rights of yourself and others. This is a great way to keep your caern from being bought out by land barons — or maybe your last chance to save your neck from a lynch mob. The difficulty of the Mental Challenges necessary to accomplish these tasks depends on factors like the precedents for and severity of the crime, not to mention legal complexity of the subject or legal action desired. Alternatively, this could be an understanding of "wolf politics" for a lupus character or of Garou law for a metis or Philodox character.

**Leadership**

This is a function of confidence, bearing and a profound understanding of what motivates others. It is more than barking orders. It measures how well you can get others to obey your decisions. It also covers how willingly people accede to your wishes, as reluctant followers are worth far less than willing ones. To use this ability they must first be under your command or in some way your subordinates, like an alpha to a packmate, a chief to his tribe, or a sheriff to his deputies. You may use this Ability to cause others to perform reasonable tasks for you. These requests may not endanger the subjects or violate the subjects' Natures or Demeanors. *Leadership* works with a Social Challenge. This Ability should not be allowed to override a player character's free will, but if a character is uncertain about following an order, the outcome of the challenge can assist in roleplaying his eventual decision.

**Linguistics**

One of the chief reasons the Savage West is such a fractious place is that many folk simply don't ken each other's lingo. This measures your ability to comprehend various spoken or written languages. Its common use is to represent tutelage in one or more languages other than your native tongue. The language(s) learned can be anything from ancient hieroglyphics to common national languages to complex dialects. In the case of languages known, they must be specified when the *Linguistics* Ability is chosen — each new Trait allows a character a new language. This skill allows you and anyone who also knows the language to speak privately. Furthermore, you can translate data for yourself or others, though a Static Mental Challenge may be required to do so. *Linguistics* also allows for identifying accents, reading lips, picking up slang and a certain amount of linguistic mimicry.

**Medicine**

Too often on the frontier someone falls victim to some ill or another, and this Ability represents your skill at treating the injuries, diseases and various ailments of living creatures without resorting to quackery or "special elixirs." Narrators can allow a living being under the treatment with someone with the *Medicine* Ability to recover a single Health Level per night with time and a Mental Challenge. The difficulty of the challenge is influenced by the severity and nature of the damage, equipment at your disposal and any assistance or distractions. Other uses of this Ability include some basic forensic information, diagnosis and pharmaceutical knowledge. Of course, knowledge of healing also implies a knowledge of what is harmful to the human form as well.

**Meditation**

Despite the constant toll taken by the war against the Wyrm and the ravages of Rage, Garou are still deeply spiritual creatures, and even the stoutest Ahroun must occasionally seek the solace of Gaia within. This Ability is the talent to focus and center one's thoughts, calming the emotions, controlling the mind and relaxing the body. Garou may use this Ability to channel and renew their Gnosis. For every 10 minutes spent in meditation, the Garou may convert one Mental or *Meditation* Trait into a Gnosis Trait. To meditate, one does not necessarily need to be in any special position or have any special philosophy; this is a very personal Ability, and one for which you must develop your own technique.

### Melee

Whether from years on the warpath, service in the Army or participation in a lot of saloon dust-ups, you are skilled at a broad range of armed combat skills. You are proficient in the use of a variety of weapons, from tomahawks to broken bottles to klaives. The *Melee* Ability comes with knowledge of proper care for your weapons as well. A character without this Ability may not use any of the advantages of Abilities in armed combat, including retests.

### Occult

There are many supernatural secrets in the Savage West, and with the *Occult* Ability, some of them are yours. *Occult* implies a general knowledge of things such as curses, shamanism and fortune telling, as well as information more specific to the supernatural beings that inhabit the world. Examples of applications include identifying the use and nature of visible magicks, rites and rituals, understanding basic fundamentals of the occult, and having knowledge of cults, tomes and artifacts. Most uses of the *Occult* Ability involve a Mental Challenge. The difficulty of this challenge can be subject to many factors, such as obscurity, amount of existing data and the character's individual scope of understanding (Garou know more about their own rites, for example.).

### Performance

This Ability actually covers the entire gamut of artistic expression, including writing, singing, acting, dancing, playing musical instruments and similar skills. It grants you the gift to make your own original creations and/or express these creations to your peers, in a chosen medium. The genius of your creativity or the power with which you convey it is determined by a Static Social Challenge. Some particularly sensitive types, such as Galliards and Toreador vampires, can even become entranced by the use of this skill — after first being defeated in a Social Challenge. In addition to actual performing ability, this Ability also measures how well you know the society surrounding your particular art form and how you fit in with that crowd. Advanced levels of *Performance* always involve some form of specialization. This Ability can also be used to critique the works of others.

### Primal Urge

*Primal Urge* describes your natural instincts and connection to your ancestral past. It measures your ability to function not only as a wolf, but as a half-wolf. Those Garou skilled in this Ability are very attuned to the bestial part of their inner nature, and can retest perception-related challenges, as well as challenges to change forms. *Primal Urge* always reduces a Garou's time to change forms or pass through the Gauntlet.

Homid characters may not start the game with this Ability, except with Storyteller permission.

### Repair

You possess a working understanding of what makes things tick. This Ability covers everything from fixing steam engines to shoring up a sagging beam, assuming, of course, that you have the time, tools and parts. You can fix or slightly alter most of the trappings of frontier society. This also allows you to excel at sabotage, should you choose to do so. Using this Ability usually calls for a Static Mental Challenge, the difficulty of which depends on such factors as the subject of your attention's complexity, the tools and parts available, the extent of the damage and the time spent on the repairs.

Lupus characters may not start the game with this Ability.

### Ride

Although the train has made major inroads into the wild spaces, the majority of personal transportation in the Savage West is still based on animal power. Thus, you do not need this Ability just to be able to lead a team of oxen and/or mount up to travel from town to town, as it is assumed most characters have at least that basic level of familiarity with this skill. Instead, one who has this Ability is an adept rider capable of fighting on horseback, navigating difficult terrain, and attempting other hazardous feats while in the saddle. You have also learned how to repress your Garou nature to prevent spooking your mount, although all other animals are still wary and hard to deal with around you unless you also possess the *Animal Ken* skill. However, combined with *Animal Ken*, you can use this Ability to teach a horse a number of tricks to perform. Factors influencing the difficulty of a *Ride* Challenge include a horse's disposition, road conditions and the sort of stunt desired. Because of the speed implied in horseback travel, Storytellers may allow characters with this Ability and access to a horse to cut "out of game" travel times from one scene to another.

Lupus characters may not start the game with this Ability, or any familiarity with it.

### Science

While science was something of a curious cousin to what we now know it to be, the unlimited potential of the westward expansion attracted quite a few brilliant minds, each with their own theories and training. You happen to be one of them: you have a degree of factual and practical expertise in a single field of the hard sciences. This Ability measures not only theoretical knowledge but also how well you can put it to practical use. This knowledge allows you to identify properties of your field, perform experiments, fabricate items, bring about results and access information a player could not normally utilize. A Static Mental Challenge is necessary for all but the most trivial uses of this skill. The difficulty of the challenge depends on resources (equipment, data and so forth) available, complexity of the task and time. A field of study must be chosen when the *Science* Ability is taken. A few examples include physics, biology and chemistry. Other fields can be allowed at the Storyteller's discretion.

Lupus characters may not start the game with this Ability.

**Scrounge**

*Scrounge* allows you to produce items through connections, trading, wits and ingenuity. While society as a whole may have evolved beyond such a standard, many of the frontier towns and trading posts in the Savage West still depend on the barter system to function, and those who lack the wealth to purchase the things they desire or need develop this Ability instead. Materials acquired with *Scrounge* aren't always brand new or exactly right and often require some time to come by, but this Ability sometimes works where *Finance* and outright theft fail. A Static Mental or Social Challenge is necessary to use *Scrounge*. Some factors that influence the difficulty of the challenge include rarity and value of the item sought, and local supply and demand.

**Subterfuge**

You can speak with a silver tongue like the Devil himself when you choose; *Subterfuge* is the art of deception and intrigue, and relies on a social backdrop to work. When participating in a social setting or conversation with a subject, you can attempt to draw information out of him through trickery and careful probing. Information, such as one's name, nationality, Negative Traits, friends and enemies can be revealed by a successful use of *Subterfuge*.

The first requirement of gleaning information in this way involves getting your target to say something dealing with the desired knowledge, such as entering a conversation about foreign culture when you are really itching to find out where he comes from. If you can accomplish this, you may then propose your true question and initiate a Social Challenge. If you win, then your target must forfeit the information (hopefully by roleplaying his *faux pas*). To use the Ability again, you must once again lure the target into a conversation. *Subterfuge* can be used to scent out a character's Negative Traits, but may not reveal more than one Negative Trait per session. Furthermore, it may be used to defend from others with *Subterfuge*.

Conversely, the *Subterfuge* Ability may also be used to conceal information or lie without detection.

**Survival**

The wilderness is a lonely place without civilization around, and can downright deadly for the uninitiated. You have the knowledge and training to find food, water and shelter in a variety of wilderness settings. Each successful Static Mental or Physical Challenge allows you to provide the basic necessities for yourself or another living creature for one day. This Ability can also be used to track down someone in a wilderness setting. The nature and difficulty of the challenge is usually set by a Storyteller. You should choose a concentration each time you take this ability: desert, arctic, plains, forest, etc. While you your training allows you to know the essentials of surviving any clime, most likely you're better acquainted with one or two familiar ones, which is a factor in determining the difficulty of the *Survival* Challenge; other important factors are the abundance or scarcity of resources, time of year, equipment and type of wilderness.

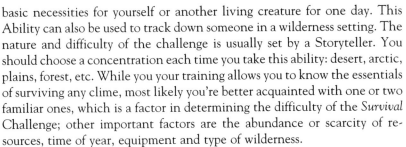

## Gifts

See above for Beginning Gifts; choose one auspice Gift, one breed Gift and one tribal Gift (for a total of three Gifts). See also "Gifts" on pp. 142.

Note that the listed Gifts are simply the Basic ones. There are more powerful Intermediate and Advanced Gifts, although these are only possessed by more knowledgeable Garou.

## Backgrounds

Each character has background details that make her unique. They represent special advantages the character possesses by virtue of birth, hard work or plain luck. They help define the character and set her apart as an individual. Background Traits should be chosen to flesh out the player's concept of her character, rather than to bolster a character's power and effectiveness. Most Backgrounds may be lost or added to during the course of play. Backgrounds do not generally increase through experience, so players are not charged experience when they gain new Background Traits through successful play.

At this stage, select your five Background Traits. Members of certain tribes are excluded from selecting certain Background Traits, and members of other tribes are required to take others. Players can select the same Background more than once to illustrate a stronger level of that Background, though Pure Breed and Past Life may never rise above five Traits, and there are no fetishes that are rated above five Traits in power.

### Pure Breed

Garou take great pride in their family lineage. Possession of this Background means your character is directly descended from one or more great Garou heroes, a birthright which is becoming all the more rare as tribal bloodlines mix and Kinfolk families spread apart, and your character receives an extra degree of praise and attention because of it. Pure Breed is not a matter of documents and claims, but an innate distinction all Garou instinctively sense and recognize. A character with Pure Breed gains a retest on Social Challenges against Garou and Kinfolk, one for each level of the Background she possesses. However, those "of the blood" are expected (demanded might be a better term) to live up to the high ideals and examples of their ancestors, which can be very trying on even the stoutest Garou; at the Narrator's option, the benefits of this Background may be suspended for a character who isn't acting in accordance with her birthright and what Garou consider noble, at least until she gains more Honor Renown and thus "proves herself" again.

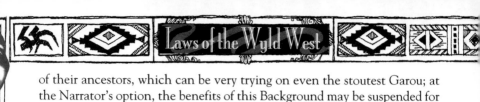

### Past Life

All Garou honor those gone before them, but you're a living link to the past, and have the ability to converse with ancestors long gone as if they were standing next to you. You may even call on their knowledge in times of need. Once per session per level of *Past Life* you possess, you may try to use an Ability you do not have or have already expended. To do so, you must roleplay out the process of contacting your ancestor for aid, and win or tie a Simple Test. Note that this Background does not confer any ability to see or converse with any other types of spirits or wraiths unless you also have the appropriate Gifts or Merits to do so.

## Fetish

Garou lore is rife with items of mystical power and legendary histories, and many tribes pass such artifacts down to their younger members as a tangible means of handing down tradition, provided the young ones seem worthy. If you are chosen to carry one of these items, you have received a great honor and should take your responsibility very seriously. A Garou entrusted to carry one of these items may draw upon its powers. The Storyteller assigns a fetish appropriate to the level of Background taken; picking your own fetish is not allowed, although you may attempt to persuade the Storyteller with an excellent story as to why your character would have a particular item, but in the end her decision is final.

### Rites

The Garou have many mysteries, rites and celebrations, and with this Background you know some of them intimately. You are versed in the traditions and order of these rites, and can identify the ones that you know about by drawing upon your knowledge of them (the player must win or tie a Simple Test to do so). Furthermore, you may have been taught how to perform a few of these rites.

**One Trait:** Has knowledge of Basic Rites and can perform one Basic Rite.

**Two Traits:** Has knowledge of Basic Rites and can perform two Basic Rites.

**Three Traits:** Has knowledge of Basic and Intermediate Rites, and can perform three Basic Rites or one Basic and one Intermediate Rite.

**Four Traits:** Has knowledge of Basic and Intermediate Rites, and can perform four Basic Rites or two Basic and one Intermediate Rites.

**Five Traits:** Has knowledge of Basic, Intermediate and Advanced Rites, and can perform five Basic Rites or three Basic Rites and an Intermediate Rite.

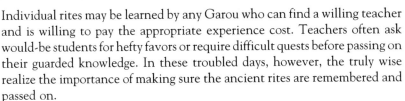

Individual rites may be learned by any Garou who can find a willing teacher and is willing to pay the appropriate experience cost. Teachers often ask would-be students for hefty favors or require difficult quests before passing on their guarded knowledge. In these troubled days, however, the truly wise realize the importance of making sure the ancient rites are remembered and passed on.

Rites later learned by a character do not count against this Background; they simply reflect the character's growing knowledge. Instead, this Background simply indicates that the character begins play with certain Rites.

### Kinfolk

You are in contact with certain humans or wolves who, while descended from the Garou, did not receive the "changing blood," and so for all practical

#### Kinfolk Modifiers

Metis may not begin the game with this Background.

- Black Fury Kinfolk with Abilities above three are always females.
- Bone Gnawer Kinfolk all have at least one *Lowdown* Influence if homid.
- Children of Gaia Kinfolk all have the extra Trait: *Compassionate*.
- Fianna Kinfolk all have at least one Trait of Performance if homid. Lupine kinfolk all have the extra Trait: *Robust*.
- Get of Fenris Kinfolk all have at least one Trait in fighting-related Abilities.
- Iron Rider Kinfolk are all homid, except for those in who are in zoos or pets, who may only have fighting-related Abilities. All homids gain one Trait in business-related skills automatically. If abused in a business deal, these Kinfolk become enemies of the Garou.
- Red Talons may have only Lupine Kinfolk, but may call upon five per Trait of Background.
- Shadow Lord Kinfolk will betray the Garou if the Shadow Lord gives them the opportunity, but will do anything commanded by a Shadow Lord as long as the werewolf is watching.
- Silent Strider Kinfolk can never be called on twice, but will always help to their fullest.
- Silver Fang Kinfolk all gain one Trait in society-, monetary- and political-related Abilities automatically.
- Stargazer Kinfolk all gain one Trait in mystical-related Abilities.
- Uktena Kinfolk all gain one Trait in *Occult*-related Abilities. When the Background is played, the Narrator secretly makes a Simple Test against the Kinfolk's Trait of Ability. A loss means the Kinfolk is Wyrm-tainted and will betray the Uktena if given a chance.
- Wendigo Kinfolk may not have Influences in the non-Native American society, but gain one Trait in native and *Survival* Abilities.

purposes are normal members of their respective species. They are immune to the Delirium, however, and know your origin; they are willing to help you however they can, though most are not in positions of power. Groups of Kinfolk can be invaluable for Garou who wish to deal with the human world but cannot risk frenzy. In the close-knit family groups of the Savage West, this Trait is actually quite common; the West is a lonely place without folks to share your troubles and triumphs with, and often Kinfolk are the only people this side of a fellow changer who can really understand you.

For each level of this Background, you may call upon a Kinfolk with a specific Ability, Numina or Influence that is desired. A Simple Test must be won for each level of special talent needed. Each Trait of this Background may only be utilized once per session; a character with five levels of Kinfolk may only test five times to find a Kinfolk with *Medicine* Ability, as each success equals one level of *Medicine* Ability present. Storytellers may require more than one success for each level of particularly rare Abilities, Numina or Influences sought, and may decide that multiple Kinfolk are available for more common Abilities — three Kinfolk with one level in *Melee* rather than one Kinfolk with three levels.

Once a Kinfolk has been accessed, he may only be found again if you win the same number of tests. Otherwise, that particular individual is not available or has moved away the next time you call. Kinfolk can only become permanent fixtures in a game if you have enough experience to buy them as a Kinfolk Influence, the number of Influences required to do so being determined by the Storyteller.

### Totem

You (or your pack) has a totem spirit that watches over you. When a pack is formed, its members often choose a totem spirit to adopt them. This spirit is then summoned by all the members of the pack, and is created using the total score of the pack's *Totem* Background. Costs to build the spirit are as follows:

**One Trait** Provides three Traits to divide among the totem's Willpower, Rage and Gnosis (minimum of one each).

**One Trait** Provides 10 Traits of Power.

**One Trait** The totem can speak aloud (you do not require the Gift: *Spirit Speech* to converse with it).

**One Trait** The totem can locate and appear in the presence of any pack member.

**Two Traits** The totem spends the majority of its time with the pack, and is ready to help out.

**Two Traits** The totem has a degree of respect among fellow spirits (may retest a single Social Challenge with another spirit per session).

**Two Traits** Provides one Charm.

**Three Traits** Per extra pack member who can use the totem's powers in the same turn (see page 263).

**Four Traits** Totem's mystical connection to the pack members is so strong that they effectively have the Gift: *Mind Speak* with one another (at Storyteller's discretion).

**Five Traits** Totem can contact and interact with the physical world for brief periods of time when the need is great.

**Five Traits** Totem is feared by agents of the Wyrm (allows pack members to incite fox frenzy on Wyrm creatures, as per Charm: *Incite Frenzy*; cost is three Gnosis; Mental Challenge versus target's Willpower).

For more information on building a totem spirit, see page 263.

### Renown

A Garou's renown defines the Rank and therefore the station of an individual within Garou society. **Wyld West** characters usually begin at Rank 1, or cliath. Cliath are Garou who have undergone their *Rite of Passage* and proven themselves to their fellow Garou. They have been accepted into the pack, and are treated as adults.

Renown is divided into three categories: Wisdom, Glory and Honor. A beginning player chooses Renown Traits just as he would choose Traits for any other attribute. However, the type of Renown Traits that a player can choose depends on the character's auspice.

See the "Auspice" section above, for beginning Renown. Also, see pp. 216 for details of gaining Renown at moots.

### Renown Traits

**Wisdom**: *Crafty, Inspired, Inventive, Pragmatic, Profound, Respected, Revered, Sacred, Scholarly, Spiritual, Venerable, Wise*

**Glory**: *Bold, Brash, Brave, Courageous, Daring, Exalted, Feared, Fearless, Glorious, Imposing, Impressive, Spirited, Superb*

**Honor**: *Admirable, Commendable, Dutiful, Eminent, Esteemed, Fair, Honorable, Impartial, Just, Noble, Objective, Proud, Reputable, Trusted, Virtuous*

## Rage, Gnosis and Willpower

The following Traits allow the Garou to perform miraculous feats beyond human capacity. These Traits are not represented as adjectives. Instead, they are a pool from which the character may draw. These Traits can be represented by cards, which are torn up when the Trait is used, or players can simply record these Traits on their character sheets.

A character's auspice determines her starting Rage Traits, her breed determines her starting Gnosis Traits, and her tribe determines her initial Willpower.

## Rage

Rage is the all-consuming passion inherent in every Garou. It is also the psychic energy used to change form, powering the transformation from breed form into other shapes. Rage is a tool of destruction, of anger and violence. It can be a dark impulse pushing a Garou to acts of senseless bloodshed and murder. When used constructively against the forces of the Wyrm, this violence can be a useful thing, destroying the enemies of Gaia and protecting the world from the spread of the Wyrm and its minions. But Rage must be tempered, because if it overwhelms the wielder, he becomes nothing more than a mindless instrument of destruction and a perfect tool of the Wyrm. The plains of the Savage West have been stained with countless gallons of innocent blood, and one more careless, bloodthirsty Garou won't make anything better.

### Using Rage

Rage can be used in many ways, depending on a character's needs. Several examples of how Rage can be used in the course of a story are listed below.

• **Changing Forms** — Changing forms is easier with the use of Rage. By expending a Rage Trait, you are able to change into another form immediately. Otherwise, changing into another form takes one full action per form shifted (so going from Homid to Crinos normally requires two actions). You may, however, take your natural form automatically without spending Rage.

• **Extra Action** — Rage can give a character the ability to perform extra feats during a challenge. This means that a character can challenge several players to different tests at the same time with no penalty. The number of players challenged is determined by the number of Rage Traits spent, but may add up to no more than one-third of the character's total Physical Attributes.

• **Extra Attacks** — A werewolf can also use Rage to attack with greater frequency and ferocity. A Garou who has just won a Physical Challenge in combat can immediately risk a Rage Trait and make a second challenge to attempt to inflict a second wound on a foe. This follow-up challenge occurs before a new challenge can begin. Furthermore, the Garou who risked the Rage Trait cannot be wounded as a result of this second test, unless his opponent has also risked Rage (or used the vampiric Discipline *Celerity*). If a foe declares extra attacks during a combat turn, the Garou may continue to spend Rage to match them as long as he has Rage.

• **Remaining Active**: When a character becomes Incapacitated from losing a challenge, she may use a Rage Trait to recover one Health Level so as to continue fighting. Doing this to negate an aggravated wound results in a battle scar unless the player wins (no ties) in a Simple Test.

Once a character loses or uses all of his Rage, he is no longer able to change forms. Garou without Rage Traits are considered to have "lost the wolf" within and revert to breed form, whether that be lupus, homid or Crinos if a metis.

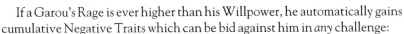

If a Garou's Rage is ever higher than his Willpower, he automatically gains cumulative Negative Traits which can be bid against him in *any* challenge:

**One Rage over**: *Bestial*

**Two Rage over**: *Shortsighted*

**Three Rage over**: *Clumsy* (Blind with rage)

### Regaining Rage

There are multiple ways in which a Garou can regain Rage, most of which are fairly simple to simulate in a game of **Wyld West**. They include:

• **The Moon**: When a Garou first sees the moon at night, something deep in her soul surges. The character regains one Rage Trait, or all spent Rage if the moon is in her auspice. (**Storyteller note**: If your game runs once per month, one particular auspice might have an unfair advantage if every session happens during its phase of the moon. It sometimes behooves Storytellers to "improve" nature a little bit in situations like this.)

• **Confrontation**: At the beginning of any new conflict (not necessarily physical combat) in which a challenge is involved, the character regains a Rage Trait. Only one Rage Trait is regained during the confrontation, regardless of the number of challenges.

• **Wounds**: The first time a Garou is wounded in an evening, she regains a Rage Trait. This is only done once per day/session.

• **Humiliation**: The character may regain a Rage Trait during a particularly humiliating situation. The award of this Trait is strictly at Narrator option.

## Gnosis

Gnosis is the power of Gaia within a Garou. It is Her presence made real and tangible, and a Garou gains Gnosis as part of his connection with Her. A character's beginning Gnosis is determined by his breed, because it is his birth that establishes his initial connection to Gaia. He may gain extra Gnosis Traits by spending experience and becoming more spiritually aware in a roleplaying sense. Characters can accomplish this either through meditation or through the guidance of another. The essence of the spirit world is still much closer to reality in the Savage West than in later times, but it is troubled as well, for the coming of the Storm Eater has upset spirits all across the land.

Gnosis Traits are used with Gifts and in rites, and one Gnosis Trait can be spent to step sideways into the Umbra immediately (the Garou must still be looking at a reflective surface).

Garou have both Gnosis Traits and a Gnosis Pool. The Gnosis Pool is a permanent number, and determines the maximum number of Gnosis Traits a Garou can store within herself at one time. Gnosis Traits are temporary, and can be bid and spent in Static Challenges, just like other Traits.

Garou can regain their spent Gnosis Traits in the following ways:

• **Meditation**: A Garou may spend a Mental Trait and get a Gnosis Trait if she spends 10 minutes meditating alone. Of course, the Mental Trait spent must be a relevant one. (You must have the *Meditation* Ability to regain Gnosis in this manner.)

• **Fetish**: A Garou may gain Gnosis from a fetish, such as the *Tear of Renewal*.

• **Spirits**: A Garou may gain Gnosis through the "death" of an Engling spirit. After either summoning the Engling or running across it in the Umbra, the Garou must convince the spirit to give itself up for the Garou's benefit. If it agrees, the Engling makes a gift of itself to the Garou, and, in death, recharges all the Gnosis Pools of the Garou involved. The Spirit Keeper (see page 234) has the option of complicating this process.

• **Rites**: A Garou may gain Gnosis through the *Rite of the Cup* (see "Spirit Rites," p. 176), although this Gnosis is actually shared, and must come from another Garou or a spirit, as opposed to directly from Gaia.

### Gnosis in the Umbra

In the Umbra, a Gnosis Trait may be spent to change the reality of the Umbra in some fashion. For example, a Garou may use a Gnosis Trait to step through an Umbral wall, hide her Umbral form briefly or provide some light in darkness.

You may not spend Gnosis and Rage in the same challenge (or in place of one another) unless the system description specifically says otherwise. (Some Gifts are exceptions to this rule.)

## Willpower

Willpower measures the capability of a character to overcome the urges and desires that tempt her and her inner strength of purpose. In times of catastrophe, ordinary people have been known to perform extraordinary feats, such as lifting a boulder off a loved one or running through a burning building to save a trapped child. One can even fight death if she truly has the will to live. Willpower gives a character the extra strength necessary to overcome obstacles and succeed where others would give up and fail.

Each character begins the game with a number of Willpower Traits. For Garou, the number of Traits depends on the character's tribe. Willpower Traits can be used for almost anything that the player deems important. A few examples of how Willpower can be used by Garou are provided below. With Willpower, you can:

• Negate the effects of frenzy (by using a Willpower Trait, the character gains a new tolerance of a situation that would ordinarily throw her into frenzy).

• Replenish all lost Traits in any one category: Physical, Social or Mental. This may be done once per category per game session.

• Ignore the side effects of wounds, such as Incapacitation, for one challenge.

• Gain a retest against any one Mental or Social Challenge.

Once a Willpower Trait has been used, it is gone until the end of the story. It is possible that a Narrator may choose to give a character Willpower during the course of a story as a reward for extraordinary roleplaying. Such a reward should be given for portraying the character's Nature or Derangement appropriately, or for any other exceptional reasons that the Narrator deems suitable.

# Final Touches

Your character should now have her basics more or less ready to go. In the final stages of character creation, you have the opportunity to improve certain statistics and add more Abilities, Backgrounds, Merits and/or Flaws and Influences. You also need to add her personal details and develop more of your character's history. Still, at this point the hard part is over; what's left is icing on the cake.

## Negative Traits and Flaws

The number of Traits and Abilities your character has can be increased by one for each Negative Trait that you add to the three Attribute categories (maximum of five), or each point of Flaws you take on (to a maximum of seven at character creation).

See also "Flaws," pp 188.

**Physical Negative Traits**: *Clumsy, Cowardly, Decrepit, Delicate, Docile, Flabby, Lame, Lethargic, Puny, Sickly*

**Social Negative Traits**: *Callous, Condescending, Dull, Naive, Obnoxious, Paranoid, Repugnant, Shy, Tactless, Untrustworthy*

**Mental Negative Traits**: *Forgetful, Gullible, Ignorant, Impatient, Oblivious, Predictable, Shortsighted, Submissive, Witless*

For descriptions of these Negative Traits, see pp. 66.

With one Negative Trait, you can:
- Take one additional Trait.
- Take an additional Ability.
- Take an additional Background.
- Take one Trait of Merits.
- Buy an Influence Trait.

With two Negative Traits, you can:
- Take an additional Rage Trait.
- Take an additional Gnosis Trait.

With three Negative Traits, you can:
- Take an additional Basic Gift from your breed, auspice or tribe.
- Take an additional Willpower Trait.

## Influences

At this stage, you can, if you wish, buy Influence Traits for your character. Each Influence Trait costs a Trait. Whether that Trait is gained from taking Negative Traits or Flaws is up to you.

A Garou with Influence Traits has gained a certain degree of control in aspects of normal human society. While many Garou shun taking such an active role in human affairs, others see it as the only way to keep accurate tabs on certain organizations and groups. Most forms of Influence in this game reflect contacts and allies not of Kinfolk stock, although you can combine the benefits of these two Traits if you desire. (See also *Kinfolk* Background, page 83.)

One area of Influence may be chosen for every Trait invested in Influences. Note that Influence does not give you full knowledge of a particular area (Abilities handle that), but it does give you sway over humans who do, if nothing else.

Some uses of Influence may not actually cost anything to use, but rather require that you possess a certain level of the Influence in question. In these cases, it is likely that a Narrator may require a challenge of some sort to represent the uncertainty or added difficulty involved when exercising Influence.

To use Influence actively, you should explain to a Narrator what sort of effect you wish to create. She decides the number of Traits needed, which can be subject to sudden change depending upon circumstance, the time involved (both real and in-game) and any tests required. In certain cases, the Storyteller may decide that two or more types of Influence are necessary to accomplish a goal. This adds an element of realism, and encourages characters to diversify their interests more widely than they might have otherwise in order to obtain the Influences they need.

A character with Influence is usually given Influence cards to represent his areas of control. Influence cards used during a game are returned at the beginning of the next session. Influence may be loaned or traded to others. To do this, the card is given to another player and is not returned to its owner until after it is spent or voluntarily returned, or one month passes. In order for a trade of Influences to occur, the Influence card in question must be signed over by the owner and the new owner's name is written on the card as well. Traits permanently signed away in this fashion are gone, though one can receive as well as give Influence.

Sometimes characters may wish to try to counteract the Influence of other characters. In such cases, it generally costs one Trait per Trait being countered. The character willing to expend the most Influence Traits (assuming she has them to spend) achieves her goal; all Traits used in this sort of conflict are considered expended.

In practice, the use of Influence is never instantaneous and rarely expedient. Even with trains, telegraphs and the Pony Express, news still takes much longer to travel in the Savage West than in modern times. You may be able to use *Political* Influence to wire the governor to send a cavalry unit to help chase down a gang of bandits, for example, but it's unlikely they'll arrive inside a week at the earliest. For sake of game flow, however, a Storyteller may allow trivial uses of Influence to only take half an hour to occur. Major manipulations, on the other hand, can become the center of ongoing plots that require several sessions to bring to fruition.

It also bears noting that while a character may have any level of Influence on hand, he is still limited by whatever resources are available; a character may wish to use five *Church* Influences to access an ancient monastic text, but it's not likely to be on hand at the local tent mission, although there might be someone there who knows where to go to find it. For this reason, the Storyteller may wish to rule some Influences inapplicable in certain locations or situations, or even prohibit a particular Influence altogether in the chronicle if it would prove too problematic or have too few local resources to be useful. As always, common sense and the needs of the story are the best guide, and Storytellers are encouraged to let their players use nearly any Influence if they can find creative enough ways to obtain it; however, simply saying "I use my *Political* Influence to drive out the local mayor" and expecting the Storyteller to comply just doesn't cut it.

The guidelines below by no means limit the number of Influence Traits that can be spent at one time or the degree of change a character may bring about. They are merely an advisory measure to help Storytellers adjudicate the costs of certain actions. The highest number listed on each Influence is just a recommended maximum effect to allow in-game play. Higher ratings are only useful to speed up a process (double Trait cost to halve the time needed). Garou characters may not possess more than their total Attribute Traits (Physical, Social and Mental) in Influences at any one time — there's only so much you can keep a handle on.

Actions followed by an asterisk (*), below, indicate that their effects can generally be accomplished without expending an Influence Trait; simply having the Traits is enough "pull."

Possible areas of Influence include the following:

### Bureaucracy

The organizational aspects of local, state or even federal government are never far behind the advancing edges of the cities, and they fall within the character's sphere of control. She can bend and twist the tangle of rules and regulations that seem necessary to run our society as she sees fit. The character may have contacts or allies among government clerks, surveying teams, road crews, surveyors and numerous other civil servants.

*Cost* *Desired Effect*

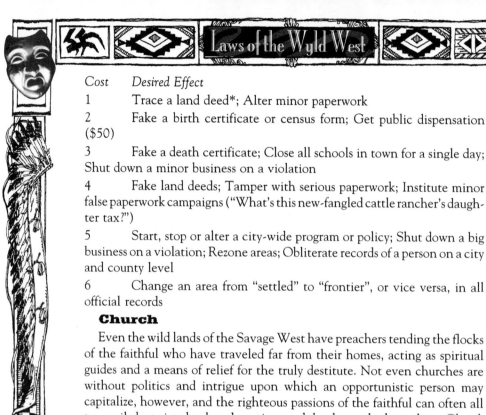

1 Trace a land deed*; Alter minor paperwork

2 Fake a birth certificate or census form; Get public dispensation ($50)

3 Fake a death certificate; Close all schools in town for a single day; Shut down a minor business on a violation

4 Fake land deeds; Tamper with serious paperwork; Institute minor false paperwork campaigns ("What's this new-fangled cattle rancher's daughter tax?")

5 Start, stop or alter a city-wide program or policy; Shut down a big business on a violation; Rezone areas; Obliterate records of a person on a city and county level

6 Change an area from "settled" to "frontier", or vice versa, in all official records

### Church

Even the wild lands of the Savage West have preachers tending the flocks of the faithful who have traveled far from their homes, acting as spiritual guides and a means of relief for the truly destitute. Not even churches are without politics and intrigue upon which an opportunistic person may capitalize, however, and the righteous passions of the faithful can often all too easily be twisted to less than pious ends by those who know how. *Church* Influence usually only applies to mainstream faiths; other practices sometimes fall under the *Occult* Influence. Contacts and allies affected by *Church* Influence include: ministers, priests, evangelists, witch-hunters, nuns, friars and various church attendees and assistants.

*Cost* *Desired Effect*

1 Identify most secular members of a given faith in the local area; Pass as a member of the clergy;* Peruse general church records (baptism, marriage, burial, etc.)

2 Identify higher church members; Track regular members; Suspend lay members

3 Open or close a single church; Find an average church-associated witch hunter; Dip into the collection plate ($25); Access the private information and archives of a church; Organize a vigil for a single event (funeral, protest, etc.)

4 Discredit or suspend high-level members; Manipulate regional branches

5 Organize major revivals; Access ancient church lore and knowledge

6 Borrow or access church relics or sacred items

### Finance

Someone has to be on the other end of any good bank robbery, but there's more to money than having it stolen by men in masks. The world teems with the trappings of affluence and the notion of living high on the hog drives those in the grip of gold fever as they go west. Those with the *Finance* Influence speak the language of money and know where to find capital. They have a degree of access to banks, nationwide companies and the truly wealthy citizens of the world. Such characters also have a wide variety of servants to draw on, such as company presidents, bankers, investors, land barons, bank tellers, stock brokers and loan agents. Please note that in this day and age, however, most investors were quite exacting as to whom they lent money, much less authority; characters who are overly scruffy or have a drifter's air will seldom be trusted with the kind of privileges this Influence represents.

*Cost* *Desired Effect*

1 Earn money; Learn about major transactions and financial events; Raise capital ($300); Learn about general economic trends;* Learn real motivations for many financial actions of others

2 Trace an unsecured small account; Raise capital to purchase a small business (small general store or saloon)

3 Purchase a large business (a company store that services an entire town)

4 Manipulate local banking; Ruin a small business

5 Foreclose on just about anything you can lay eyes on; Ruin a large business; Purchase a major company (mining concern, controlling share of a railroad)

6 Spark an economic trend; Build a small town

**Health**

What few hospital resources exist in the Savage West are often overworked, understaffed and plagued by the belief in quackery and other medical superstitions that many people still harbor. Furthermore, while most medicine is evolving toward the model the modern world is familiar with, some prominent doctors still honestly hold some amazingly strange notions to be matters of fact. However, medical science isn't nearly as primitive in this time as many people believe, and the dedication of the doctors and nurses who tend to the ill during times of cholera, typhoid and dysentery is nothing short of miraculous. Characters with this Influence have access to the resources of this fledgling industry and those involved in it: doctors, nurses, volunteer caregivers, lay monks or nuns, orderlies, midwives, pharmacists, and patients.

*Cost* *Desired Effect*

1 Access what health records a person may have;* Fake most medical records and the like; Use public functions of health centers at your leisure

2 Gain access to some medical research; Get a copy of coroner's report; Have mundane or routine injuries treated without a leaving a trail

3 Corrupt results of tests or inspections; Alter medical records; Have a person treated for highly complicated or suspicious wounds without raising an eyebrow (or leaving a record)

4 Acquire a body; Completely rewrite medical records; Abuse donations for personal use ($100); Have special research projects performed; Have people institutionalized or released; Fake a death certificate

### High Society

An clique of people exists, who, by virtue of birth, possessions, talent or quirks of fate, hold themselves above the great unwashed masses. *High Society* allows the character to direct and use the energies and actions of this exceptional mass of talents. Among the ranks of the elite, one can find dilettantes, the "old money families", performers, artists of all sorts and trend-setters.

*Cost* *Desired Effect*

1 Learn what is currently popular;* Obtain tickets for any concert or performance; Learn about all concerts, shows or plays well before they are made public*

2 Track most celebrities and luminaries; Be a local voice in the entertainment field; "Borrow" $300 as idle cash from rich friends

3 Crush promising careers; Hobnob well above your station*

4 Minor celebrity status; Organize a social gala or town festival

5 Ruin a new club, gallery, festival or other high society gathering; Grab a headline in a local paper

### Industry

The Savage West is slowly being tamed by the ambitions of the settlers and the industries that follow them, and the sweat of countless laborers acts as the grease that keeps this great machine working. A character with the *Industry* Influence has some sway in directing this body of activity, from mining to construction and more. However, the control of the railroad industry does not fall under this Influence; that is the purview of the *Railroad* Influence. *Industry* is composed of workers, foremen, engineers, contractors, construction workers and manual laborers.

*Cost* *Desired Effect*

1 Learn about local industrial projects and movements*; Know local workers and foremen personally*

2 Have minor projects performed; Dip into petty cash ($75); Arrange small accidents or sabotage on the job

3 Organize a "worker's holiday" or minor strike; Appropriate machinery or equipment for a short time

4 Close down a small factory; Revitalize a small factory

5 Manipulate large local industry as you see fit

6 Cut off production of a single resource or industry in a small region

### Larcenous

Even in the most cosmopolitan of ages, society has found certain needs and services too questionable to accept, or had members who believed their strength or cunning entitled them to whatever they could take from their fellow men. In every time, some organization arises among these various criminal enterprises to provide for such demands, regardless of the risks. Among this often ruthless and dangerous crowd are the likes of shady gunslingers, ethnic gangs, bookies, smugglers, bandits, fencers and launderers.

*Cost* *Desired Effect*

1 Locate small-time wickedness (knives, whores, bootleg liquor, petty gambling); Hear about any recent criminal captures, kills, kidnappings or cattle rustling of note

2 Obtain pistols; Hire muscle to rough someone up; Fence minor loot; Arrange for a crooked dealer at card table of your choice

3 Obtain a rifle, shotgun; Get the service of a sharpshooter with questionable morals; Prove that crime pays (and score $350); Round up a fair-size gang of outlaws for one task

4 Put a mark on someone's head; Spread the criminal word far and wide; Find a corrupt law enforcement officer; Gain respect among city gangs or bandits in the wild, and have a word in almost all aspects of their operations; Get hold of impressive weaponry (gatling guns, artillery)

5 Know an important Someone in the Big Family back East; Control one local criminal industry (prostitution, gambling, etc.) with an iron fist

6 Control or at least have a decisive say in almost all criminal activity within one small town

7 Run criminal activity out of the county courthouse and have your own office to boot

### Law Enforcement

The Savage West is commonly seen as a wild, lawless place, devoid of the rules of civilization and hunting grounds for all manner of bandits and desperadoes. Into this storm comes a number of individuals who are dedicated to bringing order to the territories and protecting those they are appointed to defend. Often outnumbered and outgunned, these men and women rely on cool courage, quick wits, lightning reflexes and a keen knowledge of what the public considers "justice" to do their job. Of course, not all constables are immune to the sins they fight against, and a character with this Influence is able to manipulate traditions, connections, favors and other avenues to get lawmen both honorable and corrupt to perform special services for him. Behind the long shadow of the silver star one can find sheriffs, deputies, jailers, Texas Rangers and marshals.

*Cost* *Desired Effect*

1 Learn the habits of the local law;* Hear constabulary information and rumors

2 Get a blind eye turned to minor violations; Have officers "check something out"

3 Get the latest on a current investigation; Have someone harassed or detained

4 Access confiscated weapons or contraband; Have some serious charges dropped; Start an investigation; Get money, either from the evidence room or as an appropriation ($100); Gather a group of "concerned citizens"; Post fake "Wanted: Alive" or "Wanted: Dead or Alive" notices for a short time

5 Institute major investigations; Arrange setups; Locate corrupt officers in a town; Have officers fired; Have someone run out of town (tarred and feathered optional)

6 Gather a large posse to hunt someone down; gather officers from several counties away; Post fake "Wanted: Dead" notices

### Legal

Many a criminal has gone to the gallows claiming to have been railroaded by the system, but unbeknownst even to the most government-fearing individual, there are those who quietly tip the scales, even in the hallowed halls of justice, and the courts, law schools, law firms and justice bureaus within them. However, characters who use this Influence to openly flout the law and get away with it had best beware, as citizens' mobs will eventually organize to run habitual criminals out of town Ñ or worse. Inhabiting the domain of this Influence are lawyers, judges, bailiffs, clerks and district attorneys.

*Cost* *Desired Effect*

1 Get free representation for minor cases; Know basic court procedures (but not theory or practice)*

2 Avoid bail for some charges; Have minor charges dropped

3 Manipulate legal procedures (minor wills and contracts, court dates) Access public or court funds ($100); Get representation in most court cases; File minor lawsuit against someone without any real basis (this will most likely take some time and cost for them to sort out, though)

4 Tie up court cases; Have most legal charges dropped; File serious lawsuits without basis

5 Close down all but the most serious investigations.

### Lowdown

While lured by promises of wealth, opportunity and wide open spaces, many of those who make the trip west find themselves unable to make it on their own for a variety of reasons. Herded into the ethnic ghettoes of the cities as cheap labor or living lives of need in ramshackle houses on the frontier, ignored by their "betters," this whole part of society makes its own culture and lifestyle to deal with the harsh lot life has dealt it. In the saloons and badlands you can find mountain men, the homeless, servants, prostitutes, poor families, petty criminals and the forgotten.

*Cost* *Desired Effect*

1 Has an ear open for the word on the street*; Identify the gangs and know their neighborhoods or territory and habits; Find the general location of a local mountain man

2 Live mostly without fear on the underside of society*; Keep a contact or two in most aspects of street life; Access minor stolen goods

3 Often gets insight on other areas of Influence, even if indirectly; Arrange some services from street people or gangs; Get hard to find personal weapons (imported guns, Spanish blades)

4 Mobilize groups of homeless or working poor; Panhandle or hold a "collection" ($25); Gain respect of one gang or bandit group, and thus go unmolested by them

5 Agitate local street scene; Call a "whore's holiday" all across town (and thus typically get whatever else it is you're asking for, if anything, *very* quickly); Know someone in almost any town you go to

6 Find out the hardest-to-find information there is to know about a topic of street life (the location of the hideout of the most wanted outlaw gang in the territory, or the possible location of a lost gold mine discovered by a local mountain man years ago)

### Newspapers

The media serves as the eyes and ears of the world, and the power of newspapers to influence people and the decisions they make is impressive; by our modern standards, even the hardened people of the Savage West are still far more trusting when it comes to the press and their bias. Even to the illiterate, newspapers stories are often considered gospel, especially concerning matters of foreign relations or policy back East. While yellow journalists and dime novelists still proliferate, and rampant jingoism is the rule when it comes to covering public affairs, there are a few souls dedicated to bringing truth to the people about their world and the people who change it. This Influence measures a character's ability to abuse the machinery of newspapers (and to a lesser extent, telegraph reports) to guide or confuse public opinion, or even to break through barriers and print the truth when no one else wants to hear it.

*Cost* *Desired Effect*

1 Learn tomorrow's news today;* Submit small articles (within reason)

2 Suppress (but not stop) small articles or reports; Get hold of investigative reporting information; Get the ear of local reporters*

3 Initiate news investigations and reports; Get your hands on the petty cash ($25); Access printing or telegraph resources; Censure a reporter indefinitely; Run a serialization of a work (your own or someone else's)

4 Print outrageously fake stories (local only); Publish a serious story criticizing a respected or important regional personality in a major newspaper; access a famous reporter or "muckraker" back East.

### Occult

Most people are curious about the supernatural world and the various groups and beliefs that make up the occult subculture, but few consider it anything but a tall tale, superstitious nonsense or branch of science waiting to be explored. This could not be farther from the truth. *Occult* Influence, more than any other, hits the Garou close to home and could very well bring humanity to its senses about just who and what shares this world with them. The occult community contains cult leaders, alternative religious groups, charlatans, would-be occultists and spiritualists.

*Cost* *Desired Effect*

1 Contact and make use of common occult groups and their practices; Know some of the more visible occult figures*

2 Know and contact some of the more obscure occult figures;* Access resources for most rituals and rites; Attend local occult ceremony without causing a stir

3 Know the general vicinity of certain supernatural entities (Kindred, fae, mages, mummies, wraiths, etc.) and possibly contact them; Can find vital or very rare material components; Milk impressionable wannabes for bucks ($50); Access occult tomes and writings; Research a Basic Rite or Gift

4 Research an Intermediate Rite; Separate truth from folklore

5 Access minor magic items; Unearth an Advanced Rite

6 Research a new or unheard-of ritual or rite from tomes or mentors

### Politics

The political process in the Savage West is a far cry from the spin doctors and constant opinion polls that plague modern politics, but the familiar game of good ol' boys, fat cats and who knows who is still in full swing. In other words, it's politics as usual, and in the impassioned politics of the westward movement many are willing to lay down their lives instead of simply their opinions. Some of these individuals include statesmen, pollsters, activists, party faithful, lobbyists, candidates and politicians themselves.

*Cost* *Desired Effect*

1 Minor lobbying; Identify real platforms of politicians and parties;* Be in the know*

2 Meet small-time politicians; Have a forewarning of processes, laws and the like*; Use a rally of the faithful or other fund raiser for your own gain ($300)

3 Sway or alter political projects (local parks, renovations, small construction)

4 Enact minor legislation; Dash careers of minor politicians

5 Get your candidate in a minor office; Enact encompassing legislature in one particular field

6 Block the passage of major bills; Suspend major laws temporarily; Use state bureaus or subcommittees to your own advantage at will

7 Usurp county-wide politics; Subvert statewide powers, at least to a moderate degree.

8 Call out the cavalry; Declare a state of emergency in a region

**Railroad**

The coming of the iron horse was a contentious moment in the history of the Savage West, as it brought the supplies that the ever-expanding network of cities and towns needed in order to push westward, but it also spelled the end of the ancient territories that the native populations had counted as their homes. Regardless of what history's judgment will be, however, the influence the railroad industry wields is indisputable, and characters with this Influence can control this critical lifeline. While technically this Influence falls under the domain of *Industry* and *Transportation*, it is such an important Influence and such a different industry from any other known in the Savage West that *Railroad* Influence is considered its own Trait, although it can certainly be paired with those to be used to greater effect, especially *Transportation*. All sorts of people fall under the purview of the railroad industry: engineers, switch men, porters, conductors, railroad executives and freight loaders.

*Cost* *Desired Effect*

1 Know train schedules and destinations*; Learn about a mundane cargo; Hop a free ride on a local route*

2 Delay a train for a short time; Have a passenger kicked off a train; Learn the real plans for local railroad expansion; Have cargo inspected

3 Use a network of bribed officials to offload cargo or smuggle at will; Have a voice in one particular branch of a railroad company; Bar a person from passage on one entire line; Ensure safe passage from mundane hazards for one trip

4 Begin a new route for an existing track; Dip into railroad bounty ($250); Switch the tracks on trains at a whim; Ensure travel protected from (most) supernatural dangers for one trip

5 Exploit railroad rules and policies to exert complete control over one train for one trip, including destination and the disposition of all passengers and cargo onboard

6 Have a say in appointing (or deposing) a railroad company president; Dominate local railroad affairs

7 Obtain funding and permits to begin an entirely new line

### Scholarly

While it is a common perception that most people in the Savage West were ignorant folks, a surprising number of them did in fact receive at least some schooling and at least a touch of letters during their lifetime. The local school teacher is a respected person in a community, and the education young people receive often carries a strong moral and religious content as well, making this the largest time in people's lives they are indoctrinated with impressions and values. Whether formal or simply understood, apprenticeships to manual craftsmen from farmers to blacksmiths also provides a significant degree of education in the Savage West. And while universities are still primarily a feature of the East, many bright and intellectually dedicated souls join the westward expansion, either conducting research or hoping to found new places of higher learning on their own. A character with this Influence can manipulate the education process and those involved in it to suit her desires. Note that, as with the *Finance* Influence, a character who hopes to have contacts beyond the local level had best put forth at least the appearance of respectability, as the higher levels of education are much more discriminating about who they accept and associate with than in the modern age. In this class of Influence, one finds teachers, professors, students of all ages and levels, Jesuits, traveling scholars, members of Greek orders, and many young and impressionable minds.

*Cost* *Desired Effect*

1 Know the location and general level of education offered in local schools;* Access the local school marm (for information, you dirty dog); Learn the true level of schooling a given citizen has had

2 Know a craftsman or scholar with useful knowledge or skills to teach (especially to an apprentice or fellow scholar); Access any resources of local schools; Pass as a "learned" individual in most circumstances (regardless of the truth of this perception)*

3 Have a student expelled; Keep a student who should be expelled in school; Have "connections" to a university (guaranteed acceptance); Access the resources of a local craftsman in a "learning" capacity; Control what is taught at local schools

4 Establish your own school; Discredit a local authority on a particular subject; Find the location of material to research a given topic; Attract a scholar in a particular field to come to the area under some pretext

5 Produce a fake university degree; Contact an eminent scholar; Use university labs and libraries freely (where appropriate); Abuse money from a generous grant ($500)

6 Arrange your own class at a university; Discredit a professor; Cancel a class

7 Found a university (keeping it from being laughed at is a function of faculty, resources, reputation and dedication, however); Control all education in a large county

### Transportation

The Savage West is a vast place, and without transportation systems to keep it all going, many cities would die out and territories remain unsettled for a long time to come. From stagecoach lines to clipper ships to local stables, you have your hand in getting people and things from place to place, and one word from you can stop shipments or smuggle goods with impunity. In an era so dependent on getting goods to and from their markets before spoilage or theft occurs, this is indeed a great deal of power to wield, albeit usually a subtle one. As the railroad industry is still new, tightly controlled and fiercely set against being at the mercy of any other type of transportation, this Influence does not give actual control over railroad cargoes once they reach the rails or the railroad industry itself (that is the domain of the *Railroad* Influence); however, it does give one broad-reaching powers over every other type of transportation in the Savage West, and thus the potential to make railroad men *very* uncomfortable if exercised properly. This is also the type of Influence that most ordinary people still use and associate with, which can give a character some added benefits as opposed to the rather insular *Railroad* powers. Of course, combining these two Influences can make for quite a profitable alliance, and allow a character to get nearly anywhere or ship nearly anything with a minimum number of hassles. Keeping these systems working are coach and team drivers, sea captains, wagon train leaders, pony express riders, conductors, border guards and untold others.

| *Cost* | *Desired Effect* |
|---|---|
| 1 | An old hand at what goes where, when and why; Can travel locally quickly and freely by a variety of means*; Know prominent local trails, rails and shipping routes* |
| 2 | Can track an unwary target if he uses anything but his own horse (and even then if you can find the right stable); Arrange a passage safe (or at least concealed) from mundane threats (robbery, kidnapping, etc.) |
| 3 | Seriously hamper an individual's ability to travel or ship goods; Avoid most supernatural dangers when traveling (such as hunters and vampires) |
| 4 | Temporarily shut down one form of transportation (wagon trains, ships, stage coaches, etc.); Deny a railroad line one cargo for a short time; Route money your way ($100) |
| 5 | Reroute major modes of travel; Smuggle with impunity |
| 6 | Extend your control to nearby areas |
| 7 | Isolate small or remote regions for a short period |

### Tribal

This Influence covers your control over the affairs of one Native American tribe. There are literally hundreds of tribes in the Savage West, which means you must specify an individual tribe when this Influence is taken. Typically this means you were born a member of this tribe, making Wendigo and Uktena the most likely candidates for this Influence, but characters from other tribes may take this Influence with an excellent story and Storyteller approval. Characters may take this Influence for several different tribes to reflect a wide degree of Influence among native populations, or the Storyteller may allow them to count a handful of small, closely related and allied tribes as one tribe for the purposes of this Trait, if this does not disturb game balance. European Garou should be warned that possessing this level of familiarity with native folk is considered akin to treason by members of some tribes (not to mention many ordinary humans), and also marks you as a sympathizer to any other native tribes that might be hostile to your allies. Obviously, the people within the domain of this Influence are all members of the tribe in question, from chiefs, matriarchs, warriors, women and children on down, even to mixed-blood relatives still loyal to their tribe.

*Cost* *Desired Effect*

1 Know the layout and boundaries of tribal lands*; Learn rumors and recent events around the fire; Identify members of the tribe, even those of mixed blood*

2 Learn the true reason behind recent tribal decisions; Gather wisdom from some of the older members of the tribe on a particular topic; Cross unhindered through tribal territory, even with nontribal companions*

3 Inspire a small group of warriors to join you for a specific, worthy cause; Get the ear of the chief or matriarch; Learn minor ancestral secrets (herbal remedies, minor spirit names); Cross through the territory of a friendly or neutral tribe unmolested*

4 Have a loud voice in tribal policy discussions; Borrow minor items of power (small talens created by tribal shamans); Access moderate tribal secrets (names of allied spirits); Take some trading material ($25 value, usually in pelts or the like)

5 Call a war council of the tribe; Access major tribal secrets (the location of a bound and slumbering great Bane); Gain the honor of carrying a minor mystical item for the tribe for a time (strong talen or weak fetish);

6 Call up a full-fledged war party for a cause related to the tribe's welfare; Replace the current chief or matriarch with one of your choosing; Control all the details of a single mundane event on a regular basis (marriages, hunting, planting)

7 Start a tribal migration; Arrange a council of tribes in the region and have a voice at that council yourself; Learn the greatest tribal secrets (whispered legends about the fall of the Croatan, for example); Arrange an alliance with your tribe and a tribe they are bitterly opposed to;

8 Introduce new elements into tribal mythology; Carry the tribe's most prized heirloom for a time (mid-range to powerful fetish, at the Storyteller's discretion)

# Spark of Life

These are the little peccadilloes and personality details that you can add to your character to make him seem more like flesh and blood and less like just a collection of Traits. These features could be anything, such as a habit of smiling when frustrated, chewing on sunflower seeds, tipping your hat to a lady, or having a particularly strong handshake — anything that adds an extra splash of life to your character. As long as you don't descend into camp and self-parody, enjoy these little details; they really add a human (so to speak) dimension to your character that other players quickly recognize and enjoy.

## Fleshing it Out

### Background

Now is when you fill in all the little details, such as where your character came from and what he does on a regular basis. By casting yourself in the role of your character, you should try to find the answers to the following questions:

*What was your childhood like? Did you have any sort of formal schooling after the Change? Many people were illiterate in the West, but a surprising number weren't and received some kind of schooling in their life. If you are a lupus, how well did you adjust to what you are, and how do you perceive the world of humans?*

You should also give some reasons for your character to be a part of the pack. Always consult your Storyteller before you get your heart set on anything; she might already be planning a story about how your pack forms.

### Motivations

*What do you want to do, and why? Is there more to your life as a Garou than merely fighting the Wyrm? If not, should there be?*

The Garou are in the grip of a tragic struggle, with Pure One fighting European and all Garou battling against the minions of the Wyrm and the Storm Eater, but that doesn't absolve them of any of the responsibilities of having lives once they're off the front lines. Many have goals both inside and outside of their packs, and ties of blood and kin are important in this time. Most Garou have their own views of the world and opinions on how to affect it. Many are eager to earn the respect of their fellows.

### Appearance

*What do you look like when you're in Homid form? How do you dress? How do you carry yourself? What does your wolf form look like?*

Many of these details can be gleaned from your background, but even more should be added here. You should ultimately select an appearance (and costume) that reflects and represents every aspect of your character. Obviously this is not intended to be taken literally, but a Bone Gnawer should definitely have a different wardrobe selection than, say, an Iron Rider, and both should be quite different from a Wendigo.

### Equipment

If you already have a fetish (from your Background Traits), then that's something you automatically have. However, your character might have other odds and ends that she carries around. Any selections must be approved by the Storyteller, and don't be surprised if you can't have everything you want. Some of it might not be appropriate to the nature or scope of the story — not everyone can have a pearl-handled pistol on each hip and a bandoleer of bullets.

## Breeds

A Garou's breed determines part of her basic personality, and often colors her perceptions and beliefs about the world. There are three breeds: homid, metis and lupus. A werewolf's breed is determined by that of her mother, with the obvious exception (metis).

### Homid

The most common breed, homid Garou are born to a human or homid mother and suffer from her lack of connection to Gaia. Because humanity has separated itself from the Wyld and become more focused on the trials and tribulations of civilization, members of the homid breed are disassociated from their wild inner selves, but possess an innate ability to get along with their fellow homids that can prove quite invaluable as the cities grow and the wild places are threatened by the shadow of the Storm Eater.

However, this detachment is also why so many homids are lost cubs, who do not know their true heritage. Many times a homid child will have his First Change in a strange place without the aid of other Garou or knowing Kinfolk, and the shock can drive the unprepared new Garou into Lunacy. These Lunatics are often prey for the Wyrm if they are not found and adopted into a tribe or pack, and are responsible for being the basis of many a dime novelist's lurid tales of massacres and monsters in the dark nights of the Savage West.

Yet homids are the most adaptable breed. As a whole, they roam over more terrain and inhabit more places than a lupus would find possible, and it is their will to explore and innovate that constantly carries the Garou Nation to new horizons, even if their cousins too often carry the taint of the Wyrm or the Weaver with them.

**Natural Form**: Homid

**Beginning Gifts**: *Jam Gun, Persuasion, Smell of Man, Staredown*

**Initial Gnosis**: One

## Lupus

These are Garou whose mother is either a wolf or a lupus Garou. This breed is more strongly represented in the Savage West than in the modern era, due to the large packs of wolves that still roam over parts of the northern and western territories. They are, however, all the more tragic for their numbers, for even now the near genocidal slaughter of wolves throughout North America is beginning as ranchers seek to eliminate these "pests" and settlers look to allay their fears of attacks in the night. Wolves once had the largest natural range of any terrestrial mammal except man, but the introduction of these new factors in their habitat and the gradual encroachment of humanity will all too soon prove to be a lethal mix. Currently, however, wolf populations are quite strong in the West, and the numbers of lupus Wendigo and Uktena are still higher than their European counterparts.

Part of playing a lupus character is understanding lupine nature. You must keep in mind some of the facts about wolves that make lupus different from homid or metis Garou.

Wolves are nocturnal or crepuscular (meaning that they come out at twilight), although diurnal (or daytime) activity is not uncommon, especially during cool weather and in winter. Lupus Garou are often night creatures, tending to be sluggish and sleepy during the day. They are almost entirely carnivorous. Some lupus Garou have adapted enough to eat foods other than meat, but they usually like their meat bloody, warm and freshly killed.

Lupus do not understand many human concepts at first. The concept of time is difficult, as is money and operating technology (they refer to such as "Weaver-stuff"). Human laws, bureaucracy and territory views are completely alien to lupus Garou.

Furthermore, lupus do not communicate as humans do. In fact, they have to learn human tongues by painstakingly taking Homid form and trying to form strange words. They are used to howling, posturing and marking territory with their scent glands to get their point across.

Lupus characters howl during courtship and mating, as a warning, as part of worshipping the moon and in celebration. In addition to howling, wolves bark, growl and whine. Barking is associated with surprise and warning. Growling occurs during challenges, and is associated with threatening behavior or asserting one's rights. Whines are associated with greetings, hungry cubs, playtime and other signs of anxiety, curiosity or inquiry. These are intimate noises that lupus Garou make to other wolves and to each other.

Lupus posture to show dominance; the most common pose is to place one's paw on another lupus as that lupus rolls over to accept dominance. Lupus also mark possessions and territories with their scent glands, which, in Crinos form, are located on the wrists and the neck.

The dominant members of a lupus pack are the alpha male and alpha female. In a lupus pack, only the alpha pair breeds with wolves, and this pair also suppresses breeding by all other pack members. However, all pack members help care for pups and feed them as well. Unlike packs composed of homid and metis Garou, many lupus packs have Kinfolk wolves as members.

Lupus Garou respect other Garou more when they take Lupus form to communicate. They generally have a hard time considering their actions in terms of future results or as a result of past actions. They live in the present for the most part, and often take the most logical and commonsensical course of action rather than involve themselves in complicated schemes. They do not often make elaborate plans; instinct usually guides them.

Lupus believe that Gaia watches over them and will provide for them. They are perhaps the most spiritual of the breeds. They are known to respect Theurges of all breeds more than they do the other auspices, and they show respect for all spirits encountered in the Umbra. The growing menace of the Storm Eater, as well as the increasing violence against their kin, upsets the lupus greatly, and are sources of great anger and sadness for this breed, which can cause them to be quite brutal and direct, even with homid Garou.

**Natural Form**: Lupus

**Beginning Gifts**: *Heightened Senses*, *Catfeet*, *Scent of Sight*, *Spook the Herd*

**Initial Gnosis**: Three

**Restrictions**: A lupus cannot begin the game with the following Abilities or Backgrounds: *Bureaucracy*, *Fast-Draw*, *Finance*, *Firearms*, Influence (any kind, barring Storyteller permission), *Ride*, *Repair*, *Science*.

## Metis

When a Garou mates with another Garou, the result is a metis. This mating is proscribed by the Litany, and is considered a perversion among the Garou. In these wild days, when so many Garou are dying and not many are born among the lupus or homids, it is very tempting for some of the remaining Garou to consider producing another Garou this way. Still, the fact that metis are born disfigured is proof enough for most Garou that such offspring are somehow tainted by the Wyrm. Many septs — Pure One or European — have a custom of testing within an inch of his life at any opportunity, or allowing the Children of Gaia to "adopt" the miserable creature.

Despite their stigma, metis usually grow up fully aware of their Garou heritage, and have the unmistakable proof (natural Crinos form) that they are Garou from the day they are born. This headstart in the world of the Garou is a powerful thing, because metis do not have to go through the traumatic First Change as the homids or lupus do, and they are often taught Beginning Gifts before they even show signs of changing. Metis sometimes take their first trips into the Umbra as children, as it is a simple thing for them to step sideways even before they first learn to walk. It is a good thing that a metis has Garou parents; not many human parents could handle a toddler whose natural form is a growling Crinos. Garou mothers usually assume Crinos form in order to give birth to metis, but the births are always difficult and dangerous, especially in the chancy medical conditions that prevail in these times.

Metis are considered the cursed of Gaia because of the sin that caused their births. They are, by nature, infertile, and they each have at least one disfigurement. This disfigurement is always detrimental.

**Natural Form**: Crinos. Unlike homid or lupus breeds, metis regenerate damage in their breed form, but they also take aggravated damage in every form. They are truly an amalgam of human and wolf, and there is no true "natural" form for them to assume.

**Beginning Gifts**: *Create Element*, *Curse of Hatred*, *Sense Wyrm*, *Wildcat Eyes*

**Initial Gnosis**: Two

### Metis Disfigurements

All metis characters have some sort of disfigurement. You must choose one from the list below, or make up your own and have it approved by a Narrator. All mandatory Negative Traits that come from a disfigurement do not count toward the normal bonuses gained by Negative Traits. In other words, you cannot gain extra Traits simply by choosing to play a metis, but you can add additional Negative Traits to a metis character.

**Bad Hearing**: You must take the Negative Trait: *Oblivious*, and lose all ties related to hearing. You must roleplay your disability. This can actually be useful as you can encourage other Garou to repeat themselves. Of course, many Garou have frenzied for simpler reasons — like being forced to endure the company of a metis for too long.

**Chitinous Skin**: You have developed a hard chitinous surface on your skin that cracks and sheds constantly. You gain one Health Level against hand-held weapons, but not bullets. Take all the disadvantages of *Hairless* on this list and the Negative Trait: *Decrepit*.

**Cleft Lip**: You have a cleft lip. Speaking is difficult for you, but at least you can snarl. You are down one Trait and lose all ties on Social Challenges related to your speech or appearance. You should roleplay this disability; it's hard to understand you when you get excited.

**Hairless**: Your body hair is mangy, patchy or totally nonexistent. When in Homid form you have the Negative Trait: *Sickly*. When in Lupus form you must take the Negative Trait:

*Repugnant* instead. Furthermore, you are one Trait down in any challenge when the temperature outside drops below 50 degrees (10 Celsius).

**Human Face**: You retain a human face in all your forms, and therefore must take the Negative Trait: *Repugnant*. You also do not gain any Trait bonuses for perception while in Lupus or Crinos forms. This mutation is disgusting to Garou, who will be horrified at the sight of you, and might well assume you to be a mockery or Black Spiral Dancer.

**Hunchback**: You cannot take any of the following Social Traits: *Elegant*, *Beguiling*, *Gorgeous* or *Seductive*, nor may you have the Physical Traits: *Graceful*, *Lithe* or *Nimble*. You must take the Negative Trait: *Repugnant* as well as either *Lame* or *Clumsy*.

**Madness**: You are slightly mad. You must either win a Static Mental Test or spend a Willpower Trait whenever you find yourself in a stressful situation. Otherwise, you will have a temporary Derangement imposed on you by a Narrator. This problem can cause many Garou to distrust you.

**Magnetic**: You are magnetic to any and all earthly metals, *except silver*. Spoons skitter to you, compasses go wild, and rusty nails always find your feet. Many Garou see this as a sign of the growing perversion of nature, and you must constantly roleplay the minor annoyances it causes you. This deformity can be helpful, but in general is much more a pain than it's worth. Furthermore, anger only makes the attraction worse — you are two Traits down defending against down foes using metal weapons or bullets to hit you in any turn you are in frenzy or use Rage.

**Malformed Limb**: You cannot take the Physical Trait: *Dexterous*, and you must take the Negative Trait: *Lame*. Your movement rate is halved, and you lose all Dexterity-related ties except combat.

**No Claws**: You have no claws, and you do not do aggravated damage when you strike with your paws. Curiously enough, your bite doesn't cause aggravated damage, either. You may never acquire a Gift which allows extra damage to be done by either tooth or claw.

# Auspice

## The Touch of Luna

It is often difficult to explain the nature of auspice to those who don't have Garou blood coursing through their veins. Some, in their ignorance, assume it merely to be some garbled form of astrology. Others with some understanding of such things dislike the destiny of purpose they think auspice represents. Many young Garou who are disdainful of anything that hints at constraint make similar mistakes. One's auspice is not a predestined and inflexible path that a Garou is forced to follow. Instead, it is a beacon that serves to illuminate her path through life. The influence of an auspice comes as much from within as it does from without.

Auspice also serves as an important focus of Garou social life. The Garou as a whole lack the vast diversity of potential interaction that their human counterparts enjoy, especially in the often clannish and insular communities of the Savage West. Therefore, it is not uncommon for Garou of a like auspice to gather together for fellowship. These meetings are informal and not at all closed to other Garou. The "Society" section provides more details on these meetings.

In addition to the phase of the moon, many mark a difference between waxing and waning auspices. When waxing, the moon provides a more positive, aggressive and direct auspice. When waning, the moon inspires a more negative, introspective and indirect auspice. Thus, a waxing Galliard may be a great public performer, while a waning Galliard may only create songs for herself and dwell on things in quiet places.

It should be noticed that the brighter, more clearly seen planets (Mars, Venus, Mercury and Jupiter) are sometimes also noted in the night sky on the day a Garou is born, as well as whether those planets are rising or falling in the sky. Saturn is ignored, as it is considered to be the "Star of the Wyrm."

## Ragabash

**Nickname**: Trickster, New Moon

Although annoying, the Trickster strives to bring and understand wisdom through the folly of self-importance and humility. The Ragabash keeps others on their toes by pulling pranks that highlight the "personality traps" over which others would otherwise trip.

Mischief may be expected from the Ragabash, but it is not often appreciated. They are tolerated but not trusted. The major strength of a New Moon is the flexibility that comes with her nonstructured behavior.

Ragabash are regarded as necessary nuisances, and given much more of a free rein to bend the Litany and traditions. Elders tend not to notice Tricksters working their pranks, but remember that Ragabash are still bound to the sacred laws. A New Moon that pranks to be mean rather than to aid Luna in teaching others to understand her wisdom had best watch his back. Most Garou are not known for their sense of humor.

The Coyote totem has been known to consort with Ragabash, as do his Children the Nuwisha, and these Garou are fond of playing jokes on everyone they meet — mages, vampires and especially faeries, with whom they seem to have a running prank contest.

**Beginning Gifts**: *Walk under the New Moon, Spider's Song, Scent of Running Water, Carried on the Wind*

**Stereotype**: A Ragabash is regarded as a shifty, untrustworthy prankster who must be watched every minute. In reality, however, only those Garou with no sense of humor have the most to fear.

**Initial Rage**: One

**Quote**: *I win again? Well, don't that beat all. I think I'm gonna go and buy my Emma some flowers, and take her to a real nice dinner in town. It's a shame you didn't tell your wife you had this money on you earlier, sir, because I think the both of you would be a little happier right now if you'd just saved it for her like you were supposed to.*

## Theurge

**Nickname**: Seer, Crescent Moon

Theurges explore the paths of the spirit, and are the most familiar with the Umbra. They serve as healers, prophets, exorcists, diviners, spiritual counselors, purifiers, artificers and summoners. Like the human shamans of native cultures, Theurge Garou stand aloof and mysterious. As the problem of the Storm Eater grows, however, and the spirits become restless and angry, more and more Theurges are being forced to step into the mainstream of Garou society in the battle to stop the encroachments of this powerful entity.

Because they are allied with the spirit world, Theurges often have conversations with people who aren't "there" and develop complicated superstitions which at best can spook cautious locals, and at worst provoke them to darker actions, especially if the Theurge belongs to a different culture than the community. Some of these superstitions are Bans laid on them by spirits (see p. 237).

**Beginning Gifts**: *Mother's Touch, Name the Spirit, Sense Wyrm, Sight from Beyond, Spirit Speech*

**Stereotype**: Although Theurges are powerful in the spirit world, more physically oriented Garou often see Theurges as strange, unearthly and weak in combat. This is not the case; many Theurges learn the martial arts in order to potentially intimidate and/or do battle with spirits. Still, it is not a coincidence that many of the Theurges of a sept tend to gather together in medicine circles, for only one Theurge can truly understand another.

**Initial Rage**: One

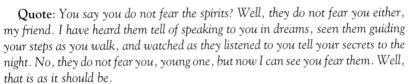

**Quote**: *You say you do not fear the spirits? Well, they do not fear you either, my friend. I have heard them tell of speaking to you in dreams, seen them guiding your steps as you walk, and watched as they listened to you tell your secrets to the night. No, they do not fear you, young one, but now I can see you fear them. Well, that is as it should be.*

## Philodox

**Nickname**: Keeper of the Ways, Half Moon

Much about the Garou is a matter of balance: balance between wolf and man, between spirit and flesh, and between creation and destruction. Born when Luna's face sits on the threshold between light and darkness, Philodox are the physical incarnation of balance, and they are renowned among the Garou for their unbiased outlook. Indeed, the words of Philodox are often taken to heart by even the most radical Garou factions. Philodox value this honor, and strive to maintain their image as fair and impartial judges in the eyes of other Garou. The Philodox who does otherwise may be ostracized by other Half Moons.

A Philodox is often the mediator and peacemaker in packs. As more multitribal packs become common in the Savage West, Philodox are valued all the more for their ability to keep everyone from each other's throats and on the front lines against the Wyrm. Those who prove their wisdom and attain old age are called upon as judges and arbitrators on a wide variety of matters. Indeed, few would argue their inestimable value to the already fractious Garou.

**Beginning Gifts**: *Resist Pain, Scent of the True Form, Strength of Purpose, Truth of Gaia*

**Stereotype**: The Philodox are often seen as mediators between others. They are typically perceived as being the most honorable of all the Garou. Though Philodox cannot help but see the world in terms of balance, they are loath to express their views unless others ask them to. This reluctance to become involved often makes them seem unconcerned to other auspices. Sometimes, by "playing the Devil's Advocate," they actually hinder split-second decisions that are necessary.

**Initial Rage**: Two

**Quote**: *What does it matter who first laid claim to this land? All of it is sacred to Gaia, and it is our duty first and foremost to ensure that it remains safe. We can either work together to refresh the caern as a new, united sept, or we can paint the canyon with our blood and leave it to the Wyrm as spoils of our folly. The choice is yours.*

## Galliard

**Nickname**: Moon Dancer, Gibbous Moon

The Garou born under this phase of the moon are imbued with the spark of creation. The greatest poems, songs and tales of the Garou have sprung from their fertile minds. Their thoughts are like quicksilver, racing and fluid, dashing headlong into places where few other Garou give a passing glance. The Moon Dancers lead septs in their howls during moots. Their energetic and inspirational performances infect an entire sept, filling the Garou with a sense of belonging and tradition. This is an important role in a time when so many Garou are losing their sense of direction and purpose.

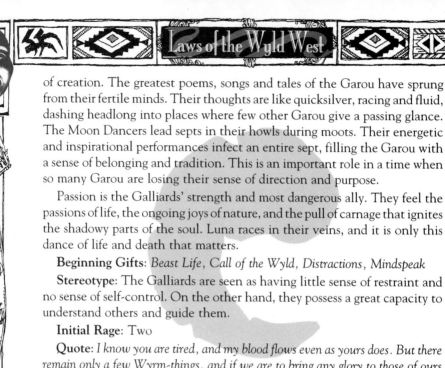

Passion is the Galliards' strength and most dangerous ally. They feel the passions of life, the ongoing joys of nature, and the pull of carnage that ignites the shadowy parts of the soul. Luna races in their veins, and it is only this dance of life and death that matters.

**Beginning Gifts**: *Beast Life, Call of the Wyld, Distractions, Mindspeak*

**Stereotype**: The Galliards are seen as having little sense of restraint and no sense of self-control. On the other hand, they possess a great capacity to understand others and guide them.

**Initial Rage**: Two

**Quote**: *I know you are tired, and my blood flows even as yours does. But there remain only a few Wyrm-things, and if we are to bring any glory to those of ours already fallen, we must deny the foul creatures this pass. Now, on your feet, my brothers, and together we shall send them screaming to Malfeas, or be there to greet them if we fail!*

## Ahroun

**Nickname**: Warrior, Full Moon

Ahroun are the teeth and claws of the moon's rage, the fury of the wounded earth itself. If Ahroun live long enough to temper their anger with wisdom, they become the most dangerous creatures alive. But in youth they tend to live for the thrill of battle and life-and-death action. These warriors are known for their temper, their embracing of death as part of the Ahroun's due and their fanatical belief in the war leader's code — "First one into battle, last one standing."

In the often violent world of the Savage West, Ahroun are both the doom and the salvation of the Garou; it is this auspice's skill at arms and strategy helps the Garou win their battles, but all too often the headstrong Ahroun lead their fellows into a great many fights that could have been avoided with a subtler tack.

**Beginning Gifts**: *Inspiration, Razor Claws, Spirit of the Fray, Trick Shot*

**Stereotype**: The Ahroun are all that is mighty, proud and foolish in Garou. They make effective wartime leaders but sometimes stumble in peacetime situations; there is often too much beast in Ahroun for them to appreciate the worth of things besides battle.

**Initial Rage**: Three

**Quote**: *I've heard enough of this talk. I don't know or care who started the feud, but I swear by Gaia that tonight it will end, or may those mockeries have my pelt for barter! Now, who will ride with me?*

# Tribes

There are 13 Garou tribes available to characters. These tribes organize the remaining Garou who fight against the Wyrm. Originally all tribes were one. Strife and personality conflict drove wedges into this Pangaea tribe, and as the separate groups moved out across the globe and later mixed with the indigenous cultures, many (nearly irreconcilable) differences formed. During that time, most tribes were very regional, each controlling and living in a certain portion of the world. However, in recent centuries, as human civilization began pushing westward and transportation grew more efficient, old hatreds and new rivalries boiled to the surface, and now as many Garou raise claw against each other as against the forces of the Weaver and the Wyrm. Even the most tolerant Garou of a multitribal pack still takes great pride in her origins, and insulting someone's family tree is one of the surest ways to provoke a fight these days. However, a Garou's tribe is the extra extended family, the heritage, that gives him purpose and prevents him from becoming a lone marauder.

## Black Furies

Ferocious Greek warrior-women and protectors of wild places, the Black Furies found the New World to be a mixed blessing. Within the ranks of the settlers, many women received much more respect for their roles in the survival of the community than they had before, but too often towns continued old-fashioned laws and customs relegating women to lesser roles. When the great westward expansion began, the Black Furies stood divided — many wished to continue to push the cause of women's suffrage and other tribal aims back East, where the political machines existed to realistically realize such aims, while another faction argued the time had come to uphold the Mother's other sacred charge, to protect the places of the Wyld from the less-than-enlightened paws of the other tribes. After a great debate, a fair contingent of the tribe went west; those Furies who stayed in the East typically grant their sisters a great deal of respect, and help them any way they can should the need arise.

Women in the West have a great deal more respect and personal latitude than is commonly believed in modern times, but even the Furies must battle the occasional chauvinist bent on "showing the little lady her place." Those Furies found in the Savage West are a hardy, honorable lot. Their duty to the Mother demands no less of them, and even the most prejudiced Get of Fenris admits they stand by their word. The Furies are also commonly misunderstood for their attitudes toward males, as what few men are in the tribe are their own metis cubs. All other male children, who in times past would have been killed, are typically given to the Children of Gaia or another tribe for adoption out of deference for the Garou's waning numbers.

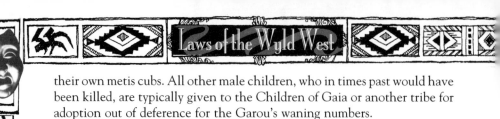

The other tribes, especially male-dominated ones such as the Get, typically believe the Furies simply hate men, but this is not the case. They just believe that women understand the tribe's mission in a way men cannot, and the majority of Furies do not harbor undue hate, contempt or even pity for men — if there is any simple understanding of their opinion of men, it is that they see them as fulfilling a different role in Gaia's plan, one that they often must be reminded of. Nonetheless, the standard perception of Furies as hard-nosed and unyielding is not entirely without basis — there are very, *very* few addled or tender-footed Furies out there.

**Totem**: Pegasus

**Initial Willpower**: One

**Tribe Advantage**: Bond of the Mother

Black Furies recover one Willpower Trait per day spent at a site holy to Gaia, such as a temple of Artemis or a glen consecrated to Selene. The site need not be a caern, but must a natural site pure of the Wyrm's taint that is tended by Furies or their kin at least twice a year. They may also trade Willpower with other Black Furies (and sometimes with other worshippers of Artemis).

**Tribe Drawback**: Rage of the Burning Times

All too often, men force women to bear the brunt of their desires, and while the Mother preaches tolerance to Her children, the Furies have a long memory of the injustices men have visited on women. They lose all ties to resist frenzy when a stressful situation involves a male.

**Backgrounds**: No restrictions.

**Tribe Gifts**: *Kneel, Sense of the Prey, Sense Wyrm, Song of the Seasons*

**Wolf Form**: Black Furies tend to be dark, predominately black, with white, silver or gray highlights or streaks. They are inevitably broad-shouldered and graceful.

**Organization**: The Black Furies are run by two major bodies called Calyxes. The Outer Calyx is made up of 13 Ranked Black Furies from all over the world, chosen by lot. The Inner Calyx consists of five Furies chosen directly by Artemis Herself.

**Territory**: Most Black Furies avoid the male-dominated politics of the cities, preferring secluded lives in the depths of the wilderness. This sometimes leads to a conflict with Red Talons or Pure Ones in the area, but most such disputes are minor and tempered by the obvious respect the Furies have for the sanctity of the land. Some Furies, kindred spirits to their sisters back East, live in cities, the better to push the causes of women's suffrage and other issues dear to the tribe.

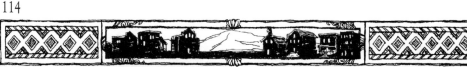

**Protectorate**: Black Furies consider themselves protectors of the Wyld, which they see embodied in the land itself and concentrated in places of Gaia. They tend the wild lands in the Savage West, hoping to keep the same taint that grew across much of Europe from being spread by the unwitting members of the other tribes and their fellow settlers. The conflict between Weaver and Wyld spirits in the Storm Umbra angers the tribe, and the Furies try to banish the touch of the Weaver and the Wyrm from the spirit world whenever they can. They see themselves as protectors of women; any man foolish enough to commit crimes against women near them is often used as a convenient tool to sharpen their claws.

**Outlook**: The Black Furies have long-standing bonds with the Children of Gaia and the Silent Striders. The former share their politics and love of the beauty of Gaia, the latter have always lent aid to Furies in need and stood by the wisest Furies without ever raising the issue of gender. The Furies respect most of the other tribes' wishes as long as they do not go against the will of Artemis, but they have a powerful distaste for the Get of Fenris, whom they see as chauvinists without honor or an understanding of the Goddess.

**Quote**: *None for you tonight. Why not? Well, I hear talk that last night you slept off your whiskey with someone other than your wife, and this talk also says it isn't the first time. I suggest you use this sober moment to leave town and never come back, because the moment I find the slightest proof to these stories you had better be six counties away, or they'll be finding bits of you all across the territory. Hear me?*

## Bone Gnawers

Everything the other tribes claim to disparage in the Garou, the Gnawers have been the bottom-rung, runts-of-the-litter tribe since the earliest days, picking at the leftovers of Garou and homids alike, calling the filthiest, most desolate places home. Allegedly of jackal stock, the Gnawers have thinned their lupus blood a bit from living in cities for so long, but the frontier and the mountain men they claim among their number have this trend in a bit of a turnaround. Gnawers are typically found running with packs of wild dogs or in the seediest parts of towns, and have extended families of kin in both parts, to which they extend a fierce loyalty.

Abused and put upon in nearly every corner of Garou society, these inveterate scavengers have learned to trust no one but each other and those in their impoverished situation. They look with cynical and more than slightly amused eyes at the representatives of other tribes they come across, who often come to them seeking information and goods they are unable to find any other way. Only the Iron Riders typically ignore the class division between the tribes, as they are longtime companions in city living, but even then the Gnawers know their relationship is far from equal. After all, it is rare for the Riders to come calling when they aren't looking for information.

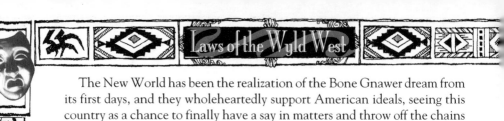

The New World has been the realization of the Bone Gnawer dream from its first days, and they wholeheartedly support American ideals, seeing this country as a chance to finally have a say in matters and throw off the chains that bound them in their old homelands. As such, Gnawers from all areas of the country are violently opposed to slavery, and support the abolitionist cause with a near-fanatical zeal that surprises many of the other tribes, who often see the Gnawers as lazy and slow-witted.

The other tribes forget that these children of Rat have endured under the worst conditions both homid and Garou society have created, and even prospered in their own way. Most members of this tribe make their true living selling and trading secrets and other loose ends they come across to other tribes, be it the schematics an Iron Rider needs to make her latest invention or the location of the local mockery den the Silver Fang war party intends to wipe out. No matter what the other tribes may say, though, the Gnawers' tolerance of their lowly conditions does not extend to tolerance regarding the Wyrm. Indeed, the Wyrm often strikes deep in the wants and vices of poor communities, and the Gnawers fight many more battles than the other tribes ever know.

**Totem**: Rat

**Initial Willpower:** Two

**Tribe Advantage**: Ear to the Ground

Bone Gnawers always have an inkling of what is going on where they live. As a result, they can gain an instant Influence Trait in any area for the purposes of gathering information. This can be done once per Trait of Rank per session. Their Influences are never people *per se*. These Influences demonstrate the tribe's knack for "just knowing where to look," and cannot be used for anything other than information-gathering. These extra Influences are lost at the end of the session, regardless of whether or not they are used.

**Tribe Drawback**: Bad Company

Bone Gnawers are often regarded as filthy and lowdown because of their lifestyles and habits. A Bone Gnawer's Rank is therefore treated as one less than normal by the other tribes. This does not actually affect a Gnawer's Rank, but does apply in moots and social interaction, and may be a handicap when it comes to holding positions in septs of Garou other than Bone Gnawers.

**Backgrounds**: May not buy Past Life or Pure Breed, or begin the game with *Finances* Influence; must spend two Traits on Kinfolk.

**Tribe Gifts**: *Cornered Rat, Odious Aroma, Scent of Sweet Honey, Stone Soup*

**Wolf Form**: Bone Gnawers look much like mangy wolf-dogs, often passing for such in open view of the townsfolk they live by. Though this does little to endear them to humans, they are more likely to be shooed away as a nuisance rather than shot as a danger. Their coats are a mishmash of clashing colors, and they are often quite disheveled, possessing a curious odor.

**Organization**: Bone Gnawers organize their tribe along familial lines, with Garou receiving honorifics such as "Mother," "Father," "Grandmother" and so on as they rise in Rank. These titles are not formally bestowed, simply something Gnawers intuitively understand and recognize. Likewise, these titles confer no true power, but most Gnawers are smart enough to realize one of their own who's survived long enough to earn such a distinction should usually be heeded. Unlike most other tribes, who still hold the old ideals of Garou/homid separation in matters of tribal politics, Gnawers keep their mortal families quite close in the matters of their septs, especially mundane issues. This is perhaps just another survival mechanism, as Gnawers are often frowned upon in more formal septs, and thus many form septs of their own.

**Territory**: Bone Gnawers can be found in boom towns, railroad ghettoes and hermit's shacks. Sometimes they live as mountain men, or pull together enough Kinfolk to form their own not-quite-rich communities, but most often they live wherever they won't be run out of town quickly.

**Protectorate**: Bone Gnawers look after those whom everyone else chooses to forget, and consider themselves the champions of the salt of the earth. They love underdogs, and will sometimes join a particular cause just to rile the other tribes (though not to the extent of aiding the Wyrm, of course).

**Outlook**: Put upon by their fellow Garou for so long, the Gnawers accordingly hold the other tribes in somewhat low esteem, even going so far as to openly mock the policies of overly serious or high-minded tribes. Iron Riders are frequent allies, as are the occasional Children of Gaia concerned about similar causes, but neither tribe usually makes lasting friendships. Bone Gnawers never forget an honest deal, but have a ken for spotting when someone's trying to sell them snake oil, and love using others' low expectations of their abilities to make such arrogant folk look foolish. They use this underestimation to set up deadly traps for minions of the Wyrm.

**Quote**: *Well, the way I sees it, the pass up in the hills is the only way ya can get yer pack past the lookouts and right to the mockery's hideout. Whatzat? You have some extra hardtack on ya after all? Well, now that I have some grub in me, I think I could find the strength to lead ya there, if ya'd also let me have a nip from that canteen there, that is.*

## Children of Gaia

One tribe alone dares consider the notion of unifying the disparate tribes of the Garou Nation. One sole group of changers calls for compromise and understanding between Garou and their human kin. One tribe considers the heresy that violence is not the only means to serve the Mother. This tribe is the

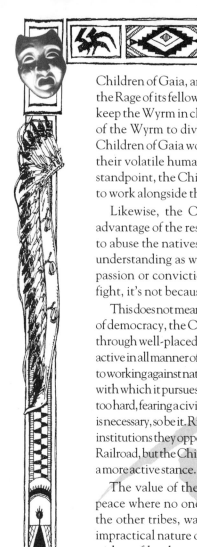

Children of Gaia, and since the earliest days of the tribes, it has sought to cool the Rage of its fellow Garou, trying to balance the worlds of wolves and men and keep the Wyrm in check. Claiming that the division of the tribes was a scheme of the Wyrm to divide Gaia's greatest defenders and make them useless, the Children of Gaia work hard to make all tribes see past their petty conflicts and their volatile human kin to the larger menace the Wyrm presents. From this standpoint, the Children continue trying to get the Uktena and the Wendigo to work alongside the Europeans they so resent.

Likewise, the Children counsel their fellow Europeans against taking advantage of the resources of their native brothers, or allowing their own kin to abuse the natives' Kinfolk. Many of their fellow Garou see this resolve for understanding as weakness or soft-headedness, but none can argue with the passion or conviction the Children pour into their mission. When they do fight, it's not because they enjoy it, but because all other options have failed.

This does not mean the Children ignore mortal politics; quite the contrary. Lovers of democracy, the Children had a hand in the very Constitution of this country through well-placed Kinfolk attending the Constitutional Convention, and are active in all manner of social movements, from abolitionist causes to women's suffrage to working against native relocations. The only issue that splits this tribe is the strength with which it pursues its goals — most within the tribe oppose pushing their causes too hard, fearing a civil war, but a minority of younger Children believe that if violence is necessary, so be it. Right now, the tribe's official stance is to speak out publicly against institutions they oppose and secretly support movements such as the Underground Railroad, but the Children will not raise claw against their own if they choose to take a more active stance.

The value of the Children of Gaia to the Garou is their ability to make peace where no one else dreamed it possible, and to act as a conscience for the other tribes, wanted or not. Most Garou, even those that disparage the impractical nature of their idealism, trust that a Child sincerely expresses the wishes of her heart when she speaks, and few ever suspect the Children of scheming or other manipulations. When a Child of Gaia has decided a cause merits violence, her fellow changers know to get the hell out of her way, as the resolve brought by knowing all other choices have been exhausted lends the Child a strength of purpose few other tribes can hope to match.

**Totem**: Unicorn

**Initial Willpower**: Two

**Tribe Advantage**: Diplomacy

The Children of Gaia are steadfast proponents of peaceful negotiation and discourse. To represent this, Children of Gaia begin with the additional Social Traits: *Diplomatic* x 2, which cannot be lost. (This Advantage can allow Children of Gaia to go over Trait maximums.)

**Tribe Drawback**: Price of Peace

Children of Gaia do not cause a Delirium reaction, and therefore must exercise great care not to break the Veil. Many Children see this as a mixed blessing, since it allows them more opportunities to interact freely with humans, but one never knows when or how it will cause problems.

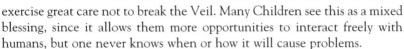

**Backgrounds**: No restrictions.

**Tribe Gifts**: *Calm, Luna's Armor, Mother's Touch, Resist Pain*

**Wolf Form**: Children of Gaia reflect their connection to Gaia in their wolf form, and their fur tends toward shades of brown and gray, often spotted or striped with white. Majestic and strong, they seem to radiate an inner calm and confidence rather than the savage ferocity of the other tribes.

**Organization**: Tribal meetings of the Children of Gaia are undisciplined affairs to the eyes of other tribes, as the tribe appreciates the energy and innovation of its younger members in addition to the wisdom and experience of its elders. Anyone is allowed to speak on any subject so long as she addresses others with due respect, but would-be demagogues beware, for the Children dislike listening to those who have no interest in at least considering the opinions of others.

**Territory**: The Children of Gaia can be found nearly everywhere, easing tempers, healing hearts and fighting noble battles against a variety of threats. More and more, the Children find themselves trying to defuse the tensions caused by territorial expansion and keeping the country from tearing itself apart (as they see it).

**Protectorate**: All humanity. The Children do their best to enlighten humans to Gaia's ways, and to remind their fellow Garou of the necessary role humans play in Gaia's scheme and in the continuation of the Garou Nation itself. Most often, the Children lead by example, as they have been doing for countless thousands of years.

**Quote**: *Blast you both anyway! What did I tell you about fighting? This site is holy to Gaia, and you'll have to steal the last heat from my body before there's blood shed between septmates here! If you want a battle so badly, why don't you search out the Warder and see about those Banes he was talking about at the moot last night? That's better!*

## Fianna

Lorekeepers and master bards of the Garou, even by the standards of other Galliards, the Fianna tribe bears its heritage proudly. It is also the tribe to go to whenever one wants to learn ancestry or points of fact about some ancient legend. Descended from the Celts, the Fianna spread all over the British Isles in ancient times, and came to the New World alongside the influx of Irish, Scottish and Welsh immigrants. Their deep love of their Kinfolk has kept them close to them even as they moved westward, and while many Fianna are quite open-minded, more than a few share the prejudices of their human kin regarding native populations.

This fact has brought them into increasing conflict with the Pure Ones, making this portion of the tribe almost as bad as the Get when it comes to settlements and native relocation. Indeed, even their faerie heritage has come to haunt them, for more than one battle has been fought with the Uktena over differences between native fae and the European changelings that follow the Fianna and their kin.

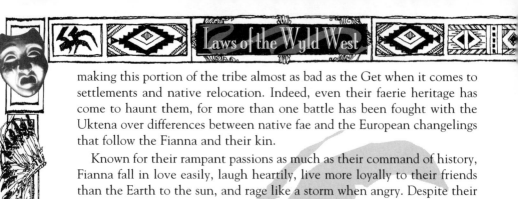

Known for their rampant passions as much as their command of history, Fianna fall in love easily, laugh heartily, live more loyally to their friends than the Earth to the sun, and rage like a storm when angry. Despite their reputation as bards and poets, their Ahroun are fierce to behold, and the generations the tribe has spent battling invaders in their homelands testifies to their will to fight.

Their thirst for carnal pleasures also gets them in trouble, and more than one Fianna in the Savage West has fallen prey to gambling, drinking and even banditry to support his lusts. Traditionally, however, Fianna love the company of others more than the activities they indulge in their presence, and when a Fianna tells a story around the campfire, all others hush and draw close to listen. Fights and loves are lost and won, but all of life is a chance to add another tale to the endless collection, and the Fianna intend to make their lives a glorious chapter indeed.

**Totem**: Stag

**Initial Willpower**: Two

**Tribe Advantage**: Heirloom

The Fianna are extremely close knit and strongly family-oriented. As a result, all Fianna begin with heirlooms that are the equivalent of a three-Trait fetish in total value. You can spend additional Background Traits if you would like these heirlooms to be even more powerful; however, you can never have a fetish with more than five Traits. Losing such an heirloom causes a loss of two Honor Renown, and no more Renown can be earned until the Fianna asks for forgiveness and receives it from his family elder.

**Tribe Drawback**: Wyld Heart

The Fianna are creatures of passion. They ride the turbulent emotional sea of life's joys, angers, loves and sorrows. Therefore, any attempt to emotionally influence a Fianna will succeed on a win or tie, unless he can overbid. If a Fianna spends a Willpower Trait to avoid frenzy or exert emotional control, the situation still renders him one Trait down in any challenges during the rest of the scene.

**Backgrounds**: No restrictions.

**Tribe Gifts**: *Family Tree*, *Glib Tongue*, *Howl of the Banshee*, *Resist Toxin*

**Wolf Form**: The Fianna typically are large and stocky in wolf form, looking much like Irish wolfhounds or even the legendary dire wolves. Their fur is often blood-red or black, and they have striking green to greenish-gray eyes.

**Organization**: Family is very important and blood is everything to this tribe. Fianna and their Kinfolk meet once every lunar month to settle disputes and rejoice in their Celtic heritage, spinning tales of their deeds and bringing greater glory to themselves and the tribe. The governing body that oversees this tribe, the Council of Song, is a group of elder Garou. Members are elected by the tribe, and each member comes from a different auspice. Their responsibility is to decide all matters concerning the tribe, including intertribal politics, as well as affairs pertaining to other facets of society, both human and Garou. The councilors are well-respected among the Fianna, and their word is considered law, but their word is sometimes slow to travel at the farthest edges of the frontier, where Fianna do their best to run their own affairs in the councilors' absence.

**Territory**: Fianna prefer rural, picturesque areas, but typically only places where they can have their own land. Always restless for a new tale or new adventure, many young Fianna can also be found among prospecting expeditions, or in a town with a lively saloon.

**Protectorate**: First and foremost to these clannish Garou is the protection of their Kinfolk, and a Fianna will go to extremes to keep her fellow immigrants safe. They move along the railroads with Irish laborers, and since they often find themselves aiding the Bone Gnawers and the Children of Gaia, they try to lend a hand watching over those protectorates as well.

**Outlook**: Fianna look for adventure and passion in life, and anyone who attempts to curtail their appetites is automatically on their bad side. They typically get along well with other immigrant tribes, especially the Bone Gnawers, but have a lot of trouble seeing eye to eye with the Pure Ones, who they see as responsible for many massacres of their kin and other innocents. Although characterized as wild and rebellious, Fianna know when to shut up and take orders, and fill the ranks of some of the fiercest packs the frontier has seen, in all auspices and capacities.

**Quote**: *Lass, you've got to listen to me a moment. I know it's hard for you, but if you don't tell us which way Dougherty rode after he killed Sean, we won't be able to avenge your brother, and then this whole bloody mess will have been for nothing. Toward the foothills? That's a good lass. Now be strong, girl, and I swear that by the next time I see you, your brother will be able to sleep right peaceful in the hereafter.*

## Get of Fenris

Descended from Nordic stock, the Get of Fenris are a ferocious, tenacious tribe of warriors that respect only one thing more than battle: victory. While many of the Get came west with immigrants fresh in the Americas, others hail from families that have settled the country for decades already. What unites these family groups and their Garou relatives is their determination, as well as their love of strength and hard work. To the Get of Fenris, the only rights one has are the rights one earns for oneself, and they have little tolerance for most of the abolitionist and women's suffrage movements, or the complaints of native populations who have lost their lands. If the slaves are to be freed or the women are to vote, they reason, then they must earn it themselves, rather than demand that others give it to them. Likewise, if the Pure Ones were truly pure and worthy of their land, then they'd be strong enough to keep the Get from taking it.

The latter attitude, as well as their love of settling in cold lands reminiscent of their homelands, has placed the Get of Fenris and the Wendigo in direct conflict with each other many times, and typically neither side will give conversation, ground or mercy to the other without a bitter battle. The Get are also not close to such tribes as the Black Furies and the Children of Gaia, for obvious political reasons. Although individual members of the tribe may be prejudiced, the Get as a whole bear no special antipathy toward other races or populations — they simply feel that life is a cold and constant battle, and that no one deserves special consideration.

Indeed, for their part, the Get are honorable to a fault, and would sooner die than break their word. They are not bloodthirsty so much as relentlessly determined, and they ask for no more quarter than they give. Their constant physical toil and need to test themselves against each other and the world has given the Get great courage, and when the time for action comes, they do not hesitate, regardless of cost to themselves. Even their bitterest foes don't doubt their skills at warfare and tactics, and many Get legends feature tales of doomed heroes fighting their finest hour as they fall. To the Get, it is not the cost or even the cause, but the courage taken in pursuing it that makes them great.

**Totem**: Fenris Wolf

**Initial Willpower**: One

**Tribe Advantage**: Warrior's Heart

The Get of Fenris are some of the toughest warriors of all the tribes. Many joke that this is because their youngest take quite a pounding, but they are really among the best because of their battle-tested souls. Because of the effects of the Get of Fenris bloodline and their rigorous lifestyle, each Get gains one additional Health Level.

**Tribe Drawback**: Hardened Heart

The Get of Fenris' desire to destroy the Wyrm or die trying has created such conviction that Get tend to be intolerant of anything they perceive as being gained ignobly, or that falls under the category of "weakening Gaia's defenses." Players with Get characters should choose something that is not inherently Wyrm-tainted (e.g., cowardice, treaties, abolitionists, displaced natives) as an object of blind contempt and scorn. When the object of this contempt is near, the Garou must win or tie a Simple Test or do whatever he can to rid himself of the annoyance (one Willpower Trait may be spent to negate this Drawback as if it were a frenzy situation).

**Backgrounds**: May not begin the game with more than three Influences.

**Tribe Gifts**: *Cry of the Killer, Razor Claws, Resist Pain, Safe Haven*

**Wolf Form**: Among the largest wolves, even compared to other Garou, the Get are typically gray-coated wolves of immense size, savagery and power, and even the youngest Get typically shows a few scars on his pelt as a testament to his tribe's ferocity.

**Organization**: This tribe meets regularly on every full moon. These meetings are very strict, with an air of military discipline about them. Ahroun are given the greatest respect among the Get, as they are the tribe's fiercest warriors. However, each of the auspices has a role in battle. Even a Get of Fenris Ragabash can be a fierce opponent. During their moots, the Get plot war strategies and recount deeds of great Glory. They also settle any major disputes within the tribe by combat.

**Territory**: Get of Fenris lay claim to any territory they can take, although they tend to prefer northern lands, where they can be close to their Kinfolk. They are among the worst land-grabbers in the eyes of the Pure Ones; however, if the inhabitants prove themselves worthy opponents, the Get will cease pressing for a particular territory and move on.

**Protectorate**: Like the Fianna, the Get will go to nearly any length to protect their Kinfolk, as long as their actions would not further the Wyrm's goals. The Get have also taken to claiming caerns they find as being "inadequately defended against the Wyrm," even over the protests of their fellow European tribes. This Get "protection" is also extended by will of the tribe to all areas they feel are in danger of being corrupted by the Wyrm.

**Outlook**: The Get are a fatalistic lot, given more to hard work than get-rich-quick nonsense, and typically expect few to understand their determination — the proof they earn testing themselves is enough for them. Those few who seem to grasp the Get way of life, such as rugged pioneers who refuse to bow to the elements, or ranchers who carve out a living where no one else will, are accorded much respect and friendship by this tribe. Likewise, those who prove honorable equals in battle earn great admiration from the Get, but the tribe has little patience for gunslingers, carpetbaggers and others who earn their living on the underside of society. Courage and honor are everything to these Garou, and they choose their company accordingly, regardless of tribal lines. The exceptions to this rule are the Black Furies, who seem to have a peculiar hatred of the Get, and the Wendigo, who are currently embroiled in too many conflicts with the Get to make many allies at this time.

**Quote**: *You have come many times to our land, and each time you claim you will give my family more money for our ranch, but nothing comes of it. Now I see you have come with guns and torches, to send us from our lands by force. How unfortunate for you that it is a full moon tonight; I fear you will find we have a few more family members here now than you had reckoned on.*

## Iron Riders

Not all Garou dread the spread of humanity and the emerging cities and towns that growth entails. The Iron Rider tribe is dedicated to bringing about an understanding between Garou spirituality and homid technology, and points to the septs and even caerns it has established in cities as proof that Gaia exists even in the midst of modern living. The Iron Riders see the direction the world is going, and claim human cities and culture as the new wilderness in need of Garou protectors. As even the most rural members of other tribes and their Kin now need the occasional service performed for them in the cities, and since the Riders have always helped such requests to the best of their ability, most other tribes swallow their accusations of outright Wyrm corruption at the strange ways of the Iron Riders.

This does not mean the other tribes have any great love for them, however. The Red Talons see them as the champions of a humanity that has decimated their wolf kin, and tend to hold them responsible for any and all actions of humanity. Likewise, the Pure Ones dislike them for encouraging the cities that are snaking across the plains, and even their fellow European tribes warn them that the black clouds of factories and trains threaten to taint the breath of Gaia. Most seriously of all, Theurges point to the powerful negative effect the Weaver energies at work in the Storm Umbra are having on the native Wyld spirits. The Iron Rider tribe is hard at work trying to figure out a way to balance out the two forces, as well as root out and destroy the Wyrm influences worsening the situation.

However, the Iron Riders refuse to let technology itself take the blame for its misuse at the hands of a small number of individuals, and work hard at creating and funding new inventions such as the telegraph and the transcontinental railroad. Learning the secrets of new such devices is one of life's great pleasures for an Iron Rider, and they like to keep up to date with all the latest trends and politics in mortal society. Many young Iron Riders (especially Ahrouns), fascinated by the merging of ritual challenges and modern technology, have taken up gunslinging as a way of life, and have developed unique Gifts to reflect this passion. And while they may share their territory with members of other tribes, none of their fellow Garou can ever quite understand the way an Iron Rider loves the song of his city.

**Totem**: Cockroach

This might seem an odd choice at first, but Cockroach is incredibly adaptable, resilient and nearly impossible to wipe out. Some Iron Riders hold Spider in high regard as well, which does not endear them to the Pure Ones, who blame her for helping spread the Weaver across the Pure Lands.

**Initial Willpower**: Two

**Tribe Advantage**: Weaver's Children

Iron Riders begin the game with one additional Influence Trait. Furthermore, an Iron Rider can purchase more Influence during character creation at the rate of one for one. Once play begins, Iron Riders can purchase Influence with experience (other Garou can gain Influence only through roleplaying). One Trait of Influence can be purchased for three Experience Traits, subject to Storyteller approval, of course.

**Tribe Drawback**: Weaver Affinity

Iron Riders regain Gnosis only in cities and towns, which can lead to some hard times for those Iron Riders interested in seeing the wild vistas of the Savage West. Caerns are the exception to this rule. The Riders' Weaver ties lead many Wyld-minded Garou such as the Black Furies to distrust them, though

**Backgrounds**: Iron Riders cannot buy Past Life or Pure Breed, but they start with an additional Influence, as noted in the Tribe Advantage.

**Tribe Gifts**: *Control Simple Machine, Iron Fur, Persuasion, Sense Weaver*

**Wolf Form**: Iron Riders typically appear as small- to medium-sized wolves, with mottled but well-groomed coats, reflecting the tribe's cosmopolitan heritage.

**Organization**: The Iron Riders are generally organized in a very human way. They tend to think of themselves as a corporation, with directors, middle managers and employees. Competition is friendly, with less backstabbing and bloodletting than the Shadow Lords, but still quite strong. Their caerns are now located almost exclusively within cities, a fact that causes shock and consternation among their fellow Garou. The tribe's leadership has always been solidly Ragabash, which helps account for its unpredictable habits and unconventional lifestyles, and in truth this is the only way it can keep up with the ever-increasing pace of human development. This also buys the tribe extra leeway from their fellow Garou (who see such leadership as only natural for Ragabash, even if otherwise a little suspect).

**Territory**: The Iron Riders live in the cities and major towns cropping up across the Savage West, and can also be found around the new universities being established in the territories. Some Iron Riders travel as surveyors for the railroad companies, finding that their Garou nature makes them well-suited to crossing such harsh terrain, even if their Weaver Affinity makes Gnosis scarce during such journeys.

**Protectorate:** The Iron Riders watch over the brightest innovators of human society, particularly in the realm of technology: inventors, wealthy investors, mechanics and the like. They aid all those who seek to advance human scientific understanding, and do their damnedest to keep the talons of the Wyrm out of the cities and the arena of scientific experimentation.

**Outlook**: Iron Riders see themselves as the next stage in Garou evolution. They believe that Gaia is changing forever and if the other tribes don't see this, then they'd better be prepared to reap the whirlwind. Their irreverent outlook on tradition has earned the Riders many enemies among the tribes, as has their enthusiasm for adopting human customs and technology. For their part, the Riders are having a great time, as their protectorate — slowly building for the last several hundred years — is finally starting to take off, and they're convinced they can make the ride Wyrm-free if they try hard enough. They tend to ally with the Bone Gnawers out of common habitat, but generally this tribe is left to themselves by their fellows — which is exactly how they like it.

**Quote**: *Forget klaives. With pistols you've got a real test of skill, not just a contest of raw strength. And it's the same as the old-fashioned duels you fight: The challenge, the staredown, the battle. Only with pistols it's whoever has the bravest heart and quickest hands wins, not some lumbering oaf who happened to have been born twice as tall as a cactus. Best of all, you can't even be killed without silver bullets, so you don't have to disembowel your packmate over who gets to lead the next war party. Now, wanna give it a try?*

## Red Talons

Angry howls in the night, the Red Talons stand against the spread of humanity in any form, and many of them would like nothing more than to drive the oncoming hordes of settlers back into the sea in a massive wave of blood. Composed entirely of lupus stock, the Talons despise the clumsy, insolent apes that have spread across Mother Gaia, and recognize only the traditions of their fellow wolf kin, disdaining or even raiding the human communities that encroach their lands. Back in the Old Country, the Talons were the staunchest proponents of the Impergium that culled the ranks of the humans, but have been driven from many of the wild places by the entrenchment of humanity, with native wolves driven to extinction in many countries.

The Talons came by Moon Bridge to the New World around the same time as the first settlers, and found what seemed to be a paradise: a vast, untamed land full of wild wolves and apes that, while still prone to many human foibles, respected the ways of Mother Gaia in a way most Europeans had forgotten. Quickly making peace with the Uktena and Wendigo, the Talons traveled all across the continent, breeding with the abundant wolf population and establishing Kinfolk packs of their own wherever they went. Content with this new life, they ignored the first violence between European and Pure One, seeing it as nothing more than monkey foolishness. That was their great mistake.

Now the Talons face a determined and ever-growing number of settlers intent on taming the frontier, who view wolves as a threat to family and livestock alike. Supernaturally, the influence of the Weaver and the threat posed by the Storm Eater has grown too great to ignore, and the cities bring a small but growing number of vampires (called Leeches), mortal enemies of the Talons. And while the numbers of native wolves are still strong, they stand at a dangerous transition point, and the Talons recognize this. They hurry to make alliances with the Wendigo and Uktena to attempt to drive the Europeans from their land, and to teach the lupus of these tribes of the evils the homids represent. It is a desperate battle, and one that Red Talons pursue with growing ferocity as the settlers advance and the Talons' territories grow smaller and smaller.

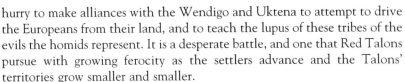

**Totem**: Griffin

**Initial Willpower**: Two

**Tribe Advantage**: Gaia's Fury

Red Talons gain an additional Rage Trait during character generation and always have a maximum Rage of one higher than the other tribes.

**Tribe Drawback**: Wyld Affinity

A Red Talon is completely at home in the wild. Unfortunately, he cannot find peace in cities or towns; as a result, a Red Talon cannot regain Gnosis in any such environment.

**Backgrounds**: Red Talons may not buy Influences.

**Beginning Gifts**: *Beast Life, Eye of the Hunter, Scent of Running Water, Sense of the Prey*

**Wolf Form**: Red Talons tend toward red to ruddy brown fur, and prefer to spend as much of their time as possible in Lupus or Hispo form. Their most distinctive feature is the fact that, no matter what form they're in, Talons always have at least one bright red patch of fur on their bodies.

**Organization**: As this tribe is very close to its lupine roots, every group is led by an alpha. The strong lead and the weak follow; all challenges are quickly settled, winner take all.

**Territory**: The Red Talons enjoy the wide spaces of land to which they still lay claim in the Pure Lands, far away from the encroaching cities of humanity, and in any case will not spend any more time than absolutely necessary in a city or town. However, the spread of the Weaver and the Storm Eater bothers them, and they will go afield to investigate this as necessary.

**Protectorate**: The Talons are sworn to protect the unspoiled wilderness, and would rather die than let the poisons of the Old World take root there. They also have adopted the native wolves as their own, and vowed to protect them from the homids. Many feel a kinship with Uktena and Wendigo lupus and try to teach them what they can, but this has mixed results at best. Still, they look after those tribes' protectorates when they can.

**Outlook**: The other tribes proved themselves weak by allowing Wyrm-taint to take the wild places of the Old Country, and now they expect to do the same here? While the Red Talons occasionally get along with some of the European Garou, particularly the lupus of the Black Furies and the Silent Striders, for the most part they will be found only in their company when it is absolutely necessary to fight minions of the Wyrm the tribes cannot handle apart. Otherwise, the Talons keep close to their lupine Kinfolk and try to keep the invaders from claiming any more of their land, something they often share with the Wendigo and the Uktena. Red Talons *despise* the railroads that cut gashes in the flesh of Gaia and herald the approach of humanity; many tales of lonely work crews being ravaged by savage wolf packs are based on Talon attempts to curb this defilement of Gaia's face. Naturally, this stance puts them at odds with the Iron Riders, and conflicts between the two tribes are growing in ferocity.

**Quote**: *No apologies, ape, only blood. You take as many suns to die as you have wolf pelts in pack (growl). Oh, look like you going to suffer.*

## Shadow Lords

The law of nature dictates predators and prey, dominance and submission, those who lead and those who serve. Any who don't bow to this order must be eliminated. The Shadow Lords count themselves among the former of every one of those examples, and are more than happy to execute the clause that follows. This ambitious tribe has nothing less than the leadership of the Garou on its mind, and will stop at little to secure it, even skirting the edge of the Wyrm in some instances. The Lords see the Savage West as a new opportunity, a wild land crying out for control and order, two things the Lords are quite willing to supply — with themselves at the top of the chain, naturally. Whether such order means a bandit gang instilling terror in the populace, or a ruthless term as sheriff meting out justice... well, that depends on the Lord in question.

Originally hailing from Eastern Europe, the Shadow Lords cut imposing figures and make formidable fighters, but it is their skill at manipulation and social maneuvering that sets them apart from their fellow Garou — and casts a dark cloud over the reputation of the tribe as a whole. Few other Garou trust a Shadow Lord, for while they know better than to break their word to the other honor-driven tribes, the Lords are masters at obeying the letter rather than the spirit of an oath, or at finding loopholes and semantic technicalities to exploit in their execution of a decree.

For their part, the Lords are now the ones to bring discipline and enforce the Litany on the other tribes, a position that allows them to serve as judge of their fellow Garou and thus avoid most legal difficulties entirely. They are considering making their bid for the leadership of the tribes now, while the Silver Fangs are still suffering the effects of the anti-monarchy sentiment high in the country, but are careful in their actions, waiting to ensure that just the right moment arises.

Indeed, the rise of the Storm Eater is seen by the tribe as a grave insult to Grandfather Thunder, not to mention a strike at their dominance in many areas of the Savage West. The most paranoid among them have even considered the possibility that it is a creation of the Silver Fangs, sent to destroy them, but there is no evidence to support this view at this time. Still, the Lords are nothing if not careful, and so they are slow to relax their guard.

**Totem**: Grandfather Thunder

**Initial Willpower**: Two

**Tribe Advantage**: Social Guile

By spending one Gnosis Trait, a Shadow Lord can double her Social Traits up to a maximum addition of six Traits. These Social Traits may be used for bidding in a single Social Challenge. This includes resolving ties or crushing an opponent in an overbid. For some reason, this advantage fails when used against Garou of equal or higher Pure Breed.

**Tribe Drawback**: Unworthy

Because of the unforgiving nature of their tribe, Shadow Lords suffer double Renown loss for any failing or transgression on their part (if caught).

**Backgrounds**: Shadow Lords may not begin the game with more than three Influences.

**Beginning Gifts**: *Aura of Confidence, Clap of Thunder, Fatal Flaw, Mark of Suspicion*

**Wolf Form**: Shadow Lords are typically stocky wolves with dark fur and a menacing air to them, which seems oddly commanding to those around them.

**Organization**: The Shadow Lords boast of a chain of command that would make any modern corporate division proud. No member is ignorant of his position, power or, most importantly, responsibilities within the tribe. At the lower end, eager young pups stand ready fill to any vacancy that opens in the tribe's ranks, including vacancies that they sometimes create. Those already in positions of power are constantly on guard against capable upstarts. All in all, the Shadow Lord drive for dominance creates a constant current of change and uncertainty, as those in power inevitably miss a step and are brought down. The Shadow Lords believe in the right to rule through outmaneuvering, outgunning, overpowering, backstabbing and/or assassination — and the right to keep a position in the same ways. If a leader is truly adept, he'll see such threats coming and deal with them — if not, he must not have been such a good leader after all and is better off replaced.

**Territory**: Shadow Lords can be found wherever they sense an opportunity, but love most of all to find a places where they can rule over all that they see: mountain passes, forest dens, or views of dark, cold lakes. However, as it is difficult to thunder imperious commands at trees and boulders and retain one's dignity (much less get results), Lords often ensure that humans or wolves are about to carry out their wishes.

**Protectorate**: Most Shadow Lords are responsible for themselves, their pack, their tribe and their territory. Nothing else matters, except conquest. Some Lords are even more exacting, and care only for themselves, feeling everyone else should likewise fend for themselves and that if they don't, well, they deserve to be dominated by someone who understands the world a bit better. Some Shadow Lords, members of a camp called the Judges of Doom, go about enforcing the Litany and passing judgment on other Garou, and are widely feared for their ruthless natures.

**Outlook**: Whatever the situation, Shadow Lords will always strive to be on top, or, if attempting a takeover would be unwise at the moment, at least to secure a position where leadership will eventually be possible. This does not mean they are incapable of feeling friendship or even love for their fellow beings, but they will always have an eye on the equity of such relationships, and will never accept a submissive role for long. Even the most sensitive, open-minded Shadow Lord recognizes that her fellow Lords will try to use those close to her against her in schemes of their own, and so strives to protect those she cares about from the claws of her fellows as well as other dangers. The overtly compassionate and understanding do not last long in this tribe, and even the youngest cub knows it.

**Quote**: *So, you found out about my conversation with the sheriff regarding our mutual friend Dougherty? Yes, I told the sheriff to release him, but only so that we could track him back to his hideout and wipe out the entire gang. What good is hanging one man when you can have his whole gang as well? What's that? Killed one of your kin while he was loose? I'm terribly sorry. I had no idea that he would be back to his evil ways so quickly, but that's not my fault.*

## Silent Strider

Although the other tribes argue about whether or not the Silent Striders have always known about the paths and trails of the New World, or whether they are as new to the land as the European tribes, the tribe itself remains characteristically silent about it and continues its ages-old mission of delivering goods and information to other Garou. Known for their ability to traverse any terrain with a speed that far outstrips even the newest homid contraptions, the Silent Striders have acted as the Garou's messenger service from the oldest days, and a promise from a Strider that a delivery will be made is as good as handing the object to the recipient yourself.

However, outside of their reputation as dauntless and honorable couriers, Striders are mistrusted by many of their fellow Garou on account of their solitary ways, as well as their habit of appearing with news of some great evil well before any other Garou are aware of it. While Silent Striders are excellent sources of information, picking up news and gossip from all the areas they travel to, many tribes are afraid to speak openly around them, fearing any secrets or other information they share will become the latest news at the next sept over. For their part, the Striders often remain true to their name and will not divulge any information without due cause, but convincing the other tribes of this has proven difficult. The Striders feel the knowledge they gain and the lands they travel makes up for this loss of camaraderie, but the pack instinct runs strong within them as with all Garou, and many Striders have started joining multitribal packs, with which they bond intensely.

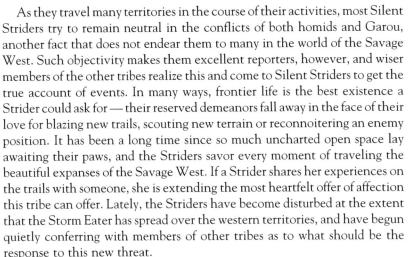

As they travel many territories in the course of their activities, most Silent Striders try to remain neutral in the conflicts of both homids and Garou, another fact that does not endear them to many in the world of the Savage West. Such objectivity makes them excellent reporters, however, and wiser members of the other tribes realize this and come to Silent Striders to get the true account of events. In many ways, frontier life is the best existence a Strider could ask for — their reserved demeanors fall away in the face of their love for blazing new trails, scouting new terrain or reconnoitering an enemy position. It has been a long time since so much uncharted open space lay awaiting their paws, and the Striders savor every moment of traveling the beautiful expanses of the Savage West. If a Strider shares her experiences on the trails with someone, she is extending the most heartfelt offer of affection this tribe can offer. Lately, the Striders have become disturbed at the extent that the Storm Eater has spread over the western territories, and have begun quietly conferring with members of other tribes as to what should be the response to this new threat.

**Totem**: Owl

**Initial Willpower**: Two

**Tribe Advantage**: The Omen of Doom

Once per session, a Silent Strider can "back up" one action (*I had a bad feeling about doing that*), somehow manage to have a common item in his possession at the right moment (*I just had a feeling we might need a bag of salt today*), or restart a challenge sequence that he did not initiate (O.K., *this time I do not walk into the saloon and right into the ambush.... I stop and tell everyone I have a bad feeling about it*). In other words, a Silent Strider gets little "spooky" feelings after something bad happens in-game and can back up the scene one step to avoid taking an action, or to have remembered to pick up something that becomes instrumental to the success of the scene (Storyteller discretion). An important use of this capacity allows a Silent Strider to negate a combat situation that he did not initiate *before it starts* in order to prevent it or make it come out differently. If the Strider initiated the challenge, he can only back up events to right after the initial challenge, because of a hunch he had about the first outcome. No information is retained about "events that did not happen" thanks to the use of this Advantage.

**Note**: This power can be either unwieldy or potentially extremely powerful. Narrators should keep an eye out for characters abusing The Omen of Doom and penalize them appropriately (say, by making them "forget" important items, giving them false hunches, and so on). The Strider Tribe Advantage should be used no more than once per session, if that often.

**Tribe Drawback**: Haunted

Because of their ancient interactions with the dead of Egypt, Striders must (once per lunar cycle) succeed in a Simple Test or attract the attention of wraiths. The Silent Strider can see and hear this wraith, which bothers and harasses the Garou until he either helps the wraith with one of her Fetters (an item or person that connects her to this world) or he leaves and remains outside the area of the wraith's haunting (usually about 50 miles) for an entire lunar cycle. A Strider must also succeed at a Simple Test every time he becomes stuck in the Gauntlet or likewise attract a wraith when he emerges.

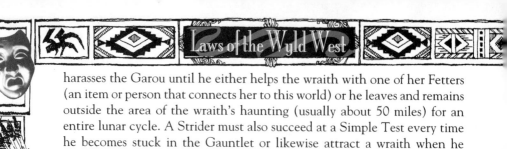

For more information on wraiths, see **Mind's Eye Theatre: Oblivion**. Otherwise, use this sample Gaffling Spirit:

**Willpower** 5, **Rage** 4, **Gnosis** 3, **Power** 15

**Charms**: *Airt Sense, Sap Will, Suggestion*

Silent Striders will never reveal a haunting to other Garou.

**Backgrounds**: Silent Striders may not buy *Past Life* or Influences that are not accessible nationwide (Storyteller approval required).

**Beginning Gifts**: *Dust-Talking, Messenger's Fortitude, Sense Wyrm, Speed of Thought*

**Wolf Form**: Resembling the majestic jackals of Egyptian art, Silent Striders often seem like portraits of Anubis come to life. Their pelts reflect their diverse heritage, coming in many varieties, but somehow never seem motley or unkempt.

**Organization**: Silent Striders have no formal structure, something which shocks many other tribes but is simply a necessity of their far-ranging habits. Instead, Striders simply follow those with the most experience in the matters at hand.

**Territory**: Silent Striders can be found throughout the Savage West on both sides of the frontier, delivering goods and messages, or seeking knowledge in all its forms.

**Protectorate**: Explorers and vagabonds of all types enjoy the Striders' protection, but these solitary Garou seldom choose those who aren't searching after enlightenment. Striders also sometimes protect traveling entertainers and sideshows, as many of them spring from similar stock.

**Outlook**: Most Silent Striders keep to themselves, offering their advice when it is needed and avoiding whatever they consider frivolous or unnecessary. They are very adaptable, and though they travel light they have gear on hand to fit any of their needs. As even their youngest have often traveled impressive distances, they tend to have very balanced viewpoints on the cultures and situations they encounter. Striders enjoy conversation with a thoughtful partner, and are often surprisingly good at gathering all kinds of information, but their solitary lifestyle and abrupt manner tends to alienate those who would be lasting friends. However, none can discount their ability at efficiently dealing with situations, or the loyalty they display for those who accept them and their wandering lifestyle.

**Quote**: *"That trail is safe for the first three days, but then you enter Apache territory, and after last night's cavalry action, I wouldn't bet on how safe that* *would be. Now, I'll show you a faster way to get there that's far less dangerous, but listen well, for I don't have time to repeat myself."*

## Silver Fangs

Leaders of the Garou since time immemorial, the Silver Fangs outwardly embody the best of all the Garou ideals, and carry themselves with faultless confidence wherever they go. A disapproving look from a Silver Fang can silence a room, one of her smiles can break a dozen hearts, and an angry Fang scatters foes like a thunderstorm. Even their pelts are a wonder to behold, as they are always immaculately white and majestic, seeming to radiate purity and nobility. The Silver Fangs have bred with the richest and noblest families of Europe for centuries, and proudly claim a part in most of history's shining moments, mortal and Garou. Even in the New World, some Fangs have taken to breeding with native chiefs in order to extend the tribe's bloodline to the rulers of this new land. The greatest terrors and the mightiest enemies of the Garou fail to ruffle most Silver Fangs, and it is this steadfast leadership that the other tribes have learned to count on and rally around.

Unfortunately, while the Fangs continue to stand tall against external foes, the tribe is greatly pained within. Despite the attempt by some members of the tribe to refresh the bloodline by breeding with different families in the New World, native and otherwise, most of the tribe continues to breed with the same families they have for centuries, and the tribe is now threatened by inbreeding. Even now, most of the tribe exhibit odd mannerisms and personality quirks that, while not dangerous, are starting to be noticed by members of the other tribes. However, the tribe is still strong enough that these foibles are not commented on, at least not to the face of the Fang in question, and most other Garou are hoping the transition to the New World will refresh the line. In the meantime, the Savage West is dangerous enough, and the martial prowess and stalwart leadership of the Fangs are too sorely needed to worry about why the sept leader sleepwalks so often.

Currently, the tribe faces two major concerns apart from battling the advances of the Wyrm and the twisting of the Weaver: the reunification of the tribes and the changing spirit of the Garou Nation toward leadership. The first is more easily quantified; the Silver Fangs wish to reunite the Pure Ones with their fellow tribes, and are puzzled as to why most of them want nothing to do with the idea. After leading the Garou for so many years, they find it hard to believe that these tribes won't accept their *noblesse oblige*.

The second is the growing disrespect that many Garou born in the States have for the old-fashioned system of royalty and courtly protocol. Beneficiaries of the democratic system, these Garou simple don't follow with the same unquestioning hesitation that they used to, a fact which mystifies the Silver Fangs, who see their leadership as something beyond such petty concerns as mortal politics. Still, even the most insolent New World Garou is struck dumb at the sight of Silver Fang in her full glory, and if the Garou are to overcome their petty struggles and strike decisive blows against the Storm Eater and its minions, their best hope lies in the noble courage of this hallowed tribe.

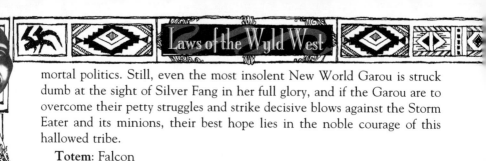

**Totem**: Falcon

**Initial Willpower**: Two

**Tribe Advantage**: Progenitor Wolf

Because of the tribal role as traditional leaders and commanders of the Garou for at least the last 15,000 years, a Silver Fang may call for one free retest in all Social Challenges with Garou or Kinfolk (even Black Spiral Dancers).

**Tribe Drawback**: Touch of Greatness

The bane of the Silver Fangs, a byproduct of centuries of breeding (and inbreeding) with royalty, manifests itself as odd quirks. All Silver Fangs must begin the game with a Quirk, chosen at character creation. This Quirk can be any of the following, but others can be taken at Storyteller discretion. These Quirks serve as Negative Traits.

**Background**: Silver Fangs must spend at least three Traits in Pure Breed.

**Beginning Gifts**: *Imposing Gaze*, *Lambent Flame*, *Luna's Armor*, *Sense Wyrm*

**Wolf Form**: As indicated before, Fangs appear as stunningly beautiful pure-white or silver wolves, with long jaws, graceful builds and green or blue eyes. They usually wear some form of jewelry, even in wolf form.

**Organization**: Silver Fangs honor their aristocratic heritage in their tribal organization. Those with the best lineage and those who have been in power longest are invariably heeded over others. While no one argues with giving an elder her due, many young with new ideas have been drowned out by the rhetoric of the old guard, one of the reasons this tribe has had trouble facing the problem of its weakening blood in recent years.

**Territory**: Silver Fangs choose places to live that are themselves majestic and beautiful, such as panoramic vistas or ancient redwood forests.

**Protectorate**: Silver Fangs claim to hold the other tribes as their responsibility, but as their bloodline invariably entangles them in mortal power structures, many Fangs look after their mortal families and their interests as well. An individual deemed by the Fangs to be particularly noble or courageous may fall under their protection as well, though this is quite rare, as the Fangs generally expect mortals to fend for themselves.

**Outlook:** While not always aloof, many Silver Fangs have trouble dealing with those who do not show them the proper respect, and thus have unjust reputations for detachment. After all, Silver Fangs are expected to persevere where all others would fail, and as a result, they have developed a sort of *noblesse oblige* attitude that many Garou find condescending. However, you haven't seen courage until you've seen a Silver Fang shrugging off the attacks of a gang of lesser minions so that he can challenge an enemy leader. Think of the Lone Ranger with fur and claws.

**Quote**: *We are not many, but damn the lowly cur who doesn't think we are the equal of such flea-infested mockeries! Not only will we hold our ground, we will win the day, and anyone who doesn't believe that is welcome to die an honorable death by my claws first, as I will not share this battle with them. We ride out tomorrow night victorious, or not at all!*

• Absent-Minded — In highly stressful and traumatic situations, you forget details unless you succeed in a Simple Test. (*Forgetful*)

• Mood Swings — Your energy changes without regard to situation. You begin each story feeling geared up (*Impatient*), normal (*Witless*) or lethargic (*Submissive*). You can change this by either spending a Willpower point or changing your present situation (going into another story line, for example). Starting mood is determined at Narrator discretion.

• Fixation — You tend to get excited, latch onto someone or something new and spend too much time involved with them or it (such as wanting to play a live-action game every week and getting pissed when you have to miss a session). (*Gullible*)

• Apprehension — If you spend any time around someone or something, you begin to consider how things can go horribly wrong. You wonder if your friend really likes you, if your boss is bad-mouthing you behind your back or if your pack really listens to you. In other words, you expect others to let you down, so you often act like they already have. (*Condescending*)

• Imperialist — You believe in Manifest Destiny in all the worst ways, and will not rest until you have made the land safe for "civilized" folk and taught the "savages" the true way to live. (*Callous)*

• Jealousy — You cannot help wanting the best and the most. Those that have it better than you did not earn it, as you did. (*Tactless*)

• Arrogant — You *have* to be right. When you are proven wrong, you reinterpret your original observation to have been right all along, or maybe others just misunderstood you. (*Ignorant*)

• Hot-Headed — When you have been wronged, you get seriously angry. You will not forget the Veil, but you will not voluntarily spend Willpower to prevent frenzy when angered. (*Violent*)

• Unstable Personality — Every time you enter a new story line (not each new session), you pick up a different Quirk. Pick one item from this list at random.

## Stargazers

An island of tranquility in the stormy seas of Garou society, the Stargazers are a tribe seldom mentioned by their fellows, for their dedication to inner truth and spiritual peace surpasses even the Children of Gaia. Descended from Garou dissatisfied with the infighting of the tribes and the senseless carnage it caused, the Stargazers turned to a different path, seeking enlightenment and spiritual harmony. They also pledged to rid themselves of the Wyrm-taint that the hatred the other tribes now held for each other was breeding in their hearts. This quest caused a great divide between them and the rest of the Garou Nation, and the Stargazers are easily the smallest tribe. Most Garou have never seen one, and even fewer know anything more about them than their name. Indeed, most of the members of the tribe now walking the Savage West were in fact born to another tribe but converted to this one seeking a different way of life.

For their part, the Stargazers do not bemoan their small numbers. They understand that their way is not for all Garou, and that those who are truly kin to them in blood or spirit will eventually join them, without preaching or recruitment. However, the meditative solitude and even temper that this tribe often enjoys is not without a high price Ñ in preferring the company of fellow Stargazers, they risk losing contact with the very core of their Garou being, for like the Silent Striders, even the most disciplined Stargazer cannot deny the pack instinct within herself. A lone Garou, even one as wise and physically trained as the average Stargazer, is also a tempting target for the minions of the Wyrm, which helps reduce this tribe's numbers even further in these brutal times.

Heeding the advice of their elders, who foresaw this problem in visions and omens, many younger Stargazers now seek to join multitribal packs. This is both an effort to help calm the tensions of the Savage West as well as see to it that their fellow Garou seek enlightenment without falling to the Wyrm. Some Stargazers seek to teach the Pure Ones not to fall into the same folly as the Europeans, seeing this as a chance to prevent a similar decline, while others stand ready to help whichever side presents the best plan for combating the Storm Eater.

Indeed, the puzzling nature and origin of this fearsome Wyrm-creature only incites the curiosity of these wise Garou, and many Stargazers have made it their duty to find out as much about this entity as they can. Whether this assembled knowledge will be of any use to the quarreling tribes is another story, but until such time the Stargazers remain patient as always.

**Totem**: Chimera

**Initial Willpower**: Three

**Tribe Advantage**: Inner Peace

A Stargazer begins the game with *Meditation* Ability x 2 and *Enigmas* Ability.

**Tribe Drawback**: Obsessive Mind Games

Stargazers are always trying to solve puzzles or define puzzles to solve. They are (when stumped) slightly unfocused on situations at hand. If a Stargazer loses a challenge involving the *Enigmas* Ability, he is down three Traits on all challenges for the rest of the session.

**Backgrounds**: Stargazers may not begin the game with fetishes or Influences.

**Beginning Gifts**: *Catfeet*, *Inner Strength*, *Measured Step*, *Sense Wyrm*

**Wolf Form**: Stargazers can have almost any fur color, a tribute to their diverse origins, but those born in the tribe usually have at least one white "star" somewhere on their coats. Such a star is considered especially portentous if it is found on the head or heart, and is said to be a sign of great wisdom or courage. They are usually lean but toned, and most seem to radiate serenity.

**Organization**: While Stargazers place great weight on the wisdom of their elders, their young are free to choose their own path through destiny, wandering where they will in their service to Gaia. Sometimes members of this tribe will gather to discuss recent events or share their wisdom, but such events are more like debating societies and tea circles than formal organizations.

**Territory**: Stargazers wander places where few men (or even wolves) have set foot before, plumbing the fresh mysteries to be found there and testing themselves against the challenges the unknown provides. Any time a Stargazer settles in one place, it will be a place where she can collect her thoughts in solitude, such as a desert cave or by a tiny mountain lake.

**Protectorate**: Stargazers protect hermits and philosophers, wise nomads and any who seek to peacefully learn the ways of Gaia and enlightenment. As many of their kin are now found among the Chinese labor camps or in small Native American tribes, the Stargazers will often defend these places as well, but will not share their wisdom directly even with those they find to be as trustworthy as Garou. Instead, they wrap their knowledge in complex metaphors and even haiku, the better to keep it safe from those who would warp such knowledge to their own ends.

**Outlook**: Stargazers are typically patient, wise and open-minded, and it is rare to meet one who is not physically trim, even if untrained in martial skills. They desire peace when possible, and if they feel an enemy can be redeemed they will go to great lengths to avoid causing permanent harm; however, if they deem a foe beyond redemption, that target usually is not much longer for this world. Stargazers try to channel and balance their Rage constructively, but are often quicker to use it than the Children of Gaia, for they realize that Rage is a natural part of Garou, and repressing it only builds it to dangerous levels. Combat is often the only viable reality, especially in the Savage West, but that does not mean the Stargazers must enjoy it. While many other tribes give them mistrust or at least curiosity, Stargazers do not mind the company of any tribe, as long as they have some interest in enlightenment.

**Quote**: *Do not be fooled by flashy weapons and blustery words. The true warrior does not rely on such things, but strikes his enemies like water. He is a tidal wave across their strongholds, a sudden downpour coming among them, a wide river quietly wearing away all their defenses. You can always break a gun or silence a fool, but you cannot hurt a rainstorm.*

## Uktena

Legends say that of the three tribes of the Pure Ones, the Uktena were the wise Elder Brother, the Croatan the balancing Middle Brother, and the Wendigo the fiery Little Brother. As they settled the Pure Lands, the Uktena took to exploring the southern territories, even going so far as what is now South America in their quest for knowledge. Known for their potent rites and magics, the Uktena made alliances with all manner of spirits and even other Changing Breeds, helping cleanse the land of Wyrm-creatures. They also joined with their Brothers to bind many great Banes, including the Storm Eater, for while such creatures were too strong to simply destroy, the Uktena were able to harness the energy of the land to construct mystic prisons to subdue the great spirits. It was their sacred duty to maintain this web and keep the slumbering Banes from awakening, a task they upheld well until the coming of the first Europeans.

All too quickly, things changed. The Croatan sacrificed themselves to stop Eater-of-Souls, a powerful Wyrm-creature, and Little Brother Wendigo went wild with rage over their loss. The Wyrmcomers began taking over caerns and destroying sacred sites, disrupting the bindings and unwittingly loosing more and more Banes as they went westward. The Uktena tried in vain to warn the Europeans of the consequences of their actions, but as many of them and their kin have fallen to the claws of the invaders, they are deeply dubious of any offers of friendship from their Old World "cousins." They have taken to adopting members of the population that are oppressed by the Wyrmcomers, such as slaves, and while the tribe is still largely composed of Native Americans, that fact is slowly changing. They work with the Silent Striders to gather information, and occasionally indulge a visiting Child of Gaia emissary, but look on all other tribes with at least suspicion, if not outright distrust and anger.

Currently, the Uktena fear what might happen should the greatest of Banes become free, and track the Storm Eater with almost feverish intensity, trying to figure out the proper course of action. They control too few of the sacred sites to bind it once more, and even with those the Wendigo control they still could not hope to succeed; only with the aid of the caerns currently controlled by the Wyrmcomers could they attempt another such great binding, a level of cooperation none of the elders foresee at this time.

As a result, the Uktena study the Wyrm harder and harder looking for a weakness to exploit, a practice that often brings accusations of Wyrm-taint from other tribes, who already regard their duty to "tend" slumbering Banes as suspect. It is a sad fact that many of their Kinfolk have fallen to the Wyrm in recent years, unable to handle the kind of knowledge their Garou relatives discover. While it brings shame upon the whole tribe, the Uktena are unswayed in their dedication to uncovering the secrets of the Wyrm and using them against it. Ultimately, of course, it is the suspicion that the other tribes place on them, more than anything else, that makes Wyrm-taint more likely in the hearts of the Uktena.

**Totem**: Uktena

**Initial Willpower**: Two

**Tribe Advantage**: Umbral Sight

Uktena can peek into the Umbra from the real world using the same rules as peeking out of the Umbra. This power allows them to see others moving within the Umbra.

**Tribe Drawback**: Mystic Curiosity

Uktena desire to learn ancient lore and rituals drives them ever deeper into uncharted waters. If an Uktena is not in the process of learning something related to the occult — Lore, Gifts, rites, empowering a fetish — she becomes fidgety and short-tempered. Uktena are down three Traits in all challenges under these conditions.

**Backgrounds**: No restrictions.

**Beginning Gifts**: *Flick of the Fish's Tail, Pass As the Shadow, Sense Medicine, Sense the Tunneler's Passage*

**Wolf Form**: Although their most dominant feature is their dark, piercing gaze, the lupus forms of the Uktena are quite attractive themselves, with deep reddish-brown coats. Those with mingled ancestry may have slight alteration in pelt color, but their eyes remain distinctive.

**Organization**: Uktena maintain very tightly organized septs, and rely heavily on their own messengers, spirit messengers and the Silent Striders. They also perform regular rituals to renew their connections with the land. It is rumored the Uktena have secret septs in carefully hidden places that are still as pure and as untamed as the land was during prehistoric times. This tribe is ruled by a central lodge that is a collection of elders from all the Uktena-dominated septs, although other Uktena are often invited to attend. Obviously, Theurges dominate most of the politics of this tribe, though all auspices are welcome to contribute any way they can.

**Territory**: Anywhere they can watch over their sleeping spirits is a place the Uktena can be found. While the Wyrmcomers make this increasingly difficult as time goes by, the Uktena are fiercely dedicated to their mission, and will take great risks to perform it. Most live with their Native American Kinfolk if they can, even if it means relocation.

**Protectorate**: Uktena protect the same tribes of Pure Ones they have lived with for millennia, and now also watch over those tribes formerly under the protection of the Croatan, as well as slaves who have joined the tribe. Above all else, however, is the tribe's obligation to defend their sacred sites, and even Kinfolk realize this is their top priority in any situation. Kin come and go, but allowing another being like the Storm Eater to be released would spell certain doom for the forces of Gaia in the New World.

**Outlook**: Uktena work closely with the Wendigo, with whom they share a timeless bond, as well as the Silent Striders, though that is more of a professional relationship than anything else. Uktena are intensely curious, and love all manner of magics, rites, Gifts, spirits, fetishes and arcane lore. They will trade handsomely or take substantial risks to acquire a new secret or artifact, but woe to anyone who breaks his word to these Garou or deals them shoddy goods, for the Uktena and their spirit helpers make fierce enemies indeed! They are dubious at best when it comes to the Wyrmcomers, tolerating only the Children of Gaia and the occasional Stargazer without extensive negotiation. Most Uktena have considerably more detailed knowledge about the Wyrm and its minions than other Garou, but are loath to share it unless it becomes necessity, fearing to contaminate others who are not as prepared as they are.

**Quote**: *You have washed away the seals of my ancestors with our own blood, and shattered the ancient spirit-trails with your iron horses. Is it any wonder, then, that the land itself revolts beneath you, or that the spirits swarm angrily about you now?*

## Wendigo

Finding the harsh northern lands suited their survival skills and temperament, the Wendigo settled the great northern woods and the frozen lands when they came to the Pure Lands. They helped bind mighty Wyrm-spirits alongside their Brother tribes, and all seemed well after that until the first boats of the Wyrmcomers arrived. Always hot-tempered, the Wendigo clashed with the newcomers from the first days of their arrival, checked only by the wisdom of the Uktena and the pleas for patience from the Croatan. When the Croatan died to stop Eater-of-Souls, and the Uktena began corrupting their blood with some of the stock of the Wyrmcomers, the Wendigo finally decided enough was enough and went to war with all Europeans, even their Garou tribes.

It is doomed to be a valiant but losing battle, and the Wendigo have been slowly pushed back over the years, until now they have been pushed off almost all of their ancestral lands, outnumbered and outgunned. Masters of the wilderness and the spirits within it, the Wendigo conduct raids of such cunning and ferocity as to scare fellow Garou with tales of their exploits, but this does them no good against the overall spread of cities and towns that is swallowing the frontier whole. Still, even the Get of Fenris and the Fianna, who are locked in a feud with the Wendigo as they push westward, admit that the Wendigo fight amazingly well and with courage beyond the Garou norm.

Wendigo abide by their own rules of battle (which, sadly, are quite different from most Europeans), and abhor the massacres of innocents and other savage atrocities that are often attributed to them. However, they feel that once a target has been warned, Wyrm-tainted or otherwise, the Wendigo are not to blame if the target is destroyed; after all, the victim had a chance to flee. The tribe prizes honoring one's word and feats of glory above all else, and a Wendigo without these qualities is considered less than nothing by his fellows, often shunned without relent.

Like lupus Garou, who are still strong in the tribe, the Wendigo are often at a loss with the customs of "civilized" society; while they understand them on an intellectual level, they believe so strongly in the old ways that such notions as claiming exclusive rights to a piece of Gaia and the like are completely alien to them. This is but one more reason the Wendigo remain apart from the society of the Wyrmbringers, and they are still fiercely proud of their independence. They are also immensely proud of the fact that their tribe is still composed entirely of Pure One stock.

**Totem**: Wendigo

**Initial Willpower**: Two

**Tribe Advantage and Drawback**: The Wheel of Seasons

The Wendigo gains one or two positive Traits with each season, but also takes one Negative Trait. This change of Traits occurs the moment a season changes and is in effect until the next arrives.

• **Winter** — Physical Traits: *Tenacious* and *Rugged*

Negative Trait: *Callous*, *Dull* or *Witless*

• **Spring** — Physical Trait: *Energetic*

Negative Trait: *Predictable*, *Tactless* or *Impatient*

• **Summer** — Social Trait: *Charismatic*

Negative Trait: *Lethargic*, *Violent* or *Shortsighted*

• **Fall** — Mental Trait: *Reflective*

Negative Trait: *Lethargic*, *Dull* or *Impatient*

**Backgrounds**: Wendigo may not buy Influences except *Tribal*.

**Beginning Gifts**: *Call the Breeze*, *Camouflage*, *Cutting Wind*, *Song of the Seasons*

**Wolf Form**: Descended from northern timber wolves, Wendigo are usually gray, brown or a combination of the two. They are stoutly built, with powerful muscles and great jaws, and walk with confidence through any natural setting, from frozen north woods to burning desert.

**Organization**: The elders of the tribe are given the utmost respect. They hold ceremonies on sacred ground, much like their Kinfolk have for centuries. Wendigo moots are usually held during the crescent moon, thought the tribe can be led by members of any auspice.

**Territory**: Wendigo prefer the deep forests of the north woods, although they can be found almost anywhere in the company of the Uktena and/or helping battle the Wyrmcomers.

**Protectorate**: As they are entirely made up of those of Pure One lineage, the Wendigo take great pains to ensure the safety of their Kinfolk and keep their bloodlines pure. They tend to follow the warrior's path, and thus feel close to those tribes resisting the Europeans such as the Apache and the Sioux. In reality, anyone who comes through their land, especially anyone who tries to claim a part of it, and who is not an ally of the Wendigo, is in danger, regardless of the presence of their protectorate. They also protect the wolf packs of the northern territories, where many of their lupus come from.

**Outlook**: The Wendigo do not associate with Wyrmcomers, and any group that has a mix of the two is doomed to short life as a pack unless they have amazingly understanding members who are not afraid to stand up to the worst abuses of their parent tribes for their strange loyalties. Typically the Wendigo only work with the Uktena and occasionally the Red Talons, who share their desire to rid the Pure Lands of the Wyrmcomers. While not bloodthirsty, the Wendigo are proud and righteously angry, and will not give ground to Europeans in any way without a bitter struggle. They are typically very wise in the ways of the wilderness, but have fierce tempers, and disdain even the most primitive of modern tools, preferring the ancient ways whenever possible.

**Quote**: *If you had not made a noise like a thunderclap with each step, we might have been able to take the Wyrm-things by surprise. However, since you insisted on finding every dry leaf with your feet, we will have to battle them when they are fully prepared. Be prepared, and fall on them when you hear the first owl call.*

# Gifts

Gifts are normally taught by spirits. A Garou must either petition a particular spirit to teach him its power or ask an elder to summon that spirit and petition for him. (Further ideas on this process can be found in **Werewolf: The Wild West**.) Only spirits allied with the Garou will teach Gifts, and they will not teach them to Garou who have not attained the proper Rank.

Sometimes a Garou may teach another Garou a Gift he knows. Unlike spirit teaching, which takes only a short time, this method can take quite a while. In addition, Gifts learned this way cost an additional Experience Trait. Bonuses received through the use of Gifts, talens, fetishes, rites and Merits, can push characters over their present Trait maximums. The total number of Trait bonuses can never equal more than double the Garou's current Trait maximums.

Keep in mind, though, that Gifts are just that — blessings given to a Garou by spirits. They are spiritual rewards that live and breathe beneath a Garou's skin, and learning them is should never be as plain as "The Owl-spirit shows you how to fly." Imagine what it would be like to learn how to leap from a jackrabbit, or how a chameleon changes its skin, and you have an idea of the uniqueness of a Gift. A Fianna with the *Howl of the Banshee* Gift should feel the haunted breath of the spirit stirring in her throat on dark and eerie nights, while a Wendigo with *Camouflage* will find himself fascinated by the changing leaves as the spirit lore within him learns the nuances of their colors. If players to see Gifts as simple Trait modifiers and neat ways to pound their enemies, rather than intriguing spiritual experiences, it makes the Garou seem like no more than superheroes with fur and claws, instead of the mystic primitives they rightly are.

**Additional note**: Although many Garou can affect spirits, there is a distinction between spirits and wraiths. A Gift that can affect a spirit will not necessarily have any affect on a wraith.

A Garou does not need to learn all the Gifts of one level before learning Gifts of the next level. A Garou need not learn all Basic Gifts of his breed before learning Intermediate ones, and so on.

Due to space considerations, only those Gifts unique to the Savage West or changed from their modern incarnations are printed here. Other Gifts are referred to in **Laws of the Wild**.

## Breed Gifts

### Homid

#### Basic Gifts

- **Persuasion** —See **Laws of the Wild**, p. 92.
- **Smell of Man** —See **Laws of the Wild**, pp. 92-93.
- **Jam Gun** — If there's one sad truth about the Savage West, it's that *everybody's got a gun!* This Gift is the retaliation of various Wyld- and Ancestor-spirits angered at the slaughter, who disrupt the machines that have brought so much suffering to their land. All that's required is for the Garou to spend to spend a Gnosis Trait, and one firearm of her choice becomes useless for five minutes, or until the user takes time to unjam it. Unjamming a gun requires a Static Mental Challenge against three Traits with the *Firearms* Ability, and takes at least one uninterrupted combat turn's time to perform. Unjamming cannot be performed by those without the *Firearms* Ability.
- **Staredown** — See the Gift: *Paralyzing Stare*, in **Laws of the Wild**, p. 93.

#### Intermediate Gifts

- **Disquiet** — See **Laws of the Wild**, p. 93.
- **Reshape Object** — See **Laws of the Wild**, p. 93.
- **Tongues** — See **Laws of the Wild**, p. 93.

### Advanced Gifts

• **Spirit Ward** — See **Laws of the Wild**, p. 94.

• **Weave of Steel** — By concentrating for a minute and spending a Gnosis Trait, the Garou may mystically reinforce any manmade structure or material, making it far more durable. In addition to the Gnosis cost, the Garou must spend Physical Traits to strengthen the object: for every two Traits spent, the item effectively gains one Health Level, making it harder to destroy. If used on the Garou's clothing, every two Traits spent add a Health Level of damage the armor can absorb while adding nothing to its mass or rigidity. The effects of this Gift last the remainder of the session or until the extra Health Levels are lost, whichever comes first. This Gift may be used on an item more than once, but may not be re-used until the effects of the first usage have worn off due to time or damage.

• **Part the Veil** — See the Gift: *Reduce Delirium*, in **Laws of the Wild**, p. 94.

## Metis

### Basic Gifts

• **Sense Wyrm** — See **Laws of the Wild**, p. 94.

• **Create Element** — See **Laws of the Wild**, p. 94.

• **Curse of Hatred** — See **Laws of the Wild**, p. 94.

• **Wildcat Eyes** — The Garou may sharpen her eyesight to the degree where even total darkness presents no problem to her; she suffers no Trait penalties due to darkness while this Gift is in effect. Even other visual hindrances, such as smoke or fog, only incur half the normal penalty for the Garou. Once learned, use of this Gift becomes automatic; the player need only declare it to be in use, as there is no cost. However, while this Gift is in use, the Garou's eyes glow an eerie green, like those of a great cat, which she must describe to any who meet her.

### Intermediate Gifts

• **Gift of the Porcupine** — See **Laws of the Wild**, p. 95.

• **Grovel** — See **Laws of the Wild**, p. 95.

• **Rattler's Bite** — A wily metis who has learned the secret of this Gift has her fangs lengthen and learns how to secrete a deadly poison from them, paralyzing or slaying foes with ease. To use this Gift, the Garou must declare a biting attack and spend two Rage Traits; if the attack is successful, the target takes a wound and immediately falls helpless to the ground for the remainder of the scene, doubled up in agony. The target may attempt self-defense if necessary, but is at a two-Trait penalty on top of any existing wound penalties, and any movement or action besides labored talking and the most basic self-defense is futile. Supernatural creatures may spend a Willpower Trait to take any actions desired for the rest of the scene, but the two-Trait penalty remains. Garou may spend a Rage Trait to burn the poison from their systems and thus ignore this Gift's effects (although the wound from the bite remains). At the Storyteller's discretion, this poison can prove fatal to creatures less hardy than the Garou if left untreated. The Garou must be in Crinos, Hispo or Lupus form to use this Gift.

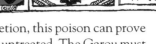

### Advanced Gifts

• **Wither Limb** — See **Laws of the Wild**, p. 95.

• **Lunacy** — See the Gift: *Lunacy*, in **Laws of the Wild**, p. 95.

• **Totem Gift** — See **Laws of the Wild**, p. 96.

## Lupus

### Basic Gifts

• **Heightened Senses** — See **Laws of the Wild**, p. 96.

• **Scent of Sight** — See **Laws of the Wild**, p. 96.

• **Spook the Herd** — By calling on the inherent fear all domesticated animals have for wolves, the lupus may send any such nearby animals into a state of panic, causing them to throw riders and break fences in their haste to get away from the Garou. The Garou must spend a Social Trait and howl where the animals can hear her. Those attempting to control affected animals need to make a Static Mental Challenge with the *Animal Ken* or *Riding* Abilities at a difficulty of the lupus' total Mental Traits, or be thrown/ trampled for one Health Level of damage. In any event, even if foes remain mounted, all challenges made from horseback are at a one-Trait penalty for the rest of the scene. Optionally, the Storyteller may rule that additional damage and other consequences may incur if the a target is caught in a particularly bad place (such as in front of a herd of stampeding cattle). Ghouled or otherwise supernatural animals (but not Garou or vampires in animal form) must be defeated in a Simple Test for this Gift to work on them.

• **Catfeet** — The Garou gains the preternatural agility of this Gift's namesake. She avoids damage from falls of 100 feet or less, and gains the Physical Traits: *Athletic*, *Graceful* and *Nimble*. These Traits can be used only in challenges that deal with balance, agility, dodging and grappling. Once this Gift is learned, it is considered to always be active, although the extra Traits gained from it can be lost in challenges like any other Traits. These clarifications should be applied to the same Gift in **Laws of the Wild**, p. 97.

### Intermediate Gifts

• **Name the Spirit** — See **Laws of the Wild**, p. 97.

• **Beast Life** — See **Laws of the Wild**, p. 97.

• **Gnaw** — See **Laws of the Wild**, p. 97.

### Advanced Gifts

• **Dispel the Golden Plague** — This Gift allows lupus to stop the invasion of greedy homids entering their lands seeking that curious yellow substance they seem to find so attractive. Long thought to have been a Black Fury Gift, this Gift was in fact taught to them by lupus seeking to help stop the spread of homid "gold fever." The Garou must spend a Gnosis Trait and make a

Static Challenge of her permanent Gnosis Traits varying with the amount of gold in the area she wishes to destroy; a normal room with people carrying some gold coins is easy, while a bank vault full of gold bars or a natural gold deposit is much more difficult. If successful, the gold in the area turns to dust and swirls away in a cloud that defies any normal attempt to capture it, as the spirits carry it far away. The Garou cannot direct where the spirits take the gold. A sealed area such as a bank vault will keep the gold from escaping, but will not prevent it from turning to dust.

- **Elemental Gift** — See **Laws of the Wild**, pp. 97-98.
- **Venom Jaws** — As the Metis Gift: *Rattler's Bite*, except the poison secreted by this Gift is supernatural in origin, and thus can affect any creature the Garou can bite: Banes, vampires, other Garou, etc., even if the target is a normally immune to poison. Likewise, Garou cannot spend Rage to ignore the effects of this poison.

# Auspice Gifts

## Ragabash

### Basic Gifts

- **Scent of Running Water** — See **Laws of the Wild**, p. 98.
- **Walk Under the New Moon** — See the Gift: *Blur of the Milky Eye*, in **Laws of the Wild**, p. 98.
- **Spider's Song** — By spending a Gnosis Trait, the Garou may put her ear to a telegraph pole or wire and eavesdrop on any messages carried on the line. The Garou need not know Morse code, as a Spider-spirit tending the lines actually whispers the message to her. However, the Garou may not alter or intercept the messages.
- **Carried on the Wind** — This devious Gift allows the Garou to block communication between any parties in the Ragabash's vicinity. The wind might pick up, mechanical noises might increase, or background sounds may swell, but however it happens, talking, howling and even telegraph messages become incomprehensible. Gesturing and scent communication are still possible, however, as is writing. When activating this Gift, the Ragabash or a Narrator must approach the target(s) and tell them their newfound communication difficulty. The targets will not, however, be able to deduce that the Ragabash is the cause of their problems unless he makes it obvious somehow. This Gift costs two Social Traits, plus one for each additional target beyond the first two, and lasts 10 minutes.

### Intermediate Gifts

- **Hide in Plain Sight** — See the Gift: *Blissful Ignorance*, in **Laws of the Wild**, p. 98.
- **Man with No Name** — The Garou with this Gift has mastered the ability to go from town to town without leaving a trace of her identity, as people forget

they met or even saw the Garou. Any time the Garou takes her leave of someone, she can call for a Simple Social Test (no traits at risk, Social Traits compared in the event of a tie); success means the person is unable to remember what the Garou looked like, what her name was (if given), any specific details she mentioned, or where she went. If the target is a regular mortal, the Garou wins all ties, regardless of who has more traits. The Garou should inform the target as to what she does or doesn't remember before she leaves, and the target must roleplay this memory lapse honestly. Other supernatural creatures can cancel this power's effects by spending a Willpower Trait, though even then all the relevant details seem hazy and dreamlike.

• **Open the Moon Bridge** — See **Laws of the Wild**, p. 99.

• **Bald-Faced Lie** — This Gift makes the Garou capable of cheating and lying in the most outrageous, obvious ways and getting away with it. By beating the target to be cheated or lied to in a Mental Challenge and spending a Mental Trait, the Garou may get away with everything from picking his own cards in a poker game to telling a wealthy old widow that he's her long-lost father. If the Garou wishes to cheat or lie in front of a crowd, use the rules for a group challenge, but if the Garou wins all the targets are affected whether they like it or not. Only one lie or cheat may be attempted per use of this Gift, and it only functions for outright cheating and truly blatant lies; more subtle work is the function of Abilities. This Gift lasts for one scene/hour, whichever is longer, at the end of which time the target will realize what really happened. The other danger of this Gift is that the Garou must lie or cheat *first*, then make the challenge for the Gift; failure thus means there'll be a lot of people who are very unhappy with the Garou....

### Advanced Gifts

• **Luna's Blessing** — See **Laws of the Wild**, p. 99.

• **Mark of Shame** — See the Gift: *Whelp Body*, in **Laws of the Wild**, p. 99.

• **Thieving Talons** — A Garou with this Gift can steal the powers of other supernatural creatures and use them for herself; this is not a great way to win a popularity contest, but often acts as a prelude to a masterful trick — or devastating attack. Anything from other Garou Gifts to vampiric Disciplines to fae Arts can be taken. The Garou must first specify the power to be stolen (use game terms for clarity if necessary; it is unlikely the Garou knows that vampiric strength is known as the *Potence* Discipline, but in character she certainly knows what she means) and win a Mental Challenge against her target. If successful, she gains full command of that power for each turn that she spends a Gnosis Trait. The Garou instantly understands how to use the power, but she must still spend all costs and make all required tests to use the power. If the power requires an expenditure of Blood, Pathos, Glamour or the like, substitute Gnosis Traits instead. This operating knowledge fades at the end of the scene where this Gift is used, and the Garou does not gain any of the target's memories associated with the power, only knowledge of how it works.

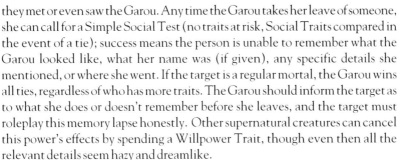

## Theurge

### Basic Gifts

- Sense Wyrm — See **Laws of the Wild**, p. 94.
- Spirit Speech — See **Laws of the Wild**, p. 100.
- Mother's Touch — See **Laws of the Wild**, p. 100.
- Sight from Beyond — See **Laws of the Wild**, p. 100.
- Name the Spirit — See **Laws of the Wild**, p. 97.

### Intermediate Gifts

- Command Spirit — See **Laws of the Wild**, p. 100.
- Exorcism — See **Laws of the Wild**, p. 100.
- Pulse of the Invisible — See **Laws of the Wild**, p. 100.
- Grasp the Beyond — See **Laws of the Wild**, p. 101.

### Advanced Gifts

- Spirit Drain — See **Laws of the Wild**, p. 101.
- Savage the Mind — See the Gift: *Feral Lobotomy*, in **Laws of the Wild**, p. 101.
- Malleable Spirit — See **Laws of the Wild**, p. 101.
- Spirit Vessel — See **Laws of the Wild**, pp. 101-102.

## Philodox

### Basic Gifts

- Resist Pain — See **Laws of the Wild**, p. 102.
- King of the Beasts — See **Laws of the Wild**, p. 102.
- Truth of Gaia — See **Laws of the Wild**, p. 102.
- Scent of the True Form — See **Laws of the Wild**, p. 96.
- Strength of Purpose — See **Laws of the Wild**, p. 102.

### Intermediate Gifts

- Call to Duty — See **Laws of the Wild**, p. 102.

• **Mend the Forked Tongue** — A Philodox with this Gift may force a target to tell the truth, despite the target's desires. With a successful Social Challenge and the expenditure of one Social Trait, the Garou can force the victim to tell the complete and utter truth as he knows it about one subject (not one question) of the Garou's choice. Each additional subject, however, requires that this Gift be reused. Those attempting to resist this Gift must spend two Willpower Traits instead of the usual one, but doing so renders them immune to this Gift for the remainder of the story. However, they may still be detected as lying if such Gifts as *Truth of Gaia* are used.

• Roll Over — See **Laws of the Wild**, pp. 102-103.

• **Balance Man and Beast** — Calling on the balance of man and beast required of all Philodox in pursuit of their duty, the Garou can summon fury or concentration as necessary, through sheer force of will. By meditating for at least five minutes on his role as arbiter of the Garou, the Garou may then make a series of Simple Tests — on a win or tie, one Trait of Rage or Willpower (whichever the character desires) is recovered, up to his usual maximum. The Garou may make as many Simple Tests as he has permanent Gnosis Traits. This Gift may only be used once per scene/hour. Alternately, the character can choose to spend a Willpower Trait to become immune to involuntary frenzy for the remainder of the scene, or a Rage Trait to fly instantly to frenzy whenever necessary. These latter abilities require no tests or expenditures to activate — only five minutes of preparatory meditation once per session.

### Advanced Gifts

• **Rally to the Cause** — One of the few ways Garou can bring the disparate groups of the Savage West together, the Garou can call upon immense powers of inspiration to deliver moving speeches that unite even the bitterest enemies to her cause. The Garou must make a Social Challenge against those to be affected (group challenge rules apply) after explaining her cause; those who she defeats, or who willingly choose to follow her, receive an extra Willpower Trait for the duration of the mission, and are two Traits up on all friendly social interactions with each other. They also may choose to waive the Rage cost of instantly entering frenzy once while working toward the Garou's goal. This Gift's effects last for the remainder of the session or until the mission is completed, whichever comes first. Assuming the goal is not a complete anathema to any of the parties involved (such as asking Wendigo to help the Get of Fenris wipe out a native village), the Garou can conceivably bring together any combination of tribes and packs, even ones who are normally bitterly opposed to each other. Dissenting characters can choose to spend a Willpower Trait to ignore the effects of this Gift. Preferably, the player should do her best to roleplay the speech, and at the very least she must explain her goals before making the challenge.

• **Wall of Granite** — See **Laws of the Wild**, p. 103.

• **Honor Bound** — See the Gift: *Geas*, in **Laws of the Wild**, p. 103.

## Galliard

### Basic Gifts

• **Beast Speech** — See **Laws of the Wild**, p. 103.

• **Call of the Wyld** — See **Laws of the Wild**, pp. 103-104.

• **Mindspeak** — See **Laws of the Wild**, p. 104.

• **Distractions** — See **Laws of the Wild**, p. 104.

### Intermediate Gifts

• **Call of the Wyrm** — See **Laws of the Wild**, p. 104.

• **Dreamspeak** — See **Laws of the Wild**, p. 104.

• **Fighting Words** — See the Gift: *Song of Rage*, in **Laws of the Wild**, p. 104.

• **Come Hither** — See the Gift: *Eyes of the Cobra*, in **Laws of the Wild**, p. 104.

### Advanced Gifts

• **Bridge Walker** — See **Laws of the Wild**, pp. 104-105.

• **Heart Twister** — See the Gift: *Head Games*, in **Laws of the Wild**, p. 105.

• **Song of the Storm** — The Garou can sing up the energies of the Storm Umbra, using the flurry of Wyld energies to work changes on herself, her environment or those around her. To use this Gift, the character must first spend two Gnosis Traits and win a Static Mental Challenge against the difficulty of the local Gauntlet. If she succeeds, she must specify the general type of change she desires and contact the Storyteller, who then must decide how the change is carried out by the Wyld-spirits. For example, the Moon Dancer may ask that the Black Spiral Dancers be subdued, but whether the walls spring to life and bind them, their legs turn to lead, or some other effect occurs is up to the Storyteller. This usually means a "Time-out" should be called as the Storyteller announces any changes to the location or characters in it. While nearly any sort of change is within the purview of this Gift, extra attention should be taken to ensure all changes are fair and in keeping with the spirit of the Gift, as a general rule, supernatural creatures can shrug off personal alterations caused by this Gift at the end of the session with the expenditure of a Gnosis or comparable Trait unless the Storyteller says otherwise. The only true rule is that the Gift is always beneficial — to the Moon Dancer, that is.

## Ahroun

### Basic Gifts

• **Razor Claws** — See **Laws of the Wild**, p. 105.

• **Spirit of the Fray** — See **Laws of the Wild**, p. 105.

• **Inspiration** — See **Laws of the Wild**, p. 105.

• **Trick Shot** — No shot is impossible to the Garou who knows this Gift, from putting a bullet down the barrel of an enemy's gun to hitting a dime on a post six fields away. The Garou may add a number of Traits equal to her total Glory Traits to any challenge where she is attempting such a difficult or outrageous shot; the only rule is that this Gift never applies to any challenges which would directly injure another. The Garou may use this Gift to indirectly harm someone, such as shooting out the rope to bring a chandelier down on someone, but cannot simply plug his foe with this Gift, no matter how creative it might seem to do so. ("I shoot the varmint through the heart!" doesn't count, not even from a half-mile away through six doors and two beer bottles.)

### Intermediate Gifts

• **Sense Silver** — See **Laws of the Wild**, p. 106.

• **Stoking Fury's Furnace** — See **Laws of the Wild**, p. 106.

• **True Fear** — See **Laws of the Wild**, p. 106.

• **Silver Claws** — See **Laws of the Wild**, p. 106.

### Advanced Gifts

• **Hail of Bullets** — Using this mighty Gift, the Garou may stride untouched through vicious gun battles, wade through a sea of arrowheads, even cross through gatling cannon fire without a scratch. By spending two Gnosis Traits, the Garou becomes immune to all metal or stone projectiles for the remainder of the scene. They simply do not touch the Gifted Garou, veering away harmlessly or vanishing inches from his skin. If an opponent is using silver ammunition, the Garou must win or tie a Simple Test for each such attack, but doing so means he suffers no ill effects from it. Note that melee or brawling attacks of any kind are unaffected by this Gift, and that the Gifted Garou is perfectly able to fire back at her opponents.

• **Strength of Will** — See **Laws of the Wild**, p. 106.

• **Sun Dance** — See the Gift: *Kiss of Helios*, in **Laws of the Wild**, p. 106.

## Tribe Gifts

### Black Furies

Basic Gifts

• **Sense Wyrm** — See **Laws of the Wild**, p. 94.

• **Song of the Seasons** — After spending a Gnosis Trait, the Garou ignores the effects of natural climate extremes, as long as they aren't severe or sudden enough to be considered attacks. Even against such attacks (bursts of cold, storms, etc.), the Garou is one Trait up to resist for the duration of the Gift. This Gift lasts for one session/day.

• **Sense of the Prey** — See **Laws of the Wild**, p. 107.

• **Kneel** — This Gift allows the Garou to force a blatant gesture of submission out of a target, and is commonly used by Furies to humble males they find offensive. The Garou must point at the target and beat him in a Social Challenge; if the Garou is successful, the target must sink to his knees and remain there until the Garou releases him. He can speak all he wants, but until the Garou leaves the vicinity or voluntarily cancels the Gift, he can do nothing else but kneel. This Gift is also canceled if the target is attacked in any way. Supernatural creatures may spend a Trait of Gnosis (Glamour, Blood, etc.) to resist this Gift, but mortals are helpless until the Gift is ended as above. To date, this Gift has never been taught to a male, not even a male metis.

#### Intermediate Gifts

• **Devil Talons** — The Garou using this Gift summons her Rage to the surface and allows it to literally drip off her claws, making them venomous and capable of delivering wounds that burn for hours afterward. This Gift costs one Rage Trait per scene to activate, but once it is engaged, every time the Garou does damage with her claws she may choose to spend an additional Rage Trait — her damage does not increase, but the target suffers wound penalties twice as severe as normal: two-Trait penalties increase to four, etc. These heightened wound penalties last for one scene, though non-regenerating creatures may feel them for much longer than that.

• **Spirit Ripper** — The Garou with this Gift has the ability to use her bond with the Wyld to her advantage, using her kinship with chaos to blast other spirits apart. The Garou must spend a Gnosis Trait and beat the spirit in a challenge of Gnosis versus Gnosis; if successful, the Garou may spend a variable number of Mental Traits, each one doing five points of damage to the spirit's Power. This damage cannot be soaked by any spirit Charm, but unless the spirit is materialized, the Garou must be in the Umbra to use this Gift. Using it on those possessed by spirits, such as mockeries, requires only a Gnosis Trait and a Mental Challenge, and if successful inflicts one aggravated wound. This Gift has no effect on Wyld-spirits.

• **Wasp Talons** — See **Laws of the Wild**, p. 107.

### Advanced Gifts

• **Healing Breath of Mother Gaia** — The Garou can call the healing power of Gaia to dispel Wyrm-taint and injure creatures of corruption, or bless a place of Gaia with peace. The Garou must make a Static Challenge of her permanent Gnosis rating against a Storyteller-assigned difficulty, which depends on the amount of taint in the area; a recent battlefield is not too difficult, but an Anchorhead to Malfeas is near-impossible. If successful, the Garou may spend Gnosis traits to cleanse the Wyrm-taint and return the area to normal; each point spent reduces it by one degree, with the total degrees of an area being equal to the difficulty number of the Static Challenge. (e.g. spending three Gnosis on a site that had a Static difficulty of three "cures" it, or improves a site that had a difficulty of six down to three.) Furthermore, any Wyrm-creatures within 10 feet of the Garou at the time of this Gift's use take one Health Level of damage per Gnosis Trait spent. This healing is not instantaneous, but should take place over the course of a session or two, during which time the local Umbra gradually improves. If used on a place of Gaia, such as a caern, all difficulties to frenzy are increased by two (only one Gnosis Trait is required for this effect).

• **Wyldstorm** — This devastating Gift allows the Garou to channel the raw power of the Storm Umbra in a spiritual tempest, which spills over into the mortal world in a brief but lethal assault. The Garou must first step sideways to use this Gift, then spend at least five uninterrupted minutes singing up the storm, at the end of which period she spends one Rage, one Willpower and one Gnosis Trait. At this time, the Spirit Keeper is contacted to determine the length and severity of the storm; these factors typically depend on the purity of Garou's cause and the size of the enemy the Garou wishes to affect, but the resulting storm inflicts a total of one to three aggravated Health Levels of damage to any targets within range. Range is roughly the Garou's line of sight from where her physical position would be, though this can be modified at the Spirit Keeper's discretion; the Gift lasts 10 minutes. Obviously, a time-out should be called to announce the storm's arrival, and any characters with Gifts like *Pulse of the Invisible* will definitely feel it coming. The storm may take any form, from sleet in the desert to lightning from a blue sky, at the Spirit Keeper's choosing, but the damage remains the same regardless.

• **Beast Witch** — See the Gift: *The Thousand Forms of Gaia*, in **Laws of the Wild**, p. 107.

## Bone Gnawer

### Basic Gifts

• **Hide in Plain Sight** — See the Gift: *Blissful Ignorance*, in **Laws of the Wild**, p. 98.

• **Stone Soup** — See the Gift: *Cooking*, in **Laws of the Wild**, p. 108.

• **Cornered Rat** —When cornered, the Garou can call on the "fight or flight" instinct in all creatures, presenting a formidable target, especially to those who thought they were closing in for a kill. The Garou spends one Rage Trait and instantly gains the Physical Traits: *Ferocious x 2* and *Tough* for the remainder of the current battle. The Garou also instantly enters a berserk frenzy once this Gift is used. Note that the Garou must be fighting a losing battle, ambushed, cornered or otherwise backed against the wall to use this Gift.

• **Odious Aroma** — See **Laws of the Wild**, p. 108.

### Intermediate Gifts

• **Glass Talons** — By spending a Gnosis Trait, the Garou may transfigure his talons into glass, making them capable of delivering terrible wounds as they slice open flesh and splinter apart in the wound. The first time the Garou injures someone with his altered claws, he does the normal amount of damage, but unless the target takes time to clean the wound, the glass shards still in it deliver an additional non-aggravated level of damage for each combat turn/four seconds that they are untended. Cleaning the wound requires that the target remain fairly still and perform no hostile action for one turn (defending only), during which time any attackers are two Traits up, and the victim must win or tie a Simple Test to remove the glass. Since the Garou's claws shatter as a result of the attack, he is incapable of using them during the next combat turn as they regenerate, at which time he must use this Gift again to turn them into glass once more.

• **Gift of the Termite** — See **Laws of the Wild**, p. 108.

• **Run for Ground** — Any good Bone Gnawer always knows the way out of a situation, and this Gift proves it. The Garou using this Gift may attempt to call a Fair Escape any time he is within reach of a hiding place (reach: roughly five feet) or other cover. By concealing himself and spending a Gnosis Trait, the Garou can effectively disappear, emerging from behind some other little nook or hiding place farther away. He cannot reappear in plain sight; only out of another hiding place will do. This Gift may be contested by speed-related powers such as *Speed Beyond Thought* or vampiric *Celerity*, but at the end of any such series of challenges the Garou will still escape, unless held with supernatural strength or somehow Incapacitated by his foe.

• **Reshape Object** — See **Laws of the Wild**, p. 93.

### Advanced Gifts

• **Hometown Hero** — By calling on her role as the defender of the lost and downtrodden, the Gnawer may summon great bursts of strength in the defense of her fellows. Spending a Rage Trait and loosing a mighty roar at her foes, the Garou gains a number of *Brawny*, *Tough* or *Ferocious* Physical Traits equal to her rating in the Kinfolk Background, plus an additional Trait for each person she is directly defending in combat, up to a maximum of twice the Garou's regular Traits (before the addition of any extra Traits due to shapeshifting and the like). This Gift may be combined with the effects of other Gifts, but may only be used if the Garou is at least indirectly defending one of her Kinfolk or another member of the Bone Gnawer protectorate; stopping a gang of mockery bandits preying on a poor peasant village is acceptable, but settling a personal grudge or defending a gold mine is not. This Gift may only be used once per session, and when the combat it is used in has passed, the Garou becomes ravenously hungry and will need to eat for at least half an hour before feeling sated; failing to do so puts her down one Trait on all challenges until she has indulged her hunger.

• **Survivor** — See **Laws of the Wild**, p. 109.

• **Gold Fever** — Bone Gnawers have long suffered the abuses of the wealthy, and more than a few have learned how to turn the tables, at least for a while. The Garou using this Gift must spend a Rage Trait and a Physical Trait; for the next hour, whenever he touches someone he can spend a Physical Trait to infect the victim with "gold fever." If the target resists being touched, the Garou must first win a Physical Challenge to affect the subject. If the target fails a Simple Test when touched, he begins to sweat and shake and find his mind wandering to thoughts of money almost uncontrollably. To represent this, the target gains the Traits *Sickly x 2*, *Delicate* and the Derangement *Obsession: Money* for the remainder of the session. Bone Gnawers and their Kin are completely immune to this Gift, as are any other individuals the Storyteller deems to be "impoverished"; this Gift only functions on those who have more money or trade goods than it takes to keep themselves in very meager food and shelter, as this is the Bone Gnawers' revenge for the harm that the wealthy have caused them. This Gift is so named because of the gold color of the sweat those affected perspire. (There is no gold in the sweat, though. Nice try.)

## Children of Gaia

### Basic Gifts

- **Resist Pain** — See **Laws of the Wild**, p. 102.
- **Mother's Touch** — See **Laws of the Wild**, p. 100.
- **Calm** — See **Laws of the Wild**, p. 110.
- **Luna's Armor** — See **Laws of the Wild**, p. 110.

### Intermediate Gifts

- **Lord of the Wilds** — See the Gift: *Beast Life*, in **Laws of the Wild**, p. 97.
- **Spirit Friend** — See **Laws of the Wild**, p. 110.
- **The Guilty Mind** — See **Laws of the Wild**, p. 110.
- **Serenity** — See **Laws of the Wild**, p. 110.

### Advanced Gifts

• **Gaia's Balm** — With this Gift, the Garou may bring an end to the suffering and madness of spirits in the Storm Umbra, either by healing the spirits or destroying them entirely. By spending a Gnosis Trait and a Willpower Trait, the Garou may make a Social Challenge against the spirit's Gnosis; if successful, the Garou may then make a series of Static Social Tests against a difficulty of the spirit's Gnosis. Each successful test strips 10 Power from the spirit, and if the spirit reaches zero Power, the Garou may choose either to heal the spirit's mind and restore it to full Power or (if the Narrator deems a cure impossible) destroy the spirit permanently. This Gift only works on spirits driven mad by the Storm Umbra, and has no effect on Wyrm-spirits. A Garou will not receive Notoriety for most uses of this Gift, as it is considered a kindness (or at least a mercy killing) by the spirit community as a whole.

• **Halo of the Sun** — See **Laws of the Wild**, p. 110.

• **Life for Life** — With this awe-inspiring Gift, the Garou can curb the excesses of even the worst killers, provided she is true to herself. The Garou must first approach her target, telling him of Gaia's forgiveness and swearing oaths of friendship and kinship to the target (beasts and mindless creatures are thus immune to this Gift). Whether or not the target agrees, the Garou may then spend a permanent Willpower Trait and engage the subject in a Social Challenge. If the Garou wins, the subject is overcome by the beauty of life, and may not willfully bring harm to another living thing again until after the Garou herself makes her next kill, though the target may defend himself if necessary. Likewise, the Garou and her packmates may not attack or harass the target, or the Gift is immediately canceled. This Gift may not be resisted by spending a Willpower Trait, although supernatural creatures may spend a permanent Willpower Trait to retest the challenge. This Gift has no effect on creatures created entirely of the Wyrm's essence (such as Banes themselves), though such things as vampires and mockeries are certainly possible targets.

• **Unicorn's Grace** — See **Laws of the Wild**, p. 110.

## Fianna

### Basic Gifts

• **Family Tree** — By naming her ancestors back several generations, Garou or otherwise, the Gift's user can renew her sense of mission and belonging in the world. This Gift may only be used once per session, and requires at least a minute of naming ancestors before it takes effect; however, once that is complete, the Garou may choose to either replenish any spent levels of the Past Life Background or regain a spent Willpower Trait. The player must actually recite a family tree each time this Gift is used, preferably one that becomes reasonably consistent from one use of this Gift to another; failing to name and respect one's ancestors properly is considered a subject of derision at best, or grounds for spirit Notoriety or a loss of Wisdom Renown at worst. This Gift should take at least one minute to perform, if not more.

• **Glib Tongue** — See the Gift: *Persuasion*, in **Laws of the Wild**, p. 92.

• **Howl of the Banshee** — See **Laws of the Wild**, p. 111.

• **Resist Toxin** — See **Laws of the Wild**, p. 111.

### Intermediate Gifts

• **Call of the Old Country** — By singing or howling, the Garou is able to cause either deep feelings of kinship or terrible feelings of loss in her listeners, evoking memories of their ancestral homelands with her song. This Gift works regardless of where the targets come from; Europeans may feel pride in or acute homesickness for lands they left behind, while Pure Ones might feel the old connection between their folk and Gaia. The Garou must first spend a Gnosis Trait, and the player must actually sing for at least a minute for this Gift to work; after that time, the Garou may call for a Social Challenge with her listeners, although if the Garou is able to name the actual homeland of her targets, this knowledge replaces her bid (meaning she has no Traits at risk). If successful, the Garou may cause her targets to either gain or lose one Willpower and Rage Trait, depending on which mood she decides to put them in. The effects of this Gift last for one hour/scene. Players should try to choose songs sung for this Gift as appropriately as possible, as many modern songs not only ruin the mood of a Savage West setting, but also fail to convey the basic sentiments the song itself should. Note also that humans cannot gain Rage Traits from this Gift — that benefit is only useful to other creatures with Rage.

• **Mirage** — This Gift allows the Garou to conjure up static illusionary images that appeal to all five senses. Examples include a man leaning against a wall, barrels of TNT or even a small building. By static, this means an illusionary guard could pace back and forth, or speak the same phrase over and over, but could not be made to stop pacing and check his weapon. This illusion cannot harm others, even indirectly, though they might harm themselves due to their belief in the illusion (by trying to walk on an illusory bridge, for example). The Garou must spend a Gnosis Trait to create the illusion, and every five minutes past the first that he wishes to maintain it costs an additional Gnosis Trait. Anyone who sees it must defeat the Garou in a Mental Challenge in order to see through the deception, but *Heightened Senses* offers no benefit, as the illusion appeals to all the senses equally. Note that those attempting to disbelieve the illusion must have some reason to doubt the illusion to begin with, although any characters who try to interact with it directly (such as picking up the barrels or trying to enter the building) automatically receive a chance to disbelieve in it. The Garou may not create or maintain illusions that are out of his line of sight. The Storyteller may also require that truly grand creations, such as an entire troop of cavalry, require additional Gnosis Traits to create/maintain.

• **Prospector's Luck** —The Garou can call on an ancient alliance with faeries of the earth to find deposits of precious metals. By spending a Mental Trait and concentrating for one minute, the Garou can activate the Gift. For the remainder of the scene, she may sense deposits of silver or gold in the area with a win or tie on a Simple Test. She may also attempt to find large hidden caches of these same materials in her line of sight with a Mental Challenge against the person who originally hid the treasure. The Storyteller must determine exactly how much gold or silver is present (if any), as well as the total value of any particular find. This Gift offers few other direct benefits, but it doesn't take an Andrew Carnegie to figure out what kind of fiscal possibilities emerge if the Garou stumbles on a large vein of gold....

### Advanced Gifts

• **Balor's Gaze** — See **Laws of the Wild**, p. 112.

• **Gift of the Spriggan** — See **Laws of the Wild**, p. 112.

• **Warp-Fury** — This desperate Gift calls on a level of Rage and power few Garou ever achieve, and evokes a frenzy no human has ever survived to tell of. The Garou must first spend three Rage Traits and make a Static Physical Challenge against a number of Traits of his choosing (minimum three, maximum of 18); for every three Traits in the difficulty of the challenge, the Garou enters the warp-frenzy for one turn. (One turn is defined as the time it takes a single attack/action challenge to be completed, retests and follow-ups included.) During this time, the Garou suffers no wound penalties, doubles his Physical Traits, adds two "Healthy" Health Levels, and regains at least one Rage Trait every turn. Once the frenzy has ended, the Garou instantly suffers three aggravated wounds which cannot be soaked. If the Garou survives that, his Rage and Willpower are lowered to one Trait each until he's rested for at least two hours. This Gift, if survived, also incurs at least one minor battle scar for the Garou each time.

The effects of this Gift are not cumulative with the Gift: *Might of Thor*; only one or the other may be used at any given time.

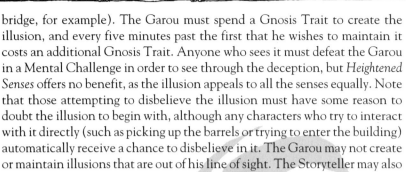

## Get of Fenris

### Basic Gifts

• **Cry of the Killer** — See **Laws of the Wild**, p. 112.

• **Razor Claws** — See **Laws of the Wild**, p. 105.

• **Resist Pain** — See **Laws of the Wild**, p. 102.

• **Safe Haven** — With this Gift, the Garou can establish an early warning system against approaching Wyrm-tainted creatures. This can only be done at a place the Garou has had time to become intimately acquainted with (read: lived *at least* for a few days), costs one Gnosis Trait to establish, and costs one Gnosis Trait per session/day to maintain. During that time, whenever a Wyrm-creature crosses the designated boundary, the Garou gets a Static Mental Challenge (difficulty five Traits) to detect it. Otherwise, it is identical to the *Rite of the Guardian's Heart* (see the Rites section), except with the aforementioned change in difficulty, and the questions asked may not pertain to anything but the presence of a threat and its location or general direction.

### Intermediate Gifts

• **Halt of the Coward's Flight — See Laws of the Wild**, pp. 112-113.

• **Might of Thor** — See **Laws of the Wild**, pp. 113.

• **Rage of Fenris** — The Garou can call on the might of Fenris, the ultimate warrior wolf, to aid him when battle looks darkest. By snarling or shouting defiantly at his foes and spending two Gnosis Traits and a Willpower Trait, the Garou immediately gains the Traits: *Ferocious*, *Relentless* and *Brutal* as well as five Rage Traits (even if this takes him over his normal maximum). He also immediately enters a berserk frenzy, but will not succumb to any temptations of the Wyrm such as wanton carnage or cannibalism while in this frenzy, as Fenris guides his claws. All extra Traits are lost at the end of the current combat, and the Garou immediately exits the frenzy as well. This Gift may not be used unless the odds are at least two-to-one against the Garou or a Narrator rules that the enemy is clearly vastly superior to the forces of the Garou (such as a massive Bane or three).

### Advanced Gifts

• **Fenris' Bite** — See **Laws of the Wild**, p. 113.

• **Hero's Stand — See Laws of the Wild**, p. 113.

• **Roar of Vengeance** — Summoning a primal howl from the depths of his soul, the Garou can roar with impossible force, shattering bones and scattering his enemies to the winds. By issuing a suitable Fenris roar (let's have a hearty bellow, players) and spending a Gnosis Trait and a Willpower Trait, the Garou may make a series of Simple Tests against a single target, one for each permanent Rage Trait he possesses; each success inflicts one level of aggravated damage, which may not be reduced or negated by any means. This Gift may be used only on minions of the Wyrm, and attempts to use this Gift improperly force the Garou to make the tests against himself, and to endure the loss of a permanent Glory Trait.

## Iron Riders

### Basic Gifts

• **Control Simple Machine** — See **Laws of the Wild**, p. 114.

Items include: locks, doorknobs, pistols, small levers, rifles, safe doors, clockwork devices, pulleys and watermills.

• **Iron Fur** — The Garou may transform his pelt to steel, gaining a good deal of extra protection but sacrificing a bit of manual dexterity and speed. While in effect, this Gift grants the Garou two extra Health Levels and the Traits: *Enduring, Tough and Resilient*. However, the Garou may not bid any Traits related to fine manipulation, quickness or agility such as *Dexterous* or *Lithe* while this Gift is in effect. This Gift costs one Gnosis Trait to use, and may only be used to any real effect in Crinos, Hispo or Lupus forms.

• **Persuasion** — See **Laws of the Wild**, p. 92.

• **Sense Weaver** — As the chosen tribe of the Weaver, Iron Riders can sense its presence wherever they go. This Gift works in ways identical to the Metis Gift, *Sense Wyrm*, except the Garou may detect the presence of the Weaver instead. This allows him to detect semi-civilized towns about a mile away with a win or tie on a Simple Test, and to roughly judge what types and amounts of technology are nearby. With a successful Mental Challenge, the Garou can also sense creatures who collect the Weaver's essence: Pattern Spiders, some mages, ancient vampires (who also stink of the Wyrm), and what the fae know as "banal" folk.

### Intermediate Gifts

• **Reshape Object** — See **Laws of the Wild**, p. 93.

• **Ten Thousand Bullets** — A Garou with this Gift can call on friendly metal-spirits to suspend the laws of reality a bit, allowing her to keep firing from a gun that should already be emptied. Each time the Garou runs over the regular ammunition count for her weapon, she may spend two Mental Traits for bullets to suddenly "appear" in her gun, fully reloading it. These bullets are always normal in every way (no silver rounds), and they can only be used in a gun that the Garou is holding in her hands, although the Garou may then pass her weapon to another. This Gift can also be used by devious Garou to mystically reload guns previously shown to be "unloaded," which is one of the many reasons that Garou distrust Iron Rider gunslingers. At the Storyteller's discretion, larger weapons such as gatling cannons may require larger expenditures, or the spirits may simply refuse to reload them. This Gift may only be used with firearms; more primitive projectiles are not covered by this Gift.

• **Gift of the Iron Horse** — Calling on the spirits of the railroad, the Garou may acquire information from along its tracks, or even borrow the strength of a speeding train for a time. The Garou may make a Static Mental Challenge against a difficulty dependent on the distance to be covered to hear anything happening along the rail as if he were standing there; he must simply place his ear to the track, and the spirits will convey the information to him as best they can. Additionally, by stepping between the rails of a railroad line, the Garou gains the ability to run at twice normal speed without tiring and gains the Traits *Tireless*, *Quick* and *Brawny*. These benefits last only as long as the Garou stands between the rails, but they are automatic once learned. At the Storyteller's discretion, this Gift may also allow the Garou to cut travel time by one-half between scenes by using the railroad track to travel.

• **Double Walker** — The Garou may take on the likeness of an individual he has studied closely. By spending a Gnosis Trait and performing a Static Social Challenge (against a difficulty of 10 Traits), he may assume the subject's exact likeness, including clothes or other belongings (which, if magical or technological, will not function). Someone familiar with the original person senses something is amiss only if she wins a Simple Test. Individuals with powers that reveal the hidden Garou may uncover the truth (if the individual thinks to use her power on the disguised Garou). The Gift lasts for the rest of the session. This Gift does not grant the Garou any Abilities, languages, armor or powers above and beyond those he already possesses.

Players using this Gift should wear cards or name tags that describe what they are supposed to look like in their new forms.

### Advanced Gifts

• **Calm the Flock** — See the Gift: *Reduce Delirium*, in **Laws of the Wild**, p. 94.

• **Dynamite Blast** — The Garou may summon the destructive power of dynamite at will, blasting his foes with killing force or destroying structures with frightening speed. The Garou must spend two Rage Traits and make a Mental Challenge against his target. If successful, his target and those within a step of him take three aggravated wounds from burns and concussive force; those within another two steps take two aggravated wounds; and those within three more steps take a single aggravated wound. If the Garou loses, the blast is muffled and all who would have been within range take half damage, rounded down. (This damage is still calculated from where the original target stood). Those caught within the radius of the blast may surrender all offensive challenges that turn and win or tie a Simple Test to leap to the next radius level (those within a step can go to two, those at two to three, etc.), but the primary target of the Gift may not escape full damage unless she won the Mental Challenge as described above.

• **Quell the Storm** — By calling on a pact with the Weaver, the Garou may impose order on the Storm Umbra, at least for a time. This Gift counters Umbral storms and even dispels them by using the power of the Weaver to ward off the Wyld. Spending two Gnosis Traits and making a Static Gnosis Challenge against eight traits, the Garou may attempt to calm Umbral winds in his immediate vicinity (up to 10 steps around him); if successful, he may then enter an Extended Gnosis Challenge versus the same difficulty — each additional test won allows another 10 feet to be added to the radius of calm. If used against a Wyld-spirit, the Garou must still spend two Gnosis Traits, and then make a Challenge of his Gnosis versus the spirit's. If successful, he enters an Extended Gnosis Challenge as above, but each test won strips four Power away from the spirit. Obviously, this Gift is looked upon very poorly by Wyld-spirits and Wyld-affiliated tribes such as the Black Furies and the Red Talons.

• **Repel Metal** — As per the Ahroun Gift: *Hail of Bullets*.

## Red Talons

### Basic Gifts

• **Beast Life** — See **Laws of the Wild**, p. 97.

• **Scent of Running Water** — See **Laws of the Wild**, p. 98.

• **Sense of the Prey** — See **Laws of the Wild**, p. 107.

• **Eye of the Hunter** — Using innate wolf instinct to find the weakest member of a herd, the Garou can attempt to probe the weakest and strongest targets in a group. By stating a particular Trait category (Mental, Physical, Social) and making a Mental Challenge, the Garou may then ask the targets to count off their group from strongest to weakest in the stated category. They need not tell the Garou the exact numbers of Traits they possess, but must answer honestly. Obviously, this Gift requires use of the group challenge rules, and the Garou cannot scan more targets at one time than she has total Mental Traits. If used on a lone target, the Garou may ask which Trait category she is strongest in, or discover one Negative Trait in a category stated before the outcome of the challenge is determined (if there is a Negative Trait to discover). This Gift may not be used on the same target or group of targets more than once per session.

### Intermediate Gifts

• **Monkey Songs** — See the Gift: *Babble*, in **Laws of the Wild**, p. 116.

• **Beastmind** — See **Laws of the Wild**, p. 116.

• **Curse the Weaver** — See **Laws of the Wild**, p. 116, but use the table below.

| | |
|---|---|
| 3 Traits | Pistol, lantern, lock |
| 7 Traits | Rifle, steam engine, clockwork device |
| 10 Traits | Gatling cannon, camera, entire train |

### Advanced Gifts

• **Share the Wolf's Skin** — See the Gift: *Curse of Dionysus*, in **Laws of the Wild**, p. 116.

• **Quicksand** — See **Laws of the Wild**, p. 116.

## Shadow Lords

### Basic Gifts

• **Fatal Flaw** — See **Laws of the Wild**, p. 117.

• **Aura of Confidence** — See **Laws of the Wild**, p. 117. This Gift also allows the Garou a free retest on the staredown challenge if the optional gunfighting rules on page 228 are used.

• **Clap of Thunder** — See **Laws of the Wild**, p. 117.

• **Mark of Suspicion** — Whispering accusations, the Garou can brand an unseen mark of suspicion on a target, causing others to treat the subject with caution and interpret his actions in a more negative light than they might have done before. By spending a Gnosis Trait and defeating her opponent in a Social Challenge, the Garou can bestow upon the target the Negative Social Trait: *Untrustworthy*, and this Gift also puts the subject one Trait down on all Social Challenges. The effects of this Gift last for one scene and are not cumulative. Repeated uses of this Gift can extend the effect's duration, however.

### Intermediate Gifts

• **Luna's Armor** — See **Laws of the Wild**, p. 110.

• **Icy Chill of Despair** — See the Gift: *Roll Over*, in **Laws of the Wild**, pp. 102-103.

• **Shadow Cutting** — By calling out "Ptooie!" in reach of her opponent's shadow and spending a Gnosis Trait, the player may have her Garou spit into her opponent's shadow and thus allow her to inflict damage on her opponent simply by striking his shadow. She may only use fetish weapons, silver or natural weaponry to inflict this damage; other attacks have no effect. The target is two Traits down on any attempts to defend against attacks directed at his shadow. An actual shadow must be present for this Gift to be used, but the Garou may use all the advantages the Gift gives her once the shadow falls within her range. She may damage an opponent whose shadow falls across her path even if its owner is hiding behind a corner, and any fool who comes after the Garou at sundown is begging for trouble. An opponent may attempt a Physical Challenge to avoid the start of the Gift, but only if he sees it coming and knows enough to try; most folks in the Savage West would be insulted by someone spitting on their shadows, but certainly wouldn't try to avoid it unless they had been victims of this Gift before.

• **Open Wounds** — See **Laws of the Wild**, p. 117.

### Advanced Gifts

• **Strength of the Dominator** — See **Laws of the Wild**, p. 117.

• **Wounding Lies** — Shadow Lords may live for intrigue, but they detest being lied to. This Gift ensures that those they deal with quickly banish any notion of such foolery. By spending a Gnosis Trait and defeating the subject in a Social Challenge, the Garou may establish a link for the remainder of the scene: after each statement the subject makes to the Garou, the Garou's player may ask the target if he lied, which he must answer honestly. Each time the subject lies to the Garou, he takes a level of aggravated damage (no test to resist). Half-truths or significant omissions open visible and stinging but not actually damaging wounds that the Shadow Lord notices. Garou may ignore the effects of this Gift by spending a Gnosis Trait, but other characters may resist this Gift only at the Storyteller's discretion.

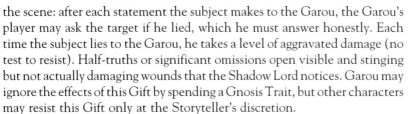

## Silent Strider

### Basic Gifts

- **Sense Wyrm** — See **Laws of the Wild**, p. 94.
- **Speed of Thought** — See **Laws of the Wild**, p. 118.
- **Messenger's Fortitude** — See **Laws of the Wild**, p. 118.
- **Dust-Talking** — Silent Striders travel many roads, and as the advance scouts of the Garou, they quickly learn how to identify trail markings. By spending a minute examining a set of tracks and speaking softly to the local Earth-spirits, the Garou may spend a Mental Trait to determine what has passed by recently. Animals are immediately identifiable, as are the true number of tracks present; the Garou may also gain the following information with an additional Mental Trait per question: emotional state of the group (brief summary), each member's state of health, and their general destination. With a Static Mental Challenge against the target's Mental Traits, the Strider can ask what type of creature left each track (vampire, human, Garou, etc.)

### Intermediate Gifts

- **Hide in Plain Sight** — See the Gift: *Blissful Ignorance*, in **Laws of the Wild**, p. 98.
- **Gaia's Resilience** — See the Gift: *Adaptation*, in **Laws of the Wild**, p. 119.
- **Tongues** — See **Laws of the Wild**, p. 93.
- **Speed Beyond Thought** — See **Laws of the Wild**, p. 119.

### Advanced Gifts

- **Train of Thought** — Masters at both learning and spreading rumors, Striders long ago learned how to manipulate local gossips to their own advantage as they traveled. The Garou must spend a Gnosis Trait and defeat the target in a Social Challenge using the *Subterfuge* Ability; she may then bring up a specific topic in conversation that she'd like to "tail." This Gift lasts one scene. At the end of that time, the Garou may come back to her target out of character and ask him to tell her anything he heard or said related to that topic during the scene, which he must relate honestly. Knowledge that the target possessed prior to this Gift's use is not covered, unless the target brought it up in conversation during the scene. While this Gift is in effect, the Garou must not speak, and especially may not actively bring up the topic about which the Gift was invoked. Voluntary failure to do so immediately negates this Gift. This Gift may only be used once per session. Note that the target does not know that anything supernatural occurred, and thus will have no reason to avoid the topic the Garou raised. Some appropriate topics are "*The new sheriff is going to round up a posse by dawn,*" and "*I heard the bandits have a hideout outside of town,*" but "*Tell me where local Wyrm-things are,*" or "*Give me the names of all the werecreatures in town*" are not, unless the target specifically knows what those terms mean.

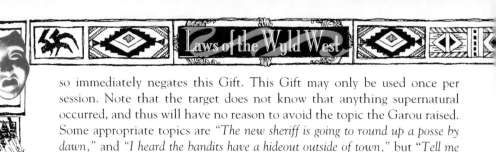

• **Open Moon Gate** — See the Gift: *Open the Moon Bridge*, in **Laws of the Wild**, p. 99.

• **Reach the Umbra** — See **Laws of the Wild**, p. 119.

## Silver Fangs

### Basic Gifts

• **Sense Wyrm** — See **Laws of the Wild**, p. 94.

• **Lambent Flame** — See **Laws of the Wild**, p. 119.

• **Luna's Armor** — See **Laws of the Wild**, p. 110.

• **Imposing Gaze** — See the Gift: *Paralyzing Stare*, in **Laws of the Wild**, p. 93.

### Intermediate Gifts

• **Roll Over** — See **Laws of the Wild**, pp. 102-103, but this version of the Gift does not cost Gnosis to use.

• **Silver Claws** — See **Laws of the Wild**, p. 106.

• **Foe of the Wyrm** — See the Gift: *Wrath of Gaia*, in **Laws of the Wild**, p. 120.

• **Mastery** — See **Laws of the Wild**, p. 120.

### Advanced Gifts

• **Proud Warrior** — See the Gift: *Ignore Wound*, in **Laws of the Wild**, p. 120.

• **Gaia's Favor** — The Garou can call upon Gaia's patronage whenever a task appears daunting and failure looms without Her aid. After failing a challenge, the Garou may speak an invocation to Gaia and spend a Gnosis Trait to receive a retest. This Gift may be used to retest any sort of challenge, but may not be used on challenges that are not vital to defeating a potent minion of the Wyrm or advancing the greater cause of the Garou Nation; any attempt to abuse this Gift immediately loses the unfortunate Garou a permanent Trait of Wisdom Renown, and she may not use this Gift again until she has performed some quest to atone for her misdeed to Gaia.

• **Whelp the Insolent** — See the Gift: *Paws of the Newborn Cub*, in **Laws of the Wild**, p. 120.

• **Luna's Might** — See the Gift: *Luna's Avenger*, in **Laws of the Wild**, p. 120.

## Stargazers

### Basic Gifts

• **Sense Wyrm** — See **Laws of the Wild**, p. 94.

• **Catfeet** — See **Laws of the Wild**, p. 97.

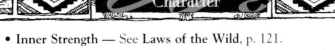

• **Inner Strength** — See **Laws of the Wild**, p. 121.

• **Measured Step** — See the Gift: *Surface Attunement*, in **Laws of the Wild**, p. 121.

### Intermediate Gifts

• **Counting Coup** — See the Gift: *Merciful Blow*, in **Laws of the Wild**, p. 121.

• **Mastery of the Mortal Coil** — With this Gift, the Garou may exert amazing control over her body and its functions. By spending a Willpower Trait and meditating for at least five minutes, the Garou gains the following benefits: by controlling her breathing, she becomes immune to gases; by controlling her metabolism, she becomes immune to poisons; and by controlling her pain reflexes, she may ignore wound penalties from lost Health Levels. These effects last for five minutes per permanent Willpower Trait the Garou possesses. The Garou does not collapse due to this Gift, but simply forces her body to work much more efficiently than before. The effects last for one session.

• **Preternatural Awareness** — See **Laws of the Wild**, p. 121.

### Advanced Gifts

• **Wisdom from the Heavens** — See the Gift: *Wisdom of the Seet*, in **Laws of the Wild**, p. 121.

• **Rage at Shadows** — See the Gift: *Circular Attack*, in **Laws of the Wild**, pp. 121-122.

• **Vision of the True Spirit** — With this Gift, the Garou may force a target to confront the true nature of her spirit, and the impact the actions she has taken have had on those around her. This Gift presents the target with a vision representing the goodness or evil of her spirit; the Garou does not know or control what the target sees. To use this Gift, the Garou must touch her target, spend a Gnosis Trait, and beat her in a Mental Challenge. If successful, the target is struck with a vision; the target should consult the Storyteller as to the nature of the vision, but it is always powerfully cathartic and symbolic. The vision lasts for five minutes; during that time, the target may do nothing but defend herself at a one-Trait penalty, but using this Gift to gain a combat advantage is considered dishonorable in the extreme. A person who willingly embraced evil might not feel shaken after the vision has passed, but one who slowly slid to corruption might have a change of heart, and a good person feels refreshed and renewed (perhaps regaining a Willpower Trait or similar benefit, at the Storyteller's discretion). Players are encouraged to be honest in their estimation of their characters' true natures, and kind players tell their Storytellers in advance when and upon whom they plan on using this Gift, so that a vision can be properly prepared.

## Uktena

### Basic Gifts

• **Sense Medicine** — If the Garou succeeds in a Mental Challenge

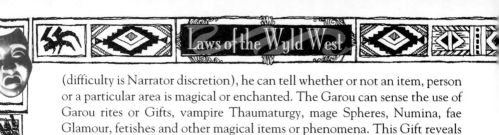

(difficulty is Narrator discretion), he can tell whether or not an item, person or a particular area is magical or enchanted. The Garou can sense the use of Garou rites or Gifts, vampire Thaumaturgy, mage Spheres, Numina, fae Glamour, fetishes and other magical items or phenomena. This Gift reveals the type of supernatural powers present, but nothing specific beyond that.

• **Sense the Tunneler's Passage** — See the Gift: *Sense Wyrm*, in **Laws of the Wild**, p. 94, except the Garou may make one or more Static Mental Challenges to track Wyrm-taint to its source if it has left the area in question; a loss cancels this Gift immediately. The trail also cannot be tracked into the Umbra.

• **Flick of the Fish's Tail** — See the Gift: *Spirit of the Fish*, in **Laws of the Wild**, p. 122.

• **Pass as the Shadow** — See the Gift: *Blissful Ignorance*, in **Laws of the Wild**, p. 98.

### Intermediate Gifts

• **Flame of the Sun Dance** — See the Gift: *Call Flame Spirit*, in **Laws of the Wild**, p. 122.

• **Sharing Raven's Supper** — See the Gift: *Secrets*, in **Laws of the Wild**, p. 122.

• **Call the Four Brothers** — See the Gift: *Elemental Gift*, in **Laws of the Wild**, pp. 97-98.

### Advanced Gifts

• **Fist of the Winds** — With the expenditure of one Gnosis, the Garou can move objects weighing up to 500 pounds. A successful Mental Challenge (against six Traits, + one per 100 pounds) is required to redirect the object successfully.

• **Call on Ancient Medicine** —The Garou can call on powerful ancestral magic to aid her in working her medicine, making her capable of truly powerful feats of magic. The Garou must spend two Gnosis Traits and win a Static Mental Challenge (versus 10 Traits). Any levels of the Past Life Background may be added to the Garou's bid for this challenge. If successful, the Garou becomes a potent sorcerer Ñ she wins all ties involving rites; detecting, summoning, dispelling or controlling spirits, deals an additional level of aggravated damage in combat to all spirits or beings possessed by spirits (such as mockeries); and all Gifts cost one less Gnosis to use (minimum of one if the Gift normally costs Gnosis). She also regains one Gnosis Trait for every five minutes spent resting or meditating. The effects of this Gift last for one scene, and this Gift may only be used when the Garou is attempting a particularly bold or vital action concerning the spirit world, as the ancestors will not allow it otherwise.

• **Kachina's Luck** —The Garou can create a small doll with which she may invoke luck and success for a target. The doll requires part of the target (or a close personal effect), one week of work to construct and a Gnosis Trait to finish. The Garou then makes an Extended Mental Challenge against seven Traits to determine the luck in the doll. Each success invests one Trait in the doll, while a loss ends the process. Once complete, the doll allows the target to add the Traits within to their total Traits for any challenges desired, but once they're used they vanish. For example, Smoky Lightning has a kachina with five Traits in it. One combat challenge, she uses two of the Traits to put her two Traits up in the contest, leaving three Traits in the doll. Once those three are used, the kachina ceases to be magical. Using the kachina does not count as an action. The target must possess the doll to use its power, though she need not know it's magical, and a target may not benefit from more than one kachina doll at a time.

## Wendigo

### Basic Gifts

• **Call the Breeze** — See **Laws of the Wild**, p. 123.

• **Song of the Seasons** — As per the Black Fury Gift of the same name.

• **Cutting Wind** — See **Laws of the Wild**, p. 123.

• **Camouflage** — See the Gift: *Blissful Ignorance*, in **Laws of the Wild**, p. 98, except it only functions in wilderness settings.

### Intermediate Gifts

• **Winter Frost** — See the Gift: *Chill of Early Frost*, in **Laws of the Wild**, pp. 123-124.

• **Sky Running** — By concentrating for one turn and spending a Willpower Trait, the Garou can literally run across the sky at 50 miles per hour. He must move continuously, however, or he will fall. The Garou leaves a trail of fire in the sky behind him. This Gift lasts for four hours.

• **Bond with the Earth** — When in a wilderness setting, the Garou can commune with local spirits for information on the area. To use this Gift requires that the Garou expend a Gnosis Trait and win a Simple Test (no Traits are risked). If he succeeds, he may ask one of the following questions and can expect an honest answer (unless the only spirits nearby are Wyrm-spirits, who will always mislead the Garou). The Garou may continue to make tests and ask questions until he loses. Each test equals one question. The Spirit Keeper must be contacted to use this Gift.

Typical questions include:

— What is the general population of (type of supernatural creature) in this area? (Note, however, that some very powerful creatures cannot be uncovered by these means.)

— Is (a person of certain description) nearby?

— Are there any (objects of a general type) nearby?

— Roughly how many people and/or animals have passed by (or have been in) this area in the last day?

The key is to ask general questions about general subjects.

### Advanced Gifts

• **Invoke the Spirits of the Storm** — See **Laws of the Wild**, p. 124.

• **Spirits of Decay** — See the Gift: *Rot Weavertech*, in **Laws of the Wild**, p. 124, but the Garou may affect any type of object he desires, regardless of complexity.

• **Ghost Shirt** — As per the Ahroun Gift: *Hail of Bullets*. This Gift is taught by Buffalo-spirits, angered by the slaughter of their kin by distant guns, and is intended to allow the Garou to close to the more honorable melee range without being troubled by the treacherous bullets of Europeans.

# Rites

Rites are the formal yet highly individualized mystic ceremonies of the Garou race. They are like recipes, utilizing the bounty of Gaia to create a spiritual repast for Her most beloved children. The rites bear the flavor of the auspices and tribes that perform them. No one would mistake the reflective meditations of the Stargazers for the savage pageantry beloved by the Get of Fenris.

Regardless of the trappings of a set of rites, they share a common direction and bent, and are often recognizable by other Garou even in the most unfamiliar forms.

Rites can be broken down into several categories according to their nature. The categories are assigned as Accord, Caern, Death, Mystical, Punishment, Renown, Seasonal and Minor, although Garou are hardly limited to one particular type of rite. As one might expect, different auspices show affinities for particular categories. Most noteworthy among these are Theurges (Mystical, Seasonal and Caern Rites) and Philodox (Accord and Punishment Rites). Other auspices often learn assorted rites befitting their natures, but not nearly as often as do Philodox and Theurges, who are expected to learn this ancient lore from spirits or their elders.

### How to Throw a Rite

Most of the rite descriptions below are deliberately devoid of step-by-step instructions ("First you howl at the moon, then you scratch behind your left ear…,"). Such rote roleplaying isn't fun for anyone, and can turn a game of the **Wyld West** into nothing more than a glorified game of Simon Says.

Instead, Storytellers and Ritemasters are encouraged to improvise or pre-script their rites, taking into account their settings, characters and cohorts. A personalized rite is always more appropriate than a generic one.

## Enacting a Rite

All but the simplest of rites are performed by a group of three or more Garou, one of whom coordinates the effort and is designated the Ritemaster. The Ritemaster is the only member of the group who must know the rite. As a result, she directs the actions and channels the energies of the others.

Performing a rite takes about 20 minutes for each level of the rite. Minor rites take 15 minutes. An untested or inexperienced Garou can take twice as long to perform a rite that is unfamiliar to him.

Each rite requires a minimum number of Traits, which can be determined by cross-referencing the rite type and level on the chart on page 170. The Garou who attempts to lead the rite must meet or exceed this minimum Trait requirement to perform it, and succeed in a Static Challenge against the rite's rating and type. These Traits are not spent in the process of the rite. Rather, they are merely the minimum that the Ritemaster must have to perform the ceremony. If the Ritemaster does not have enough Traits, but is within three Traits of the total needed, he can still attempt the rite. However, it will take him twice the usual amount of time to do so.

Additionally, a rite can take less time to perform if the Ritemaster has more Traits than needed. For every two Traits over the minimum number required, the Ritemaster can subtract 10 percent from the time it should take to perform the rite. No more than half the time needed for a rite can be shaved off in this manner.

The more Garou involved in a rite, the easier the rite is to perform. For every two Garou beyond the minimum number required to perform the rite, the Ritemaster gains a free additional Trait to use in the ceremony.

If the Ritemaster succeeds in her challenge, the rite proceeds. If she fails, the rite also falters, no benefit accrues, and the Ritemaster herself suffers a Trait loss equal to half the number necessary to perform the rite.

The following table shows the types of Traits that are used in different types of rites.

| Rite | Trait and Challenge Type |
|---|---|
| Accord | Social |
| Caern | Varies |
| Death | Social |
| Frontier | Social |
| Mystical | Mental |
| Punishment | Social |
| Pure Ones | Social |
| Renown | Social |
| Seasonal | Physical |
| Minor | None |

### Minimum Number of Traits

If a ceremony requires a minimum number of Traits from the Garou present, this pool of Traits is separate from the Traits that are actually risked. This pool is not part of the actual test, and the Traits of attending Garou are not actually part of the bid. The Traits risked in a rite are those of the Ritemaster only.

### Minimum Number of Participants

Some confident or desperate Garou attempt rites even when they do not have the necessary resources to perform the rite properly. If a group attempting a rite does not have the minimum number of Garou necessary to do it properly, the Ritemaster must spend a number of Mental Traits equal to the number of participants he is lacking in order to perform the rite successfully.

| Rite Level | Min. # of Traits | Min. # of Participants |
|---|---|---|
| Basic | Five | One |
| Intermediate | Eight | Three |
| Advanced | 11 | Five |

## Rites of Accord

These rites draw their power from connecting to the primal state of Gaia. That cycle is characterized by harmonious coexistence and rejuvenation. To channel this power, the Garou must utilize a talen, fetish or an object that is unspoiled by the ravages of man or the Wyrm. Rites of Accord are based on the Ritemaster's Social Traits for making challenges.

### Basic Rites

**Rite of Cleansing:** The Wyrm and its minions leave their indelible taint on everything they touch, and have begun to spread since the first European set foot in the New World (or so say the Pure Ones). While this rite cannot affect the Wyrm or its minions directly, it can remove the taint of their presence. Once the taint is removed, the area, person or object once tainted may not be further infected for the rest of the session. Native Garou might use medicine rattles or sweat lodges to purify a subject, while European Garou might immerse the subject in water or require a period of fasting and atonement. The Gnosis cost of this rite varies with the size of the target the Garou wishes to affect. The challenge is made against the Power Traits of the contaminator-spirit.

| | |
|---|---|
| No Gnosis | One person or one man-sized object |
| One Gnosis | A small room or two people |
| Two Gnosis | A large building or three people |

If a minion of the Wyrm is present in the contaminated object or area, it must first be defeated in order for the rite to work. Also, if the minion is not banished in time, it can re-infect the target.

**Rite of Reconciliation:** Too often in the contentious lands of the Savage West, the Garou find themselves embroiled in all manner of feuds, at a time when Garou population grows thin. This rite offers two feuding Garou a chance to resolve their differences, usually by openly airing their grievances, forswearing further violence somehow, and then symbolically burying their aggression. Native Garou often name each other's lineage as a symbol of respect, while Europeans clasp hands and elaborately forgive each other. The two Garou involved, if they sincerely wish to settle their differences, must each win a Static Willpower Challenge with a difficulty equal to their permanent Rage Traits to convince the Ritemaster, and thus Gaia, of their sincerity. The Ritemaster must spend a Social Trait and talk of the new future the two rivals now have before them as they complete the rite. If successful, the feuding Garou will be eligible for an Honor Renown Trait at the next moot; if not, they must let their actions speak for their intent in the coming seasons.

**Rite of Renunciation:** Often known as the Rite of New Hope by immigrants looking for a new life, this rite allows a Garou to take on a new auspice while leaving her old auspice (and any previous Rank) behind. It is also used by those wishing to move beyond some great shame and experience a rebirth of sorts. Those partaking of this rite are often frowned upon by the more conservative factions of Garou society, and may (as a so-called Shifting Moon) even experience open hostility as one who would not bear the weight of his burdens assigned by Luna. This rite requires no challenge or Gnosis, but it must be entered into freely. Often the Garou must symbolically "kill" her old self and come before her fellows as a new person; exactly how she chooses to express the creation of the new identity is itself a critical part of the renunciation process, and is highly personalized to each Garou.

Once the rite is complete, the subject is a fostern of her new auspice, with the minimum number of Renown Traits. A Shifting Moon no longer learns Gifts of her previous auspice as easily (see the Experience Point chart on page 243), but does retain any old ones, and may now learn Gifts of her new auspice at regular cost.

## Caern Rites

These rites are aligned with the most sacred sites of the Garou and Gaia. Caerns are the bosom from which all Garou are nourished. Were the caerns left to ebb and die out, the Garou race would not be long in joining them.

Caern Rites may be performed only within the bounds of a caern. This condition implies that those performing a rite have the permission of the presiding Garou, as caern piracy is one of the foulest breaches of Garou etiquette. Furthermore, for every level of the caern, the Ritemaster receives a free Trait to use in the rite's contest, in addition to any other bonus Traits she might have.

## Basic Rites

**Moot Rite:** This rite is required to open a moot. It must be performed at a caern at least once per month, or the caern will wane. During the course of the rite, two Gnosis Traits must be sacrificed for each level of the caern. For every month this rite is ignored, the caern drops one power level until it is dormant. The Gnosis Traits sacrificed may come from any Garou present for the moot. All moots open with a howl carried by the sept, but after that tribal and sept procedures vary widely (see the heading "Organization" under a tribe's description for ideas of how they might open their moots).

**Rite of the Opened Caern:** Caerns are fonts of enormous mystical energy. Each caern has its own power; Knowledge, Strength, Healing, Gnosis, Rage and Defense are some examples. A brave Garou can attempt to harness those energies with this rite; prayers, invocations, fasting and some form of minor but significant sacrifice are all traditions in this instance. In order to formally open the caern, a Garou must enter a Social Challenge against the caern's rating (one to five in Traits), with the benefit of the caern's bonus Traits as well. If she wins, the Garou can utilize one level of the caern's power in future challenges appropriate to the caern's special purpose. This bonus lasts until the Garou travels more than 100 miles away from the caern. If the Garou fails, she suffers a number of aggravated wounds equal to the caern's rating divided by two (round up).

See "Caerns", pp. 248.

## Intermediate Rites

**Rite of the Guardian's Heart:** The Garou can use this rite to forge a mystic sensory link between herself and the area around the caern. No challenge is necessary to enact this rite, but interpreting its results can be difficult. For every Mental Challenge (against 14 Traits) the Garou wins or ties after enacting the rite, she can ask a short yes/no question of a Narrator. Questions can concern only the caern, the bawn and their surroundings, contents, current state and history. Most Garou marked by this rite carry some symbol of guardianship or part of the caern on their person at all times.

**Rite of the Opened Bridge:** This well-protected rite has served the Garou since ancient times, helping distant septs keep in touch with each other and providing a means of quick travel (1/1000th normal time) in times of need. The rite, which must be performed at two caerns simultaneously, works through a Lune-spirit to establish a bond between the two locales.

In order to perform this rite, a Pathstone (also called a Moongem) is needed at both caerns. The two performing Garou must win or tie the challenge to open the bridge. If successful, either the *Rite of the Opened Caern* or the Gift: *Open Moon Bridge* will be able to activate the bridge throughout the next 12 months. If either Garou loses, the two caerns may not be linked for a full year, and the Ritemasters may be subjected to the *Rite of Ostracism*. The maximum range of the bridge is 1000 miles.

See "Caerns" for Moon Bridge distances, pp. 248.

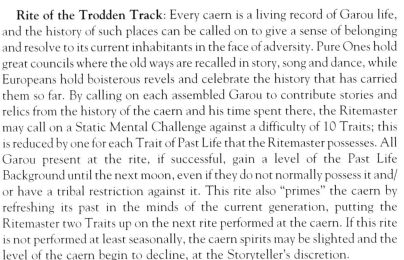

**Rite of the Trodden Track**: Every caern is a living record of Garou life, and the history of such places can be called on to give a sense of belonging and resolve to its current inhabitants in the face of adversity. Pure Ones hold great councils where the old ways are recalled in story, song and dance, while Europeans hold boisterous revels and celebrate the history that has carried them so far. By calling on each assembled Garou to contribute stories and relics from the history of the caern and his time spent there, the Ritemaster may call on a Static Mental Challenge against a difficulty of 10 Traits; this is reduced by one for each Trait of Past Life that the Ritemaster possesses. All Garou present at the rite, if successful, gain a level of the Past Life Background until the next moon, even if they do not normally possess it and/ or have a tribal restriction against it. This rite also "primes" the caern by refreshing its past in the minds of the current generation, putting the Ritemaster two Traits up on the next rite performed at the caern. If this rite is not performed at least seasonally, the caern spirits may be slighted and the level of the caern begin to decline, at the Storyteller's discretion.

## Advanced Rites

**Rite of Caern Building**: This rite creates a caern, a power base for Gaia. It can be performed only at locations that have inherent potential to become caerns; stretches of soot-stained factory land and desolate wasteland generally don't fit the bill. The initial setup for this rite tells the Garou about the area's potential. Once the intent to perform this rite has been announced and a site has been selected, the Storyteller must decide if a caern can be made in the area, and if so, how powerful it could be (Level One to Five). The Garou can then decide if they wish to attempt to build the caern at that spot or look elsewhere.

Once engaged in the rite, which must be performed after nightfall, the Ritemaster is helpless and must be defended from any minions of the Wyrm, which almost invariably arrive to disrupt the rite. If any Banes, mockeries or Black Spiral Dancers are within 20 miles of the event, they home in on it and attack the Garou mindlessly, fighting to the death to prevent the caern's creation. This includes vampires "of the Wyrm," but not those who are merely "Wyrm-tainted." For every hour of the rite, the Ritemaster may make up to five Simple Tests (a maximum of 40 tries). At dawn, the number of successes is tallied, and if the total is 20 or more, all is well. See below for the newborn caern's rating. Excess successes are discarded; a caern's rating can't be raised above its maximum potential. In other words, even if the Ritemaster scored 40 successes on a site with potential to be only a Level One caern, it would still be only a Level One caern.

| | |
|---|---|
| 20+ Successes | Level One |
| 24+ Successes | Level Two |
| 28+ Successes | Level Three |
| 32+ Successes | Level Four |
| 36+ Successes | Level Five |

When the 20th success is made, a total of 50 Gnosis Traits must be spent by the Garou present (minimum of 13 Garou). If less than 50 Gnosis Traits are available from *within* the Garou participating (stored Gnosis doesn't count), each suffers an aggravated wound. Each wound thus taken provides three more Gnosis points, and the process continues until the requisite 50 is reached. Once the caern's level is established, the Ritemaster must also spend a permanent Gnosis point for each level of the caern.

If fewer than 20 successes were made to create the caern, divide the number of successes that were achieved by the number still needed; these get divvied up evenly among the participating Garou as levels of aggravated wounds. The rite has failed, the Gnosis has been wasted, and those who failed must pay the price. Wounds received this way inevitably leave a single tear-shaped scar. A "Tear of Gaia" makes one worthy of one Glory Renown Trait.

To have participated in a successful *Rite of Caern Building* is a legendary feat deserving of three Glory and two Honor Renown. The Ritemaster also deserves four Wisdom Renown, even though these might be posthumous rewards. The Ritemaster for a *Rite of Caern Building* cannot initiate challenges, defend, flee, use Gifts or fetishes or otherwise act while the rite is in progress. If he does so, the rite ends instantly, with results as described above. As a *Rite of Caern Building* can easily be the focus of an entire chronicle's efforts, the Ritemaster, Storyteller and Spirit Keeper should work together to make it as vivid and involved an experience as possible. If the game can support such things, special music, different setting layout and extra costume attention are all strongly encouraged, plus as many extra details can be conjured up, from ritual Pure One chanting to European consecration ceremonies and beyond. Bear in mind all the rules of **Mind's Eye Theatre** still apply, but some special attention should be given when this rite is performed or the significance of it can be lost.

## Rites of Death

Having spent their lives so close to the spirit world, Garou understand death as an essential part of Gaia's cycle, and show appropriate homage to it.

### Basic Rites

**Wake Rite**: Though the idea of a formal wake came with the Europeans, many Pure Ones have similar practices of considering the life of a fallen companion, and while the Europeans often mix sadness with joy and festivity to celebrate the life of their friend, the ceremonies of the Pure Ones are often somber, quiet affairs. This rite consists of reciting the tales of the departed's life, remembering his good qualities and allowing all present to make their farewells without undue sorrow. It offers no game benefits, but is an essential part of Garou society, where lives are often far too short and those who remain behind need the comfort of knowing those who care for them will come together to honor them should they, too, die in Gaia's service. If this rite is neglected, the spirit may become lost and haunt his old companions until they give him this honor and speed his spirit to Gaia. Treat such Garou as wraiths. (See **Oblivion** for details.)

## Rites of the Frontier

The European Garou came across incredible distances into a harsh new land to make their lives here, and thus they need to keep family and tribe close. This is not a strict school of rites, but rather a collection of lore Theurges and Galliards have patched together as they struggle to help their septs and families survive and prosper in their new homeland. Most of these rites are more geared to adapting the land to the newcomers rather than the other way around, which makes them something of a sore spot with the Pure Ones.

### Basic Rites

**Rite of New Territory**: Too often, desirable land is claimed by more than one group of Kinfolk, and while this rite does not determine ownership of such critical things as caerns or septs, it does help to decide whose kin are allowed rights to which frontier outposts and towns. This rite is performed by two "Ritemasters", one from each contending faction, who need not have any actual knowledge of rites or rituals at all. This is because this rite is a fist-against-fist brawl in Homid form, with whoever falls first being declared the loser, whose kin must move elsewhere. It is always performed in plain view of the Kinfolk being represented, and while some of these matches have become deadly battles, it is generally considered the responsibility of those present to keep the match clean and nonlethal. There are no mechanics to this rite other than the battle between the two fighters, but a mutually agreed-upon Philodox is most often called on to oversee the match, for obvious reasons.

**Rite of the Homeland:** This rite brings a sense of the Old Country to the frontier, and is often used as the cornerstone when building a new community or even a caern, where members of a particular tribe or country can feel at home. The area so chosen can be no larger than the encircled arms of the Garou conducting this rite. If the rite challenge is successful, over time it subtly changes to resemble some small portion of the homeland: trees grow instead of cacti, tulips bloom in the garden, or perhaps a lawn greens like an old homestead. This is not without cost, though, as the Gauntlet rating of the area increases by one. If used in or around a caern, any member of a tribe that took part in this rite who is using the *Rite of the Guardian's Heart* (above) receives a free retest on all challenges allowed by that rite. If this rite can be undone, as some Pure Ones claim, there has yet to be any proof of such a deed being successfully carried out.

### Mystical Rites

These rites call spirits and Umbral entities to the Garou who performs them. These are considered solitary affairs, performed by a lone Ritemaster (a ceremony can be performed elsewhere). The results often manifest only in complete privacy.

## Basic Rites

**Baptism of Fire**: This rite is used to help Garou keep track of their young, who will one day share in the task of defending Gaia. It leaves a spiritual mark on a child that is only lifted upon the completion of the *Rite of Passage*. Until that time, a marked cub who is lost or absent may be found as if the performer were using the *Ritual of the Questing Stone*. Rumor has it that Black Spiral Dancers (and worse) may take advantage of this rite to track down Garou young for their own purposes. Some naturalistic tribes mark this Gift with a tattoo (which disappears along with the spiritual mark), while others attach a special surname or other honorific when addressing those marked by this rite.

**Rite of Spirit Awakening**: This rite awakens the spirit in an object or place. If the rite is performed on an object, the sleeping spirit "wakes up" and is now visible in the Umbra. The object's spirit is now available to be communicated with, commanded or bound. An object's spirit is usually a Gaffling or Jaggling. If this rite is performed on a fetish or talen that has been discovered, it allows the Ritemaster to speak briefly with the inhabiting spirit and perhaps learn some of the item's secrets. Iron Riders are particularly adept at speaking to technology spirits, and often awaken even the engines they ride on.

In addition, natural herbs that have been specially dried and treated with this rite gain special powers of various kinds. These herbs are assigned a Gnosis Trait rating depending on the quantity of the herbs gathered. For example, plantain can heal a number of Health Levels equal to its Gnosis Pool; a single leaf might contain only one Gnosis, while a five-pound bundle could hold five Gnosis. The Storyteller will have to decide what sacred foods and herbs do in the context of her story, and must list what is available in a given area.

**Rite of the Cup**: This rite allows two or more entities to exchange or otherwise transfer Gnosis, either receiving or giving it. The rite requires at least one Garou. Other participants can be Garou or spirits.

The *Rite of the Cup* requires that each Garou participant spends one of the following Mental Traits: *Calm*, *Disciplined*, *Insightful*, *Intuitive*, *Patient*, *Reflective* or *Wise*. If the Garou in question does not possess one of these Mental Traits, he may not take part in the rite.

The actual order of the rite is as follows: A ritual cup is prepared, which can be any kind of container, from an ale stein to a crystal wine glass to a clay basin. The container is filled with water. At this point, everyone involved in the rite decides to whom his Gnosis goes. If there is a dispute, the person who is performing the rite decides how the Gnosis is shared. Once the rite begins, the Gnosis cannot be removed or redirected. The Gnosis "travels" through the water into the appropriate individual and the rite ends. The passage of the Gnosis into the water is purely symbolic; no one needs to take an actual drink to get his Gnosis.

Gnosis may be stored by performing this rite with the assistance of an invested, bound spirit who agrees to hold the Gnosis, which is accessed again by another use of the rite (investiture is discussed under *Rite of Binding*). There is no effective limit to the amount of Gnosis that can be transferred, but a Garou or an invested, bound spirit cannot hold more Gnosis than his Gnosis Pool allows.

**Ritual of the Questing Stone**: By enacting this rite, the Garou forms a sympathetic magical link between the subject item or person and himself. The Garou must know the name by which the item or person is called. He then holds out a small stone tied to a string. If he succeeds in a Simple Test, he feels a slight tug on the stone from the direction of the subject. After the rite has been performed, the player of the Garou may ask any other player or Storyteller (out of play, of course) where the subject was last seen. The person who answers must answer honestly. The rite's effect lasts for the duration of the session if the Garou has either a piece of the subject or one of his treasured possessions. Otherwise it only lasts for one out-of-game hour.

It is recommended that those who perform this rite carry some sort of Narrator-approved identification, such as a card or a prop, to indicate that the rite has been cast and that pertinent questions should be answered truthfully.

**Rite of the Talisman Dedication**: When a Garou changes forms, her possessions are normally left behind or destroyed. This rite binds items to the Garou so that they will change with her and go with her into the Umbra. The cost of the rite is one Gnosis per five pounds or cubic foot of material. Items such as a set of clothes, a handgun, a knife or jewelry cost one Gnosis. Something the size of a rifle, boiler plate or rucksack costs two Gnosis. Surveying gear, full sacks or anything up to man-size costs three. The final determination of cost is up to the Storyteller. Some Garou inscribe the affected objects with their names or other personal glyphs, while other Garou simply add some extra decoration to the object such as a certain feather or a metal pin

The rite is permanent, unless the Garou ends the effect. In no case may a Garou have more Gnosis Traits' worth of items bound to her than her total Gnosis score. (Note that if an "inappropriate" technological item, such as a silver-plated pistol or rifle, is bound by a Garou who isn't a Bone Gnawer or Iron Rider, that individual may lose Renown.)

**Rite of Becoming**: This powerful rite can be performed only at an Anchorhead domain, a place where the veil between worlds is thinnest. It allows the Garou to travel into the Deep Umbra. The Storm Umbra is a potentially dangerous place; the Deep Umbra is worse. Garou hurling themselves into this realm better be well-prepared and capable of dealing with malefic entities. In addition to the normal challenge, this rite costs three Gnosis to use.

**Rite of Binding**: This rite binds a spirit to a specific real-world object or a specific place in the Umbra. The object must be brought into the Umbra after being dedicated by the *Rite of Talisman Dedication*.

There are three kinds of binding:

**Anchoring**: This prevents a spirit from leaving and gives the Ritemaster the power to communicate with the bound spirit at will. Thus, the spirit can use its senses to report to the Ritemaster. This binding, which allows the spirit to use its Charms, Abilities and Traits, is temporary, although it can be made permanent later (see "Imprisonment," below). Septs often bind spirits in this manner to have them watch over their bawns.

This kind of binding costs one Gnosis Trait, plus one extra Gnosis Trait if the bound spirit is a totem or Incarna avatar. The Ritemaster must ask and receive permission to bind the spirit in such a fashion. This can either be a result of roleplaying or of several successful Mental and Social Challenges. This version of the *Rite of Binding* gains the Ritemaster no Notoriety. This is the equivalent of "working in the mornings" to a spirit.

**Investiture**: A spirit is bound into an item, which then becomes a specific talen. The enchanting Garou spends a Gnosis Trait and one other appropriate Trait in the investiture, and must get permission from the spirit so invested (see "Anchoring," above). The result is a talen. A talen must have a spirit of an appropriate affinity (Bane Arrows must have spirits of War in them, etc.). The spirit stays bound until the talen is used.

**Imprisonment**: A spirit is bound into an item, which subsequently imprisons that spirit. The spirit cannot break free unless someone breaks the object or the binding. A Garou wishing to imprison a spirit usually beats the spirit into submission, and then, when the spirit has only a little Power remaining, enacts the *Rite of Binding* and imprisons it. The Garou can communicate with a spirit bound in this manner, although the prisoner cannot use its Charms. It can, however, use its Gnosis in Social and Mental Challenges, particularly with unsuspecting Garou who might be persuaded to break its prison and set the spirit free. By the time a spirit is freed after many years of imprisonment, it is usually restored to full health and Power, and is quite angry at the person who originally bound it.

Regardless of whether a spirit is evil when it is bound, a Ritemaster gains an automatic Notoriety Trait just by performing this version of the *Rite of Binding*.

The *Rite of Binding* requires 10 minutes of game time and the attention of the Spirit Keeper.

**Rite of Summoning:** One of the most potentially powerful of rites, the *Rite of Summoning* enables a Garou to call up a spirit from the Storm Umbra. The *Rite of Summoning* is possible only because of the respect that most spirits have for the Garou; they are, after all, the defenders of Gaia. It is only when this respect is abused or when Garou do not return the spirits' respect that problems develop, particularly in the chaotic and unpredictable realm of the Storm Umbra.

The *Rite of Summoning* takes 30 minutes of game time. It is not something that is done in the middle of combat, nor can it be done off the cuff.

| Spirit Type | Basic Difficulty |
|---|---|
| Jaggling | 4 |
| Gaffling | 5 |
| Totem avatar | 6 |
| Incarna avatar | 7 |
| **Affinity** | **Difficulty Modifier** |
| Healing | +1 |
| War | +2 |
| Enigmas | 0 |
| Tribal totem | -3 |
| Pack totem | 2 |
| Wyrm | +3 |
| Weaver | +2 |
| Wyld | +3 |
| Storm-touched | +3/-3 |
| **Miscellaneous Factors** | **Modifier** |
| Summoned the spirit before | -1 |
| Knows spirit's name | -3 |
| Lupus breed | -1 |
| Theurge auspice | -1 |
| On a mission for Gaia | -2 |
| To fight the Wyrm | +2 |
| To fight another Garou | +3 |
| Will take any spirit | -4 |
| Per extra Gnosis Trait spent | -2 |
| Each Notoriety Trait of the summoner | +3 |

Summonings should only be thoroughly thought out, prepared and researched. Likewise, this rite should be as vivid and involved as possible, whether the character uses such methods as the spirit-naming songs of the Pure Ones or the archaic invocations of the Europeans. Casual or frivolous summonings can be considered disrespectful by spirits, and will have far-reaching repercussions.

The *Rite of Summoning* begins with the would-be Ritemaster informing the Spirit Keeper that he is preparing for a *Rite of Summoning.*

The Spirit Keeper then asks the Ritemaster the following questions:

What type of spirit are you trying to summon?

What is the affinity of the spirit are you trying to summon?

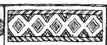

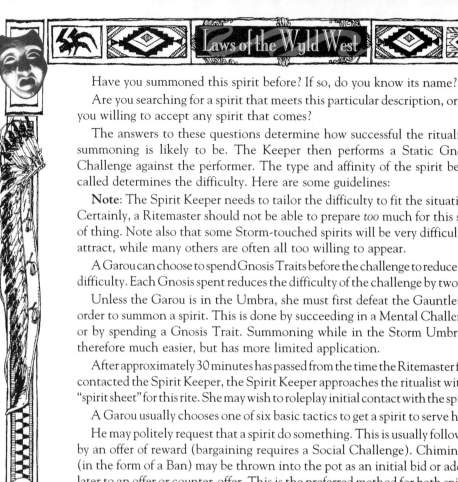

Have you summoned this spirit before? If so, do you know its name?

Are you searching for a spirit that meets this particular description, or are you willing to accept any spirit that comes?

The answers to these questions determine how successful the ritualist's summoning is likely to be. The Keeper then performs a Static Gnosis Challenge against the performer. The type and affinity of the spirit being called determines the difficulty. Here are some guidelines:

**Note**: The Spirit Keeper needs to tailor the difficulty to fit the situation. Certainly, a Ritemaster should not be able to prepare *too* much for this sort of thing. Note also that some Storm-touched spirits will be very difficult to attract, while many others are often all too willing to appear.

A Garou can choose to spend Gnosis Traits before the challenge to reduce the difficulty. Each Gnosis spent reduces the difficulty of the challenge by two.

Unless the Garou is in the Umbra, she must first defeat the Gauntlet in order to summon a spirit. This is done by succeeding in a Mental Challenge or by spending a Gnosis Trait. Summoning while in the Storm Umbra is therefore much easier, but has more limited application.

After approximately 30 minutes has passed from the time the Ritemaster first contacted the Spirit Keeper, the Spirit Keeper approaches the ritualist with a "spirit sheet" for this rite. She may wish to roleplay initial contact with the spirit.

A Garou usually chooses one of six basic tactics to get a spirit to serve him:

He may politely request that a spirit do something. This is usually followed by an offer of reward (bargaining requires a Social Challenge). Chiminage (in the form of a Ban) may be thrown into the pot as an initial bid or added later to an offer or counter-offer. This is the preferred method for both spirits and Garou, and sets up a potential future relationship between them.

The Ritemaster may command a spirit to do something, appealing to its sense of duty. This is usually followed up by a threat of some kind. (*Leadership*, Social Challenge)

The summoner may challenge the spirit to a riddle game or some other contest to vie for control, usually with some offer of a Ban burden made by the summoner to balance out the service of the spirit. (*Enigmas*, Mental Challenge)

He may use a Gift to command the spirit. Of course, this has its own potential problems.

He may use his prowess and strength to intimidate the spirit (*Intimidation*, Social Challenge).*

He may attack the spirit and force it to agree to serve him. ("Bullying" requires a Physical Challenge).

* Indicates that Notoriety may be gained by using these methods.

If the spirit wins the initial challenge, it may depart immediately. If the spirit loses, it usually serves the summoner to the best of its ability and then

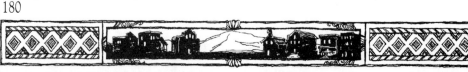

depart. A Ritemaster may continue to use commanding tactics to get the spirit to continue to serve him.

The amount of knowledge that the Spirit Keeper passes on to the summoner concerning the spirit he's attracted is determined by the relationship between the Garou and the spirit. If it's a good one, and the spirit is likely to do anything that the summoner asks, the Spirit Keeper can simply give a "spirit sheet" to the summoner. Otherwise, she has to arrange with the summoner exactly what he wants from the spirit and decide what happens as a result of the spirit's decision to obey or disobey.

## Intermediate Rites

**Rite of the Totem**: This rite binds a totem to a group of Garou (henceforth called a pack). The group begins the *Rite of the Totem* and steps into the Umbra, where it finds some trail of the spirit animal it has chosen as its pack totem. The Garou must then track the spirit animal; this is usually just a formality.

When the spirit is found, it can either agree to take the pack as its fosterlings or ask for the Garou to prove themselves worthy of recognition as a pack by performing a quest. The latter option is rare, but can make for some excellent roleplaying opportunities.

The new pack howls as one at the end of this rite, and goes immediately to the nearest tribe or sept elder to announce its new pack name and members. A feast or hunt is often planned for this occasion. If a pack of Garou want to add a member at a later time, members must agree to the addition. No challenge is needed to perform this rite, but the subject Garou must collectively purchase at least one point in the Totem Background in order to benefit from this rite. Acting out the performance of this rite, or at least reciting highlights from it, is a great way to bond a pack together, and provide them with insight into the totem that watches over them.

**Rite of the Fetish**: The *Rite of the Fetish* takes a spirit and binds it permanently into a prepared object. The object then becomes a magical thing, a fetish with specific powers. The object must be appropriate to the fetish being created. Furthermore, the item must be "purified" for three consecutive nights before it is ready to become a fetish. Fetish creation, as with spirit summoning, is not to be undertaken lightly, as an impure object offered to house a spirit can have unpredictable and unfortunate effects.

During the actual *Rite of the Fetish*, a spirit is either summoned or released near the Ritemaster in the Umbra. The spirit must be of a type and affinity appropriate to the fetish being created. The Ritemaster formally asks the spirit to enter the fetish, and sacrifices an appropriate Trait (Physical for a war fetish, Mental for a mind fetish, etc.). If the spirit complies of its own accord, the fetish behaves normally.

If the spirit is compelled in any way, however, there is a chance that the fetish will become cursed or possessed. A cursed fetish is unpleasant to use, and can lead to Wyrm-taint in anyone who wields it. On the other hand, a cursed fetish can be cleansed through repeated *Rites of Cleansing* and Gnosis sacrifices.

A possessed fetish, on the other hand, uses its powers only when it deems them to be necessary. Garou cannot argue their fetishes into performing; only a Narrator or Storyteller can decide when the fetish feels like working, and they are under no compunction to be cooperative.

The Spirit Keeper decides whether a fetish is cursed or possessed.

Casting this rite requires an hour of ritual and the sacrifice of one permanent Gnosis Trait per "level" of spirit required. See the guidelines below for required spirit types.

| Gnosis Cost | Type |
|---|---|
| 1 | Gaffling, Jaggling |
| 2 | Totem avatar |
| 3 to 5 | Incarna avatar |

Once the rite is finished, the fetish must be wrapped in red cloth (preferably silk) and must sit for an entire month. This gives the Spirit Keeper time to devise rules and game elements for the fetish, but also helps players come to grips with the level of sacrifice necessary to wield a fetish. If possible, fetishes should be represented with actual props if the rules of **Mind's Eye Theatre** permit, as it lends an excellent sense of accomplishment to the process; the Storytellers should also consider decreasing the difficulty of the rite if a player actually creates the item they are trying to make into a fetish.

## Punishment Rites

In a race as proud and honorable as the Garou, the regard and fellowship of one's peers is of paramount importance. It is no surprise, then, that Garou punishments for transgressions rely heavily on the pack, tribe and sept. Most of the time, offenders are simply punished physically or socially, but not supernaturally. The guilty party takes his lumps, accepts his punishment, and gets on with his life. This is usually enough, but for truly heinous or repeated offenses, certain rites may be brought to bear. These rites are never used lightly, but when they are, the Garou ensure that the offender never forgets his trespass.

If a Ritemaster performs a Punishment Rite on a Garou he *knows* to be innocent of her supposed crime, the rite affects the Ritemaster and any cohorts he has instead, and the rite's effects last twice as long as normal. Those who punish the innocent accidentally do not suffer this penalty.

### Basic Rites

**Rite of Ostracism**: This rite serves as a punishment by peers for those Garou who commit lesser crimes. The duration of the rite's effects varies with the severity of the crime. It can be permanent, if necessary. The Garou

**Note:** Nobody likes to be picked on. While roleplaying is recommended as much as possible when enacting rites, these rites exist as way of punishing a wayward *character*. A decision to use a Punishment Rite should be a measure of the feelings of local Garou society, not the attitudes of troupe members themselves. It is of paramount importance to remember and ensure that all punishments, insults and other shameful expressions are directed at the character, not at her player. If it looks like a Punishment Rite is getting out of hand and/or causing tempers to flare, substitute straight challenges instead. (A time out to allow everyone to cool off also might not be a bad idea.) There is no honor in picking on a helpless player, enforcing one of these rites vindictively for out of game reasons, or gloating about a character's misfortune at the end of the evening. In other words, it's obnoxious. Don't do it.

is simply ignored by other Garou, not allowed to participate in any formal functions, and may not use her Renown Traits while under the sentence of ostracism. For all practical purposes, the guilty party ceases to exist. This is an especially common practice among the Pure Ones, but is by no means exclusive to them.

Players whose characters are subjected to this rite find themselves left out of plots and unable to participate in Garou sections of a session. Conversely, the ostracized Garou may wish to put his solo time to good use, but the pack instinct that dwells in even the most solitary Garou soon begins to suffer after this rite has remained in place for some time.

**Stone of Shame:** This rite is one of the more creative forms of punishment among the Garou and is reserved for crimes against honor. The rite binds minor spirits of suffering and shame to a large rock, to which the offender is bound with a heavy chain collar. Any member of the tribe may hurl physical attacks as well as verbal insults at the guilty Garou. The punishment lasts one night, during which the subject loses a Renown Trait. This Trait is not regained until the end of the next session. No challenge is necessary to enact this rite.

**Voice of the Jackal**: A Garou can be subjected to this rite if found guilty of an act of cowardice, or of one action shameful not just to herself, but also to her sept or tribe. When the rite is performed, the Garou is cursed with a shrill, high-pitched voice (which she must roleplay), and is two Traits down on any Social Challenges involving speech. The effects of this rite last for two lunar cycles.

## Intermediate Rites

**The Hunt**: This rite is commonly enacted by a solemn circle of Garou, and is used on a Garou who is guilty of a terrible crime against his people, when amends can be made only through his death. Victims of this rite are denied shelter or aid by any other Garou. Furthermore, it is the duty of all Garou taking part in the rite to hunt down and execute the Hunt's target. After the object of the Hunt is caught and killed, his Honor is restored to him. Those few who escape the Hunt are never welcomed back, and will be killed on sight by any aware of their crime (news of which quickly spreads, if the subject is not infamous already).

**Satire Rite**: A favorite rite of the Half Moons and Moon Dancers, this ritual is a long and humiliating session where all present heap ridicule and shame upon the Garou subject. These poignant insults and ribald tales become part of the permanent oral history of the Garou. No challenge is necessary, and the Garou who is subjected to this rite loses a Glory or Honor Trait permanently.

### Advanced Rites

**Horror Beyond the Veil**: When used on a human, this rite dispels the protection of the Veil so that she can see the Garou in all their glory. The effects of the rite last for an entire night, but few spectators survive the fury of the Garou for that long. Remember, only Crinos form causes a Delirium reaction. Obviously, the precise details of this rite are shrouded in secrecy, but it is known that the first presentation of the Garou in their true form is geared to cause as much terror as possible. Many humans die of fright even before his first pursuer reaches him.

**Gaia's Vengeful Teeth**: This rite is reserved for those Garou guilty of the foulest and most horrible crimes, such as consorting with the Wyrm, or killing or causing the death of Garou. The rite has a permanent effect, and causes any natural surface the victim comes in contact with to be transmuted momentarily into razor-sharp slivers of silver. Furthermore, the effects of the rite prevent the Garou from stepping sideways. Garou thus cursed are typically run to the ground —literally. Every turn requires a Static Physical Test against 10 Traits, or the victim takes an aggravated wound. Victims of the rite who stand still suffer injuries at a rate of one aggravated wound level every three rounds. This rite begins by spreading a trail of silver powder that the victim must walk down as she leaves her sept behind, and ends with the ritual burning of whatever remains of the victim are left upon her death.

## Rites of the Pure Ones

The Pure Ones evolved a very different culture in the thousands of years apart from their European kin, and while the last hundred years have seen a furious mesh of the rituals of the two and some amazing similarities in their patterns, these rites are still known almost exclusively by Pure One septs. They are often quite intricate and elaborate, designed to coax out the powers of the spirits of the harsh West, and are considered inscrutable by many Europeans, who prefer their more straightforward ceremonies. However, as the blessing of Gaia proves, these rites are just as potent when performed successfully.

### Basic Rites

**Seam Between Worlds**: This rite is used to rally the spirits of natives and cubs and attempt to show Europeans the error of their ways, and must be performed in sight of a boundary between native and settled land. By drawing a stylized boundary line with a talen or fetish, the ritemaster must then perform the rite challenge; if successful, all Garou present must step into the Umbra. When they do, they see the line of "progress" as it truly is on the land, and Garou touched by this line feel the changes in themselves; some Iron Riders and other modernists feel it as a positive glow, but most Garou feel it is as an oily, unhealthy touch, and Pure Ones refresh their temporary Rage from the resolve to act it inspires in them. There is no tangible effect on the non-Pure Ones, but how they feel will largely be determined by their attitude toward "progress."

**Facing the Final Journey:** This rite is used when a Garou knows he is facing near certain death, and is committed to dying honorably. This rite is usually conducted with the Ritemaster and the Garou alone, although entire packs sometime take part on either side of the rite, and is a solemn affair, full of speeches about the doomed one's life and deeds, the cycle of life, and the honorable conclusion of a life well-lived. The Ritemaster must make an Extended Social Challenge against the recipient (the recipient may not choose to submit in this challenge); for each success, the target gains a temporary Trait of Rage, Gnosis and Willpower. These extra Traits may exceed the Garou's normal maximums in these categories, but not more than twice the normal maximum in each category. There is no dishonor in surviving the trial this rite is used to prepare for, but it is never used lightly, for it requires the Garou to seriously consider his life and contemplate his death. This rite often involves periods of fasting, time in sweat lodges and other ritual purification.

## Rites of Renown

These rites serve to reward those Garou who distinguish themselves in any of the Garou virtues. Many Garou dream of receiving the accolades of these rites. If a Garou is so honored for an action he did not perform, these rites fail and remove Renown in equal measure to what they might have bestowed.

There is no rules mechanic for the performance of any of these rites. Instead, they are a vital part of the experience of roleplaying Garou. The details and forms of these rites are left to individual Storytellers; what is important is what the rites stand for.

### Basic Rites

**Rite of Accomplishment**: When a Garou performs a great deed against the Wyrm or shows uncommon valor, her peers may choose to perform this rite in her honor. The *Rite of Accomplishment* is generally enacted in the stories and songs portion of a moot, and is almost invariably presided over by Galliards. Its purpose is to award a Garou Renown for a recent deed. The Ritemaster extols the virtues of the supplicant, and while no challenge is made, any Garou who dispute the claim to Renown can do so. If the majority of Garou present ignore the disputant, the subject receives the Renown Trait; if not, she may not try again for that Trait for at least one lunar cycle.

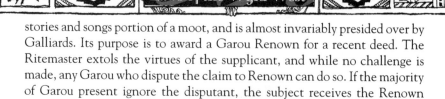

**Rite of Passage**: This rite serves as the "coming of age" ceremony for Garou. It is the time when a Garou's true nature is awakened, and she is introduced to her fellows as well as her heritage. Usually, some quest or trial must also be performed instead of a challenge, though the details of this trial can vary greatly. Before she passes through this rite, a young Garou may not question or challenge her elders, and she has no voice within Garou society.

### Intermediate Rites

**Brand of Honor**: This Rite is becoming increasingly common on the frontier, where the rough life has toughened even the hardy Garou. Although pioneered by Europeans, it is now in use on both sides of the frontier, and is one of the highest honors a Garou can earn. Typically, it is earned in defense of a caern, although similar great actions for a sept may warrant this rite as well. The Garou honored with this rite is branded with the sept's unique pictogram, which remains visible in all her forms. The Garou so branded sustains an aggravated wound and must make a Static Willpower Challenge to avoid frenzy; if successful, however, the Garou earns a Glory Trait for her valor. Some Garou have taken to wandering about collecting pictograms from as many septs as possible; each additional pictogram earned gives the owner a chance to test for an additional Glory Trait (meaning the second can be worth two, the third three, etc.) at the next moot.

## Seasonal Rites

In ancient times, the Garou — men, women and wolves — had to stay keenly aware of the seasons. Failing to do so meant starving in the bitter winter cold, broiling in the summer heat or not being prepared to take advantage of the fertile spring or abundant autumn. On a grander scale, the seasons reflect Gaia's own eternal cycle of yearly renewal.

### Basic Rites

**Rite of the Hunting Grounds:** The Garou using this rite may choose to mark an area as her own, her pack's, her sept's or her tribe's. After the rite is finished, Garou and natural wolves instantly recognize the ritualist's mark for what it is. Others with enhanced sensory powers realize something is strange, but do not recognize its importance without winning an *Occult* Mental Challenge (against eight Traits and risking two).

**Rite of the Equinox:** This is not so much one rite as a tradition of associated rites performed at the turning times of the year. Each tribe and sept has different ceremonies for each equinox, but some common themes, moods, and requirements of each celebration follow:

**Winter Solstice**: This rite, performed at the darkest time of the night, is a solemn and vigilant time for the Garou, as they renew their commitment against the minions of the Wyrm during the long nights and short days. Other than the initial challenge, there are no game mechanics associated with this rite, although it is arguably the worst time of the year a Wyrm-creature could choose to be in the area of a caern.

**Vernal Equinox**: Garou are creatures of great vitality and emotion as well as guards and warriors, and this rite of spring allows the Garou to celebrate the rebirth of Gaia and the beginning of a new year for the earth itself. This rite is typically an occasion for great merriment and passion, and many Kinfolk are allowed into the caern at this time, ensuring that the festivities last long into the night; many cubs are conceived on this equinox. This is also a time where tribes close to the fae folk, such as the Fianna and the Uktena, often invite their "cousins" to attend the festival, ensuring an even wilder time for all those present as the two sides try to out-jest and out-romance each other.

**Midsummer's Eve**: A time of great power and strength for the Garou, Midsummer's Eve has become a rite where many tests of ability, contests of strength and wit, and other trials between members of the sept are common. Growing more common with the times are incidences of intrigue and tribal politics during this rite, and as it commonly recognized as a time to challenge leaders and elders, it is not unheard of for this rite to descend into violence.

**Autumnal Equinox**: Often an even more solemn and sad time than the winter solstice, the autumn rites are typically a time when the sept looks to the growing shadow of the Wyrm spreading across the continent, the touch of the Storm Eater around them (if they even know of it), and contemplation of the dying year and coming winter. Many great old tales of Garou history are told at this time, and packs often swear to courageous or even foolhardy quests in an effort to quench the fear that this rite fosters in their hearts.

## Minor Rites

These rites each take about 15 minutes to perform, during which time the Garou character must be out of play. The modifiers these rites grant are not cumulative, but an individual Garou can receive the modifiers from a number of different Minor Rites equal to her Rank.

**Chant of the Run:** This rite is often used before a journey is begun. The werewolf must stamp or shuffle his feet while turning slowly in a circle and chanting to Gaia for guidance. Once completed, the Garou must step sideways, where glowing tracks will show him the best way. The Garou gains a free retest on any travel-related tests as long as he performs this rite every morning of the trip.

**Prayers for Rain:** This rite can be enacted by one werewolf or a pack, and is performed by dancing in a circle and calling to Gaia to bring rain. It is entirely the Storyteller's discretion as to whether or not this rite actually works, though it does seem to rain more often in days following this rite, and any uses of Gifts that control weather to bring rain after this rite receive a free retest.

**Welcome Luna:** If a Garou performs this rite, which consists of howling an elaborate greeting to the moon, over three consecutive sessions, she gains a free retest that can be spent on any Social Challenge.

**Hail the Sun:** This rite is identical to *Welcome Luna*, but is done at sunrise. This gives the Garou one free retest when sensing for Wyrm-taint or Wyrm-creatures. This free retest returns each session so long as the Garou does not miss performing the greeting each session.

**Hunt Blessing:** The Garou chooses a common item (a bowl, knife or candle will do), and prays in praise to Gaia over the item for three consecutive sessions. The Garou thereafter receives one free retest per session when hunting. If the item is lost or is not taken hunting with the Garou, he must start the process over with a different item.

**Tear for the Prey:** The Garou steps into the Umbra just after making a kill, whether in the hunt or on the battlefield, and thanks the spirit of the fallen for giving its life for the Garou. This is considered a sign of respect to Gaia, Her children and to life itself. If a Garou does this for four consecutive sessions, the Garou gains one free retest whenever dealing with nature-related spirits. To keep this advantage, the Garou must perform this rite over every beast of Gaia (not including Wyrm-spawn) that she slays.

## Merits and Flaws

Merits and Flaws are optional defining Traits that give you a way to make your character unique. A Merit is a descriptive Trait that applies to your character and gives him a slight advantage in some area, while a Flaw gives your Garou a slight disadvantage. You may buy Merits only during character creation, unless you earn them during a story (and with Storyteller approval). To buy Merits during character creation, you may spend only Traits from Flaws (maximum of seven), Backgrounds (maximum of five), Abilities (maximum of five) or Traits earned by taking Negative Traits (maximum of five); the maximum number of Merit Traits allowed is seven. Your character will not suffer if you do not have any Merits or Flaws, but putting all your points into Merits and Flaws will assuredly handicap you in other areas.

You can also take Flaw Traits and use them to buy other Traits — Abilities and Backgrounds — at a one-for-one ratio.

Merits and Flaws might be restricted in some stories, or not purchasable at all. Make certain that you talk with your Storyteller before buying any Merits or Flaws, as some of the ones listed below may be disallowed. Merits and Flaws are optional parts of a character, and **Wyld West** can be played quite well without a single Merit or Flaw.

Remember that you must have Storyteller approval on all Merits and Flaws you want for your character. Once gameplay starts, Merits and Flaws may be purchased or bought off only with Storyteller approval, and at double the Trait cost listed in Experience.

You may never purchase a Flaw that duplicates a Flaw already inherent in your character because of breed, tribe, etc. You are also not allowed to double up an existing advantage with a Merit.

Again, because of space considerations, only those Merits that have specifically been changed for or added to the **Wyld West** setting are listed in full here.

## Aptitudes

Use the Merits and Flaws listed on pp. 141-142 of **Laws of the Wild**.

Merits: *Ability Aptitude* (1), *Ambidextrous* (1), *Pitiable* (1), *Daredevil* (3), *Jack of All Trades* (5), *Peacetalker* (5, as *Natural Peacemaker*), *Outmaneuver* (5)

Flaws: *Illiterate* (1), *Inept* (5)

## Awareness

Use the Merits and Flaws found on pp. 142 of **Laws of the Wild**.

Merits: *Acute Sense* (1), *Local Gossip* (5, as *Pulse of the City*), *Umbral Sight* (5)

Flaws: *Weak Sense* (1), *One Eye* (2), *Deaf* (4), *Blind* (6)

## Garou Ties

Use the Merits and Flaws found on pp. 143 of **Laws of the Wild**.

Merits: *Favors* (1-7)

Flaws: *Twisted Upbringing* (1), *Enemy* (1-5), *Social Outcast* (3), *Unworthy* (3)

**Tribal Ties (2 Trait Merit)**: Through hard work and shared experience, or perhaps simple patience, you have managed to become accepted by another tribe; they will not necessarily teach you tribal Gifts or other secrets, but they will do their best to aid and shelter you when necessary, and they and their Kinfolk are friendly to you unless provoked. You are two Traits up on any Social Challenges dealing with honestly befriending or gaining the trust of any members of this tribe or their Kinfolk. This can be a very handy Merit in the wide open spaces of the Savage West, where your own kin can be few and far between, but it will also mark you as a sympathizer to any forces unfriendly to this tribe. This could even lead to loss of Renown if the befriended tribe is badly at odds with your own, and your kin find out. The Trait cost of this Merit should be increased for truly unlikely combinations (Bone Gnawer to Silver Fang, most Europeans to Wendigo), not to mention that such a friendship should require an exceptional story.

**Tribal Enmity (2 Trait Flaw):** For one reason or another, you have attracted the ire of another tribe, and while they will not simply walk up and attack you, they will do their best to make your life miserable however they can, and seem naturally disposed to dislike you. They also will most certainly use force if they feel you offer the slightest threat to them or their Kinfolk. You are two Traits down on any Social Challenges involving this tribe other than Gifts, and may bring dishonor on packmates or others close to you if they are members of this tribe. Obviously, the tribe chosen should be one that is present fairly frequently in the chronicle, and Storytellers should disallow players from taking this Flaw more than once without a truly excellent story.

## Human Society

Use the Merits and Flaws on p. 143 of **Laws of the Wild**.

Merits: *Weaver's Children* (5)
Flaws: *Stubborn Relatives* (2, as *Persistent Parents*), *Ward* (3), *Hunted* (3)

**Gunslinging Reputation (1-3 Trait Merit or Flaw):** Whether or not it's accurate, you've earned notice in gunfighting circles, and now carry a certain reputation with you wherever you go. If you take this Trait as a Merit, you are widely respected and even feared for your prowess, and may add the Trait value of the Merit to all Social Challenges involving intimidation. Additionally, you are considered to be up the number of Traits of this Merit in the staredown challenge if you are using the optional gunfighting rules on page 228. However, you must constantly deal with being challenged by young upstarts seeking to make their own reputation at the cost of your hide. If this Trait is a Flaw, you are seen as something of a joke in gunfighting circles, and unless you win a quick draw in a person's presence, you are down a number of Traits equal to the value of the Flaw to any intimidation challenges with that person. Your opponent is up the same number of Traits on the staredown challenge if the optional gunfighting rules are used, as she perceives little threat from you. You also have trouble getting serious gunfighters to accept your challenges, as they see you as a waste of time and bullets, making your reputation unlikely to improve any time soon. Bear in mind that, Merit or Flaw, this Trait does not affect the actual speed of your hands in any way, just how fast other people *think* you are.

**Outlaw (2-5 Trait Flaw):** Innocent or not, you got accused of some serious wrong in the past, and whoever it was you angered has put a warrant out for your arrest and/or a bounty on your head. Your likeness is becoming a familiar sight in the areas you travel, and wherever you go, you face the threat of law enforcement officers and freelance bounty hunters trying to bring you in. While they are not aware of your Garou nature (that is the *Hunted* Flaw, above), they are quite bothersome at times, and killing one will only bring others closer. The seriousness of the warrant and/or the size of the reward determine the value of this Merit: being "Wanted: Alive" is worth two Traits, the classic "Wanted: Dead or Alive" is worth three, and being "Wanted: Dead" is worth four. The Storyteller may also add one Trait to these values if the reward is particularly high, as it generally increases the quality and zeal of your pursuers. You must also decide how you came to be wanted, who put the mark out on you, and under what conditions it could be removed (if any).

## Mental

Use the Merits and Flaws on p. 144 of **Laws of the Wild**.

Merits: *Time Sense* (1), *Light Sleeper* (2), *Calm Heart* (3), *Warrior's Heart* (5)

Flaws: *Deep Sleeper* (1), *Amnesia* (2), *Confused* (2), *Absent-Minded* (3), *Blind Commitment* (3), *Low Self-Control* (3), *Weak-Willed* (3)

**Iron Will (5 Trait Merit, updated):** Once your mind is made up, nothing can thwart you from achieving your goals. You may automatically resist the effects of the vampiric *Dominate* Discipline with the expenditure of a Willpower Trait (rendering you immune to that vampire's *Dominate* powers for the remainder of the evening), and you are extremely resistant to other powers that affect your mind or emotions, gaining one free retest in such challenges.

## Physical

Use the Merits and Flaws on pp. 145-146 in **Laws of the Wild**.

Merits: *Double-Jointed* (1), *Bad Taste* (2), *Fair Glabro* (2), *Lack of Scent* (2), *Longevity* (2), *Huge Size* (4), *Metamorph* (6)

Flaws: *Animal Musk* (1), *Strict Carnivore* (1), *Disfigured* (2), *Monstrous* (2), *Short* (2), *Deformity* (3), *Partially Lame* (3, as *Partially Crippled*), *Wolf Years* (3), *One Arm* (4), *Mute* (5)

## Psychological

Use the Merits and Flaws on pp. 146-149 of **Laws of the Wild**.

Merits: *Code of Honor* (1), *Higher Purpose* (1), *Berserker* (2), *Inner Peace* (5)

Flaws: *Compulsion* (1), *Dark Secret* (1), *Intolerance* (1), *Nightmares* (1), *Overconfident* (1), *Shy* (1), *Speech Impediment* (1), *Low Self-Image* (2), *Pack Mentality* (2), *Soft-Hearted* (2), *Vengeance* (2), *Driving Goal* (3), *Hatred* (3), *Phobia (Mild)* (3), *Quirk* (3), *Short Fuse* (3), *Territorial* (3), *Phobia (Severe)* (5)

## Supernatural

Use the Merits and Flaws on pp. 149-152 of **Laws of the Wild**.

Merits: *True Love* (1), *Danger Sense* (2), *Faerie Affinity* (2), *Magic Resistance* (2), *Medium* (2), *Moon Bound* (2), *Luck* (3), *Natural Channel* (3), *Spirit Mentor* (3), *Destiny* (4), *Charmed Life* (5, as *Charmed Existence*), *Gaia's Fury* (5), *Totem's Siblings* (5), *Resistant to Wyrm Emanations* (5), *Mysterious Guardian* (6), *True Faith* (7)

Flaws: *Slip Sideways* (1), *Foe from the Past* (1-3), *Forced Transformation* (1-4), *Banned Transformation* (1-6), *Mark of the Predator* (2), *Sign of the Wolf* (2), *Haunted* (3), *Limited Affinity to Gaia* (3), *Pierced Veil* (3), *Dark Fate* (5), *Taint of Corruption* (7)

**Silver Tolerance (7 Trait Merit, updated):** You have partial immunity to the adverse effects of silver. You still receive aggravated wounds from silver, but you do not suffer any sort of Trait penalty when fighting against an opponent with a silver weapon. This Merit should be watched carefully, as it can be exceedingly powerful in certain chronicles, and is one of the rarest Traits a Garou can possess.

# Example of Character Creation

Sarah, searching for an alternative to the Dark Ages machinations of the vampiric Jyhad but not looking for another modern werewolf fable, decides she wants to try something a bit different, and joins a local group for a game of the **Wyld West**. Pete, the Storyteller of that game, comes by to help her out with any questions she might have during the character creation process, and together they sit down and start working on a concept.

### Step One: Concept

Sarah spends a bit of time on this, trying to find just the right role to portray. Having played **Laws of the Wild** before, she's somewhat familiar with the basic themes of Garou life, but Sarah is still a bit careful of assuming too much — this is the Savage West, after all! First she considers what breed her character will be, and settles on homid, something she's sure she can play accurately. Working with that basic notion, she starts envisioning a wanderer, someone who goes from town to town in search of a good tale, good drink and a good scrap. The Fianna tribe seems a natural choice given these interests, and proud of her own Celtic heritage, Sarah feels she will be able to depict that side of her character very well. Thinking on this combination for a minute, a name suddenly comes to her: Patricia McKinnon. She jots that down in her notebook, makes a note to think of "Garou name" later, and looks to the next area.

Nature and Demeanor take a bit more time; from the impression of Pat that Sarah's getting, Pat definitely has a Jester Demeanor, as she always has a ready joke and never takes anything overly seriously. However, a Nature is harder to come by — Sarah wants Pat to be a more complicated character underneath, not simply a one-dimensional bit of comic relief. After some more consideration, she gives Pat the Deviant Nature, underscoring her light-hearted manner with a steely personality and a powerful determination to walk her own path. These are just the kind of qualities a woman used to traveling alone in the Savage West would need, and Sarah makes a note to buy Traits reflecting those attributes later on in character creation. She'll also have to decide just what it is Pat embodies or believes in that makes her so committed to living outside society's norms, but as her wandering stranger concept already somewhat fulfills this role, it'll do for now. Now all that's left to ponder in Pat's basic concept is her auspice.

Sarah considers the Galliard auspice, with its high Rage and love of stories, but decides that a Fianna Galliard is too typical a character, and anyway Pat's sense of humor prevents her from taking even the creative duties of a Moon Dancer seriously enough. The more Sarah thinks about it, there's only once choice that makes sense, and with an evil chuckle Sarah writes down Ragabash as Pat's auspice. Having finished her basic concept, she gives it to Pete to look over, in order to ensure it doesn't clash with the pack and storyline he's developed. Fortunately for Pat, the game centers around a rather motley pack in a run-down town that no other sept wanted, and so a Deviant Ragabash just happens to fit right in. Now it's time to start picking some other Traits, to help define Pat's essence in game terms.

## Step Two: Attributes

Sarah has to prioritize Pat's Attribute categories now, to determine her basic strengths and weaknesses. Normally, Ragabash take Social as their primary, but Pat is already a bit of a rebel, and Sarah decides this is just another area Pat shatters expectations in. She assigns Physical as Pat's primary Trait category, Mental as her secondary and Social as her tertiary. Seeing Pete's quizzical look, Sarah explains that Pat has learned most of all how to take care of herself and stay in shape on the frontier (Physical), that she's always alert for a swindle or an ambush (Mental), and that she used to have a lot of problems relating to people due to her different beliefs (Social). Sarah then says that Pat has overcome some of her problems with people now, which will be illustrated by increasing her Social Traits later. Pete agrees, liking the development he's seeing, and Sarah now goes on to picking specific traits for each category.

First she does Physical, with seven Traits. Thinking about how Pat is built and how she fights, Sarah chooses Athletic, Ferocious, Nimble, Quick, Tenacious, *Tough, Wiry*. This gives her a well-rounded fighter, natural athlete and all-around tough customer, which suits Pat's independent lifestyle just fine. Next is Mental, with five traits, and she picks the Traits *Alert, Creative, Cunning, Observant, Wily*— good ones for any Ragabash! Finally comes Social, with but three Traits. Sarah thinks hard on this one; she knows she wants to improve this category later, but first she has to show what Pat started with. She settles for *Beguiling, Gorgeous* and *Seductive*, and now Pat is ready for the next step.

## Step Three: Advantages

Staring down five choices for Abilities, Sarah spends a bit more time on this area, since there are so many which seem to fit Pat's personality. Deciding to cover the bases first, she elects to give Pat a broad range of Abilities, letting her attempt a wide variety of tasks. First Sarah takes a level of *Melee*, as she envisions Pat wielding a wicked pair of Bowie knives for her usual weapons (departing from the standard everyone's-got-a-gun Western stereotype, much to Pete's relief). Next, Sarah takes a level each of *Gambling* and *Ride*, letting Pat indulge in the games of her choice and make it to the next town in a hurry when some of her Ragabash tricks are discovered. As Pat has spent so much of her time on the road, Sarah puts the last of her Abilities into two levels of *Linguistics*, selecting as her languages Irish Gaelic (from her childhood with the Fianna) and Swedish (taught by some grateful Get Kinfolk near that same community).

Surveying the wide range of Gifts available to her character, Sarah can't quite decide what to choose — so many of them seem handy to a person with Pat's lifestyle. As most Garou are more inclined to learn Gifts in tune with their own personal philosophies, Sarah ultimately decides to let Pat's personality and past history dictate the Gifts she knows. For Pat's breed Gift, Sarah chooses *Jam Gun* — Pat's had one too many sore losers aiming to get even with her before, and it allows her knives to be even more effective. Moving on to her auspice Gift, Sarah selects *Walk Under the New Moon*, a handy talent when it comes to Pat sneaking around or saving her hide from a group of enemies. Finally, she chooses *Resist Toxin* for her tribe Gift, as Pat's a tough customer, and has learned how to handle more than a strong glass of liquor in her time on the frontier.

Now for Backgrounds. Right away Sarah chooses four levels of Kinfolk, reflecting Pat's huge family, which has continued to support her even through her days as the latest Fianna hellion to walk the Savage West. With such a family, in most places she visits Pat usually has no trouble in finding someone who, if not related, at least knows of her family and is willing to lend her a hand. The final Trait goes to a level of the Totem Background, since although Sarah doesn't yet know what her pack's name or totem is, she wants Pat to be ready to carry her share of supporting their totem avatar. Pete takes note as well, adding that Trait to the pool the pack has already assembled.

Seeing that choosing Renown is the next part of character creation, Sarah checks her auspice requirements and sees that Ragabash get to choose three Traits in any combination. She decides to give Pat one Trait in each category, to show the broad range of adventures that this wild Fianna has already had at her tender age. Her final choices are *Crafty*, *Proud* and *Spirited* all of which are easily explained by Pat's forceful and light-hearted personality.

## Step Four: Finishing Touches

It's time to record starting totals and fill in any remaining details. Sarah starts by recording Pat's starting Rage, Gnosis and Willpower totals, which are decided by her auspice, breed and tribe, respectively. Checking the appropriate charts, she finds a Ragabash starts with one Rage Trait and fills that in Ñ a little low for someone like Pat, but that's always something that can be improved during gameplay. Likewise, homids such as Pat start with one Gnosis Trait, but as Pat isn't overly spiritual, this suits her just fine for now, so Sarah jots that down. Fianna begin play with two Willpower Traits, which Sarah feels captures Pat's level of determination, and she fills that Trait in. Sarah also marks her sheet to indicate these Traits are all full when play begins, as all characters start with full Rage, Gnosis, and Willpower. Looking up the Fianna Tribe Drawback, *Wyld Heart*, Sarah notes on her character sheet Pat's decreased resistance to emotion-based powers and a difficulty increase if Pat suppresses her passions. Sarah doesn't mind too much, though, as this Drawback plays right into her conception of Pat anyway, high-spirited and often unable to keep her emotions in check.

At this time, Sarah also takes a look at the Fianna Tribe Advantage, *Heirloom*, which allows her to begin play with an item equivalent to a three-Trait fetish. Looking over the fetish lists, she sees that Fang Daggers cost three Traits, and gets a wonderfully wicked vision of a character with Pat's skill at knives wielding such a blade. However, as fetishes are normally chosen by the Storyteller, Sarah presents her case to Pete, explaining how Pat learned her *Melee* skill as a way to prepare herself to be worthy to receive her family heirloom, and how she proudly displays and cares for the Fang Dagger while on the road, adding a nice roleplaying quirk to her character at the same time. Pete, seeing her enthusiasm and impressed by her quick but eloquent history, gives his permission to own a Fang Dagger for her Tribe Advantage, writing up and signing a prop card to this effect for her to use in play.

Now it's time to decide whether Sarah wishes to take any Merits, Flaws or Negative Traits to further delineate her character. On consideration,

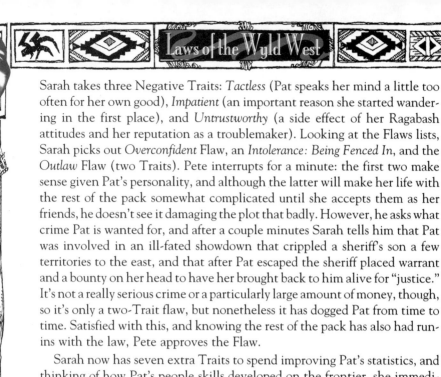

Sarah takes three Negative Traits: *Tactless* (Pat speaks her mind a little too often for her own good), *Impatient* (an important reason she started wandering in the first place), and *Untrustworthy* (a side effect of her Ragabash attitudes and her reputation as a troublemaker). Looking at the Flaws lists, Sarah picks out *Overconfident* Flaw, an *Intolerance: Being Fenced In*, and the *Outlaw* Flaw (two Traits). Pete interrupts for a minute: the first two make sense given Pat's personality, and although the latter will make her life with the rest of the pack somewhat complicated until she accepts them as her friends, he doesn't see it damaging the plot that badly. However, he asks what crime Pat is wanted for, and after a couple minutes Sarah tells him that Pat was involved in an ill-fated showdown that crippled a sheriff's son a few territories to the east, and that after Pat escaped the sheriff placed warrant and a bounty on her head to have her brought back to him alive for "justice." It's not a really serious crime or a particularly large amount of money, though, so it's only a two-Trait flaw, but nonetheless it has dogged Pat from time to time. Satisfied with this, and knowing the rest of the pack has also had run-ins with the law, Pete approves the Flaw.

Sarah now has seven extra Traits to spend improving Pat's statistics, and thinking of how Pat's people skills developed on the frontier, she immediately adds the Social Traits *Expressive* and *Witty*, at a total cost of two Traits. This raises her overall total Social Traits to five — not bad at all. She then puts a trait into the Rites Background and asks Pete if Pat can know the *Rite of Talisman Dedication* before play begins, figuring that Pat has learned how to keep all her gear with her throughout her changes in form. A character cannot normally know rites when play begins (Storyteller permission is needed), but Pete agrees, as he knows the pack will have trouble finding elders to teach new rites and thus needs all the ones they can get to start with. Her next extra Trait goes into another level of the *Linguistics* Ability, and after asking Pete what native tribes are in the area the game is centered around, Sarah chooses Navajo for the language, explaining it by saying a native mysteriously aided Pat while coming to this territory during her escape from the vengeful sheriff back East, and how Pat picked up a good deal of his lingo as they traveled together. For her last three extra Traits, Sarah selects the Ragabash Gift: *Scent of Running Water*, which is just another trick Pat has picked up along the way. Sarah's ready for the final stage.

## Step Five: Spark of Life

All the game mechanics, Traits, powers and skills are now laid out. Sarah has a much clearer picture of Pat than when she first started, but there are still some things not covered, things that can't be captured by rules and character sheets; specifically, the details that make Pat live and breathe to the other players. Sarah has to think about ways to convey her character's personality to the other players, and a host of little identifying quirks that come with roleplaying her. How does Pat dress? Does she have an immigrant's accent, or have the languages she's learned combined into a distinctive blend? Does she snort instead of laugh, or sigh when someone starts lecturing her? When she walks, does she accent her feminine physique, or belly up to the bar like any other dusty old soul? There are countless subtleties that can be added to make a character seem more real, and which make for an entertaining and memorable personality for everyone in a game to interact with. Furthermore, a little more work on a character history can't hurt — the Traits Sarah has selected paint the outline of an interesting past, but fleshing it out is still definitely possible. What are the names of the vengeful sheriff and his son? What other places has Pat seen? Does she have any real friends outside of the pack? What are some of her favorite stories of her adventures?

Most importantly of all, Sarah realizes that she hasn't given Pat her Garou name yet, the title she earned from her Rite of Passage, and looks at the personality and history she's created so far. Sarah feels that ultimately Pat is searching for what's right for her and her alone, and isn't afraid to break any kind of boundaries along the way to finding out what that is, something the Garou have recognized. A minute later it comes to her: Fights-for-Truth. Sarah likes the sound of it, and now Pat's as ready as she'll ever be to begin. Sarah has played enough **Mind's Eye Theatre** before to realize that characters are really never finished, especially before play begins, and that all sorts of details and behaviors unforeseen during creation emerge in play as the character matures and the player practices playing her Traits. She turns her sheet over to Pete to inspect, and seeing that all the totals add up and she's got enough of a history and personality to get started role-playing, he approves it. Fights-For-Truth stands ready to walk the trails of the Savage West, and the next session will see another one of Gaia's warriors coming through the saloon doors....

# Chapter Three: Rules

There are times when a player wants to have her character do something that can't be accomplished through simple roleplaying, such as attacking another person, picking a lock or riding through a thunderstorm at night. When this happens, you need rules.

Rules are an imperative part of any game; they define what characters can and cannot do. Still, the primary focus of this game is to tell a good story, and it's always best to try to defeat your opponents through roleplaying and manipulation rather than by direct confrontation. When confrontation does occur, though, rules are necessary to govern those situations.

## Time

Time in **Mind's Eye Theatre** works as it does in real life. It moves forward inexorably, relentlessly. For the most part, everything is played out in real time, and players are expected to stay in character unless they have a rules question.

It is assumed that a player is always "in character" during the course of a story. A player should never drop character when interacting with other players. Doing so ruins the atmosphere for everyone involved. Challenges may be talked through, but a player is always considered to be active in the game. If a player needs to take a break, he should inform a Narrator. That player should not interact with any of the other players while out of character.

The only other exception to the "in-character rule" is when a Narrator calls for a "time-out." This may be necessary to resolve a dispute or to change the scene if the story calls for it. When "Time-out!" is called, all players within hearing distance must stop whatever they are doing until the Narrator calls out, "Resume." Time-outs should be kept to a minimum, since they interrupt the flow of the story.

# Challenges

During the course of most stories, there comes a time when two or more players come into conflicts that cannot be resolved through roleplaying alone. The system detailed in this chapter allows for the resolution of conflicts simply and quickly, whether they're firefights or tests of will. This sort of face-off is called a challenge, and it makes for a very simple system of conflict resolution. In most cases, a Narrator does not even need to be present when a challenge is played.

Roleplaying does not necessarily have to end when a challenge begins. Experienced players can seamlessly integrate a challenge into their roleplaying so that outsiders don't know that anything unusual is going on. At the players' option, hand signals can be used to indicate when certain Traits and powers are being employed.

In order for this system to work, players need to work together. They have to educate each other on the rules and agree on what Traits can be used in a challenge. Compromise and cooperation are the bywords of the game. Arguments over whether or not a particular Trait bid is appropriate wreck both the momentum and the mood of a game.

The challenge system presented in this chapter is part of the basic rules for the **Mind's Eye Theater** system. Although alterations would need to be made to recreate the historical elements of the Savage West with other games in the series, with just a little extra effort players can have werewolves interact with vampires, wraiths, changelings, mortals and other types of characters. (See the Setting chapter for more details.) This system of challenges is also included in **Laws of the Night, Oblivion** and **The Shining Host**.

## Using Traits

Before you can begin to learn how challenges work, you must first understand what defines a character's capabilities. A character is created by choosing a number of adjectives that describe and define that person as an individual. These adjectives are called Traits, and are fully described in Chapter Two. These Traits are used to declare challenges against other characters or against static forces represented by a Narrator.

## Initial Bid

A challenge begins by a player "bidding" one of her Traits against her opponent. At the same time, she must declare what the conditions of the challenge are — firing a gun, attacking with a klaive, etc. The defender must then decide how she will respond. She can either relent immediately or bid one of her own Traits in response.

When players bid Traits against one another, they may only use Traits that could sensibly be used in that situation. Essentially, this means a player can usually only use Traits from the same category as her opponent's Traits. Most challenges are categorized as Physical, Social or Mental, and all Traits used in a challenge must be from the same category. Experienced players may offer each other more creative leeway, but that sort of arrangement works strictly by mutual agreement; don't try it out on an unsuspecting newcomer.

If the defender relents, she automatically loses the challenge. For example, if she were being attacked, she would suffer a wound. If she matches the challenger's bid, the two immediately go to a test (described below). Those Traits bid are put at risk, as the loser of the test not only loses the challenge, but the Trait she bid as well for the rest of the evening.

## Testing

Once both parties involved in a challenge have bid a Trait, they immediately go to a test. The test itself is not what you may think — the outcome is random, but no cards or dice are used. The two players face off against one another by playing Rock-Paper-Scissors. It may sound a little silly, but it works.

If you lose the test, you lose the Trait you bid for the duration of the story (usually the rest of the evening). Essentially, you have lost some confidence in your own capabilities and can't call upon them for a while. You can no longer use that Trait effectively, at least until you regain confidence in your Traits.

The test works like the moment in poker when the cards are turned over and the winner is declared. The test produces one of two possible outcomes — either one player is the victor, or the result is a tie.

In the case of a tie, the players must then reveal the number of Traits that they currently have available in the category used (Physical, Social or Mental). The player with the least number of Traits loses the test and therefore loses the challenge. Note that the number of Traits you've lost in previous challenges, or lost for any other reason, reduces the maximum number of Traits you can bid in ties. The trick to the declaration is that you may lie about the number of Traits you possess, but only by declaring fewer Traits than you actually have — you may never lie and say that you have more Traits than you actually do. This allows you to keep the actual number of Traits you possess a secret, although doing so may be risky. The challenger is always the first to declare his number of Traits. If both players declare the same number of Traits, then the challenge is a draw, and both players lose the Traits they bid.

**Example of Play:** Kat, a saloon keeper, is trying to chase down Lucas, a Nuwisha troublemaker, and teach him a lesson. She begins by bidding a Physical Trait ("I *Dexterously* grab hold of your arm and keep you from getting away.") and Lucas, knowing it's in his best interest not to hang around, responds in kind ("I am *Nimble* enough to evade you and leap out the saloon doors."). They do a test: both shoot scissors, a tie. They now compare Traits: Kat has six Physical Traits, while Lucas has only five. Kat wins, and the unlucky coyote not only loses a Trait from the challenge, but now must sit through a long Black Fury lecture on the virtue of playing cards honestly in her establishment.

Incidentally, certain advanced powers allow some characters to use gestures other than Rock, Paper and Scissors. Before players can use the gestures in a test, however, they must explain what they are and how they are used.

### Rock-Paper-Scissors

If you do not happen to know (or remember) what we mean by Rock-Paper-Scissors, here's the concept: you and another person face off, and, on the count of three, show one of three hand gestures. "Rock" is a basic fist. "Paper" is just a flat hand. "Scissors" is represented by sticking out two fingers. You then compare the two gestures to determine the winner. Rock crushes Scissors. Scissors cuts Paper. Paper covers Rock. Identical signs indicate a tie.

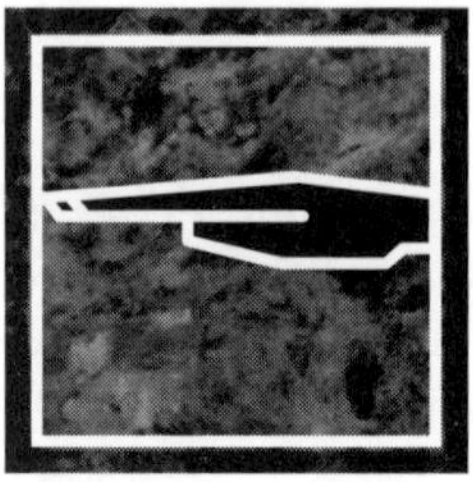

### Adjudication

If you have question or argument about the rules or the conditions of a challenge, you need to find a Narrator to make a judgment. Try to remain in character while you look for a Narrator. Any interruption in the progress of the story should be avoided if at all possible, so work problems out with other players if you can. If you do not know the correct application of a certain rule, it's usually better to wing it rather than interrupt the flow of the game. Cooperation is the key to telling a good story.

## Complications

There are a number of ways in which a challenge can be made more complicated. The basic rules are enough to resolve most disputes, but the following rules add a few bells and whistles.

### Retests

Certain Gifts, Abilities and special characteristics allow retests on a given challenge. In this case, the loser of a challenge may call for a new test, and take the results of that test instead. Any Traits bid in the initial challenge are still lost, but the loser now has the opportunity to turn the tables on his foe.

However, no source of retests can be claimed more than once on any given challenge. For instance, if a character engaged in a brawl wants to use the *Brawl* Ability to call for a retest, he cannot use another level of *Brawl* to retest again if the initial retest fails — he must rely on an overbid, the use of a special Merit or the like. However, the *Brawl* Ability could be used on the next challenge (presumably on the next attack), if necessary.

### Negative Traits

Many characters have Negative Traits; these are Traits that can be used against a character by his opponent. During the initial bid of any challenge, after you have each bid one Trait, you can call out a Negative Trait that you believe your opponent possesses. If he does indeed possess the Negative Trait, your opponent is forced to bid an additional Trait, although you must still risk your one Trait as usual. If he does not possess that Negative Trait, *you* must risk an additional Trait. You may call out as many Negative Traits as you wish during the initial bid phase of a challenge, as long as you can pay the price if you're wrong.

If your opponent does not have additional Traits to bid, then your Trait is not at risk during the challenge. Additionally if you guess more than one Negative Trait that your opponent cannot match, you gain that many additional Traits in the case of a tie or an overbid. The same works in reverse, favoring your opponent if you do not have additional Traits remaining to match incorrect Negative Trait guesses.

**Example of Play:** Sam, Iron Rider Ahroun, and Patricia, Fianna Ragabash, are in the middle of a drinking contest, which they have decided will be a Physical Challenge. The players both take a swig of the iced tea they're substituting for liquor, and Sam bids his Trait ("You think you're as *Rugged* as I am, little lady?"). Patricia smiles and responds with her Trait ("*Tough* enough to take you on, sure."). Sam then attempts to up the ante by suggesting that Patricia is *Delicate* ("Why, you're as wavy as a wheat field! You're too *Delicate* for this kind of contest!."). However, Patricia does not possess this Trait ("*Delicate*? Hah! In yer dreams! Now drink up!") Now Sam must bid an additional Trait, such as *Enduring*, if he wishes to continue the challenge.

It can be risky to bid Negative Traits, but if you're sure about what you're doing, you can raise the stakes for your opponent, possibly even to the point where she relents rather than risking additional Traits. Just make sure your sources of information are dependable.

## Overbidding

Overbidding is the system by which elder Garou (who often have considerably more Traits than less experienced opponents) may prevail in a challenge, even if they lose the initial test. An elder Garou with 16 Social Traits should be able to crush a cub with five. This system is designed to make that possible.

Once a test has been made, the loser has the option of calling for an "overbid." In order to call an overbid, you must risk a new Trait; the original one has already been lost. At this point, the two players must reveal the number of applicable Traits they possess in the appropriate category, starting with the player who called for the overbid. If you have double the number of Traits as your opponent in that category, you may attempt another test. As with a tie, you may state a number of Traits less than the actual number you have and keep your true power secret. This can be dangerous, though, unless you are completely confident in your estimation of your opponent's abilities.

**Example of Play**: "Doc" Heaurt, a Bone Gnawer Theurge, and Lily, a Silver Fang Philodox, are playing high-stakes poker, which they have decided will be a Mental Challenge. Coming down to the final hand, with all the chips on the line, poker newcomer Lily wins the challenge, but Doc, unwilling to relinquish the pot so easily, calls for an overbid, announcing that he has seven Mental Traits. Lily, worn down by earlier challenges that night, admits she has only three. Doc bids another Trait: *Clever* and they test again. This time, Doc wins, and both he and Lily lose their original Traits; however, as a result of the challenge Doc has won the hand. Now all he has to do is deal with a Silver Fang who doesn't take well to public embarrassment.

A challenger who fails on a Social or Mental Challenge must wait five real-time minutes (and not spend them arguing over the results of the previous challenge — you can't protest a ruling with a Narrator for 4:58, then drop your argument and say, "Oh, look, time's up,") before repeating the failed challenge. This does not include trials that are failed but then redeemed through overbids.

## Static Challenges

Sometimes you may have to undergo a challenge against a Narrator rather than against another player, such as when you are trying to pick a lock or summon a spirit. In such circumstances, you merely bid the Trait that would be appropriate, then immediately perform a test against the Narrator. Before the test is made, the Narrator decides on the difficulty of the task which you are attempting — in other words, the number of Traits you are bidding against (so you can overbid if you fail). The test proceeds exactly as it would if you were testing against another character. Of course, you may overbid in a Static Challenge, but beware, because the Narrator can overbid as well. The number of Traits attached to the challenge should represent the difficulty and danger inherent in the challenge.

Sometimes Narrators may leave notes on objects, such as books, doors or even fetishes. These notes indicate the type of challenges that must be won for something to occur (such as understanding a book, picking a lock or identifying a fetish). With experience, you may learn how difficult it is to open a locked door. However, difficulty ratings can be as different as lock types.

## Simple Tests

Simple Tests are used to determine if you can do something successfully when there is no real opposition. Simple Tests are often used when using Gifts. Most Simple Tests do not require you to risk or bid Traits, though some may.

When a Simple Test is called, a test (Rock-Paper-Scissors) is performed against a Narrator. In most cases, the player succeeds on a win or a tie, although in some cases, it may be necessary for the player to win for him to receive any benefit from the challenge.

# Health

A character in the **Wyld West** has five Health Levels; these represent the amount of injury the character can endure. These levels are: Healthy,

Bruised, Wounded, Incapacitated and Mortally Wounded. If a healthy character loses a combat challenge, she becomes Bruised. If she loses two, she becomes Wounded, and so on.

• **Bruised** — When a character is Bruised, he is only slightly injured, having perhaps suffered a few scrapes and bruises, but little more until he is healed. In order to enter a new challenge, he must risk an additional Trait. Thus, to even have a chance in a challenge, a Bruised character must bid at least two Traits.

**Example of Play**: Georgia, Silent Strider Ahroun, has chased down the despicable outlaw Earl "Dead Cat" Vasquez and won a combat challenge, injuring him. The battle continues; however, this time, Earl must now risk two Traits in order to defend himself. Georgia, however, still only needs to risk one Trait.

• **Wounded** — When a character is Wounded, he is badly hurt. He might be bleeding freely from open wounds, and may even have broken bones. He must bid two Traits to have a chance in a challenge. In addition, he always loses during a test on a tie, even if he has more Traits than his opponent. If he has fewer Traits, his opponent gets a free extra test. (**Note**: If Traits permit, a character can always attempt to overbid, even in a situation such as this.)

**Example of Play**: Earl has now been Wounded by Georgia, who continues to press the attack. The "Dead Cat" is in pretty bad shape now. He must risk two additional Physical Traits to have a chance in the challenge. However, he has also lost the past two challenges to Georgia. Because of this, Earl has already lost three Physical Traits. He now has considerably fewer Physical Traits than Georgia, who is in her mighty Crinos form, so he will not only lose on ties, but Georgia now gets two tests to see if she can Incapacitate poor Earl. If Georgia wins or ties either of these two tests, Earl will be Incapacitated (see below).

• **Incapacitated** — When a character is Incapacitated, he is completely out of play for at least 10 minutes. Once awake, the character is still immobile, and may not enter into challenges until he has healed at least one Health Level. He is at the mercy of other characters. He may not change forms until he is conscious.

**Example of Play:** Earl, with a snarled "I'll die 'fore you take me in!", decides to fight to the bitter end. Georgia presses her attack, and Earl wins the Physical Challenge, but because of his Wounded Status, Georgia gets a free retest. They test again and this time they tie — since Wounded means he loses all ties (not to mention Georgia has more Traits than him now anyway), poor Earl is dropped in the street, Incapacitated. One more wound and the bandit will be out of his misery for good.

• **Mortally Wounded** — When a character is Mortally Wounded, he is near death. He also immediately reverts to his breed form (his "natural form"). One

Physical Trait is lost for every 10 minutes that he is without medical assistance. Ten minutes after his last Physical Trait is expended, he dies.

## Battle Scars

Every time a character is mortally wounded, she gets a battle scar. These battle scars can add up; each one is nastier than the last. However, battle scars are also worthy of Renown, for they show, indisputably, that the Garou has faced great peril and survived. The first three battle scars are light scars. Light battle scars are rarely bothersome — they occasionally itch during the winter. The next two battle scars are deep scars. Deep scars offer a one-Trait penalty if an opponent specifically targets them. However, if an opponent does that, she will probably lose Honor Renown. Finally, once a character has been Mortally Wounded six times, serious permanent injuries result. The following list includes some possibilities. The player or Narrator can choose one injury that they feel is appropriate for the circumstances, or the effect can be chosen randomly.

- **Improper bone setting** — A limb has been set improperly. The character has the added Negative Physical Trait: *Lame*.
- **Skull Head** — At some point, the side of your head was bashed in, and even though the wound has healed, part of your skull can still be seen. The character gains the Negative Social Trait: *Hideous*.
- **Broken Jaw** — Your jaw was broken and did not reset properly. You have trouble speaking and cannot always make yourself understood verbally. This should be roleplayed.
- **Missing Eye** — One of your eyes is gone. You lack depth perception. You must risk twice as many Traits involving any vision-based challenges or range-based challenges, such as noticing something hidden or operating a firearm at anything other than close range.
- **Collapsed Lung** — Your lung was punctured in battle, and you now have trouble breathing. Wheeze a lot. You also gain a Negative Physical Trait, either *Decrepit* or *Lethargic*.
- **Missing Fingers** — One of your hands has lost several fingers. Your claw attacks will only do aggravated damage if you risk an additional Physical Trait in a challenge. You also gain the Negative Physical Trait: *Clumsy*.
- **Severe Damage** — If a character already has several major battle scars, the Narrator may elect to give her more permanent damage. This could mean completely losing a limb, suffering from spinal cord damage or even sustaining brain damage. The exact nature of the battle scar and its impact on the character are at the discretion of the Narrator.

## Healing

Werewolves heal wounds at a very rapid pace, recovering one Health Level every five minutes, unless the damage is aggravated (see below). However, Garou in breed form do *not* heal faster than a normal human or wolf; the lone exception to this rule is metis in Crinos. Additionally, a Garou must remain still while healing. While healing damage, a Garou may not engage in any other actions or participate in any challenges. Should a Garou in the process of healing be challenged, the healing process is considered to be interrupted and no partial benefit accrues from it.

In other words, a Garou who is two Health Levels down who rests for seven minutes before being discovered and challenged by a roving Black Spiral Dancer would receive the benefit of the first five minutes' rest (one Health Level) but that's all. Furthermore, assuming the Garou defeated the Dancer and resumed resting, the two extra minutes from the first period of rest don't carry over to the Garou's second bout of R&R.

## Aggravated Wounds

Wounds that cannot be healed by the Garou's natural healing powers are called aggravated wounds. Such wounds are usually caused by injury from fire, silver or the claws or teeth of a supernatural creature, such as another Garou or a vampire. A Storyteller can also deem any injury to be aggravated, depending on the circumstances. A full night of rest is required to heal one level of aggravated damage.

## Silver

Silver is the bane of all Garou. All Garou suffer one Health Level of aggravated damage for every 10 seconds they remain in contact with silver. Likewise, any wounds caused by silver weapons cause aggravated damage. When a Garou is faced with a silver weapon, the defending werewolf may only claim *half* of his normal number of Traits in ties — rounded up — making it far more likely that he will suffer injury.

## Mob Scene

During the course of many stories, there will inevitably be situations that involve challenges in which several people want to take part. Multiparty challenges can be confusing, but if you follow these simple guidelines, you shouldn't have much difficulty. These rules are most useful in combat situations, but they can be used with nearly any sort of group challenge.

The first thing you need to do is decide who is challenging whom. This is usually obvious, but when it's not, you need a quick way to work things out. Simply have everyone involved count to three at the same time. On three, each player points at the individual he is challenging.

When a defender suffers attack from multiple challengers, he must test against all of them simultaneously. In this case, the defender must risk Traits for each of the challengers to whom he wishes to respond; if the defender does not have enough Traits, he may choose to whom he wishes to respond. Then, the defender and all of the attackers throw tests simultaneously. The defender compares against each one, winning or losing as indicated by the hand signs and resolving ties normally. In cases of retests from Abilities or Overbids, the defender must use a separate Trait for each retest — a defender attempting to retest against five attackers in hand-to-hand combat had better have five *Brawl* Abilities! Note, however, that even if the defender defeats multiple attackers in this fashion, he can only choose to affect one of them (unless he is using a power that grants him additional actions within the turn); the others simply fail to affect the defender.

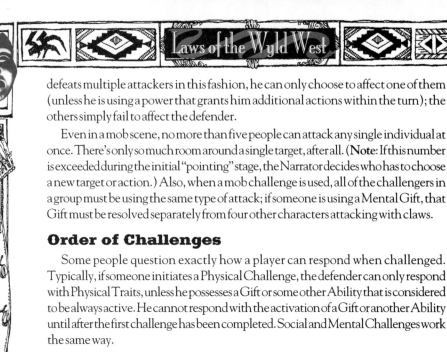

Even in a mob scene, no more than five people can attack any single individual at once. There's only so much room around a single target, after all. (**Note**: If this number is exceeded during the initial "pointing" stage, the Narrator decides who has to choose a new target or action.) Also, when a mob challenge is used, all of the challengers in a group must be using the same type of attack; if someone is using a Mental Gift, that Gift must be resolved separately from four other characters attacking with claws.

## Order of Challenges

Some people question exactly how a player can respond when challenged. Typically, if someone initiates a Physical Challenge, the defender can only respond with Physical Traits, unless he possesses a Gift or some other Ability that is considered to be always active. He cannot respond with the activation of a Gift or another Ability until after the first challenge has been completed. Social and Mental Challenges work the same way.

## Time & Movement in Combat

**Note: These rules can also be added to *Laws of the Night*, *The Shining Host* or *Oblivion*.**

### Three Step Rule

Anyone in or just entering combat is subject to the "three step rule." You may take three steps during any combat action and still attack. Moving one step is considered walking cautiously, two steps is moving directly (down one Trait in Physical Challenges), and three steps is running (also down a Trait in Physical Challenges). Any Gift, fetish, etc., that allows greater movement or multiple actions in combat affects movement accordingly. Two actions equal six steps — a Gift that allows for an additional action would allow you to take three additional steps, and so on.

### Turns

Many Gifts mention "turns;" this term denotes a single sequence of challenges, including retests and overbids. As turns most often apply to combat scenes, it also includes any extra actions gained due to powers like Rage or vampiric *Celerity*, once more including any retests and overbids of these extra actions. Once all follow-up Challenges, retests and the like have finally been resolved — a person is injured, a character is thrown, mind control established — the turn is over. Turns are not a strict unit of time, but rather a measurement of how long it takes one whole sequence of actions to go from start to finish.

**Example of Play:** Fireheart, Wendigo warrior, is tussling with a nasty mockery. He wants to bite his foe, the mockery wishes to knock him down, and so a Physical Challenge is called for. Fireheart loses the test but bets he can overbid — he compares his 10 Physical Traits to the mockery's four, and so he calls an overbid. They shoot again and Fireheart wins, but the tenacious mockery announces he's spending a level of *Brawl* to retest. However, Fireheart wins that retest as well, and things look grim for the mockery as he jots down an aggravated wound from the bite. Fireheart, wanting to put his foe down as fast as possible, spends a Rage Trait for another challenge before the next sequence of actions begins, and he wins easily against the wounded mockery, inflicting a second aggravated wound level. Neither party wishes to retest, overbid or take an additional action, and so the turn is now considered over.

If Fireheart had been using a Gift that was effective for one turn, it would have applied to all those challenges and retests, but faded after he finished his Rage Trait action and announced no more challenges in that sequence. If another mockery attacked, or the mockery he was battling continued to fight, another turn would begin.

# Chapter Four: Systems

This chapter discusses some of the additional rules and complications that sometimes come into play in the **Wyld West**. It also describes a multitude of different systems for resolving character interactions. However, this chapter is more a set of permutations than a set of rules. There is nothing contained in the next several pages that you *need* to know, only things that you might *want* to know. These are complications that can add more detail and depth to the game.

## Combat

The basic challenge system used in the **Wyld West** has already been presented in Chapter Three. This section contains a few basic modifications to the combat system, as well as some elaboration on it.

Combat is the usual intent behind Physical Challenges. Essentially, combat involves two characters in physical conflict. The players agree what the outcome of the challenge will be, each player bids an appropriate Trait, and a test is performed to determine the victor. The following section allows for variations on those basic rules, such as situations using surprise or weapons.

The agreed outcome of a Physical Challenge is often the loser being injured. This is not the only possible result, though. For instance, a Garou could say that he wants to wrest a weapon from his opponent's hands or try to trip him. The result can be nearly anything the two parties agree on, whether it's simply raking someone with claws or throwing him through a window. The results of a combat challenge may also be different for both participants. (For example, if a frenzied Get of Fenris elder is trying to rake a Child of Gaia fostern with his claws, the Child of Gaia might try to restrain her opponent instead of hurting him).

## Surprise

If a player does not respond within three seconds of the declaration of a Physical Challenge, the character is considered to have been surprised — he is not fully prepared for what's coming. Sometimes a player is busy with another activity, doesn't hear a challenge or is playing a character who just isn't prepared for the attack (i.e., the character is led into an ambush). A player who sneaks around whispering challenges to try to get the element of surprise is a lowdown varmint indeed.

Surprise simply means that the outcome of the first challenge in a fight can only harm the surprised defender, not the challenger. For instance, if a player did not respond in time to an attack, but still won the challenge, the challenger would not be injured. Furthermore, if the challenger loses the test, she may call for a second challenge by risking another Trait, since she was operating from the benefit of surprise. With the second challenge, play continues, and winners and losers of a challenge are determined as normal. Overbidding is permitted for both challenger and challenged in surprise situations.

Surprise is only in effect for the first challenge of a conflict; all further challenges are resolved normally, as explained below.

## Weapons

For obvious reasons, no real weapons are ever allowed in **Mind's Eye Theatre** games. Even nonfunctional props are forbidden if they can be mistaken for weapons. This system does not use props of any kind, nor are players required (or allowed) to strike one another. Weapons are purely an abstraction in this game. Instead, characters should use weapon cards, which display the Traits and pertinent details of a particular weapon. The damage a weapon inflicts is limited only by mutual agreement, although it is generally assumed that an injury incurred from a blow reduces the target by a Health Level.

A weapon gives its wielder extra Traits for combat or other appropriate challenges. Sometimes this advantage is offset by a disadvantage in terms of a Negative Trait. Each weapon has one to three extra Traits; these may be used in any challenge in which the weapon is employed. These Traits *cannot* be used in place of Traits when placing an initial bid. Instead, they add to the user's total when she is comparing Traits, such as in the case of a tie during a test or an overbid. In addition, some weapons have special abilities that may be used, such as causing extra levels of damage or affecting more than one target.

Disadvantages are weaknesses inherent to a weapon. These can be used by the wielder's opponent in precisely the same way as Negative Traits. The weapon's Negative Traits can only be used against the wielder of that weapon. Negative Traits for a weapon must be appropriate to the situation. For instance, if you are firing a gun and your opponent wants to use the gun's

Negative Trait: *Loud* against you, that Negative Trait could be ignored if you have taken the time to find some means of silencing the weapon.

If a Negative Trait of your weapon is named by your opponent, and that Trait applies to the situation, you suffer a one-Trait penalty (i.e., you are required to risk an additional Trait). If your opponent calls out a Negative Trait of your weapon that doesn't apply to the situation, your opponent suffers a one-Trait penalty in the challenge.

Statistics for weapons are written on cards and carried along with your character card. Weapon cards specify the capacities of each weapon. Weapon cards allow other players to see that you actually possess a weapon — when you have a weapon card in your hand, you are considered to be holding the weapon. Each weapon has a concealability rating. If the weapon is not concealable, you must have that card on display at all times. You cannot, for example, pull a rifle out of your pocket. Instead, you must carry that card in hand at all times or, optionally, you could pin the card to your shirt, indicating that the rifle is slung over your shoulder.

## Bidding Weapon Traits

During a normal hand-to-hand fight, characters bid Physical Traits against their opponents' Physical Traits. However, if a character is using a firearm, he may use Mental Traits instead. If his opponent is also using a firearm, she bids Mental Traits as well. If the opponent is not using a firearm and is merely trying to dodge, then the attacker uses Mental Traits to attack, while the defender uses her Physical Traits to dodge. This is one of the few instances in which Traits associated with different Attributes may be used against one another.

## Weapon Examples

**Knife** — This easily concealed weapon is very common, and can also be thrown.

Bonus Traits: 2

Negative Traits: *Short*

Concealability: Pocket

**Club/Ax** — These two common weapon types can be anything from chair legs to tomahawks to tree limbs; one bludgeons while the other cuts, but the essential function is the same.

Bonus Traits: 3

Negative Traits: *Clumsy*

Concealability: Long coat or duster

**Broken Bottle** — A good example of a weapon made from scratch.

Bonus Traits: 1

Negative Traits: *Fragile*

Concealability: Vest (ouch!)

**Klaive** — An artistic, powerful blade favored by the Garou.

Bonus Traits: 3

Negative Traits: *Bulky* (this Trait does not apply when the character is in Crinos form)

Concealability: Vest

**Pistol (Single-Action)** — This covers nearly any sort of handgun made before 1860, and they remained quite common in some areas even after the invention of the double-action.

Bonus Traits: 2

Negative Traits: *Loud*

Rate of Fire: 1 (See sidebar, below)

Concealability: Pocket

**Pistol (Double-Action)** — This covers some pistols made after 1860, but double-action pistols were not too common until the early 1880s and later.

Bonus Traits: 2

Negative Traits: *Loud*

Concealability: Pocket

## Multiple Attacks with Single- and Double-action Pistols

A single-action pistol must be manually re-cocked each time after it is fired, while a double-action pistol automatically advances the cylinder after every shot (much the same as a modern pistol). Double-action pistols may be fired normally up to as many times per round as the wielder is capable, within the limits of the gun's ammunition capacity. A single-action pistol, on the other hand, may only be fired rapidly in a single turn by "fanning" the hammer, which requires both hands and at least one level of the *Firearms* Ability. Each additional shot from a single-action pistol in one turn is considered one Trait down for purposes of ties and overbids, cumulatively; the second shot is one Trait down, the third shot two Traits down, and so on. A character using a single-action pistol one-handed or without the *Firearms* Ability may only make a shot every other combat action taken, even including extra actions granted by Rage. Reloading either type of pistol usually takes at least one combat turn, though the character may attempt other actions at this time, as long as they don't require both hands to perform.

**Rifle** — Favored by many types of hunters, not to mention riflemen and snipers.

Bonus Traits: 3

Negative Traits: *Loud*

Concealability: None

**Shotgun** — This powerful weapon fires a spray of pellets, making targets easy to hit.

Bonus Traits: 3

Negative Traits: *Loud*

Concealability: Long coat or duster.

Special Ability: A shotgun may affect up to three targets if they are standing immediately next to each other and are further than 20 feet from the person firing the shotgun. This is resolved with a single challenge against the group. The Traits are risked against the entire group. Up to three separate tests are performed (one test for each target). In this fashion, it is possible to simultaneously wound up to three opponents in a single challenge. The Trait risked by the attacker is used against all three opponents. If any of the three opponents win, the attacker loses that Trait. However, that Trait still applies to all three tests within that group challenge. Thus, a character can challenge up to three opponents while only risking one Trait with this weapon. Also, a shotgun can cause two levels of damage to a single target standing within five feet.

**Gatling Cannon** — This weapon is very powerful and fires a large number of bullets very quickly, but it requires a tripod mount and two people to operate.

Bonus Traits: 5

Negative Traits: *Loud*

Concealability: Not a chance

Special Ability: A gatling cannon may affect up to five targets if they're standing immediately next to each other and are further than 10 feet from the person firing the gun. This is resolved with a single challenge against a group (as described under the section on shotguns).

## Ranged Combat

Many weapons allow a character to stand at a distance from a target and engage him in combat. In such situations, the character must go over to the target (after shouting "Bang!") and engage in a challenge.

If a character has surprised her opponent, even if she loses the first test, she has the option of calling for a second test. Once the second challenge is called, play continues as normal with that new challenge. The target is considered to be surprised for the first attack, and if he has no ranged weapon with which to return fire, he is considered "surprised" for as long as the aggressor can attack him without facing resistance (that is, if he wins on a challenge, she doesn't take damage).

If the target is aware of the attack before it happens and has a ranged weapon of his own, he is not considered to be surprised for the first attack. He may shoot back right away, and challenges are resolved as stated below.

After the first shot is fired (and the first challenge is resolved), the target may attempt to return fire (assuming he is armed). The loser of a firefight challenge loses a Health Level.

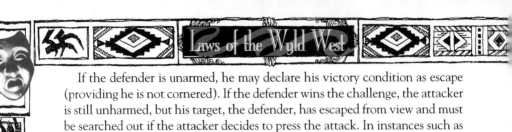

If the defender is unarmed, he may declare his victory condition as escape (providing he is not cornered). If the defender wins the challenge, the attacker is still unharmed, but his target, the defender, has escaped from view and must be searched out if the attacker decides to press the attack. In instances such as this, a new challenge cannot be made for at least five minutes.

### Cover

Fighting with hand-to-hand weapons — clubs, knives, tomahawks, klaives and whatnot — requires that combatants be within arm's reach of each other. Fighting with ranged weapons allows combatants to stand some distance apart; participants can therefore "dive for cover." When resolving each ranged combat challenge, each combatant can present one Trait of cover to add to his total number of Traits. These cover Traits may not be used for bidding, but they do add to a player's total if Traits are compared. This cover can take the form of whatever obstacles are around and within reach (*don't* actually dive for them). A Narrator might be required to describe what cover is around, but if combatants know the area, they can agree upon what cover is available. In some instances, there may be no cover around, leaving a combatant in the open with only his own defensive Traits for protection.

If cover is extensive (a brick wall, perhaps) it may be worth more than one Trait. The number of Traits available for cover is left for challengers to agree upon, or for a Narrator to decree. Hiding behind a boulder, for example, might be worth two Traits, while hiding behind a thin wood fence might only count as one. If one combatant goes completely under cover (he cannot be seen at all *and* is thoroughly protected), he is considered impossible to hit. The attacker must change his position to get another clear shot.

### Using Two Weapons

Usually, a character needs the *Ambidextrous* Merit to use two weapons (usually guns) with any sort of accuracy. However, it's possible for a character to use two weapons without such benefits, albeit clumsily.

A character using two weapons must bid two Traits for the weapon in the primary hand, and three Traits for the weapon in the secondary hand. Using an extra weapon like this is good only for one additional attack per turn, regardless of the number of extra actions that the character may have. Thus, you may fire your primary pistol three times using Rage, but you can only fire the pistol in your secondary hand once.

Note also that a character using a pair of single-action revolvers cannot fire them more than once each in a turn, regardless of Rage or *Firearms* Ability.

## Renown

Renown governs ranking among the Garou. Rank determines what level of Gifts a Garou is able to learn, how powerful she may be and how well she is respected and known throughout Garou society.

There are three kinds of Renown Traits that characters can collect: Honor, Glory and Wisdom. Each auspice has its own requirements for rising in Rank. In general, Garou try to excel in the areas of Renown that are favored by their particular auspices.

Honor is adherence to the Litany and an indication of how well a Garou upholds his own word and code of ethics. It is also traditional "chivalry," as well as the idea of remaining true to yourself and your ideals. The Philodox of a sept are chiefly concerned with matters of Honor, and they are the ones who nominate a Garou to receive Honor Renown.

Glory is willingness to throw yourself headlong into the fight against the Wyrm. It represents bravery, prowess and success in the face of certain doom. A truly glorious Garou has fought well and often, and continues to make a name for himself by defeating the Wyrm in a manner that shows style. The Ahroun of a sept are chiefly concerned with matters of Glory, and they nominate a Garou to receive Glory Renown.

Wisdom is inner strength and knowledge. When disputes are solved without bloodshed, when the Wyrm is defeated by simple means rather than violent ones, when a Garou devotes himself full-time to the service of his totem or to spiritual meditation, the Garou is considered Wise. Since the Theurges of a sept are chiefly concerned with matters of Wisdom, they are the ones who nominate a Garou to receive Wisdom Renown.

## Nominations

Nominations of Garou for Renown can be decided on by the auspices responsible for the particular aspects of Renown. This can either be done as a majority-rule vote, or by having one elder of the auspice decide who gets the Renown. It is really up to the characters as to how they do this, but a Storyteller may step in as an angered elder or spirit if Renown is dealt out too easily or is not given when truly deserved.

The general rule about Renown is this: A Storyteller can tell you, as a player, what your character's auspice, tribe or breed would normally do, but she cannot make your character give or refuse to give Renown. Only Narrator characters can interact with your character to attempt to influence such matters — and you can bet they will if you are abusing this system.

For more on awarding Renown in game, see "Moots" (page 250).

### Renown Awards

The following list can be used as a guideline for circumstances that could warrant Renown awards. These situations are by no means set in stone, and they are always up to the individual interpretation of the characters involved.

Remember, as a character earns Renown, it becomes more difficult to outdo past actions to gain more Renown from the same actions (i.e., a character may earn Glory the first time he kills a young vampire, but the second time this happens his packmates and the sept will not be so impressed). Such successes will be expected from the character. To translate this into the game, each player should keep a written list of what he did to earn each Renown Trait. In order to earn another point for the same general action, the character must excel or succeed in an extremely diverse way. (i.e., teaching several young Garou of the importance of the basic tenets of the Litany is not worthy of more than one Wisdom Renown. Mediating a conflict between two Garou fairly, then doing the same later for two elder Garou and several vampires, would be worthy of a second award of Wisdom Renown for the same general action).

Losing Renown, however, can be a very simple — and speedy — process. Every time a Garou takes an action that is dishonorable, inglorious or unwise, she can lose Renown. An appropriate Renown Trait is removed from her list, and the Garou must successfully once again perform the general action that earned the Renown in the first place in order for her to be eligible for that Renown Trait again.

If Narrators notice that a character is on an endless cycle of gaining and losing Renown over one particular action or set of actions, they may wish to intervene and declare that the character is no longer eligible for Renown from that source. Constant repetition of a pattern of actions indicates that the Garou has not learned from her past mistakes, and as such is not truly worthy of Renown.

**Glorious Actions**

Surviving an incapacitating wound

Gaining a battle scar

Surviving a particularly vicious Wyrm-generated attack (such as balefire)

Attacking a minion of the Wyrm without regard for personal safety

Defeating a minion of the Wyrm (if there was some real personal risk involved)

Traveling beyond the Near Umbra to another Realm and surviving

Performing or participating in a *Rite of Caern Building*

Owning a klaive (this is awarded once, after three moons of use)

Helping to prevent a caern from being overrun by anyone

Dying while defending a caern (posthumous)

Preventing the Wyrm from overtaking a caern (a Garou can receive more than one Glory Trait for this action if it is done without any assistance)

Accepting a sept position

Telling a good story at a moot

**Scandalous inglorious actions**

Cowering from a foe

Begging a minion of the Wyrm for your life

Participating in a failed Great Hunt

Suffering the *Rite of Ostracism*

Failing or refusing to prevent a caern from being overrun by the Wyrm

Refusing a sept position

Suffering from a fox frenzy (running in fear)

**Honorable Actions**

Showing restraint in the face of certain death

Performing a *Moot Rite* (first time only)

Performing a *Rite of Passage* (first time only)

Performing a *Trodden Track* Rite (once per season)

Performing a *Rite of Caern Building* (earned again only if subsequent caern is of higher Rank than the last)

Performing a Punishment Rite (only one per rite)

Owning a klaive (only once, after three moons of use)

Consistently helping to guard a caern, even when you'd rather be somewhere else

Helping to prevent a threat of the caern being overrun by the Wyrm before things come to blows

Teaching another Garou a valuable lesson

Reciting part of the Silver Record at a moot (once per each evening-long part)

Gaining the position of pack leader (awarded once)

Serving in a sept position faithfully for one year

Upholding the Litany during a controversial issue

Mediating a dispute fairly and impartially

Consistently keeping your promises

Being truthful in the face of adversity

Telling an epic story at a moot

Showing mercy to a wayward Garou

Protecting a helpless human or wolf

Supporting a person who is accused of a crime (who is later proven innocent)

Making sacrifices to protect the Veil

Repairing the Veil

**Scandalous dishonorable actions**

Falsely accusing anyone of being of the Wyrm

Refusing to perform a *Moot Rite*

Suffering the *Stone of Scorn*

Suffering the *Rite of Ostracism*

Accidentally breaking or losing a klaive

Not staying on watch at a caern when a more tempting activity presents itself

Refusing to help guard a caern

Failing to prevent a caern from being overrun by the Wyrm

Refusing any sept position

Challenging someone too far above or below your own Rank

Mediating a dispute unfairly

Failing to keep your promises

Being deceptive

Speaking poorly of the Garou as a whole

Speaking poorly of one's tribe, auspice or pack

"Crying Wolf" (i.e., summoning the Ahroun of a sept when there is no real danger present)

Not protecting a helpless Garou

Not protecting a helpless wolf or human as appropriate

Performing heinous acts while "Wyrm-ridden" (in such a frenzy that one's monstrous tendencies take hold, said to occur when the Wyrm "rides" a frenzying Garou)

Abandoning your pack in a time of need

Harming/rending the Veil

**Wise Actions**

Besting someone (even a spirit) in a riddle contest

Showing restraint in the face of certain death

Ending a threat without serious harm to any Garou

Revealing with certain proof that a Kinfolk or Garou is "of the Wyrm"

Purifying a Wyrm-tainted object, person or place

Successfully completing a spirit quest in the Umbra

Giving a prophetic warning that later comes true

Discovering ancient Garou lore

Performing a *Rite of Caern Building*

Discovering/creating a new rite or ritual

Discovering/creating a new Gift

Creating a fetish

Sacrificing a fetish for the good of the sept or tribe

Keeping a caern safe through trickery or imagination

Teaching another Garou a valuable lesson

Upholding the Litany

Consistently giving good advice

Healing a fellow Garou (not a pack member) selflessly

**Scandalous unwise actions**

Attacking a much more powerful force without aid

Falsely accusing another of being "of the Wyrm"

Failing to complete a spirit quest in the Umbra

Giving a prophetic warning that does not come true

Giggling, joking or otherwise being disrespectful during a rite (leeway is given on this one for a Ragabash)

For a homid, ignoring one's wolf nature for too long

For a metis, attempting to hide one's deformity

Living alone or away from your pack

Breaking the Litany

Consistently giving bad advice

Having trickery backfire

Injuring a fellow Garou during a frenzy

Having poor relations with nearby Kinfolk

Teaching Garou knowledge to one of the Wyrm's minions (including vampires)

## Confirmation

When all is said and done, and all Renown nominations have been made at a sept, the elders of each auspice present the Galliards with their nominations. At that point, the Galliards must make a decision. Will they confirm the nominations by singing of the subject's new Renown, or will they negate the nomination by refusing to recognize the story that the Renown Trait represents? Ultimately, the eldest Galliard has veto power, and can cancel a nomination at any time. In games without enough players to fill all these roles, they can either be played by the Storyteller or the Renown must be determined by vote of the characters. Do not punish characters by denying Renown just because the group is missing a key elder from an auspice.

## Scandal

Finally, even after a Renown Trait has been awarded, a Ragabash can attempt to destroy a character's Renown by speaking scandalously. These scandals must have an element of truth, and must be agreed upon by the Ragabash elder of the sept, so in a sense, the Ragabash must prove the truth of the scandalous rumors. Still, it is the Galliards who must also confirm the scandal, thus authorizing the loss of Renown. Only one Renown Trait can be affected per scandal.

The Wyrm often finds out when a scandal has occurred among the Garou. A Bane might approach a Garou to "help" him through his crisis by offering him revenge or more power to gain back his lost Renown.

## Loss of Rank

It is possible for a Garou to gain Rank and then lose it later through scandal. This is the way of the Garou — a werewolf must purify himself before attempting to rise in Rank. A Garou may continue to use Gifts of her previous Rank, but cannot perform rites or any other functions of her previous station until her Rank has been regained. In addition, if her Traits are over her reduced Trait maximum, she cannot use the "extra" Traits until she has regained her previous Rank.

## Benefits of Renown

Aside from the fact that a Garou needs to accumulate Renown Traits in order to be able to challenge for Rank, Renown Traits give a character other benefits.

First of all, Renown Traits can be used in place of Social Traits during any Social Challenge. In order to use a Renown Trait, the Garou must somehow work the Trait into the roleplaying appropriately. For example, an Ahroun trying to intimidate someone might say, "You must realize what you are doing. Are you going to deny Luke the Glorious? I've fought and killed a Night Hunter!" Even if a Renown Trait is temporarily lost during a challenge, such a loss is only temporary and does not reduce the character's Rank.

**Note**: A player attempting to use a Renown Trait instead of a Social one must make it clear exactly what he is doing; otherwise it can be difficult to distinguish a legitimate bid from character braggadocio.

Each Renown Trait that a Garou gains also gives her the opportunity to learn a new Gift, as long as the character has sufficient Experience to do so (for more information on spending Experience on Gifts, see page 243). A character must also petition the spirits to teach her a Gift. Gifts are taught, not acquired instantaneously. Moreover, a character cannot learn a new Gift unless she has a new Renown Trait to demonstrate her eligibility. If the character wishes to learn a Gift that is outside her tribe, auspice or breed, she must have two Renown Traits to gain permission.

## Tokens

A Garou can represent "favor" by creating a token, a small gift of some kind, usually a necklace, bracelet or other piece of jewelry. A token can also be as simple as a necklace, a horseshoe, a cigar or a seashell, so long as it is easily identifiable. Each token a Garou makes should look roughly the same so that it can be identified as the mark of a particular Garou. By creating a token, a werewolf can temporarily loan *one* of his Renown Traits to another Garou, to be used in Social Challenges or to lend the token's creator's "support" to other enterprises. So long as a Garou holds a token, the creator of the token may not use that Renown Trait in challenges; it's out "on loan" and is inaccessible.

The number of tokens that a character can create is determined by her Rank (see below). Cubs and cliath may not create tokens. A fostern can only make one, an adren can make two, an athro can make three, an elder can make five and a legend can make seven. A token does not permit its recipient to learn a new Gift, and it does not count toward his total Renown Traits; after all, it is just on loan. A token does grant its bearer more authority, however, and many adren who hold sept positions receive tokens from elders. Conversely, loaning Renown to those who abuse it or are later proved disreputable is a quick way to lose Renown yourself.

## The Ranks

In general, the Garou method of gaining Rank is based on auspice, but Rank is also a measure of the respect and loyalty that the Garou feel for one of their own. Rank has its privileges, as well as its duties.

### Cub — Rank 0

This is the lowest Rank, and it is not the normal starting-point for a **Wyld West** character. However, it can be fun to play someone who's just gone through her First Change. You have to roleplay learning all about the Garou, and discover the secret lore of your character's auspice and tribe.

There are benefits to being a cub. First, no one is allowed to challenge a cub, on the grounds that cubs just aren't worth the effort. Second, everyone will likely come to a cub's aid if he gets into danger. However, cubs are only allowed to learn their breed and tribe Gifts; they learn their auspice Gifts after their *Rite of Passage*. Many septs include a Garou with the title Den Mother or Den Father. A Den Mother watches over the cubs to make sure that they respect their elders and don't get into *too* much trouble.

**Note**: Playing a cub is an excellent way to be introduced to the game as a whole. If a local troupe is set up with a Den Mother, a new player can easily join the story and be tutored in the game as a matter of course while still playing. Learning about the Garou this way can be a lot of fun.

**Gifts Available**: None (at start, but may learn Basic from their breed and tribe)

**Maximum Traits per Category**: 10

**Maximum Willpower, Gnosis and Rage**: 3

**Renown Requirements**: None (must earn Cliath Rank Renown for auspice to be considered ready for *Rite of Passage*)

**Duties**: Cubs are required to learn as much as they can, and at least *try* to stay out of trouble.

### Cliath — Rank One

As soon as a Garou passes her *Rite of Passage* she is considered a "teenager" in the Garou Nation, and must prove herself worthy of promotion to a position of responsibility. A cliath cannot hold a sept office or take command of any group projects. It is the cliath's responsibility to find her place and become proficient enough in her auspice to be considered worthy of authority. This is the standard starting rank for player characters.

**Gifts Available**: Basic

**Rites Available:** Basic

**Maximum Traits Per Category**: 11

**Maximum Willpower, Gnosis and Rage**: 4

**Renown Requirements**

- **Ragabash**: Any Three Renown
- **Theurge**: Two Wisdom and One Glory or Honor
- **Philodox**: Two Honor and One Wisdom
- **Galliard**: One Glory, Two Wisdom or Honor
- **Ahroun**: Two Glory, One Honor

**Other Requirements**: A cliath must learn three initial Gifts and swear an oath of loyalty to her sept or tribe, usually at a ceremony that takes place after the completion of her *Rite of Passage*.

**Duties**: Cliath are required to give service to the sept on a regular basis. This service can entail minor jobs, such as aiding the Keeper of the Land with his duties or patrols, accepting guard duty, or helping an adren or elder with an upcoming rite. Essentially, the job description is "other duties as required," and since cliath are lower in Rank than most Garou, a cliath usually has little choice but to obey.

**Privileges**: A cliath can petition for justice, challenge for higher Rank (when she has enough Renown), and can enter the caern (usually).

**Note**: This is the starting Rank for a player. Garou expect a cliath to go out and make a name for herself; one who hangs around the caern and doesn't try to find her own way won't be well-liked. Cliath are always getting into trouble, but that's just part of being a cliath. The elders give cliath a fairly long leash, intervening only when it looks like she will screw up so badly as to be denied fostering.

## Fostern — Rank Two

This is typically the most common rank at a sept. A fostern has earned some Renown outside of his *Rite of Passage*, and now stands as an adult among the Garou. A fostern is expected to attend moots, fulfill the duties as described by his auspice, and learn the ways of his breed and tribe.

**Gifts Available**: Basic

**Rites Available**: Basic

**Maximum Traits Per Category**: 12

**Maximum Willpower, Gnosis and Rage**: 5

**Renown Requirements**:

- **Ragabash**: Any Seven Renown
- **Theurge**: Five Wisdom, One Glory
- **Philodox**: Five Honor, One Wisdom, One Glory

- **Galliard**: Four Glory, Three Wisdom
- **Ahroun**: Five Glory, Three Honor, One Wisdom

**Duties**: A fostern is required to give service to the sept on a regular basis. This service can entail all the same minor jobs he performed as a cliath, only now he is expected to be competent and responsible.

**Privileges**: A fostern is allowed to perform Basic Rites, can petition for justice, can challenge for higher Rank (when he has enough Renown), and is usually allowed access to the caern. He can also request that a Moon Bridge be opened to the destination of his choice, but the request will not always be heeded — Moon Bridges are sacred things and are not to be used frivolously.

Also note that the word "fostern" is used to refer to pack brothers and sisters, the Garou family by choice. In the sense that all members of a pack are "family," the members of a Garou's pack can be referred to as his "fostern," regardless of their Rank. Unity is sometimes more important than social standing.

## Adren — Rank Three

Adren have gained in prestige and Renown, and now are expected to take a larger part in the affairs of the sept.

**Gifts Available**: Basic, Intermediate

**Rites Available**: Basic, Intermediate

**Maximum Traits Per Category**: 14

**Maximum Willpower, Gnosis and Rage**: 7

**Renown Requirements**:

- **Ragabash**: Any 12 Renown
- **Theurge**: Seven Wisdom, Two Glory, One Honor
- **Philodox**: Seven Honor, Four Wisdom, Three Glory
- **Galliard**: Six Glory, Five Wisdom, One Honor
- **Ahroun**: Seven Glory, Five Honor, One Wisdom

**Other Requirements**: An adren must be in training to fill one of the positions at a sept. She must also challenge and defeat another adren in some sort of contest. Note that defeating this adren does not have any effect on her Glory, though being defeated may affect the challenger's Glory. This challenge may take whatever form the challenged adren desires, and may be made appropriately easy or difficult depending on whether if the adren feels the challenger is worthy.

**Duties**: An adren must give service to the elder who is training her. This takes most of her (out-of-game) time. Adren are considered eligible to become minor sept leaders and hold positions like Keeper of the Land, Gatekeeper, Guardian and Den Mother — positions that do not require a lot of actual authority. She is required to train fostern, and often must spend more time at the caern than she would like. This is one of the toughest Ranks to perform properly, because adren often have the responsibilities of an elder, but do not always have the authority to carry out those duties.

**Privileges**: Adren must be addressed with a term of respect by fostern and cliath. If an adren knows the *Rite of Binding*, she is allowed to create talens for herself and others. Her name is known outside her sept, usually within her tribe. She is allowed to learn and perform Intermediate Rites on her own. She can demand that the sept provide a place for her to live, even if it is just communal living quarters. (Demanding living space of a sept, especially in the tough environment of the Savage West, is seen as somewhat *déclassé*, and this privilege is usually only invoked by Garou with very low *Finances*.)

**Note**: Adren are usually in line for one or more sept positions. Everyone watches what an adren does, and Ragabash in particular will try to trick her or catch her doing something scandalous. An adren is expected to set a good example, making a Garou's adren years stressful ones indeed.

## Athro — Rank 4

Athro have respect and authority within the Garou Nation. Others will come to an athro for advice, and his word is respected at moots.

**Gifts Available**: Basic, Intermediate

**Rite Available**: Basic, Intermediate

**Maximum Traits Per Category**: 16

**Maximum Willpower, Gnosis and Rage**: 8

**Renown Requirements**:

- **Ragabash**: Any 17 Renown
- **Theurge**: Nine Wisdom, Four Glory, Two Honor
- **Philodox**: Nine Honor, Seven Wisdom, Three Glory
- **Galliard**: Eight Glory, Six Wisdom, Two Honor
- **Ahroun**: Nine Glory, Seven Honor, Two Wisdom

**Other Requirements**: An athro may fill one of the elder positions in a sept. These are: elder of an auspice, elder of a tribe, elder of a breed, sept leader, Warder, Master of the Rite and Master of the Challenge. One can be both the elder of a tribe, auspice or breed and also be sept leader or Master of the Rite — the duties can overlap. He cannot advance to elder Rank if one of these positions is not available. He must either challenge the current elder for the position and defeat her, or wait until a position becomes vacant. In the latter case, he may have to contend for the position.

**Duties**: Athro are typically the leaders of the packs and the ones who receive quests and assignments to fulfill from a sept's elders. The most dangerous missions are assigned and the greatest chances to gain Renown exist at this level.

**Privileges**: An athro can be judged only by a sept's council of elders. He gets the best assignments, and is considered a teacher by all other Garou.

## Elder — Rank 5

An elder is at the peak of her achievement as a Garou. Others look up to her as a paragon. She commands respect and obedience from those around her.

**Gifts Available**: Basic, Intermediate, Advanced
**Rites Available**: Basic, Intermediate, Advanced
**Maximum Traits Per Category**: 18
**Maximum Willpower, Gnosis and Rage**: 9
**Renown Requirements**:

- **Ragabash**: Any 24 Renown
- **Theurge**: 10 Wisdom, Five Glory, Three Honor
- **Philodox**: 10 Honor, Nine Wisdom, Four Glory
- **Galliard**: 10 Glory, Eight Wisdom, Three Honor
- **Ahroun**: 10 Glory, Eight Honor, Three Wisdom

**Other Requirements**: Not surprisingly, an elder is expected to fill one of the elder positions in a sept. These are: elder of an auspice, elder of a tribe, elder of a breed, sept leader, Warder, Master of the Rite and Master of the Challenge. One can be both the elder of a tribe, auspice or breed and also be sept leader or Master of the Rite or Master of the Challenge — the duties can overlap.

**Duties**: As the elder of an auspice, tribe or breed, you are required to watch out for the interests of your auspice, tribe or breed within the sept. As an elder of an auspice, you have the power to veto Renown nominations. As an elder of a tribe, you have the ability to accept new members into the tribe and to ban certain Garou from the tribe. As an elder of a breed, you are responsible for all external liaisons with others of your breed — the metis elder is a position that is rarely filled, but if it is, the metis elder must watch over and give aid to all metis characters in the sept.

**Privileges**: Elders can only be judged by a council of other elders. An elder is free to do pretty much what she pleases as long as she fulfills her duties. Furthermore, an elder automatically commands respect and obedience from everyone around her.

**Storyteller Note**: If you don't have many players, it's best if elders are Narrator characters. Too many elders in a game may disrupt it, or make things extremely difficult for cubs and cliath.

## Legend — Rank 6

Only one out of every thousand Garou ever attains the status and Rank of a living legend. A legend is no longer an individual. He belongs to the Garou Nation as a whole.

**Gifts and Rites Available**: All
**Maximum Traits Per Category**: 20
**Maximum Willpower, Gnosis and Rage**: 10
**Renown Requirements**:

- **Ragabash**: Any 31 Renown
- **Theurge**: 13 Wisdom, Seven Glory, Five Honor

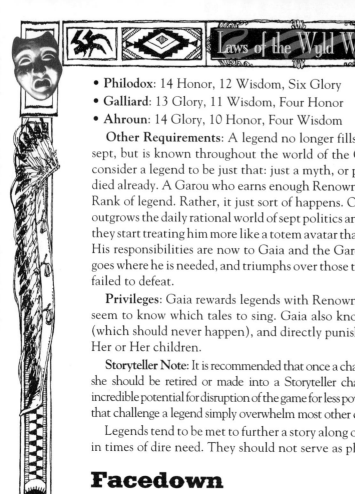

- **Philodox**: 14 Honor, 12 Wisdom, Six Glory
- **Galliard**: 13 Glory, 11 Wisdom, Four Honor
- **Ahroun**: 14 Glory, 10 Honor, Four Wisdom

**Other Requirements**: A legend no longer fills any official position in a sept, but is known throughout the world of the Garou. Many might even consider a legend to be just that: just a myth, or perhaps someone who has died already. A Garou who earns enough Renown does not contend for the Rank of legend. Rather, it just sort of happens. Over the course of time he outgrows the daily rational world of sept politics and stable packmates, while they start treating him more like a totem avatar than a flesh-and-blood elder. His responsibilities are now to Gaia and the Garou Nation in general. He goes where he is needed, and triumphs over those threats that all others have failed to defeat.

**Privileges**: Gaia rewards legends with Renown, while the Galliards just seem to know which tales to sing. Gaia also knows when a legend falters (which should never happen), and directly punishes transgressions against Her or Her children.

**Storyteller Note**: It is recommended that once a character reaches legend status, she should be retired or made into a Storyteller character. Otherwise, there is incredible potential for disruption of the game for less powerful characters; the threats that challenge a legend simply overwhelm most other characters.

Legends tend to be met to further a story along or to assist wayward Garou in times of dire need. They should not serve as player characters.

# Facedown

A facedown is an honored tradition in Garou society. It occurs when two characters lock eyes in a test of wills for the purpose of intimidating each other. The idea is to force one's rival to back down before a conflict actually comes to blows. Garou commonly employ facedowns, primarily to settle minor disputes, scold pups and show discontent with a pack's leaders.

Success in a facedown is determined in one of two ways. First, if one of the players relents while roleplaying this action, his opponent is considered to be the winner, and is allowed to gloat over his victory as he pleases. If one of the players does not relent during a facedown, a Social Challenge is necessary to determine the victor. The Social Challenge proceeds as normal, with the loser breaking eye contact and losing the contest.

## I'll See You At High Noon

Capturing the speed and drama of a fast-draw showdown is an essential aspect of any classic Western. When two characters decide to settle their differences in this style, the following optional system can be used to enhance the feel of the moment and more accurately capture the skill of the contestants. This system is strictly optional, as it is designed to be quicker and somewhat more lethal than most **Mind's Eye Theatre** situations, and a player may not be forced into this type of challenge against her will; furthermore, no other type of conflict with a firearm may use this system, *only* a traditional western quick-draw contest. It is also not intended to allow a player to min/max his character into some mythical ultimate gunfighter — even if he did, then it would be unlikely another character would be very eager to accept a challenge from her. That said, the system is broken down into three simple parts: staredown, draw and resolution.

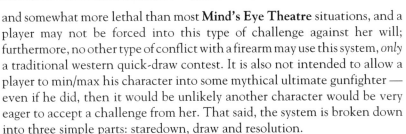

**Staredown:** This is conducted like a facedown challenge (above) — at this stage the two gunfighters are testing each other with intimidation and force of reputation, seeing who has the steadiest nerves. This should be roleplayed out if at all possible, but if neither character will relent, a Social Challenge determines the winner. Whoever succeeds at the staredown is considered to have the steadier hand and thus is two Traits up on the draw challenge. The Trait value of the *Gunslinging Reputation* Merit/Flaw also adds or subtracts to a character's total Traits at this time, and Glory Renown may be used in place of (but not added to) a character's Social bid, if appropriate. The staredown challenge cannot be retested unless one party is able to overbid, but its effects may be ignored with a Willpower Trait, which means the characters are evenly matched (at least mentally) and neither character gains the two-Trait advantage.

**Draw:** Now both characters take *one* shot, making a challenge using a special group of Traits collectively called the Gunfighting Pool, which combines the Mental and Physical Traits most appropriate for quick-draws (and *only* these Traits). These Traits are each specifically labeled "Gunfighting Trait" in the Trait listings on pages 64-71. The gun's bonus Traits are added to this pool as well. Fighters may overbid, if possible, but otherwise they get only one retest each, available by expending a level of *Fast-Draw* (not *Firearms*). If a character uses a pre-emptive power such as *Spirit of the Fray*, this allows her to make another retest for each use of the power, but confers no other benefits. Multiple shots are possible with Rage and similar powers, but may only be used if a character is still standing once the outcome of the first challenge is determined (see resolution, below). At the Narrator's discretion, a Willpower Trait may be spent to retest the draw, but only one Willpower Trait may be spent in this fashion.

**Resolution:** The loser suffers a wound, loses the Trait bid from his Gunfighting Pool, and also loses a level of *Fast-Draw* as a function of his decreased confidence. Optionally, the Narrator may enforce grim reality and rule (if it is the winner's desire) that Garou are automatically Mortally Wounded by losing a showdown, and less hardy folk than Garou are simply killed; gunfighting *is* a risky prospect, after all. If Garou are crazy enough to use silver bullets, instant death becomes an option for them as well. However, player characters should never be automatically killed this way unless the player (not the character!) knowingly and specifically agrees to allow such an outcome before the showdown takes place. If both characters are still standing, normal ranged combat rules apply and they may continue to fire until the contest is declared over, one character is felled, or another event occurs which makes the continuation of the showdown impossible.

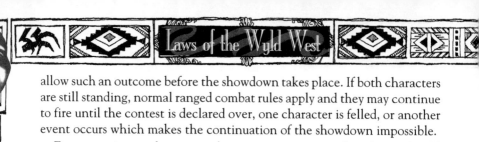

For convenience, characters who expect to engage in showdowns should record their Gunfighting Pool total somewhere on their character sheet before play begins, taking care to note if any of those Traits are lost during regular play. Multiple characters may be involved in a showdown, but unless a character spends Rage, she may only challenge one other opponent at a time. (See Mob Scene rules; see also rules for firing single- or double-action pistols more than once in a turn, above.) Characters participating in a quick-draw showdown but who do not have at least one level of *Fast-Draw* normally (not counting skill levels lost during play) are two Traits down on both challenges, due to their unfamiliarity with the unique nature of such a contest. Yes, this cancels the benefit of winning the staredown (but at least then there's no penalty).

## Frenzy

Frenzy is an uncontrollably violent state suffered by all Garou. Some claim it is the taint of the Wyrm within them that causes Garou to go mad, destroying and ravaging everything within their reach. Others disagree, believing that frenzy is the release of the animal within them all. Frenzy can happen at any time and can be provoked by anything. When it happens, it is sudden, bloody and often fatal. Not even the Stargazers are calm enough to forsake this horrible curse of the Changing Breed.

The trigger for a frenzy can be almost anything, depending on the character in question. For a Fianna Galliard, it could be a member of an audience mocking him as he performs; for a Wendigo Ahroun, it could be an ignorant, prejudiced white man making racist comments about Native Americans; for a Get of Fenris Theurge, it could be a type of Wyrm-creature or a bad moot. What triggers frenzy is entirely up to the personality of the character and the discretion of the Narrator. However, discretion is advised; a character in constant frenzy is no fun to be around, and will likely be "put down" by his fellow sept members. Players are also advised to try to be consistent when playing what causes a frenzy; frenzies are personal and situational things, but a player cannot ignore something that would normally cause frenzy simply because it isn't expedient for him to frenzy at this time.

To see if a character enters frenzy, the player performs a Static Willpower Challenge (current Willpower versus current Rage, no Traits risked).

A character can also try to instill frenzy in another character by taunting him and calling for a Social Challenge. If the attacker (the taunting character) wins the challenge, the defender must then test to resist frenzy.

If the defender wins the challenge, nothing happens and the story continues as usual.

Once in the state of frenzy, a character attacks all those around him violently and without discretion. A frenzied character does not suffer penalties from wounds (simulating the blind, uncontrollable anger of a frenzied Garou). Frenzies usually last only about 10 minutes, or until the object or person that triggered the frenzy is removed from the character's vicinity.

A character may also enter frenzy voluntarily by spending a Rage Trait. Such an action can prove useful in a combat situation in which frenzy might be necessary to achieve victory — or even just survive. It has its uses, but it is a dark gift.

**Note**: Be cautious when roleplaying frenzy. Do not jump about screaming at people, frothing at the mouth and clawing at the furniture. Remember, although frenzy is a violent state of mind, *you absolutely cannot strike other players, even in jest*. Just because your character is in an uncontrollable rage does not mean that you can forget the rules and become reckless. Use your own discretion, but act out only as much frenzy as the environment allows without upsetting your fellow players.

## The Many Forms

The Garou have five forms: Homid (pure human), Glabro (bestial human), Crinos (towering man-wolf creature), Hispo (dire wolf) and Lupus (pure wolf). Each of these forms gives a Garou a different set of advantages and disadvantages.

Changing forms requires a Simple Test and one turn for each form assumed. It therefore takes one turn and one Simple Test to change from Homid to Glabro, but a total of four Simple Tests and four turns to go from Homid to Lupus. Any test lost along the way marks the point where the Garou stops shifting until another turn has passed and the shifting process can begin again. *Primal Urge* allows retests.

Alternatively, a Garou may elect to spend a Rage Trait to make the change instantaneous, regardless of initial and final form. The player should be certain to alert those within sight that the change is taking place so that other characters can make an appropriate reaction.

Although Garou can have difficulty communicating with humans and wolves, they can always communicate with one another freely. The language of the Garou is a combination of human phonetics and lupine snarls, and thus is pronounceable in all forms.

### Homid: The Human

**Trait Adjustments**: None

**Change Description**: This is the normal state for characters who wish to interact with human society. This form is identical to human form in all ways. A Garou in Homid form does not regenerate damage, but may carry silver items without harm.

## Glabro: The Bestial Man

**Trait Adjustments**: The character gains the following additional Physical Traits:*Brawny*, *Ferocious* and *Quick*. These Traits may be bid just like normal Traits. Once lost, they are gone for the duration of the session. A Garou also gains the following Negative Traits while in this form: *Bestial* and *Tactless*. A character may still engage in fast-draw showdowns in this form.

**Change Description**: A Garou in this form is still recognizably human, but differences from average humans are apparent — he's a big, plum-ugly palooka now. The Garou gains about six inches in height and may nearly double his body weight in muscle mass. Teeth and nails grow longer and body hair becomes profuse. While Glabro form can pass for human (barely), it will be remembered as strange and scary (think Mungo from "Blazing Saddles" and you've got the right idea). In Glabro, the Garou's thick fingernails cause aggravated damage, but he can still handle most delicate manipulations.

**Roleplaying**: Full human speech is possible, but Glabro usually only speak one or two short sentences at a time, delivered in a guttural snarl.

## Crinos: The Wolf-Man

**Trait Adjustments**: The character gains the following additional Physical Traits: *Brawny* x 2, *Ferocious* x 2, *Quick*, *Relentless* and *Robust* x 2 . These Traits may be bid just like normal Traits. Once lost, they are gone for the duration of the session. A Garou also suffers the following Negative Traits while in this form: *Bestial* x 2 and *Tactless*. A Garou can initiate no Social Challenges that are not meant to intimidate while in Crinos form.

As a Garou gains Rank his Crinos form gains strength-related powers. At Rank 2 he may call for one free retest of any challenge that involves raw physical strength. At Rank 3 he gains the use of a fourth hand signal, the Bomb (which is thrown as a "Rock" but with the thumb pointing out, like a fuse). The Bomb beats Rock and Paper, and is only defeated by Scissors. At Rank 4 he gains one extra Health Level while in this form. At Rank 5 he wins all ties in Physical Challenges involving strength. At Rank 6 he inflicts an additional level of damage with every success in hand-to-hand combat. However, a Crinos cannot engage in fast-draw showdowns unless she has a firearm specially modified for Crinos paws, which is often considered quite dishonorable by every tribe outside of the Iron Riders. Furthermore, finding someone who would accept a challenge from such a hulking monster and not lose her mind to the Delirium is an interesting proposition in itself.

**Change Description**: Garou in this form often grow to a towering nine feet or more in height. The Garou's body is covered in thick fur, and her head becomes that of a snarling canine. Claws and fangs become pronounced and ready for combat. This form is most often assumed when a Garou is preparing to face great danger. Both the claws and teeth cause aggravated damage. When a character frenzies, this is typically the form she adopts as soon as she can (without spending Rage), although a few lupus prefer Hispo.

**Roleplaying**: When in Crinos form, the character takes on an appearance that evokes horrific racial memories in humans; any human seeing the Garou in this form is affected by the Delirium. Saying anything more complex than a few human words while in Crinos requires a Simple Mental Test, no Traits risked.

## Hispo: The Dire Wolf

**Trait Adjustments**: While in this form, the character gains the following bonus Traits: *Ferocious* x2, *Quick* x2 and *Tireless* x2. He is also afflicted with the following penalties: *Bestial* x2 and *Shortsighted*. Obviously, no fast-draw challenges are possible in Hispo or Lupus forms.

**Change Description**: This form is a huge, hulking, wolflike beast resembling the prehistoric dire wolf. The Hispo's head and jaws are massive, and his bite causes a second level of damage if a Simple Test is won after the initial combat challenge (this is not cumulative with any other damage enhancements, including Gifts). The Hispo can stand on his hind legs in emergencies, but he mostly stays on all fours. He weighs almost as much as the Crinos, but his wolflike legs enable him to run at one and one-half times normal wolf speeds. A Garou has paws instead of hands in Hispo, so he cannot hold objects except with his jaws.

**Roleplaying**: The Hispo form is a hunting machine and gains three extra Traits for comparison and overbids on any perception-related challenge. No human speech is possible in this form, unless a Simple Mental Test is won, and will be monosyllabic at best.

## Lupus: The Wolf

**Trait Adjustments**: While in Lupus form, the character gains the following bonus Traits: *Quick* x 2 and *Tireless*. He also incurs the following Negative Trait: *Bestial*.

**Change Description**: In this form, the Garou assumes the form of a wolf, usually a near-perfect specimen. The exact type of wolf is usually determined by the character's tribe. A character in Lupus form may not cause aggravated wounds with his claws, but may still do so with his teeth. In addition, a Garou in Lupus has exceptional senses. He may attempt to perform sensory feats that would be nearly impossible for a human: seeing in near-darkness, tracking by scent, hearing sounds too faint for the human ear, noticing beings hiding through Gifts or Disciplines, and the like.

**Roleplaying**: While in Lupus form, a character is driven mostly by instinct. A Lupus usually prefers to flee rather than fight a battle. Lupus cannot speak to humans, but may speak freely to wolves or other Garou.

**Note**: It is highly advisable to use cards pinned to shirts or colored ribbons around the wrist to designate which form characters are presently in. This way everyone knows what is going on and can remain (and react) in character. Some troupes prefer to use hand-signals to indicate forms (hands over head for Crinos, hands held out front for Lupus or Hispo, etc.).

# Beyond the Velvet Shadow

## Spirits and the Storm Umbra in the Savage West

The spirit world plays an instrumental role in the life of the Garou. A Garou can travel from the physical world to the spirit world (also called the Storm Umbra or simply the Umbra), allowing him to interact with the spiritual landscape. As a member of a pack, a Garou shares a mystic connection to the spirit world through his relationship to his pack totem; this totem also binds the pack together. Spirituality is an integral part of anything a Garou does. Even the most cynical Iron Rider living in the shadow of billowing factory clouds can see spirits everywhere she looks. To the Garou, the entire world is alive with the spirits of Gaia.

It is the Storyteller's job to bring out the spiritual side of werewolves when playing the Savage West. The spiritual aspect of the Garou is a rich and rewarding aspect of the game, but one that can be impractical to play and that can seriously damage the whole mood of the game if it is not handled well — and with consideration toward character development.

## The Spirit Keeper

If spirits play more than a minor role in your game, there should be a Narrator whose job is to adjudicate and administer all spirit-related Gifts and rites, Umbral travel, totems and spirit combat. This Narrator, called the "Spirit Keeper," is also in charge of all the spirit plotlines and anything having to do with the spirit world. The Spirit Keeper should prepare for any **Wyld West** session by defining any pre-existing spirits in the area and by creating some spirits in advance (just in case any are summoned). The Spirit Keeper also needs to know what the Umbra is like in all of the playing areas, and should be the final authority on all matters spiritual in gameplay.

## The Storm Umbra

There is a spirit world outside the perceptions of normal humanity. It lies alongside this world, separated from us by a wall of static reality called the Gauntlet. One must pass through the Gauntlet to reach the Storm Umbra or return back to Earth. The Gauntlet is said to be a membrane woven by the Weaver to separate physical reality from the Storm Umbra, but its origins are less important than its effects.

### Gauntlet Ratings

| Area | Gauntlet |
|---|---|
| Science lab | 9 |
| Large City | 8 |
| Small Town | 7 |
| Most places | 6 |
| Wilderness/Rural areas | 5 |
| Typical active caern | 4 |
| Powerful caern | 3 |
| Greatest caerns | 2 |

## Stepping Sideways

Any Garou has the power to step sideways into the Storm Umbra. In order to do this the Garou must focus his eyes on a reflective or shiny surface, then perform a Static Gnosis Challenge against half the local Gauntlet rating (*Primal Urge*, *Enigmas*, etc. allow retests). If the Garou wins, she enters the Umbra at the end of the present turn (a Storyteller may modify the difficulty if the reflective surface is something less or more difficult to focus one's eyes on; a full-length mirror is very easy to work with, while a reflection in someone's eyes is incredibly difficult). A loss indicates that the Garou cannot get through at this point and must move at least 20 steps from the area or wait five minutes in order to try again. A tie indicates that the Garou is only partially through. She must test again on the next turn; a success gets her through, a tie leaves her still trying, and a loss means she is stuck in the Gauntlet.

A Garou who is stuck in the Gauntlet is in trouble. She may try once per hour to get free by spending a Gnosis Trait and succeeding in a Simple Test. While stuck in the Gauntlet, the Garou is neither in the spirit or physical world, and cannot be affected by direct assaults from either side, but is at the tender mercies of whatever spirits in the area: the character may be attacked by Weaver-spirits, have horrible visions of places like Malfeas (the Wyrm's home realm), and/or experience other particularly unnerving events. While caught between worlds, a Garou cannot recover Gnosis. However, it is possible for a "stuck" Garou to be rescued by another werewolf, who makes a Static Gnosis Test (against seven Traits) to free the prisoner.

Two or more Garou going into the Umbra at the same time may designate a leader. Only that leader tests against the Gauntlet, and her result affects everyone. If she gets stuck, the whole group gets stuck, and no one else can become leader and attempt to pull the group free until the present leader runs out of Gnosis. Garou with the Gift: *Grasp the Beyond* can take non-Garou with them into the Umbra.

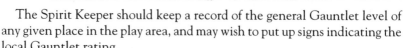

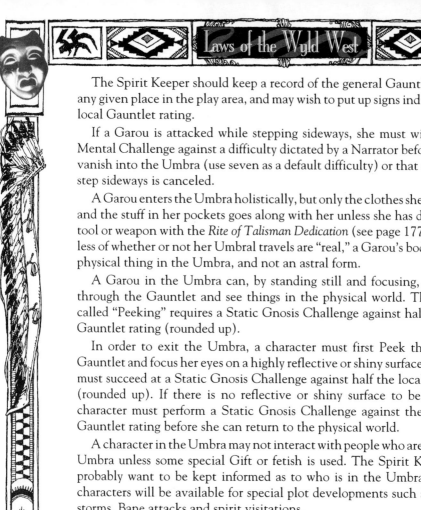

The Spirit Keeper should keep a record of the general Gauntlet level of any given place in the play area, and may wish to put up signs indicating the local Gauntlet rating.

If a Garou is attacked while stepping sideways, she must win a Static Mental Challenge against a difficulty dictated by a Narrator before she can vanish into the Umbra (use seven as a default difficulty) or that attempt to step sideways is canceled.

A Garou enters the Umbra holistically, but only the clothes she is wearing and the stuff in her pockets goes along with her unless she has dedicated a tool or weapon with the *Rite of Talisman Dedication* (see page 177). Regardless of whether or not her Umbral travels are "real," a Garou's body is a real, physical thing in the Umbra, and not an astral form.

A Garou in the Umbra can, by standing still and focusing, peer back through the Gauntlet and see things in the physical world. This action, called "Peeking" requires a Static Gnosis Challenge against half the local Gauntlet rating (rounded up).

In order to exit the Umbra, a character must first Peek through the Gauntlet and focus her eyes on a highly reflective or shiny surface. She then must succeed at a Static Gnosis Challenge against half the local Gauntlet (rounded up). If there is no reflective or shiny surface to be seen, the character must perform a Static Gnosis Challenge against the full local Gauntlet rating before she can return to the physical world.

A character in the Umbra may not interact with people who are not in the Umbra unless some special Gift or fetish is used. The Spirit Keeper will probably want to be kept informed as to who is in the Umbra, as those characters will be available for special plot developments such as Umbral storms, Bane attacks and spirit visitations.

One of the advantages of the Umbra is that Garou can do battle in it without endangering the Veil. The Umbra also makes an excellent "escape route," although the Umbra can sometimes be more dangerous than the physical world. There are locations in the Umbra that correspond to places on Earth, although exact distances can become confused in the spirit world.

As a Storytelling device, the Storm Umbra is without equal. It is a metaphoric reflection of our world. Where there is desolation or corruption on Earth, there are seething masses of Wyrm-tainted power, called Hellholes, in the Umbra. Where there are great monuments to the Weaver, such as railroads, bridges and growing cities in the real world, in the Umbra there are webs everywhere and Pattern Spiders busily weaving to maintain them. Outside "civilization," the Umbral wilderness glows with an internal light, and the power of Mother Gaia is shown in all its glory.

However, both newcomers to **Wyld West** and those experienced in **Laws of the Wild** should take care, for the Storm Umbra of the Savage West is nothing like the Umbra of the modern world. It is less tainted by the touch of pollutants and widespread Weaver influence, but this is balanced by its savage, unpredictably primal nature. The Setting chapter describes the Storm Umbra in more detail, but consider that as a rule of thumb many spirits are quite angered at the great changes going on, and more than a few have been driven mad by the chaos around them. Bizarre crossbreeds of Weaver- and Wyrm-spirits are cropping up with ever-increasing frequency, and Wyld-spirits are often downright vicious toward those they see as furthering the "taming" of the Savage West.

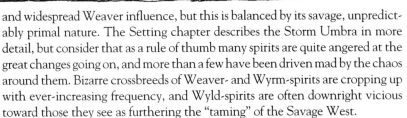

During the day, the Umbral sky is dark; at night, it is illuminated by the light of Luna. If one were to travel far enough, one would soon pass through the areas of the Near Umbra (Penumbra) and approach the boundary that separates the Near Umbra from the Deep Umbra. The Deep Umbra is a strange and wild place, the position of which corresponds to deep space in the realm of the physical world.

There are two other Umbral planes accessible from Earth: A realm that is called the "High Umbra," where spirits of ideas and concepts take form, and a realm of wicked spirits and wraiths, called the "Dark" or "Low" Umbra.

## The Storm Umbra in Play

The Spirit Keeper may wish to create a separate area that's set up to evoke the atmosphere of the Storm Umbra. Many dramatic and important scenes can be played in a place where it actually appears as though the players are no longer in this world. Narrators can create the appropriate ambiance for the area by using such elements as dry ice fog, special lighting, mood music and other decorations. However, this area should be kept separate from the rest of the game, and the Spirit Keeper should prevent anyone who is not "in the Umbra" from entering the area.

It is also possible that players will try to abuse their advantage by constantly entering the Umbra to escape potential danger. This is unwise, as the Storm Umbra contains dangers unlike anything found on the Earth. A Spirit Keeper has free reign to throw Banes and other hazards at Garou who abuse the Umbra for purely tactical "drops" and "extractions."

To indicate that he is in the Umbra, a Garou should bring his right hand across his chest. Making this gesture lets other players know that you are in the Umbra and not really "there" — which can prevent no end of confusion during gameplay.

# Spirits

Entities given form by a particular purpose and icon, spirits are Umbral beings that reflect the mundane world. All of the world is full of spirits; everything has a spiritual component, though in many cases, the spirits are asleep. Some spirits aren't sleeping any longer, and many things have awakened spirits associated with them. For example, a particularly well-loved saddle might actually have a wakeful spirit of Affection or Speed attached to it.

The difference between a waking and sleeping spirit is that one has an active consciousness and the other does not. **Wyld West** focuses on awake, active spirits only. Sleeping spirits are not dealt with, unless the special *Rite of Spirit Awakening* is used (see "Rites" in Chapter Two, pp. 181).

## Gafflings and Jagglings

The Garou think of spirits in terms of their general level of power. The weakest and smallest spirits are called Gafflings. These are mere extensions of the power of larger spirits and have little to no independent intelligence. Slightly more powerful spirits are called Jagglings. These are common, everyday spirits with which the Garou interact. One type of Jaggling, called an Engling, can provide Garou with Gnosis. The spirits that are commonly found as servants of the Wyrm are called Banes, and come in many forms, each usually associated with some dark emotion or act of depravity.

## The Incarna

There are a number of spirits that have grown in power to the point where they command many Jagglings and have a great supply of personal energy. These spirits, called Incarna, tend to have their own realms in the Umbra, and are often incarnations of ancient deities, powerful forces and archetypes, and other mythic beings. Many of the Incarna are very ancient, and therefore have correspondingly vast knowledge and powers.

## Totem Spirits

Some of the most ancient Incarna are the animal spirits that were allies of the Garou when the Changing Breeds were first born. These animal spirits pledged that they would forever lend their wisdom, power and spirit children to the aid of the Garou, Gaia's noble sons and daughters.

These animal Incarna are called totems, and they have left their lasting mark on the tribes and packs of Garou. Occasionally, a totem sends one of its avatars, an extension of its will, to serve the Garou directly. This always occurs as a result of a pack forming, as the totem avatar becomes bound to the pack as part of the *Rite of Passage* or the *Rite of the Totem*. Each tribe, caern and pack has a totem associated with it, and many Garou adopt personal totems that they quietly follow on an individual basis.

## The Celestines

Above the level of the Incarna are the Celestines — powerful and eternal spirits that embody fundamental forces in the universe. Gaia Herself is a Celestine, as are Luna and Helios. Celestines are the least "normal" appearing of the spirits. They assume abstract forms and communicate in strange ways. These entities are so transcendent and distant that it is difficult to describe them in simple terms; it is highly unlikely that a Garou is going to interact with a Celestine during the course of a game of **Wyld West**.

Because of limited space, this book has only cursory descriptions of spirits. Refer to **Laws of the Wild**, pp. 190-200, for more complete information about spirits and spirit creation.

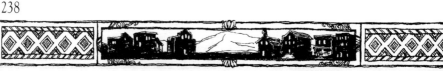

## Delirium Chart

| Willpower/ Mental Index | % of Population | Reaction |
|---|---|---|
| 1 | 10% | **Catatonic Fear**: This unfortunate just got a whopping dose of ancestral memory. He collapses into a fetal ball and whimpers, remembering nothing of the encounter later. |
| 2 | 30% | **Panic**: The person runs as fast and as far as her feet can take her, running over anything that tries to stop her, often ignoring obstacles like waterfalls and oncoming trains. The person remembers that *something* scared her. |
| 3 | 8% | **Disbelief**: The person thinks he is hallucinating, attributing the Garou to fatigue, a trick of the light, alcohol or the like. "This ain't happening! You're not real! I gotta quit drinking!" |
| 4 | 15% | **Berserk:** Blind, frenzied fear goads her to action — any kind of action, even leaping on the Garou and pounding on him. She remembers seeing something big and hairy. |
| 5 | 13% | **Terror**: Not as bad as Panic, but the human still moves away from the Garou as fast as he can. Even while running, he remembers to lock the door behind him, look for hiding places or jump on his horse and haul tail for the next horizon. He will remember seeing something monstrous, big, hairy and mean. |
| 6 | 10% | **Conciliatory**: Although on the verge of collapse, she does her best to calm and placate the beast, and remembers about half of the general information ("It was big, and brown, and like a big dog — no, a wolf!"). She may agree to anything to avoid getting hurt. |
| 7 | 7% | **Controlled Fear**: Maybe he's a former soldier or a veteran Texas Ranger. He keeps his cool (although terrified), and fights or flees as appropriate. Furthermore, he remembers most of the details of the situation. "I'm telling you, this… thing walked out of that mirror, sniffed around, and went back in when it saw me!" |
| 8 | 5% | **Curiosity**: Instead of being afraid, she's fascinated with the sight. Maybe she's a scholar of things paranormal, or just a loon who thinks the Garou is a mythical emissary of some kind (in which case she might spill the story to a yellow journalist). She might start looking for the Garou to study him (from a safe distance). However, she is more likely to rationalize it away. |
| 9 | 1.5% | **Bloodlust**: His reaction is anger rather than fear, and he remembers the encounter quite well. He'll run for his gun rather than a Bible or the door. "Hoo-whee, look at that! I'm gonna have me one of them pelts for my cabin!" |
| 10 | 0.5% | **No Reaction/Blasé**: She displays no reaction to the Garou's appearance whatsoever. If spoken to, she responds politely and casually. This person either has nerves of steel or a brain of cow pies. Needless to say, she remembers *everything* in perfect detail. "Oh, yeah, the big furry guy asked me which way the robbers went, then said good-day and left." |

# Delirium

Delirium is a state of mind that afflicts humans who see a Garou in Crinos form. Reactions vary greatly. Some humans run in sheer terror, while others cower on the ground in front of the Garou. A few completely disbelieve the incident ever happened. There are also those who become quite curious about the event and attempt to gain more information. A few souls even go hunting for the Garou in a fit of ancestral vengeance. It is therefore important that characters be careful when changing forms or running about as something other than a human or wolf. The integrity of the Veil must be preserved.

To use this chart, double the subject's Willpower Traits (typically zero or one for most normal humans), add Mental Traits (usually three to five), and subtract three. The result is the line to check on the table. Results of zero or less use the "1" line; similarly, totals of eleven or more use the "10" line.

# The Curse

Whenever a Garou's Rage exceeds the Willpower of a nearby human or wolf, that human or wolf feels uneasy and nervous around the Garou. This is considered a curse by the Garou, for it prevents stable relationships, marriages and the like. Only among their own are Garou ever able to form lasting friendships.

All characters attempting to live normal human lives (marriages, businesses, hanging out with normal friends, drinking in the corner saloon every Friday, etc.) make Willpower Tests against their Rage (no Traits risked) once per cycle of the moon. A loss indicates that something has happened to ruin or hinder the character's relationship with those among whom he has been living. The Beast has emerged, the Delirium has engaged, and the character will never be completely trusted again.

# Howls

Werewolves' howls are their most powerful and evocative means of expression. By howling, Garou may condense enormous amounts of information into a few notes. Mastering the myriad howls is the life's work of a Moon Dancer.

Howls are usually begun by one Garou, but often joined by others. Regardless of which howl is employed, harmony is disdained and cacophony is actively sought. When two Garou hit the same note, one instinctively alters pitch, thereby retaining the sought-after discord. The pack uses such tactics to make it seem larger than it is, and foes are thereby intimidated.

There are many types of howls; here are a few of the more common ones:

**Call to Hunt** — To alert others to the position of prey (low ululation).

**Chant of Challenge** — To entice a fight, used by initiator of a challenge (barks and growls of self-praise, recitation of one's lineage, and carefully aimed insults).

**Cry for Help** — To get aid (bark of a lost puppy).

**Death Song** — A passionate, defiant howl in face of certain death, this howl summarizes a Garou's life and prepares her for her reunion with Gaia. A powerful and moving howl, it often lingers long after the battle has passed.

**Howl of Introduction** — Used when entering the area of another Garou, pack or sept; to let others know that you wish for permission to enter and intend no harm (warbling howl mixed with barks).

**Lament for the Fallen** — A requiem for the honored dead (somber, low-pitched, drawn-out howl).

**Shame Song** — The Garou version of the "finger," added to any other howl (particularly annoying pitch parody) and also used to mock those who have fallen from favor.

**Snarl of Precedence** — To claim an opponent for one-on-one combat (closed-teeth howl).

**Symphony of the Abyss** — Used by Black Spiral Dancers when hunting to terrify foes (reverberating, mad whine).

**Wail of Foreboding** — General danger signal, often used to warn of natural disasters (wailing, rolling howl).

**War Cry** — To summon or rally the troops (proud energetic howls).

**Wyrm Warning** — (very sharply pitched howl, emitted in a series of brief staccato bursts).

Each area tends to have something akin to a local dialect in its howls, with particular tones and phrases equating to familiar sights, names and sounds. A great deal of information can be transmitted in this way.

As it's highly unlikely that all of the players in a game of the **Wyld West** are going to be able to master these howls (and in all honesty, do you really want to know what the neighbors will do when they hear 60 people howling in unison?), it is perfectly acceptable to call out the name of the Howl you are performing instead of actually howling. Of course, if you have the privacy and permission of all of the players, by all means let a talented player or two practice their howling skills; however, keep in mind that while a good howl adds much to game atmosphere, any player who sounds like fingernails through a bucket full of broken blackboard shards should be silenced for the greater good of the game (not to mention your sanity).

# Experience

As sentient beings, we collate the information that is presented to us in our daily lives and hopefully become better people for our experiences. Some of us do, while some of us ignore our lessons and must repeat the same mistakes again and again. During our life, we learn from the mistakes of yesterday and prepare for the challenges of tomorrow.

Experience in the **Wyld West** is represented by giving each character one to three Experience Traits at the end of each session. The number of Traits awarded is based on how well a character performed during the course of the story and how active a player was in the game. The Narrator decides how many points each player receives upon completion of the session. All players receive one Trait — this is standard. Exceptional roleplayers, those who played an exceptionally memorable part, should receive two. Three Traits should be awarded to those characters who performed acts of incredible insight and courage, making the game more memorable for everyone involved. On a normal night, each player will receive one Experience Trait.

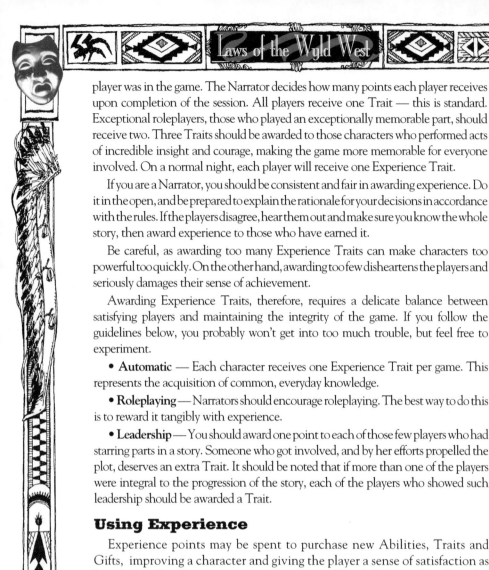

If you are a Narrator, you should be consistent and fair in awarding experience. Do it in the open, and be prepared to explain the rationale for your decisions in accordance with the rules. If the players disagree, hear them out and make sure you know the whole story, then award experience to those who have earned it.

Be careful, as awarding too many Experience Traits can make characters too powerful too quickly. On the other hand, awarding too few disheartens the players and seriously damages their sense of achievement.

Awarding Experience Traits, therefore, requires a delicate balance between satisfying players and maintaining the integrity of the game. If you follow the guidelines below, you probably won't get into too much trouble, but feel free to experiment.

• **Automatic** — Each character receives one Experience Trait per game. This represents the acquisition of common, everyday knowledge.

• **Roleplaying** — Narrators should encourage roleplaying. The best way to do this is to reward it tangibly with experience.

• **Leadership** — You should award one point to each of those few players who had starring parts in a story. Someone who got involved, and by her efforts propelled the plot, deserves an extra Trait. It should be noted that if more than one of the players were integral to the progression of the story, each of the players who showed such leadership should be awarded a Trait.

## Using Experience

Experience points may be spent to purchase new Abilities, Traits and Gifts, improving a character and giving the player a sense of satisfaction as he watches his character grow more potent. The following chart lists the costs for improving Traits, Abilities and Gifts.

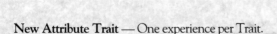

**New Attribute Trait** — One experience per Trait.

**New Ability** — One experience per Ability Trait.

**New Gift** — Three experience points for Basic Gifts, six for Intermediate Gifts and nine for Advanced Gifts. (**Note**: You must have enough Renown and be of the appropriate Rank to take a Gift. If you are of the appropriate Rank but don't have a Renown Trait that's not "spoken for," you cannot learn a new Gift. On the other hand, you can have all the Renown in the world but cannot learn Gifts past your Rank limits.) It costs an additional point to learn a Gift outside of your breed, auspice or tribe.

**New Merit/Flaw** — Double the cost of the Merit/Flaw, with Narrator approval. This should not happen instantaneously, and should be worked into a character's ongoing storyline and character evolution. The addition of a Merit or removal of a Flaw should not be treated lightly, as it represents a fundamental alteration of a character's being.

**New Rite/Ritual** — Two experience points for Basic, four for Intermediate, and six for Advanced Rites. (Note: Rites and rituals only cost experience points to buy if they are not available to be learned during game play. In that case, they may cost only time and role-playing, at the Storyteller's discretion).

**New Gnosis** — Three experience per Trait.

**New Rage** — Three experience per Trait.

**New Willpower** — Three experience per Trait.

**Buy off Negative Trait** — Two experience per Trait.

**Buy off a Notoriety Trait** — Two experience per Trait.

# Chapter Five: Storytelling

## The Litany

This is the great song of the ages, containing the traditions, codes and laws of the Garou. All Philodox are required to learn it by heart, and most Moon Dancers learn a significant portion of it. The Litany is a complex and often convoluted thing, but its intricacies serve the purpose of poetry moreso than pontification. Practical application of the Litany is much simpler than the hours-long chants would seem to indicate.

The following are some of the basic tenets of the Litany; there are many others, often varying by sept or tribe.

### *Garou Shall Not Mate with Garou*

If you produce a metis, it is sterile, cannot reproduce and therefore is of no help in continuing the Garou line. Choose a mate who can help the Garou survive into future generations.

### *Combat the Wyrm Wherever It Dwells and Wherever It Breeds*

Garou exist to fight the excesses of the Wyrm. If you allow yourself to be drawn away from that mission, you are aiding the Wyrm and weakening us all. If you blindly attack any Wyrm-creature you encounter, you will end up dead, quick. The idea is not to die for Gaia, but rather to make those poor fools die for the Wyrm.

### *Respect the Territory of Another*

You do not take what is not yours. You do not claim protection or ownership of land that is already guarded by another Garou. This causes conflicts between

Garou, which is bad for Gaia because it weakens us in our battle against the Wyrm. This point is especially contended during the westward movement, and the Pure Ones scoff at it openly, feeling the Europeans have violated it far too many times to try to ever enforce it on them.

### Accept an Honorable Surrender

We are too few in number to go about killing each other every time someone gets offended. Duels to the death aid only the Wyrm. When a fellow Garou surrenders, accept your victory graciously and go back to fighting the Wyrm.

### Submission to Those of Higher Station

Accept any reasonable request from someone who has been around long enough to have earned more Renown than you. You want to be respected for your deeds, so respect others for theirs.

### Respect for Those Beneath Ye — All Are of Gaia

Lead by example. Teach through your actions. You will not always be strong, and those you help as you climb upward will be met again on your way down.

### Do Not Suffer Thy People to Tend Thy Sickness

We no longer live in a time when the old and enfeebled must go into the wood to die. Instead, they can remain active members of the tribe, and their wisdom benefits the young. However, do not make yourself a burden to your people by expecting them to take care of you. Do not fight to remain in a position you are no longer best suited to hold.

### The First Share of the Kill for the Greatest in Station

When you are leader, it will be your right and responsibility to make the decisions concerning the spoils of war. Until then, give your leaders the rights due to them from their station and demand responsibility for their actions, or challenge them. If you serve as the leader, remember that the spoils of war should go to the Garou who can best use them to aid the whole group.

### The Leader May Be Challenged at Any Time during Peace

If you feel you would make a better leader, prove it. Take the position from the current leader — but only when the pack is not endangered by the challenge.

### The Leader May Not Be Challenged during Wartime

Do not fight amongst yourselves while trying to fight the Wyrm. Do your internal fighting in private, and always show a united face to our enemies.

Circumstances must be most dire before you move against a leader while a threat to the group exists. If you are right in this desperate challenge, you will not be punished. If you were wrong, however, the Nation will know of your punishment, and the Galliards sing of it for lifetimes to come.

### Ye Shall Not Eat the Flesh of Humans

Regardless of the original reason for this part of the Litany, it has become a clear health issue. What humans eat and do in their Wyrm-tainted cities and factories has made their meat bitter. Devouring it has made more than one Garou ill — and there is always the threat of creeping Wyrm-taint.

### The Veil Shall Not Be Lifted

The very few times that Garou have allowed humans to know of their existence, it brought tragedy and death to many involved. We are hunted, and we serve Gaia best by turning hunters against the Wyrm rather than at ourselves and our children.

### Ye Shall Take No Action That Causes a Caern to Be Violated

If your choice of actions causes the Garou to lose one of their few remaining places of power and of Gaia's strength, you will die.

Breaking the letter of the law of the Litany is not necessarily punishable by death. Major, tragic events must result from a violation of the Litany for Garou to order one of their own slain. In fact, the notion of the "letter" of the Litany is somewhat misleading, as the Litany does not exist in written form *per se*. While there are pictograms that depict each basic idea of the Litany and verbal lore which takes many days to recite, there is no strict published version of the Litany annotated with footnotes. There can never be one, for each tribe, auspice and breed has given its own "interpretations" to the Litany — making the notion of a definitive version highly unlikely. However, the spirit of the Litany is preserved from version to version; among all Garou, the Litany is used to keep the peace and resolve conflicts.

## The Silver Record

The Silver Record is the only complete record of the Garou. It exists as pictograms, each one a reminder of one tale in the history of the Garou. All the great, Glorious, Honorable and Wise achievements of the Garou heroes are recorded in the Silver Record. All the Inglorious, Unwise and Dishonorable failures of those same Garou and others are also in the Record. If something happened that was important to the Garou as a whole, its tale was incorporated into the Silver Record, no matter what.

The Record begins with Phoenix, the first of Gaia, and continues down to the present day. It tells of the forming of the Triat, the First Times, the coming of the Gurahl, the Imbalance, the coming of the Garou, the One Tribe, the War of

Rage, the splitting of the tribes, the Impergium, the forming of the Litany, the coming of the Black Spiral Dancers, the loss of the Croatan, the murder of the Bunyip and other events that have impacted the Garou.

No one Garou claims to know the entire Silver Record, but it is believed that if all Garou who knew parts of it came together, none of it would be missing. All tribes must agree as to what is worthy of mention in the Silver Record; it is one of the bonds that unites all Garou.

## Caerns

In certain areas where the Gauntlet is weak, wondrous things happen and the planet somehow seems more *alive*. The Garou know of these places and hold them dear; these holy places are called caerns. Garou defend their caerns fiercely and protect them from mages (who would drain them), vampires (who would control or destroy them), marauding spirits (who would eat their energy away), and the minions of the Wyrm (who would corrupt and destroy them).

### Caern Chart

| Caern Level | Gauntlet | Moon Bridge Distances* |
|---|---|---|
| 1 | 4 | 1,000 miles |
| 2 | 4 | 2,000 miles |
| 3 | 3 | 3,000 miles |
| 4 | 3 | 6,000 miles |
| 5 | 2 | 10,000 miles |

*The distance that can be traveled via Moon Bridge is determined by the rating of the caern being traveled from. Without a caern, Moon Bridges only allow travel up to 1,000 miles.

Be very careful in allowing your players to open Moon Bridges. Limitations of logistics and space can make it very difficult to run successful games when one pack is at the "home" caern, another is in the north woods, and a third is cavorting around back East.

Each caern has a rating from one to five, and is dedicated to a general purpose, like war or healing. A caern draws spirits of like nature to itself, and all rites performed at the caern have a slight tendency toward the direction of the caern's affinity.

Storytellers are advised to work with the players in designing the caern(s) with which the characters are going to be interacting. Caerns are rare things, and the more powerful the caern, the greater the characters' numbers and abilities must be in order to protect it from being found and overrun by the Wyrm's minions.

**Caern Types**

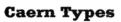

| Type | Spirits Power** | Encountered*** |
|---|---|---|
| All | Open Moon Bridge† | Nature-spirit, Ancestor-spirit |
| Enigmas | *Enigmas* Ability | Illusion, Shadow, Chameleon-spirit |
| Gnosis | Gnosis Traits | Engling, wraith |
| Healing | Health Levels | Peace, Calm, Water elemental |
| Leadership | *Leadership*, *Intimidation* | War, Bird-spirit, Ancestor-spirit |
| Rage | Rage Traits | War, Pain, Glory-spirit |
| Stamina | Damage Resistance | Protection, Guardian |
| Strength | Physical Traits | War |
| Urban | *Larceny* | City-spirit |
| Visions | Oracular Visions | Bird-spirit |
| Will | Willpower | War, Honor-spirit |
| Wisdom | *Ritual*, *Expression* | Owl-spirit Wisdom-spirit |
| Wyld | Anything | Wyldling, Any |

**One Trait/level/effect is gained (see *Rite of the Open Caern*).
***These are the spirits most often encountered near caerns of that type.
†See *Rite of the Opened Bridge*.

Access to a caern is something that is necessary for Garou to advance and learn new Gifts. Moreover, caerns can serve as neutral ground where characters can talk, where spirits can set them on quests, and other vital roles within your stories. On the other hand, your Garou storylines will die if the characters do not have access to a caern that has properties which are instrumental to the characters' plotlines and goals.

## Gathering at the Fires

Garou enjoy fellowship with one another, primarily because the only individuals who can truly understand their ways are other Garou. Only other Garou can truly share their dreams and their needs. The Garou are a lonely people, a dying breed. Their culture and community are the last refuges that keep them together in a time where families and nations are growing and drifting apart, and that remind them of all that they are fighting for.

Despite their intense devotion and sense of obligation to Mother Gaia, the Garou cannot be Her soldiers all of the time. They must take time to gather, speak to one another, decide on new paths for the future, and, for what it's worth, have fun. This is the Savage West and the land is harsh, but it's also a time of great freedom and the ability to forge one's own destiny, and no Garou will ever succeed at her tasks if she's in low spirits all the time.

Indeed, Harano, the dark depression that comes of fighting the good fight and losing, is an ever-present danger for the Garou. Although it is chiefly the job of the Galliards to watch their kin for signs of this blackness, sometimes even their perceptive eyes cannot see it coming. Therefore, it's important for a Garou to interact with other Garou and receive the spiritual and emotional support such contact provides.

## The Moot

Moots are assemblies of Garou that combine social, religious and political functions, and thus are tremendously important. Moots provide a lifeline of spirituality, strength, culture, law, tradition, honor and history that stretches back into the deepest primeval times, back to the First Pack.

A general moot structure is given below for the sept moot. This is the most common type of moot that the characters will likely attend. Such moots are generally held monthly at any given sept's caern. Any Garou can attend, but Garou not of the sept are often viewed with suspicion.

**Narrator's Note**: The moot structure below is a general guideline. Each tribe has its own way of doing things. Alter or add to it as you see fit.

### The Fool

It is tradition among the Garou that a Fool should be appointed for any moot. What the Fool does and says is never held against him. He can caper and dance, make fun of the Litany and dispute the word of anyone without retribution. Many of the more traditional septs always have a Fool, who provides a counterpoint so that the other Garou can show their feelings. In return, the Garou are supposed to affirm their heritage by refuting the claims of the Fool. Of course, when a Fool agrees with a sept, that is also an insult; after all, he is a Fool.

After the moot, the Fool's privileges are suspended, and his words in the moot are supposed to be forgotten and/or forgiven. This is often hard for Garou to do, which is why many Fools don't go completely overboard — a wise Fool nettles where he can do the most good. The Master of the Rite appoints the Fool for a moot; the position is usually held by a Ragabash, although not always.

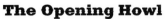

## The Opening Howl

All moots start with the howl. From among the Galliards, a Master of the Howl is chosen. The Master of the Howl is honored for his participation, and it is his voice which starts the sometimes-booming opening howl. After the last strains of the howl die down, the Master of the Rite recites the Litany. The Fool reacts vehemently to the Litany, offering wild suggestions at every point.

## The Inner Sky

This part of the moot starts in silence, and a Theurge titled the Caller of the Wyld steps forward and, sometimes with four other helpers, addresses the five directions (North, South, East, West and Within), asking for their aid in the moot. The Caller then calls up the totem or totems of the caern, and asks for their presence.

### Calling the Winds

One of the important parts of the Inner Sky portion of the moot is that it renews the connection that the Garou have with their related spirits. Below is a sample "script" for use during the Inner Sky:

Caller of the Wyld: We have gathered in this sacred place of Gaia, having called our brothers and sisters of Gaia, and we now call our brothers and sisters of Luna.

*(She faces East)*

East wind! Bringer of the dawn of clear air! East wind! You who showed us the mirror side, the other side of the Velvet Curtain, come to us! We thank you for your clear thought and bright light!

*(She turns to her right, to the South)*

South wind! Bringer of the eternal fire! South wind! You who gave us the fire of rage within, that we may strike swiftly against our enemies, come to us! We thank you for your fiery anger and your guardian protection!

*(She turns to her right, to the West)*

West wind! Bringer of the rain! West wind! You who gave us the Changing Ways, come to us! We thank you for the many shapes you've shared with us!

*(She turns to her right, to the North)*

North wind! Bringer of cold from the mountain! North wind! You who brought us the Gifts and the Sacred Ways, come to us! We thank you for your great wisdom and strength!

*(She stands with her hands above her, her eyes to the sky in the spring or summer, or with her hands pointing palm-down, her eyes to the ground in fall or winter.)*

Inner wind! Bringer of blessings from Gaia, from within us! You who hold our Mother's power within us, come to us all! We thank you for your spirit and your inner peace!

Traditionally some Garou take the part of the totems of the sept, dressing in masks and costumes to reflect the totem's nature. These are called the Shining Ones, and they symbolize the totem for the moot.

The Inner Sky is meant to be a method by which the Garou renew ties of community and respect with their totem and the spirits around them. If this thanking of the spirits is neglected at a caern for more than nine months, the power of the caern dwindles. A weakened caern can be revitalized at a moot through the normal expenditure of Gnosis by anyone who is present at the Wyrm Foe stage. This is done by spending a temporary Gnosis Trait to feed the caern forces. Once a caern is allowed to lapse into total dormancy, it must be reawakened with a moot at which one permanent Gnosis must be spent for every level of power of the caern.

**Narrator's Notes**: This is a good time to honor and thank your Spirit Keeper for the work he does at the caern. Have him play the totem and receive thanks from the Garou in this fashion. Every job should have its little perks.

## Cracking the Bone

As the moon rises toward its zenith in the night sky, the Master of the Howl signals for the stage of the moot known as Cracking the Bone. This is done with a high keening howl that ends in a jagged, shattering note, much like the splinter of a tough dry bone. This is the traditional time when those at the moot may make their grievances known, petition their peers for judgment on some matter, and propose or question sept policy.

Traditionally a Philodox elder presides over Cracking the Bone, and in doing so, bears the coveted title of Truthcatcher. He alone recognizes those who would speak, and gives them permission to do so, at least among the more structured septs. The eldest among those gathered are generally allowed to bring any grievance forth first. Some septs have a "talking bone" that is passed about to remind those present of who currently has the right to speak.

Grievances can be almost anything — requests for arbitration between two Garou, accusations of violating the Litany, requests for approval in endeavors or simple requests for advice. In any case, all members of the sept are allowed to hear any part of Cracking the Bone, and in some tribes serve as a jury of one's peers. The Truthcatcher can interrupt at any time, asking questions or demanding clarification. Once all is said and done, it is he who hands down the final decision, the final ruling, and, if appropriate, the punishment.

Different auspices show markedly different behaviors during Cracking the Bone. The Ahroun eagerly suggest trials by combat, while the Theurges remain a little distant. Philodox often become entranced by the quest for truth that they see as the core of this stage of the moot. The Ragabash shuffle, impatient at the seriousness of the whole affair, and the Galliards nearly burst as the Stories and Songs portion of the moot draws near.

## Stories and Songs

Once again, the Master of the Howl assumes the mantle of authority and declares the beginning of the time of tales. At this signal, the Talesinger rises and leads the gathered Garou in a eloquent howl that runs the entire range of the wolf's scale, from the highest inaudible whine to a low bass rumbling that is more felt than heard.

This is the time when all Garou are reminded of what it means to be the Chosen Ones of Gaia. In story and song, parable and poem, the antics, heroics and sacrifices of those who came before this generation are retold with an energy and pride that imbues the listener with the strong sense of belonging that is at the core of Garou society. The Time of Tales is not just a time to remember the past, however. New tales are told about Garou now sitting at this very gathering. Those among the sept who have excelled (or descended) beyond their peers may hear their names brought up by the Talesinger and her assistants.

The Talesinger is the moot position coveted above all others by the Galliards. To them, it is the ultimate canvas, the primary stage. By reciting the ancient lore of her kind and adding her own verses, a Talesinger can achieve a sort of immortality in the annals of the Garou's oral legacy.

Few hopeful Garou of any auspice miss this stage, however, because being included in the evening's tales (which is complimentary, at the very least) can mean gifts of Renown for the recipient. In some septs, any Garou may petition the Talesinger for the chance to tell a tale to the collected Garou. In other septs, this would be considered brash and boastful, and another Garou, preferably a Galliard, must be convinced or asked to speak on behalf of the petitioner.

Regardless of the niceties, those gathered listen to each and every tale told, and once it is done, the Talesinger asks if any present would speak against the supplicant. Offering opposition is a very serious insult, akin to calling the Renown supplicant a liar, but it is one that must be borne out. The challenger may tell her own tale, and once it is finished, the Talesinger appeals to the collected Garou for a decision. Those who support the claim to Renown call out first, and when their howls die down, those who dissent raise their voices. From this, the Talesinger judges whether to award the Renown (and suggests which Traits should be bestowed) or not.

This process is repeated for as many petitions as the Talesinger will grant, and if the "stage" is crowded, some may have to wait until the next moot.

**Note**: This is the roleplaying side of the Renown system. Characters must still have enough experience to purchase the Renown they receive at the moot, otherwise it doesn't matter how loudly the assembled packs howl. On the other hand, if the entire sept feels that a character deserves a little extra Renown, a Storyteller can certainly use her discretion.

### The Revel

While the members of the sept are still heady from the inspiring stories of the Talesinger, the Master of the Howl lets her gaze pass silently over the masses of Garou until she locks eyes with the Garou who might be this moot's Wyrm Foe. The Garou who leads the Revel represents the consummate warrior.

It is no surprise that many eager Ahroun desperately try to catch the Master of the Howl's gaze. Once eyes meet, the would-be Wyrm Foe rises and closes with the Master of the Howl. The two circle each other in an intense staredown that the challenger must win before assuming the role of Wyrm Foe. In most septs, the Wyrm Foe is chosen beforehand, and the staredown is merely for show. In a few septs, however, the Wyrm Foe has no such warning and the staredown is very real. If she is unable to defeat the Master of the Howl, another is chosen.

Once the Wyrm Foe has secured her position, most of her fellows erupt into a cacophony of howls and yelps; she is expected to quiet them with a howl that rises above the din and demands submission.

At this time, the primal passions of the Garou approach their climax, and the Wyrm Foe is the only measure of control present. She calls for mock battles, ritual hunts, displays of strength and wild dances that channel the vibrant energy of the gathered Garou.

As the energy level reaches its zenith, the Garou channel their Gnosis into the caern to maintain its connection to the Umbra. A caern requires two Gnosis Traits for each power level, in addition to one Gnosis Trait from each Garou present. Those Garou present can be issued cards to represent their Gnosis Traits. They may tear up or otherwise destroy these cards to represent the fueling process.

## Narrator's Notes: Preparing for a Moot

You may wish to hold your moots on private property outside, especially if the moon is going to be full and bright. If you can't do that, you should create an indoor moot area instead. Decorate the area appropriately, and you may get across the primeval, ritualistic feel of a moot.

Organize the people in charge of each segment of the moot. If you've never done this before, you may feel the need for a rehearsal before the whole sept gathers.

The important thing about the moot is that you keep it moving. If, for some reason, you skip a section of the moot, just go on to the next — it's not going to be a disaster. If you stop to correct too many problems or re-do sections, you'll never achieve the roleplaying mood that you're supposed to evoke: that of being a Garou among other Garou.

# Other Types of Gatherings

Aside from the moot, there are many other gatherings that occur in and around the sept. Indeed, there are almost always Garou around a caern. They come for a sense of community. They come to share concerns, report to their elders and simply to rest on Gaia's sacred ground. Here are some of the lesser gatherings that the Garou hold around their caern's fire.

## Moon Circles

Each auspice elder of a sept holds a gathering once during her phase of the moon. The Ragabash play jokes on one another, discuss dark trouble, play games and go on scouting missions. The Theurges exchange notes on spirit summoning, local spiritual happenings, occult lore and other bits of knowledge while they cast their divinations and tell prophecies. The Philodox engage in monthly verbal dueling, discuss various points of the Litany and go over the politics of the caern. The Galliards hold a bardic circle in which all present must contribute a story, song or at least a poem. The Ahroun stage contests and informal challenges, tease and insult each other, and test their strength and endurance; a favorite contest is moon-leaping, which involves jumping as high as one can toward the moon.

## Pack Tourney

Garou often get together in packs that serve as teams for a tourney, which is actually a party/contest/festival. Packs stick together, competing for status, prized fetishes and talens. A tourney is usually held after a particularly important victory against the Wyrm, or in salute to an honored visitor. A great feast of fresh game is prepared. Mead, cider, wine and the purest spring water are all served. Tourneys are good ways to win Honor, Glory and even Wisdom Renown without endangering oneself unduly. Tragically, however, tourneys are often thought a hedonistic indulgence by some in these lean times. Still, even the stern Shadow Lords and miserly Bone Gnawers call a tourney from time to time.

## Turning the Sun

In order to "turn" the sun, Helios, the Garou stage four special holidays at the solstices and equinoxes. Each holiday has a different meaning based on the time of year. In the spring, there is a wild bacchanal to which many Kinfolk and wolf–friends are invited (and at which many Kinfolk are conceived). In summer, the Garou dress in their greatest finery to honor Gaia on Her day, and many Baptisms of Fire are performed. Fetishes are blessed and hidden in the Earth in Her honor. In fall, the quieting land is honored, and the dead of the past year are remembered. In the winter, the Garou believe that the Wyrm's power grows until the solstice, at which point Gaia begins to gain strength and power again. Winter solstice is celebrated with a huge bonfire, and many Garou are invested with their new Ranks at this time. Many of the fetishes blessed and created on the summer solstice are produced and given as presents to the cubs of the sept at this time.

## Tribal Moots

In addition to the sept moot, the various tribes at a sept may hold moots from time to time to discuss tribal business. These moots are called by the tribe's elder. It is unwise to miss one of these moots, for they provide the elder a chance to guide a Garou's path toward higher Rank, and serve as means of spreading news across the whole sept. Tribal moots tend be less formal than sept moots.

### The Council of Elders

From time to time, all the elders of the sept are called together by the sept leader to cloister themselves in a clearing, cave or some similar area. The Garou elders meet and discuss problems pertaining to the sept, and they emerge only when they are all in agreement. A rattle, staff or some similar symbol is passed from hand to hand as a representation of the right to speak at such a council; none in attendance may speak unless he holds the symbol. These meetings go on into the late hours, and hard-headed elders often keep others from leaving until their points have been won.

## Harano

Harano is an inexplicable gloom and inexpressible longing for unnamable things; some say it is caused by contemplation of Gaia's suffering. Garou who suffer from Harano are prone to depression, lassitude and sudden mood swings. They may not act at all, or may explode into intense but ill-advised activity; one never knows. What is certain is that a Garou suffering from Harano is certainly not at his best, and may well be a liability to his pack, his sept and the fight for Gaia.

It is not common for a Garou to plunge into Harano, but it happens often enough for make it a concern. At the Narrator's discretion, any Garou who has suffered some sort of crushing defeat recently (losing a combat, failure of a plan, loss of a loved one, extended humiliation) must make a Mental Challenge against 10 Traits. If he fails, he slips into Harano. While this condition is not permanent, the gloom of Harano is hard to lift.

A player whose character suffers from Harano must make a Willpower Test against seven Traits each scene. If he fails, the Garou plunges into either:

• Frantic, desperate activity — The Garou must succeed on a Simple Test to avoid acting immediately on any impulse that comes to mind. Furthermore, he is down three Traits on all Mental and Social Challenges, and loses all ties;

• Deep gloom and depression — The Garou must succeed on a Simple Test to act at all. Otherwise he simply curls up and hopes the world goes away. In addition, he is down three Traits on all Mental and Social Challenges, and loses all ties.

These effects last for the duration of a scene. A new test must be made at the beginning of the next scene.

Furthermore, the senses of any Garou in Harano are inevitably distorted by his intense inner torment; all Garou in Harano are down one additional Trait in any challenges involving sight, smell or hearing.

Those who suffer from Harano may have moments of lucidity with the expenditure of a Willpower Trait. This lifts the gloom for as many hours as a character has permanent Willpower. Harano is not necessarily permanent — extraordinary Garou may free themselves from its grip after exceptional travails (at Storyteller discretion).

# Fetishes

Sometimes a spirit is bound to an item, infusing the item with part of the spirit's power. A Garou may begin a game with a fetish if her player has bought levels of the Fetish Background, although fetishes are usually acquired or even made during the course of a story. When a fetish is acquired by a Garou, the werewolf must attune it to himself by spending a number of temporary Gnosis Traits equal to the Gnosis of the item. After he successfully attunes a fetish, the Garou may attempt to activate its powers. This is done by succeeding in a Gnosis Challenge against half (rounded up) of the fetish's Gnosis Rating, or by spending a Gnosis to activate the powers automatically. The Garou must win this challenge every time she attempts to use the fetish.

**Note**: While prop fetishes might be fun to create and add to the mood of your game, it is often easier to create item cards for fetishes. These cards can detail the Traits and powers of a given fetish, making it easier to use the fetish when no Narrators are around.

### Fang Dagger

**Fetish Trait Cost**: 3 **Gnosis**: 6 **Spirit Affinity**: War, Wolf or Snake

**Melee Bonus Traits**: 3 **Negative Traits**: *Short*

A Fang Dagger is a blade carved from the tooth of some great beast. It is easily concealed.

After a character wielding a Fang Dagger has won a combat challenge, he may then activate the dagger. If the activation is successful, the damage inflicted is doubled (no more than four Health Levels of damage in one blow), as the fang "bites" deeper into the wound.

### Spirit Tracer

**Fetish Trait Cost**: 2 **Gnosis** 5 **Spirit Affinity**: Hunting, Predator-spirits

This fetish consists of a single human hair suspended in an iron ingot. When the wielder concentrates on a specific spirit, the ingot pulls in the direction in which the spirit lies until the Garou puts the fetish away.

**Phoebe's Veil**

**Fetish Trait Cost**: 3 **Gnosis**: 7 **Spirit Affinity**: Illusion, Shadow, Hiding, Chameleon

A small golden pendant in the shape of a half moon, Phoebe's Veil is attached to a leather thong, and is meant to be worn around the neck. When the fetish is activated, the wearer becomes invisible to both mundane creatures and spirits. This magic works against all senses but touch. (Use the Gift: *Hide in Plain Sight* for particulars.) The character wearing the fetish can touch things without becoming visible only if he succeeds in a Static Mental Challenge against seven Traits.

**Spirit Whistle**

**Fetish Trait Cost**: 4 **Gnosis**: 8 **Spirit Affinity**: Madness, Discord, Screech Owl

The Spirit Whistle is a small ivory whistle that makes no sound when blown unless it has been activated. When activated, it emits a wailing scream causing immense pain to all spirits within the wielder's line of sight. Any spirit present when the activated Whistle is blown must win a Static Mental Challenge against eight Traits or flee from the scream's source for the rest of the scene.

**Stone of Wealth**

**Fetish Trait Cost**: 3 **Gnosis**: 8 **Spirit Affinity**: Any Totem-spirit

This fetish appears to be nothing more than a very old "worry" stone. When rubbed (activated), it brings the user wealth. Wealth does not always mean money, which is Wyrm-tainted, nor does the summoned wealth necessarily come instantly. Instead, the stone provides the resources a Garou needs to complete her tasks. These resources usually appear in the form of funds or marketable items. The Storyteller is the final arbitrator as to how the fetish's power manifests. Each time the stone is used in a single session, the next test using the Stone during that session is against an additional two Traits.

**Gaia's Poultice**

**Fetish Trait Cost**: 2 **Gnosis**: 8 **Spirit Affinity**: Healing, East Wind, Unicorn-spirits

Gaia's Poultice is an herb-filled bandage. This wrapping, when activated, automatically heals one level of damage from an open wound on which it is placed. This fetish takes one hour to recharge between uses.

**Heart of the Spirit**

**Fetish Trait Cost**: 5 **Gnosis**: 10 **Spirit Affinity**: Any Totem-spirits

This fetish is a small, heart-shaped piece of rose quartz. The Heart of the Spirit allows the character attuned to it to store up to 10 Traits worth of Rage, Willpower or Gnosis in it (one type only; they cannot be mixed).

Storage of these Traits is accomplished by activating the fetish and spending the Traits the character wants stored. These Traits may be called upon with another activation test at any rate per turn.

### Medicine Bag

**Fetish Trait Cost**: Varies **Gnosis**: Varies **Spirit Affinity**: Depends on function

This is a catch-all term for the various types of fetish medicine pouches that are common among the Pure Ones. Each fetish of this type has a different purpose and power level, depending on what uses it has and the relative power of those uses. Some common ones are: Peace (one Trait, Gnosis 5), which allows a retest on all frenzy tests once activated; Healing (four Traits, Gnosis 8), which allows the wearer to heal twice as fast as normal; and Protection from Spirits (three Traits, Gnosis 6), which keeps an uninvited spirit from manifesting within 100 feet of the wearer. The most powerful medicine bags (five Traits, Gnosis 8) allow such things as letting the Garou walk among humans in any form without appearing to them as anything but a fellow human (although violent acts are still perceived as such), or allow the bearer to fool Wyrm-creatures into thinking the character is a kindred spirit.

Obviously, the Storyteller must determine what powers and what Trait cost a particular medicine bag has, but most that have more than one function are correspondingly expensive and need a high Gnosis to activate. These fetishes are seldom given to members of tribes other than the Uktena and Wendigo, and are usually attuned to the bearer as part of their presentation to her.

### Kinship Doll

**Fetish Trait Cost**: 2 **Gnosis:** 8 **Spirit Affinity:** Any Totem-spirits

This fetish appears to be nothing more than a crude handmade doll. However, when a Garou holds and activates it, the doll announces the location and condition of any one Kinfolk whose name is spoken by the user.

### Gnostic Bag

**Fetish Trait Cost**: 4 **Gnosis**: 9 **Spirit Affinity**: Engling, Ancestor-spirits

The Gnostic Bag is a small leather pouch with fringes, odd paintings and Garou pictograms on it. The pouch literally holds Gnosis. To activate it, the user reaches into the bag, "grabs" a Gnosis and eats it. The bag holds nine Gnosis Traits. These can be recharged if the owner expends temporary Gnosis from her pool into the bag.

### Dream Catcher

**Fetish Trait Cost**: 2 **Gnosis**: 4 **Spirit Affinity**: Protection, Guardian, Weaver

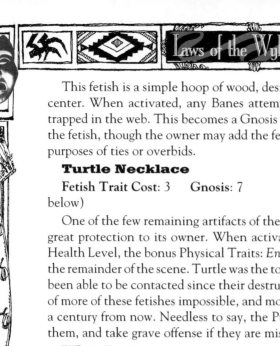

This fetish is a simple hoop of wood, designed with a web of sinew in its center. When activated, any Banes attempting to possess the owner are trapped in the web. This becomes a Gnosis Challenge against the owner of the fetish, though the owner may add the fetish's Gnosis to her own for the purposes of ties or overbids.

### Turtle Necklace

**Fetish Trait Cost**: 3 **Gnosis**: 7 **Spirit Affinity**: Turtle (see below)

One of the few remaining artifacts of the Croatan tribe, this fetish offers great protection to its owner. When activated, the wearer gains an extra Health Level, the bonus Physical Traits: *Enduring*, *Resilient* and *Stalwart* for the remainder of the scene. Turtle was the totem of the Croatan, and has not been able to be contacted since their destruction, making the construction of more of these fetishes impossible, and most doubt there will be any more a century from now. Needless to say, the Pure Ones are very protective of them, and take grave offense if they are misused in any way.

### Wise Bag

**Fetish Trait Cost**: 3 **Gnosis**: 4 **Spirit Affinity**: Wisdom, Owl, North Wind, Wolf

A Wise Bag is a bag of tokens, bones and other small items. When the fetish is activated, the owner can reach inside and gain a one small "fact" of wisdom about people in his surrounding area (e.g., breed, tribe, species, vampire, mage, ghoul, Kinfolk, etc.). This bag cannot detect the Wyrm, but can relate knowledge of someone's Negative Traits if the fetish's owner can defeat the target in a Mental Challenge. If any of the pieces inside the Wise Bag ever goes missing for more than 24 hours, the bag becomes spiritually dead and no longer functions.

### Spirit Ax

**Fetish Trait Cost**: 4 **Gnosis**: 6 **Spirit Affinity**: War, Predator

This fetish functions as a normal ax and can be used as a regular melee weapon, except that it has one extra Bonus Trait than a normal ax due to the spirits within; however, the real strength of the ax lies when it fights those possessed by Banes. In this case, the ax simply ignores the physical flesh and strikes the Bane within directly, causing no harm to the host. This allows the wielder to battle such Banes from the physical world without causing the innocent victim of possession to suffer. Those temporarily or partially possessed by the Bane are freed at the spirit's destruction, but those who have been completely possessed by a Bane for a long period of time (such as mockeries) are slain when the Bane is destroyed. Still, Garou consider this a mercy killing compared to the torments a Bane inflicts.

### War Bow

**Fetish Trait Cost**: 4 **Gnosis**: 7 **Spirit Affinity**: War, Ancestor-spirits

This fetish functions the same way as a normal bow (see below), except when used by the one it is attuned to it adds an additional two Bonus Traits, and inflicts aggravated wounds instead of regular ones.

### Tear of Renewal

**Fetish Trait Cost**: 3 **Gnosis**: 6 **Spirit Affinity**: Wolf, North Wind, Engling

These milky white, tear-shaped stones grant a Garou Gnosis. By spending a Gnosis Trait to activate a Tear, the Garou gains three Gnosis Traits, up to his maximum. The fetish can be used this way seven times before the spirit within it dies and the fetish becomes useless.

### Elk Tooth Necklace

**Fetish Trait Cost**: 2 **Gnosis**: 5 **Spirit Affinity**: Elk

This necklace of teeth allows its wearer to run and jump twice as far and twice as fast as normal. When activated in combat, its bonuses are not cumulative with those of other Garou Gifts.

## Klaives

A klaive is a sacred weapon of the Garou. There are many kinds of klaives, ranging from simple klaives to the special and powerful Great Klaives, of which only seven are known to exist. Each klaive has a spiritual affinity with War, Thunder, Falcon or Stag, and is considered attuned to whoever is carrying it (at no cost). A Garou must have a number of Honor Traits equal to the level of the klaive she carries in order to be considered its "rightful owner." If not, other Garou will constantly attempt to wrest the klaive from its current owner, either through formal challenges or outright theft.

### Simple Klaive

**Fetish Trait Cost**: 3 **Gnosis**: 6

**Melee Bonus Traits**: 3

The ritual daggers of the Garou, klaives are rare weapons. A klaive's bite is deep, and always causes aggravated wounds. A klaive is always dedicated to its wielder, and is usually tied to its owner's wrist to prevent its loss during battle. Loss of a simple klaive results in the immediate loss of one Honor Trait.

### Grand Klaive

**Fetish Traits Cost**: 5 **Gnosis**: 7

**Melee Bonus Traits**: 4 **Negative Traits**: *Heavy* (for Homid form only)

A Grand Klaive is large, usually as long as a broadsword. Not only is a Grand Klaive usually made of silver, but it is also correspondingly deadly. In addition to its obvious uses, a Grand Klaive typically has two unique powers that its wielder can activate. The first is *Luna's Fire*, which causes the blade to burst into flame. This adds two bonus Traits during combat Challenges and also causes an additional wound on all successful attacks.

A Grand Klaive's second power can be anything, but in most cases it is *Summoning*, which calls the blade to the wielder's hand through the Gauntlet. The weapon must be "stashed" nearby in the Umbra for this power to work; not even a Grand Klaive can be summoned from far away.

Usually a Grand Klaive has a second spirit imbued in it. This second spirit gives the weapon a Charm, which can also be activated be the wielder (substituting her Gnosis for Power).

### Great Klaive

Characters cannot purchase a Great Klaive; one has to be discovered or awarded. The powers of each Great Klaive are legendary, and are dangerous in the extreme. Each Great Klaive has a specific personality, and is usually attached to one of the few Garou heroes in the world. A Great Klaive can give the wielder six additional Traits in combat, has all the powers of a Grand Klaive and all the spirit Charms of an average totem spirit Incarna.

## Talens

Talens are like fetishes, but with one exception: they are strictly one-use items. A talen does not need to be activated, only attuned to the Garou. One Fetish Trait provides a Garou with a number of talens instead of a single fetish, depending on the Spirit Keeper's decision. Talens can be used by anyone who has them. If the possessor of a talen is not Garou, Willpower must be substituted for Gnosis or Rage in order to utilize the item.

#### Gaia's Breath

**Gnosis**: 5 **Spirit Affinity**: Healing, Calm

A small dried gourd marked with symbols of praise to Gaia, this talen must be crushed and spilled over a wound to be effective, but if this is done up to two Health Levels of damage are healed, even aggravated ones.

#### Clear Water

**Gnosis**: 4 **Spirit Affinity**: Water, Purity, East Wind

Contained within a flask of water, the purifying spirit within this talen instantly cleanses Wyrm-taint from bodies of water it is poured into, up to and including bodies as large as rivers and lakes. If consumed, the talen acts like the Gift: *Resist Toxin*.

#### Pine Dagger

**Gnosis**: 6 **Spirit Affinity**: Pine Tree, North Wind

This talen destroys the *Materialized* form of a spirit upon contact. When struck, the spirit must win a Willpower Challenge against six Traits or be banished back to the Umbra. This dagger is made from the heartwood of a downed pine tree.

#### Bane Arrow

**Gnosis**: 4 **Spirit Affinity**: War, Air, Pain

Appearing as normal arrows, these talens do not require a bow to use. Instead, they launch themselves. When activated and released, these obsidian-headed shafts fly immediately to the targeted Bane (either in the Umbra or materialized on Earth). Bane Arrows automatically hit and inflict two levels of aggravated damage, and no Bane can resist howling in agony.

### Death Dust

**Gnosis**: 6 **Spirit Affinity**: Bear, Wisdom, North Wind

This small jar of dust, when broken open, activated and sprinkled over the body of a recently (within a day) dead creature, allows the wielder to communicate with the spirit of the corpse for five minutes.

Note: Death Dust does not summon wraiths; rather it brings up the spiritual "echoes" of a dead soul. Wraiths can be summoned through use of this talen if they agree to appear. For more information on wraiths, see **Oblivion**.

### Wyrm Sign

**Gnosis**: 6 **Spirit Affinity**: Chimera, Uktena, South Wind

A piece of unfired pottery painted with a sigil of the Wyrm, this talen causes all creatures of the Wyrm in the area to be outlined in green fire, and thus be immediately revealed for what they are. Furthermore, the Wyrm Sign causes mockeries to scream in terror; other Wyrm creatures react less violently. If the sigil painted on the fragment is tampered with, the talen will not function properly.

### Vision Pool

**Gnosis**: 6 **Spirit Affinity**: Divination, Chimera

A simple black powder which, when added to a clear pool of water, shows a vision of the future. This talen is a great aid to divination, but often requires a Static Mental Challenge with the *Enigmas* Ability to comprehend; since it deals with the future, a Narrator should often be present when this talen is used as well.

### Basket of Bones

**Gnosis**: 8 **Spirit Affinity**: Fire

This basket is woven from plant fibers and the bones of fallen agents of the Wyrm. Decorated with beads, it has a handle carved from ash wood. Any one item of the Wyrm, such as an evil fetish, instantly burns to powder when placed in the Basket. The Basket itself turns to ash after three uses.

The item must fit completely within the basket for the Basket of Bones to work. You cannot, for example, jam this talen on a mockery's head and hope for the best.

## Pack Totems

These totems are powerful spirits who are intimately involved with the Garou and interact with them on a personal level. When a pack is formed, it is traditional for one of the totem spirits to take a particular interest in the pack. During character creation, each character has a chance to buy levels of the Totem Background which can be used to strengthen a pack's totem.

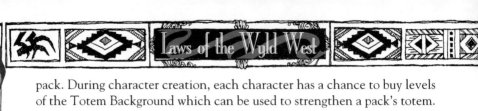

Before you play your first game as a member of a pack, you must help your pack choose a totem by the fairest means available. First, total all the Pack Totem Traits that are available to your group, then decide what kind of totem your pack should have.

As long as you are a member of the pack, you gain benefits based on the affinity of your pack totem, and your pack totem is bound to both you and your packmates. If you leave the pack (which is accomplished not by physically leaving, but by formally declaring yourself no longer to be a member of the pack), then you take your Pack Totem Traits with you, and the pack totem suffers accordingly. If you gain more pack members who have Pack Totem Traits, you may purchase new powers for your totem or upgrade its power level (Gaffling to Jaggling, or Jaggling to totem avatar). Anyone in the pack may choose to spend experience points to give the pack totem more Traits.

Pack totems usually require a minor or major geas in exchange for their patronage, depending on their unique personalities and the power they offer in return. A character can only benefit from the advantages of one pack totem and one sept totem at a time. Personal totems are connected to an individual, but do not grant the advantages of a pack totem, regardless of affiliation.

Pack totems are divided into three categories: Respect, War and Wisdom. Totems of Respect are figures accorded great honor by the Garou, and are considered paragons of honor, proper conduct, and virtue. Totems of Glory are revered as the ultimate warriors, and sought after by many packs seeking a heroic idol in their battle against the Wyrm. Totems of Wisdom are regarded as sages and riddlers without equal, and packs who turn to them for guidance are led on fascinating quests offering enlightenment and spirituality to those brave and pure enough to complete them.

## Buying a Pack Totem — The Cost

Purchasing a totem avatar costs a base of five Background Traits. Alternatively, a pack formed without a totem avatar can spend five experience points and adopt a totem later during its travels. A totem avatar is an actual spirit who serves the pack's Incarna totem. The spirit is dependent on the pack for its power. In other words, a spirit will never be more potent than the Traits the pack has invested in it. In effect, the pack invests a bit of itself in the Incarna totem and, in return, that Incarna sends a totem avatar spirit of appropriate might to aid and watch over the pack.

Five Background Traits (or experience points) provide the pack with a basic totem avatar to watch over it. The more Background Traits and experience the pack puts into the totem avatar, the more potent it will be, and thus, the more helpful it will be to the entire pack. No more than five

Traits may be dedicated to a totem per character (unless, on very rare occasions, the Storyteller gives her approval).

## Basic Totem Avatar

When a pack gets a basic totem avatar, the avatar is initially quite weak. It possesses power roughly equivalent to that of a Jaggling. However, unlike a Jaggling, a totem avatar can increase in power through contributions made directly by the characters in the pack. Additionally, the characters can purchase a special affinity for their totem. If they do so, the totem, drawing upon its affinity, endows all members of that pack with certain advantages. Each avatar has its own unique contributions to make to its pack. The bigger the contribution, the more costly the affinity.

A pack's totem avatar begins with the following basic statistics:

**Negative Traits:** May buy up to 3 maximum

**Power Pool:** 5

**Charms:** 3

**Willpower:** 5

**Rage:** 5

**Gnosis:** 5

**Abilities:** 10 levels

See Spirit Creation Table in **Laws of the Wild,** pg 192.

## Totem Affiliation

The pack must decide who its totem avatar serves. Directing a totem avatar's affiliation can be costly to the pack, but can also provide strength. The different options and their costs are listed below. These costs are in addition to the five Background Traits (or experience points) that the pack initially spends on its totem.

Each totem makes a contribution (or contributions) to the pack. In return for being chosen and choosing the affiliation of the totem avatar, the totem "adopts" the pack and refers to its members as her children. There are two types of contributions: general and exclusive. A general contribution can be used by the entire pack, such as one that grants each pack member an additional Trait or Traits. An exclusive contribution is used by only one member of the pack. The entire pack must decide who will benefit from this sort of contribution, and can use any means agreeable to come to a decision. If the pack cannot decide who should gain the benefit of the exclusive contribution, then the totem avatar withholds the benefit until the pack can come to a unanimous decision. In other words, the pack must cooperate or else lose the use of a potent advantage. Once a pack member has the benefit of an exclusive contribution, it is hers until she either relinquishes it or is no longer a member of the pack.

## Totems of Respect

### Pegasus

**Cost:** 4

The Pegasus is a noble winged horse who embodies the pure rage of the Wyld and the spirit of the Wyld flying free. Pegasus is concerned chiefly with sacred places, ever seeking to protect them.

Pegasus gives all of her children an extra Willpower Trait. Pegasus shares her knowledge of the Wyld by giving the Ability: *Animal Ken* x 2 to her children.

**Ban:** You must always aid females of all species who are in need, especially young ones, but not to the degree of furthering the Wyrm's goals.

### Stag

**Cost:** 4

Stag symbolizes life, death and rebirth to the Fianna, and they heed his grand wisdom. Stag leads the Wild Hunt, and is the representation of the masculine power of nature. Stag gives all his children an extra Willpower Trait, and shares with them his knowledge of the woods, giving each pack member the Ability: *Survival* x 2.

**Ban:** You must always aid faeries or their kin.

### Grandfather Thunder

**Cost:** 5

This totem does not allow itself to be chosen as a pack totem; it chooses which packs to adopt instead. Thunder then sends one of his stormcrows to watch over a pack instead of a relegating a totem avatar. He never travels himself, nor does he choose a pack that has not requested him. Thunder grants all of his children two Willpower Traits and two Social Traits: *Commanding* and *Intimidating*, plus the Ability: *Etiquette* x 2. All children of Thunder also gain the Negative Social Trait: *Untrustworthy*.

**Ban:** You should never tell the truth to those you do not respect. You must not respect those you can dominate.

### Falcon

**Cost:** 4

Great Falcon, the raptor, watches over honor and justice in the Garou world. Those who dare to ascend his high aeries come away with stories of glory and honor to match those of the greatest legends. Falcon sends his children to watch over the most promising packs, particularly those in which Silver Fangs are prevalent. The Silver Fangs are served by Falcon, who helps them maintain communication and thus, unity.

Falcon gives all his children two Willpower Traits and the Ability: *Leadership* x 2. Falcon's children gain the Social Traits: *Charismatic* and *Dignified*.

**Ban:** All children of Falcon must have at least one Honor Trait. Falcon does not lend his aid to packs that are not sufficiently honorable. If any member of the pack ever loses all of his Honor, he must immediately perform the *Rite of Contrition* and do something, *anything* to regain his lost Honor. Until then, Falcon will not aid the pack.

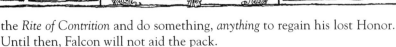

#### Thunderbird

Cost: 5

The fury of the heavens, the wisdom of the raging winds, Thunderbird is courage and dedication personified. Those who follow him face a tough road, as he constantly tests his children, but those who can face his trials are destined for lives of great Glory. All his children receive the *Intimidating* Trait and a level of the *Survival* Ability, and can call on three extra Willpower Traits per story. Thunderbird may even smite the pack's foes with lightning in a time of great need, but dislikes fighting their battles for them and will require a great service in return.

**Ban:** Thunderbird's followers cannot flee any fight unless they are clearly overmatched, and must battle the forces of decay (Banes, vampires, mockeries, etc.) and the Storm Eater whenever they find them.

### Totems of War

#### Rat

**Cost:** 5

Cunning and sharp, Rat is a totem of survival, but can be fierce in a fight when cornered. Rat provides all of his children with two extra Willpower Traits and an extra Physical Trait: *Brutal* when biting, and *Graceful* when hiding or sneaking.

**Ban:** You must never kill vermin.

#### Fenris

**Cost**: 5

Also known as Grandfather Wolf, Fenris is the warrior-wolf. He expects no quarter and gives none. He provides all of his children with one Rage Trait and the extra Physical Traits: *Ferocious*, *Tough* and *Wiry*.

**Ban**: You must never turn down an opportunity for a fight.

#### Griffin

**Cost**: 4

A symbol of great rage, Griffin is the expression of all lupus' anger and their hunger for blood. Griffin guards wilderness areas and represents the most primal and animalistic powers. Griffin gives all of his children the ability to communicate with all birds of prey and the Physical Traits: *Ferocious*, *Quick* and *Tenacious*.

**Ban:** You must not associate with humans, and homids are not usually accepted by Griffin.

#### Wendigo

**Cost**: 5

Wendigo is the cannibal spirit of the frozen north who devours the hearts of his foes. He teaches the Garou the wild tactics of the storm in battle.

Wendigo gives all of his children two extra Rage Traits and the Ability: *Survival* x 2.

**Ban:** You must aid native peoples whenever they are in trouble.

### Bear

**Cost:** 5

The Great Bear is a fierce warrior, but is also very wise in peacetime. Children of the Bear are all given the Ability *Medicine* x 2 and gain the Physical Trait: *Stalwart* (this Trait can never be lost, but can only be bid as the last Physical Trait), as well as the Gift: *Mother's Touch*, usable once per session.

Bear is a totem that has fallen out of favor ever since the War of Rage, when the Gurahl (the werebears) fought the Garou. Therefore, it is harder for any pack of the Bear to gain Honor Renown (they lose one every time they gain three), and both the Narrator and the Philodox of a sept should keep track of this.

**Ban:** Bear lays no Ban on his children, knowing that they are burdened enough.

### Coyote

**Cost:** 5

The ultimate Trickster and the shadow in the woods, that is Coyote. The tree root that trips the mighty hero, Coyote grants to each member of his packs three more Physical Traits in any challenge related to stealth, as well as the Abilities: *Larceny* x 2, *Subterfuge* and *Stealth*.

Coyote accepts any old ragtag collection that calls itself a pack, even ones comprised of creatures besides Garou. He literally accepts anyone who will have him. However, all children of Coyote soon discover that they are often used as scapegoats when bad things happen, as Coyote is considered by some to be bad luck. Packs that follow Coyote are not considered to be especially wise (they lose one Wisdom Trait for every three they earn). Of course, Coyote's own Children, the Nuwisha, will tend to be very fond of the pack, and that can make for more trouble than a herd of ill-tempered cattle in a thunderstorm.

**Ban:** Coyote makes no demands on his children.

## Totems of Wisdom

### Owl

**Cost:** 5

Stealthy and silent, Owl is the predator who flies mostly at night. He sees many things and knows many secrets, but keeps his silence. Owl grants all of his children two extra Physical Traits in any challenge dealing with stealth, silence or quiet. Each member of the pack also receives wings in the Umbra which effectively allow double movement rate and flight (it is twice as hard to find your way in the Umbra if you are not following the paths, so packs with Owl as totem tend to buy a lot of *Enigma* Ability). At the Storyteller's discretion, Owl also grants one use of *Omen of Doom* (see Silent Strider Tribal Advantage) at the cost of one permanent Willpower Trait.

**Ban**: Owl asks that his children leave animal sacrifices to him in the forest, tied in place or caged.

### Buffalo

**Cost:** 5

Patient, enduring, slow to anger and gifted with seeing the future, Buffalo's dreams of prophecy have defused many dangerous situations and guided those who would otherwise be lost. Buffalo reduces all *Engimas* difficulties related to dreams by four, grants three levels of *Survival* for the purposes of finding food and safe water, and grants each of his children three extra *Stalwart* traits per story (once lost, they cannot be bid until the next story). Most Pure Ones consider packs following Buffalo to be friends, unless given cause to believe otherwise.

**Ban:** Buffalo asks that his children protect the great herds on the ranges; they may kill a buffalo for food, provided they offer the proper respect to the spirit. This is more a charge to protect the herds from those who would slaughter them by the hundreds for sport or profit.

### Unicorn

**Cost**: 5

Proud and powerful, this totem is the symbol of unity and mystical strength among the Garou. Although some think her gentle nature belies weakness, that is a foolish assumption. Unicorn's strength lies in her purity of purpose and the sharpness of her horn. Unicorn gives all of her children the ability to move through the Umbra at twice normal speed, the Social Trait: *Diplomatic* and the Mental Trait: *Calm* in all challenges dealing with healing or trying to resolve disagreements peacefully.

Unicorn balances this by making all of her children down one Trait in all challenges dealing with trying to injure or harm another Garou (who is not Wyrm-tainted). Unicorn's children gain one free retest when performing any Gifts involving peace — healing, protection, etc.

**Ban**: Unicorn asks that her Garou to aid and protect the weak, the helpless, the abused and the exploited, but never to the extent of furthering or aiding the Wyrm.

### Raven

**Cost**: 5

Like Coyote, Raven is a great trickster, but is somewhat less brash about pulling his tricks, and thus can teach a diverse array of lore to those who seek guidance. Sustaining himself on the work of other predators, he learns much from what others leave behind. Raven's children must be resourceful, though, and cannot rely on raw strength to face their trials.

Raven's children gain a level of *Enigmas*, *Subterfuge* and *Survival*. All pack members gain an extra temporary Willpower Trait. Corax will look favorably on them as well, and may even trade information with them on occasion if they are polite and informative.

**Ban:** Raven asks that his children not carry wealth, instead trusting him to provide.

### Cockroach

**Cost:** 5

Hardy, quick and adaptable, Cockroach has been around for a long time, and will be around after the Apocalypse is but a memory. It provides all of its children with the ability, while in the Umbra, to hear the words communicated by telegraph, just by listening. They may also communicate with each other by talking into the wires. Followers of Cockroach gain the following Abilities: *Repair* and *Science*, and one free retest with any Gift that affects technology.

**Ban:** Cockroach asks that none of its brethren be slain by the pack.

### Chimera

**Cost:** 5

She of Many Faces, the Lady of Mirrors, the Ever-changing — Chimera is the totem of enigmas and a puzzle herself, all at the same time. She appears in many forms, a different one each time she shows herself. She give each pack member the ability to change what he looks like in the Umbra with a successful Gnosis Challenge (against seven Traits), the Ability: *Enigmas* x 2 and the Mental Trait: *Insightful.*

**Ban:** Chimera will not aid the pack if the members do not seek enlightenment.

### Rattlesnake

**Cost:** 7

A venerated spirit of the Pure Ones, Rattlesnake has both compassion and fury in tremendous amounts, and while his followers (like him) often have great patience, they do not forget a slight easily and seldom leave many foes standing when they finally choose to strike. Rattlesnake's children gain the Gift: *Pulse of the Invisible*, and can entrance listeners by singing or howling with a successful Social Challenge. Subjects do not become willing slaves or easy targets, simply a bit more pliant to carefully couched suggestions, putting the character two traits up on subtle Social challenges (seduction, casual cons, etc.). The pack also gains the Background Past Life x 3; this is not actual contact with ancestors, but simply a reflection of the long ancestral memory Rattlesnake possesses. Wendigo and Uktena tend to look favorably on children of Rattlesnake.

**Ban:** None of Rattlesnake's children may attack a serpent, and they must honor the Pure Ones whenever they can.

### Uktena

**Cost:** 5

This dark, powerful and ancient water spirit has the features of both a serpent and a cougar. Uktena watches over and protects his children when they are in the Umbra by giving each member of the pack one level of protection (see the Gift: *Luna's Armor*). Once this Trait is used, it can only be renewed if the character who used it stays in the Umbra for one week. Also, each time a pack member gains three experience points, he gains one more that can only be put toward learning *Enigmas*, *Occult*, rituals, Gifts or other mystical knowledge. Children of Uktena are down one Trait in all Social Challenges with Garou of other tribes.

**Ban**: Uktena asks that his children recover, hold and protect (not use) lost artifacts and fetishes from the Wyrm's minions (who sometime includes mages, but always include Tremere vampires).

# Antagonists

In **Mind's Eye Theatre**, people who work against the players' characters are called antagonists. Occasionally, players assume the roles of antagonists and face off against other players. This works especially well if the game has a large number of players. For the most part, though, antagonists are played by Narrators.

## Mockeries

Mockeries are humans who have been become servants of the Wyrm. As such, they have been granted special powers and abilities. These abilities come with a price, though, as each mockery is twisted in some foul and perverse manner. Though this perversion is not always readily apparent to the eye, all mockeries reek of Wyrm–stench to any who are able to detect it.

Most mockeries have Attributes and Abilities similar to Garou, though many may have boosted Attributes in one or more areas (usually Physical). Each mockery possesses some strange ability or power that it may use against opponents. Mockeries are not known for subtlety, beauty or intelligence. They are the foot soldiers of the Wyrm.

### Some Random Mockery Powers

**Extra Arms** Extra attacks (must bid one additional Trait for every extra attack).

**Fat Armor** The first level of damage the mockery receives per attack is always absorbed by layers of unnatural fat.

**Shark Teeth** Mockery's bite does aggravated damage.

**Berserker** Five Rage Traits that work just like those of Garou. (May frenzy as well.)

**Claws** The mockery does aggravated damage in *Brawl* challenges.

**Poison Tumors** Any time the mockery is hit, poison spatters on the attacker (effects decided by a Narrator).

Or, take a Merit and match it in a particularly nasty way with a Flaw. See "Merits and Flaws," pp. 188.

## Bane Spirits

Banes are created just as spirits loyal to Gaia are, except they are servants of the Wyrm. They assume countless forms in order to destroy and corrupt what they can. Some Banes are the avatars or personifications of such principles as Hate and Disease; others are less archetypal but just as deadly. Banes are the most common and direct enemy the Garou have. See "Spirits," pp. 237.

### Sample Bane Charms

#### Blighted Touch

**Power Cost:** 2

If the spirit succeeds in an attack on a Garou, the target must win a Willpower Test or be forced to bid two Traits in any challenge for the rest of the evening. This is not cumulative.

#### Corruption

**Power Cost:** 1

The spirit whispers an evil suggestion in a target's ear. The target must succeed in a Mental Challenge against the spirit's total Gnosis or be forced to act upon that thought somehow.

#### Incite Frenzy

**Power Cost:** 3

The spirit can cause frenzy in others. If the spirit wins a Rage Challenge against the target's Willpower (no Willpower Trait bid), the target enters frenzy instantly. The frenzy lasts one scene.

#### Possession

**Power Cost:** 5

The Bane may possess a living being or inanimate object. The spirit tests its Willpower against the target. If successful in the challenge, the spirit begins the process taking possession of the victim. *Possession* is gradual; only after six hours will the spirit be in full possession of the body and able to manifest certain characteristics and abilities through it.

During the six hours spent taking possession, the spirit must remain undisturbed. If it is found and attacked during this time, the link between spirit and host is broken. Otherwise, the spirit takes possession of the target, now called a mockery, and can only be attacked without injuring the host by striking it in the Umbra. Attacks in the Realm will damage the Bane's host as surely as they damage the Bane itself.

## Storm-Born

There are a small but disturbingly potent number of beings, known only as the Storm-Born, that have begun to appear in the Savage West. These mysterious entities are the result of the wild energies of the Storm Umbra fusing with an individual, whirling spirit and flesh into a mix that is as powerful as it is insane. Some of these beings, called Fierce Ones, appear only to crave violence and destruction and take on monstrous shapes as they wreak havoc, but they are also easily detected due to their outright violation of everything natural. Worse yet are the Clever Ones, those Storm-Born who appear to be little different than normal creatures of their type until the right moment brings their true powers to the fore, and who seem to retain rational thought even if their motives eventually become twisted and unknowable. They are as diverse as any other spirit, with their only universal weakness lying in the taboos or phobias they observe, which are as strict as any spirit's Ban and seem to be holdovers from their mortal lives - a drowned man might be mortally afraid of water, or a gambler unable to resist playing cards. Whatever their motives, Storm-Born are almost unheard of by even the Pure Ones, thus remaining a potent if not always subtle threat.

Storm-Born exist in and perceive the mortal world and the Penumbra simultaneously, which is something the sideways-stepping Garou should mind. They have both Gnosis and Power, like spirits, make use of Charms just as spirits do, and recover one Power per hour. They suffer no penalty for running out of Power; they are simply unable to use their talents until they recover enough Power. Their Charms are always complementary, such as a facility for controlling, creating, and surviving fire, and are also related to the taboos a particular Storm-Born might have. Storm-Born are potent beings, and the Storyteller should let her imagination run wild when creating them, even making up Charms and descriptions as she sees fit to capture these strange and tragic figures.

For more on Storm-Born, see **The Wild West Companion**.

## Black Spiral Dancers

The Lost Tribe was once known as the White Howlers, noble and powerful Garou who were kin to the Picts of ancient Scotland. They entered the Wyrm's den with the thought of combating it on its home territory… and were swallowed utterly by it instead, vomited back to Earth as the Black Spiral Dancers. Corrupted in both body and mind, Black Spiral Dancers are fearsome opponents; they usually attack Garou on sight.

When in Crinos, Black Spiral Dancers are monstrosities, with slaver-jawed, misshapen heads and glowing eyes. They often have patchy fur, batlike ears, jagged teeth and other deformities. In Homid form, Dancers are usually physically or mentally twisted, and their features are often describable only as "inhuman."

The totem of the Black Spiral Dancers is Whippoorwill, whose mad call they mimic during their hunts. Black Spiral Dancers are generated like other Garou, but most are metis. Their "Gifts" often resemble mutations, but the exact nature of each Gift is up to the Storyteller. Here are some suggestions:

Level One **Sense Wyrm** — Same as the Metis Gift.

Level Two **Bat Ears** — Same as the Gift: *Heightened Senses*.

Level Three **Patagia** — Flaps of skin, like those possessed by a flying squirrel. When the Black Spiral Dancer leaps from a height, these flaps allow him to glide rather than plummet. The skin flaps exist in all of the Dancer's forms.

Level Four **Crawling Poison** — The Black Spiral Dancer's claws and bite transmit a slow poison that prevent regenerative powers for the rest of the session. The Dancer must win a Gnosis Challenge against the target's Physical Traits In order to use this Gift.

Level Five **Balefire** — The Black Spiral Dancer can hurl spheres of sickly green flame. If they hit, the target must win a Physical Challenge (against eight Traits) or mutate in some harmful way (Storyteller discretion).

## Hunters and Humans

Humans present an interesting challenge to players of **Wyld West**. Garou characters encounter humans on a regular basis, and they can be valuable contacts or deadly adversaries.

Some humans, known as Kinfolk, have close ties to the Garou. These humans have Garou ancestry, but did not inherit the gene that allows werewolves to shapechange. Though most Kinfolk are wonderful allies of the Garou, there are a few who have become jealous of their brethren's power and seek to destroy or steal it for themselves. These Kinfolk are among the most insidious of the Garou's many enemies, as they tend to go without notice by the Garou until it is too late, and then use their knowledge of the strengths and weaknesses of the Garou to devastating.

See **Laws of the Hunt** for more information regarding humans and Kinfolk.

## The Enlightened Society of the Weeping Moon

Another source of great danger to the Garou is the Enlightened Society of the Weeping Moon, an ostensibly humanitarian organization that is actually wholly, willingly and completely dedicated to the service of the Wyrm. While not every member is aware of the Wyrm or believes he is following it — indeed, lower echelon members are often painfully idealistic and honest — the Society as a whole is rotten to the core, and eagerly embraces dark magics and Wyrm corruption to spread its power and influence throughout the Savage West. Typical *modus operandi* of Society operatives is to establish themselves in local politics and public works, ingratiating themselves to the populace and earning praise for their good deeds. Converts follow soon after, and soon whole towns are in the grip of the Society, with an individual member progressing through the ranks of sorcery and corruption as he becomes more and more involved. Soon settlers go to the next town, and the cycle begins again. (To simulate the magic talents of members of the Society, give them a selection of Homid, Uktena or Black Spiral Dancer Gifts, then throw in a mix of mockery powers or — even better — some dark talents cooked up by the Storyteller herself. **Laws of the Hunt** and **World of Darkness: Sorcerer** are also good references, along with some of the dark Numina from **The Book of Madness**.)

The real danger of the Society is their subtlety, as only a tiny handful of Garou have even the vaguest idea of their existence. The Society does not ride into town bearing a big flag with their logo on it and a slightly smaller "We're Evil!" banner beneath it. Nor do they immediately seek to gun down all the local Garou with silver. Rather, the Society members take their time to become established as good citizens and neighbors, only beginning to expose their true goals when they know the populace is ready to fall more directly under their sway. Many Garou have a difficult time finding ways to fight enemies they cannot square off against toe to toe, a weakness the Society knows and exploits to their full advantage; a Garou who expects to be able to walk up to a Society member and accost him on Main Street (even assuming she could find out who the members are) is likely to face a really nasty reaction from the local citizenry for "daring to lay a hand on that nice old Mr. Humphries!" In other words, by the time most Garou would normally get involved, it's too late to stop the Society in that particular town.

Obviously, the Enlightened Society of the Weeping Moon makes an excellent enemy for the Savage West, as it is a foe which cannot be defeated simply with the usual Garou display of klaives and fangs. Only by engaging in some intrigue and planning, digging through the layers of secrecy the Society has formed around itself, can the Garou hope to uncover enough of the big picture to do the Society any lasting harm. However, all too soon the Society will become an enemy that the Garou cannot afford to ignore, and that time will be all the worse unless the Garou have some knowledge of the Society beforehand. Defeating even a small portion of this growing menace is a task worthy of a veteran pack — presenting a serious challenge to the whole organization would be the stuff of legends.

## When Worlds Collide

### Vampires

The undead have been mortal enemies of the Garou since the earliest times, and for the most part the feud is still as hot as it ever was. Vampires tend to keep to cities, where they can be near a supply of blood and hunt unnoticed, while most Garou stick to the wilderness. Not only do the vampires, or "Leeches" as the Garou know them, seek to expand the cities, but many also reek of the taint of the Wyrm, sealing their fate in the eyes of the already wary Garou. There are different types of vampires, each with different powers and habits, from the strong and hideous Wormies (Nosferatu or Samedi) to the explosively violent Bruja (Brujah) to the sinister and charismatic Dark Riders (Lasombra). One "clan" of Leeches, the Dark Prowlers (Gangrel), even dares to claim parts of the wilderness as their own, and seem to have powers that allow them to mimic certain Garou abilities.

The youngest members of this race have Attributes and Abilities similar to those of Garou characters, although their elders are creatures of incredible power. Vampires have their own powers, called Disciplines, which use the power of their blood to achieve a variety of effects similar to Garou Gifts. For further information on vampires in live action, see **Laws of the Night**.

**Note About Blood Traits**: Garou have 12 Blood Traits. If a vampire drinks even one Trait's worth of Garou blood, she gains the active Beast Trait: *Furious*. The second Trait's worth of Garou blood (or the first, if the vampire already has *Furious*) throws her into frenzy until the blood is purged from her system. Storytellers are advised that the last blood in is usually the last blood out.

## Mages

Mages are practitioners of ancient arcane lore, also known as magick. They are humans of great power, and most Garou avoid them whenever possible. However, a few Garou have been known to ally with mages, and occasionally form friendships. Mages practice their own form of the Veil themselves, keeping them out of sight of mortals and most Garou. Some mages embrace mysticism and the old ways, some practice bizarre arts and philosophies unknown to the Garou, and some embrace the Weaver, the Wyld or the Wyrm with fanatical devotion, making them a threat to fellow mages and Garou alike.

Mages can add a new depth to a story, but should be used only as Narrator characters. A mage can be a useful contact should a character seek an item of a mystical nature. It is possible that a mage could request a service of some sort in exchange for the item. Such contact with mages can lead to a whole series of new stories. A mage could even be a Garou's patron, offering rituals or enchanted objects in exchange for things that the Garou has access to, such as the names of spirits. Some mages seek to steal power from Garou caerns by tapping caerns to fuel their magicks; thus, they can serve as antagonists. In particular, the Uktena have a long history of rivalries and alliances with mages, but almost any tribe has come into contact with them at some point in time.

Mages have the usual Attributes and Abilities of the average Garou, with Mental Attributes being primary. Mages always have at least three Willpower Traits, as one must be strong-willed to work magick. A mage may use his magick to warp reality around himself in whatever way the Storyteller sees fit, depending on the mages' level of power. Each mage practices within a style, though, and tends to achieve effects through methods within that paradigm; a shaman from a native tribe will call up spirits, meditate and fast, while one of the European Weaver wizards might make calculations and set to work building a machine to carry out the "magic." However, in the end the effect is the same, no matter how the mage chooses to view its execution.

## Mummies

Mummies all have one thing in common: they have received the gift of the Spell of Life, an ancient Egyptian ritual that renders the recipient immortal. Of all the individuals inhabiting this dark world, mummies are the only ones who experience a continuous cycle of life, death and rebirth. They are therefore true immortals and as such, are rarely — if ever — extinguished.

Mummies almost never involve themselves in the affairs of others, although there is a faction among them that works against a clan of vampires called the Followers of Set. On those occasions when a mummy does involve herself in Garou affairs, it is often for personal reasons — an old friendship, perhaps, or an enmity from a previous life.

Most mummies are aware of the existence of Garou, whom they call Lupines, and are aware of their various strengths and weaknesses. A mummy's typical role is manipulative rather than confrontational. However, mummies' knowledge of Garou weaknesses and their centuries-old skills make them deadly adversaries. Luckily, mummies are exceedingly rare.

Mummies have access to various potions and amulets (many of which can grant them additional traits). A mummy begins with eight primary, six secondary and four tertiary Attribute Traits. Bear in mind that, because of their immortality, it is entirely possible for mummies to have considerably more Traits than listed here. Mummies have literally millennia of life experience, and therefore can vary widely in Abilities. However, each has at least eight different Ability Traits. Some mummies even have magical powers at their disposal.

For more information on mummies, see **World of Darkness: Mummy, Second Edition.**

## Wraiths

The Restless Dead are rarely encountered by the Garou, as each race has a healthy respect for the others' abilities. The Silent Striders seem to know most about these driven souls, as members of this tribe are often haunted by the Restless Dead. There are a lot of shortened lives on both sides of the frontier, and a lot of those folk didn't go peacefully to the Great Beyond, making for more wraiths than normal in these forsaken territories.

For ideas on using wraiths in an active role in your **Wyld West** chronicle, **Ghost Towns** is invaluable. Information for use of wraiths as player characters in **Mind's Eye Theatre** games can be found in **Oblivion**. Otherwise, use spirit Charms to simulate the powers of wraiths.

Wraiths cannot be bound into fetishes unless they willingly agree to the arrangement.

## The Other Shapeshifters

### Nuwisha

Despite what the Garou believe, each species of werecreatures once had a specific purpose to fulfill — the Gurahl to heal, the Bastet to watch, the Mokole to remember, and so on. However, perhaps the most sacred duty of all fell on the shoulders of the children of Coyote — to make Gaia and Her Children laugh. Never ones to pass up a sweet job, the Nuwisha have done their best to fulfill this mission. These crafty shapeshifters use humor and pointed humiliation to keep their fellow changers honest and remind them of the error of their ways even as they battle the greater enemy. All too often a Garou is willing to overlook moral weaknesses in her elders or past Garou atrocities in the name of their "greater good," a blindness that Coyote's Children will not tolerate.

Whether they choose to teach their lessons with gentle words, clever pranks, or cunning warfare is up to each Nuwisha, and Coyote has never been one to tell his Children what to do — as long as they don't aid the Wyrm, of course. Nuwisha are rarely merciful about who or what they make the subject of their pranks, and will cheerfully list a Silver Fang Ahroun's character flaws to her face and enjoy the escape that follows. However, a target of their attentions rarely has an injury more serious than a bruised backside or deflated ego, unless they try to take violent issue with the coyote. Those who learn from the prank and know when to laugh at themselves might even earn a favor or two from the prankster in question. As those individuals who need the most teaching are often heavy with Rage and pride in their own qualities, however, these lessons often backfire, forcing the Nuwisha to hit the trails with an angry pack or two at his heels. Of course, minions of the Wyrm rarely receive gentle pranks — after all, the Nuwisha reason, some folk are better off learning in their next lifetime. Most of the time Trickster's favored ones operate in secret, only revealing their presence once their lesson has been taught (and preferably when they are a territory or two away).

Still, the Nuwisha were considered a valued part of Gaia's family until the first War of Rage came, when the Garou turned on the other changers and demanded recognition as the greatest of Gaia's Children. They accused the Nuwisha of failing to take the battle against the Wyrm seriously, an accusation the Nuwisha would not dignify with an answer, and soon the Garou declared war on them, hunting down the solitary coyotes and ravaging their numbers. Rather than fight back, however, the Nuwisha simply disappeared into the Storm Umbra, where most of them dwell. To this day there are but one or two hundred Kinfolk still living on earth they can lay claim to, and only a dozen or so of Coyote's Children wandering the trails of Gaia at one time.

Things were not always this way, however. Once the Nuwisha walked the lands openly with their fellow changers, teaching lessons where they went and sharing their gift of laughter. The Nuwisha claim that Coyote was the first to travel to the stars, so it is only natural to them that they are the greatest Umbral travelers and mystics. They are forever slipping into the realms beyond to see the strange sights and creatures there, returning to Gaia to teach what they had learned to their fellows before slipping off again. Nuwisha do not run in packs, although they are more than willing to join a group of Garou for a time (in or out of disguise) if they think it will advance their cause and generally offer them a good time.

Only one incident has marred their spiritual relations — one night the Nuwisha played a prank on Luna so grave that she still has not forgiven them, and as a result even their fiercest or wisest are still considered No Moons. Out in the wilds one can often hear the Nuwisha howling their sad songs of entreaty to Luna late at night, but she still has not forgiven them for their trespass, and ancient tradition forbids them from telling others what it was that so offended Luna.

The Savage West presents many great challenges to the Nuwisha. There is so much bloodshed, so much hatred on both sides of the frontier it seems to the wiser coyotes that a hundred of their kind could spend a hundred sleepless years teaching both sides the error of their ways and still not change things. Worse still, the Nuwisha watch uneasily as the energies of the Storm Umbra grow increasingly sinister and unstable; this has prompted more and more of them to return to the world, as they investigate and battle the forces behind the devastation of the spirit realm.

For yet more on the Nuwisha, see **Frontier Secrets** and **Changing Breed book: Nuwisha**.

**Tribal Totem:** Trickster (Most often in his aspect as Coyote, but he has many faces reflecting his different duties as a prankster and celestial scape-goat. Nuwisha almost never have pack totems, preferring a personal bond.)

**Initial Willpower:** 3

**Initial Gnosis:** Homid — 1, Latrani (coyote-born, Nuwisha equivalent of lupus) — 3.

**Backgrounds:** Nuwisha may not take Pure Breed.

**Special Quirks:** Due to their separation from Luna all Nuwisha are considered Ragabash, and Coyote denies them Rage — Nuwisha start with none and can never gain any. This makes them immune to frenzy, but they also lose the extra speed and power Rage offers. Any Gifts or other supernatural powers that cause frenzy still work, however — the Nuwisha have a spark of that same primal nature, however far down it is buried. However, their disconnection from Luna also grants them immunity to silver. There are no metis werecoyotes. Latrani Nuwisha have the same Ability restrictions as lupus Garou do during character creation.

**Special Renown:** When it comes to Renown, Nuwisha honor Ferocity (Glory) and Cunning (Wisdom), but do not recognize Honor, feeling Humor is far more important. A Nuwisha gains Humor Renown whenever he teaches someone else the error of their ways, or how the target has been blindly stumbling toward the Wyrm with their actions. Humor may also be gained when a Nuwisha creatively solves a problem, pranks a foe, or even laughs at himself and his own failings. It should not be rewarded merely for playing gratuitous pranks on one's packmates or punning throughout a story; it is a measure of the ingenuity of a Nuwisha and how well they have learned to instruct others. As a rule of thumb, use the "locational humor index" guide for awarding Humor Renown — if you "had to be there" for an incident, it probably wasn't worth Humor Renown. On the other hand, if the lesson or prank was memorable or amusing enough to merit retelling and appreciating, it's something worthy of Humor.

**Humor Traits:** *Amusing, Devious, Imaginative, Innovative, Inspired, Inventive, Open-Minded, Original, Playful, Resourceful, Sly, Subtle*

**Tribal Advantage:** Trickster's Blessing

Trickster's greatest gift to his Children is their ability to laugh at what others find serious; in times of their greatest need, Coyote grants his faithful Children the ability to defy the laws of reality. Thus, a Nuwisha might run off a cliff and fail to fall, hide behind a tree no thicker than his arm, or even vanish into "thin air" (actually into the Storm Umbra). Whatever the case, this particular quirk manifests as a chance to extricate oneself from danger — and as such, once per session, a Nuwisha may use the Trickster's Blessing to call for a Fair Escape. Of course, if the Nuwisha is later caught in the same session by the (ahem) victims of his former prank, he will have to make his own luck. Note that the actual effect is narrative- the only game effect is the Fair Escape.

**Tribal Drawback:** Coyote's Folly

Even the greatest tricksters sometimes go too far, mocking what should remain sacred or losing sight of what truly matters. This flaw is the origin of Luna's anger at the Nuwisha, and individual werecoyotes often get too caught up in their pranks for their own good. A Nuwisha must either spend a Willpower Trait or win a Static Willpower Challenge (against seven Traits) any time he wishes to avoid finishing a prank he has started. This is likewise required for the Nuwisha to avoid the urge to attempt retaliating with a greater prank when successfully duped by someone else. This is very distracting when the Nuwisha has some other mission that needs attending to, and downright dangerous if the target is very powerful or otherwise not an excellent person to have for an enemy. Finally, even changers who appreciate what the Nuwisha do aren't crazy enough to trust them. All Nuwisha have the Negative Social Trait: *Untrustworthy*, which may be called by anyone who knows their true nature.

## Forms

### Homid

**Trait Adjustments:** None.

**Change Description:** Identical to any other person, except Nuwisha tend to be leaner and more wiry than most people, and even their eldest rarely carry much fat on them. While many are still descended from the Pure Ones, the casual breeding habits of werecoyotes mean that Nuwisha of all races and descriptions now exist.

### Tsitsu (*Near Man*)

**Trait Adjustments:** While in this form, the Nuwisha gains the following bonus traits: *Vigorous*, *Wiry*, *Nimble*. He is also afflicted with the Negative Trait: *Tactless*.

**Change Description:** Much the same as the Glabro form of the Garou, except slightly more human in appearance; the Nuwisha has little trouble passing among humans, although those who know him will definitely notice something amiss. Bulk doubles in this form.

**Roleplaying:** Unlike the Garou, Nuwisha suffer no personality change as a result of transforming; to their minds, all states are as their original. The Nuwisha can still speak normally, but his voice is likely to be much deeper than normal.

### Manabozho (*Coyote-Man*)

**Trait Adjustments:** The Nuwisha gains the following bonus Traits: *Energetic*, *Nimble* x 2, *Quick* x 2, *Rugged*, *Wiry*. However, the Nuwisha also gains the following Negative Traits: *Bestial x2* and *Tactless*.

**Change Description:** Brutish and efficient, this form stands seven or eight feet tall, increasing bulk and weight by about one and a half again of the Homid form. The Delirium (known to the Nuwisha as the Trick) affects most creatures who see the werecoyote in this form, although those affected are considered to be two steps higher on the Delirium chart due to the minor role the Nuwisha played in the Impergium.

**Roleplaying:** A Nuwisha can still speak in this form, but words come out slightly slurred and with a growling undertone that makes even pleasant small talk sound menacing.

### Sendeh (*Near Coyote*)

**Trait Adjustments:** The Nuwisha gains the following Traits: *Quick x2*, *Nimble*, *Energetic*, *Tireless*, *Wiry*. The Nuwisha also gains the following penalties: *Bestial x2* and *Impatient*.

**Change Description:** Easily mistaken for red wolves in this form, Nuwisha often take advantage of this resemblance to hide among packs of wild wolves. Their weight is identical to that of their Homid form.

**Roleplaying:** While the Nuwisha cannot use human speech, he can easily imitate a baby's cry, woman's scream or man's bellow. Sendeh may also converse with both wolves and coyotes in this form.

### Latrani (*Coyote*)

**Trait Adjustments:** The Nuwisha gains the following Traits: *Quick*, *Lithe*, *Rugged*. He also incurs the following penalty: *Bestial*.

**Change Description:** The Latrani form is indistinguishable from a regular coyote, and the character's weight decreases and generally becomes much more lean and wiry.

**Roleplaying:** Human speech is right out, but Nuwisha in this form may still speak easily with both wolves and coyotes; they are brothers, after all. A coyote's howl is higher pitched than that of a wolf, but no less audible.

## Gifts

Nuwisha begin with three Gifts, same as Garou. Nuwisha choose breed Gifts just as Garou do: homid Nuwisha select one homid breed Gift, and Latrani pick one lupus breed Gift. All Nuwisha are Ragabash, so another Gift is selected from that category. Their tribal Gifts are selected from the pool of Gifts below; these Gifts are taught only to those cubs that prove themselves true to the Nuwisha way, and many are unique to the werecoyotes (although just as many were stolen from one of the other Changing Breeds — Coyote does get lazy sometimes). Most of their gifts are based on trickery and are defensive by nature, but remain quite potent nonetheless.

**Note:** It may seem like Nuwisha (and Corax, below) have a disproportionate number of tribal Gifts, but keep in mind that while it is uncommon but not unheard of for a Garou to learn a Gift from another tribe, this is not the case for these two changers. A Nuwisha may trick a Garou into teaching him a Gift, or a Corax learn the secret of a non-Corax Gift, but these are far from reliable means of learning Gifts. Other Changing Breeds are on their own when it comes to tribal Gifts, and thus Gift totals for these two groups have been adjusted accordingly. Of course, characters must still have the proper Rank and Experience Traits to purchase Gifts, and purchasing Gifts outside their breed, auspice (if any) and "tribe" costs an additional Experience Trait, as normal.

## Basic

**Rabbit Run** — As the Silent Strider Gift: *Speed of Thought*.

**Gift of the Porcupine** — As the Metis Gift. (Yes, coyotes learn it easier.)

**Swollen Tongue** — With a touch (a Physical Challenge if the target resists) and the expenditure of one Gnosis Trait, the Nuwisha can cause a target's tongue to swell, preventing all speech or howling. Furthermore, the target's hands begin to shake if they attempt to use sign language or gestures, rendering those attempts unintelligible as well. The effects of this Gift last for one scene or hour, whichever comes first.

**Odious Aroma** — As the Bone Gnawer Gift.

**Spirit Speech** — As the Theurge Gift.

**Bad Joke** — With a bad joke or pun, the Nuwisha may attempt to distract a target long enough to get away. The player must make a joke or pun *in character*, then make a Social Challenge against his target (who uses Mental Traits to defend). If the Nuwisha is successful, he may call for a Fair Escape while the target laughs, unable to help herself; the Nuwisha may also opt to use a riddles or other little mind tricks, in which case the target simply stands confused while the coyote gets away. This Gift may also be used against a group, with normal rules for challenging multiple targets. This Gift is ineffective against animals, spirits or creatures wholly consumed by the Wyrm, though most mockeries and vampires are fair game. Supernatural creatures may cancel the effects of this Gift with a Willpower Trait.

**Otter's Breath** — As the Uktena Gift: *Flick of the Fish's Tail.*

## Intermediate

**Sheep's Clothing** — This Gift allows the Nuwisha to hide in plain sight by appearing to be another type of shapeshifter: Garou, Bastet, Corax, etc. By spending a Gnosis Trait and making a Static Mental Challenge against seven traits (eight for really different forms like a raven), the Nuwisha may appear to be a perfectly normal member of that breed. This Gift allows the Nuwisha to use the caerns of other shapeshifters instead of maintaining their own. This deception fools all supernatural powers of detection, but the Nuwisha does not gain Traits from this change, and may not simulate abilities a coyote is unable to (such as the flight of a raven) unless he also possesses Gifts that allow him to do so. This Gift lasts for one scene.

**Gift of Rage** — Wait, did Coyote say that the Nuwisha cannot Rage? Well, once again Trickster proves worthy of his name, as werecoyotes with this Gift can take the same kind of extra actions and gain the other benefits of Rage that the other changers take for granted. By spending a Gnosis Trait and winning a Static Gnosis Challenge against five Traits, the Nuwisha gains three Rage Traits, which can be used and regained in all the ways Rage normally is. The effects of this Gift last for one scene, but for as long as the Nuwisha has even one Rage Trait in his body, he loses his immunity to silver — Trickster does not want his Children to learn to embrace hatred in any form.

**Laughing At Death** — This Gift causes the target to forget all her troubles and pains and simply enjoy herself for the duration of the Gift. The Nuwisha makes a Social Challenge against the target's permanent Willpower Traits; success means that the target is in her highest spirits and must celebrate for the remainder of the scene, although any attack on the target cancels this Gift immediately. The Nuwisha may even attempt to pull another character out of frenzy by spending a Gnosis Trait before making the Social Challenge; success not only negates the frenzy but induces the giddy state above. This Gift can also be used to ease the pain of a dying person, allowing them to enjoy their last few moments with full control of their faculties. Note that this Gift can easily backfire on the Nuwisha, as some people Ñ Get of Fenris, for example — tend to celebrate very violently, and in any event the Nuwisha has no control over how the target will choose to express her merriment.

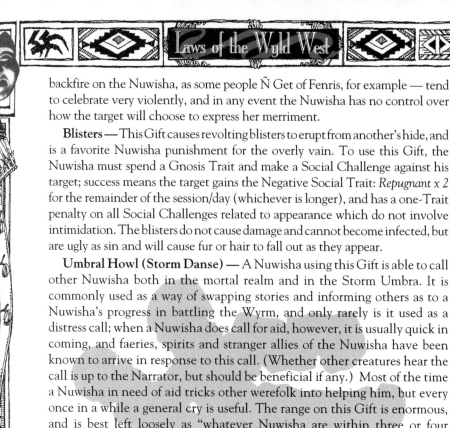

**Blisters** — This Gift causes revolting blisters to erupt from another's hide, and is a favorite Nuwisha punishment for the overly vain. To use this Gift, the Nuwisha must spend a Gnosis Trait and make a Social Challenge against his target; success means the target gains the Negative Social Trait: *Repugnant x 2* for the remainder of the session/day (whichever is longer), and has a one-Trait penalty on all Social Challenges related to appearance which do not involve intimidation. The blisters do not cause damage and cannot become infected, but are ugly as sin and will cause fur or hair to fall out as they appear.

**Umbral Howl (Storm Danse)** — A Nuwisha using this Gift is able to call other Nuwisha both in the mortal realm and in the Storm Umbra. It is commonly used as a way of swapping stories and informing others as to a Nuwisha's progress in battling the Wyrm, and only rarely is it used as a distress call; when a Nuwisha does call for aid, however, it is usually quick in coming, and faeries, spirits and stranger allies of the Nuwisha have been known to arrive in response to this call. (Whether other creatures hear the call is up to the Narrator, but should be beneficial if any.) Most of the time a Nuwisha in need of aid tricks other werefolk into helping him, but every once in a while a general cry is useful. The range on this Gift is enormous, and is best left loosely as "whatever Nuwisha are within three or four territories and a Realm or two," although the range for other allies should be much shorter. (Keep in mind how few Nuwisha there are in the Savage West at any given time.)

## Advanced

**Teasing Mate** — With this Gift, the Nuwisha can bring about a pheremonal surge in his target, making him irresistible to others. The Nuwisha must touch his target (a Physical Challenge if the target resists) and defeat them in a Mental Challenge. If successful, all beings of the same species and gender in the area must win a Static Willpower Challenge against seven Traits or desire immediate copulation with the target. (Yes, you heard right — the *same* gender.) The Nuwisha absolutely love the humor value of this trick, especially in conservative settings, but that is not its only application. The Nuwisha may also use this Gift on himself to boost his seductive powers (without worrying about those of the same gender coming after him): this use of the Gift costs one Gnosis Trait and gives the Nuwisha the following bonus Traits: *Seductive x 2*. The Nuwisha also gains one free retest on all Social Challenges related to seduction for the duration of the Gift when it is used in this fashion. This Gift lasts for one scene.

**Note:** Great care must be exercised to ensure that the rules of **Mind's Eye Theatre** are observed while this Gift is in use: the "no touch" rule still applies (more strongly than usual), and no player should ever be made to feel uncomfortable out of character because of this Gift.

**Ghost Dance (Storm Danse)** — With this potent Gift, the Nuwisha can fight in the material world and the Storm Umbra simultaneously, attacking foes on either side and then completely avoiding damage. The Nuwisha must spend a Gnosis Trait per turn this Gift is in use (a turn is equal to one normal exchange of combat challenges, including retests and extra actions), but while it is in effect he may not be harmed by any attacks short of this Gift or the Gift: *Sideways Attack*.

**Trickster's Skin** — This valuable Gift allows the Nuwisha to "swap skins" with another, taking on the voice and likeness of his target while the target assumes the Nuwisha's appearance. The Nuwisha must spend two Gnosis Traits and make a Static Mental Challenge against half the target's Mental Traits (round down). This Gift may be used at a distance, but only if the target is in sight. The effects of this Gift last for one scene, and this Gift is typically used by Nuwisha to escape an angry mob by causing them to chase "that damn coyote" while the disguised Nuwisha finds an excuse to slip away from his "friends." The Nuwisha and his target both should adopt a gesture, clothing or other posture which indicates their altered appearance for the duration of the Gift. This Gift cannot be detected by *Heightened Senses* or other powers, although the Nuwisha may be discovered by other means if they give away their true identity.

**Umbral Target (Storm Danse)** — With this potent Gift, the Nuwisha may not only fling a target into the Umbra, but may choose exactly where his target winds up: a mockery might be tossed into the Abyss, a tainted Garou thrown into the silver waters of Erebus, or a friendly faerie dropped off at Arcadia Gate. The Nuwisha spends a Gnosis Trait and must grapple his target with a Physical Challenge; if successful, the target reappears exactly where the Nuwisha intended. If the target is already in the Umbra, all that's needed is a Static Gnosis Challenge against a difficulty of five Traits and the expenditure of a Gnosis Trait. Trickster keeps a close eye on the use of this Gift, as it was intended as a rescue method and teaching tool, and a Nuwisha who abuses this Gift risks suddenly disappearing instead of his target one day…

## Rites

For the most part, Nuwisha steal Garou rites, although they have invented a few of their own, which Nuwisha guard jealously for fear the Garou might stumble on them and mess things up even worse than they have now. In particular one group of Nuwisha called the Storm Dansers act as a police force of sorts in the Umbra, exploring realms, protecting travelers and battling the endless dangers of the worlds beyond the Gauntlet. Entrance into this select group requires that a Nuwisha show exemplary courage, wisdom, and commitment to the Nuwisha ways, as well as complete the *Rite of Dansing* (below). Storm Dansers have no formal hierarchy, though the eldest among them are generally heeded in times of danger, but most of the time they respect the individualistic spirit that rests in their fellow Nuwisha and leave them to their own devices. The Garou Rites Nuwisha may learn are as follows: *Rite of Cleansing, Rite of the Opened Caern, Rite of Talisman Dedication, Rite of Spirit Awakening, Rite of Binding, Rite of Summoning, Rite of Becoming, Voice of the Jackal, Satire Rite, Rite of the Fetish, Rite of the Totem.*

The rites unique to the Nuwisha are as follows:

## Basic Rites

**Rite of Dansing (Mystic)** — This rite is the last step toward becoming a Storm Danser, and is taught only to those who have proven themselves worthy of joining the group. It is taught only by Storm Dansers, although Trickster himself has been known to teach it to worthy Nuwisha if there is a shortage of fellow Nuwisha in the area. To complete the rite, the character must spend three days fasting and meditating, spending one Gnosis Trait per day (thus this rite is usually done in the "down time" between games). At the end of this time they must also recite to the Spirit Keeper all their past experiences battling the Wyrm, traveling the Storm Umbra, and teaching their fellow shapeshifters the error of their ways. At the end of this time, the Nuwisha makes a Mental Challenge against seven Traits, which can be retested with the *Enigmas* ability. If successful, Trickster accepts the Nuwisha as a full Storm Danser, and he may purchase Storm Danse Gifts.

## Intermediate Rites

**Rite of the Dream Danse (Mystic)** — This potent rite allows the Nuwisha to know the location of all his fellow Storm Dansers, and to ask a question of them through a sort of shared dream. In game terms, the Nuwisha must enter a trance for at least half an hour and think of the question he wishes answered. The Storm Dansers individually consider the worthiness of the question and, if they decide it is worthy (Narrator's discretion), answer in the form of a riddle. Solving the riddle typically requires great ingenuity, although stumped players may request a Static Mental Challenge with the *Engimas* Ability to try to help unravel it (the difficulty varies, but is usually quite high). When solved, the riddles often offer great insight and even glimpses of the future. Many Nuwisha believe that Trickster himself answers the questions, but that remains unknown. The Nuwisha need not be a full Storm Danser to use this Rite; indeed, many applicants request full membership through use of this rite.

## Advanced Rites

**Caern Concealment (Caern)** — This rite requires at least 10 Nuwisha to perform, which ensures it isn't performed often in the Savage West, but it allows the participants to hide a caern from all but the Nuwisha themselves. It has not been performed in living memory, but wise Nuwisha teach it still, knowing it will one day see use again. Thirty Gnosis Traits are required to seal the rite, and the ritemaster must make at least four Static Mental Challenges against a difficulty of the rating of the caern x 2. Thus, to conceal a Rank Four caern, the Static Mental Challenge is against eight Traits, a Rank Five caern 10 Traits, a Rank Two caern four Traits, etc.

**Sing Back the Dead (Mystic) —** Only one Nuwisha ever knows this rite at a time, as it is taught by Trickster himself. This rite is the power to defy the rules of life and death, allowing the coyote to sing back one or more werecreatures. The Nuwisha must spend a permanent Gnosis Trait for each individual they wish to reanimate, plus one additional permanent Gnosis Trait for each Health Level of damage any of the bodies sustained past what was needed to kill them (e.g., if a Garou had one Health Level left and was killed with a shot that did three levels of damage, two additional permanent Gnosis Traits would be needed). This rite can only be performed when Coyote himself demands it, although any Nuwisha who has been given the honor of learning this rite in the first place usually instinctively knows when it is and isn't necessary.

**Quote:** *Hey, come here! Don't worry, I'm not going to hurt you! Now, why're you crying, girl? What?! Those railroad men over there were mean to you? Well, don't you worry none — I've got a few tricks up my sleeve for big old bullies like that! Now, what would you rather start with, the itching powder, the marbles or the rope snare?*

## Corax

As Gaia matured and the divisions spread between the members of the Triat, an ever-growing problem developed: too many sides were keeping secrets from each other, and Gaia suffered as hidden tormentors and other shadowy factions ate away at the face of creation. Only one species, the cunning ravens, possessed the curiosity and intuition to sort through this web of deceit, and because of this talent they became the favored children of Helios in their quest to expose the darkness that threatened to engulf Gaia. Everywhere they traveled the Children of Raven brought the blinding light of discovery with them, and soon the darkness learned to fear their watchful, piercing gazes. And even though they did not carry the blessing of Luna as most of the other shapeshifters did, in time the Corax became the trusted allies of their fellow Changing Breeds, rooting out danger and corruption so that the others could destroy it. In those golden times, the raven-folk enjoyed the secrets of humanity and helped preserve Gaia's order, trusting their appetite for knowledge to keep them safe.

However, during the War of Rage, the paranoid and arrogant Garou twisted information to their own ends and accused the other Changing Breeds of hiding secrets from them, an attitude the Corax tired in vain to correct. Thus, Raven's Children witnessed firsthand the slaughter caused by Garou pride, and while they were largely exempt from the fury of the werewolves — the Corax were simply too useful to alienate — they never trusted their "cousins" the same way again. Ever wary of another tragic misunderstanding, the Corax now guard carefully what secrets they give to their allies, checking to see if they are ready for a particular piece of knowledge before volunteering it. Indeed, because of this rift the Corax increasingly act on the information they gather themselves instead of leaving it up to the Garou as tradition demands. Even with this old scar, however, the two groups still work together far more often than any other changers, and they are a viciously effective team when properly paired. After all, though the Garou are often considered somewhat oblivious and in need of a bit of guiding to find targets of real significance for their Rage, the Corax figure that the times demand no less than teamwork, and hey, everyone's part of Gaia's family, right?

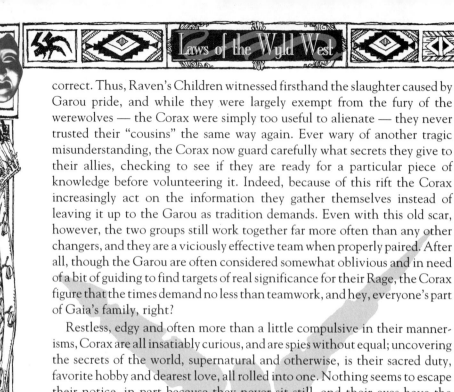

Restless, edgy and often more than a little compulsive in their mannerisms, Corax are all insatiably curious, and are spies without equal; uncovering the secrets of the world, supernatural and otherwise, is their sacred duty, favorite hobby and dearest love, all rolled into one. Nothing seems to escape their notice, in part because they never sit still, and their eyes have the disturbing habit of roaming the room even when they're speaking to someone right in front of them. Set apart from their fellow changers by the tie to Helios, the Corax treasure the difference in perspective this brings them, and they take his charge to bring corruption to light very seriously. If one Corax doesn't know a secret, chances are another will, and if neither of them know it then nothing short of death will be able to keep them from finding it out. Corax see the lore they gather as the fuel which keeps the fire of Gaia's defenders roaring high, and no secret is useful if the messenger is killed before it can be delivered — thus, unlike Garou, Corax tend to flee rather than fight when possible, the better to spread the word and mount an organized assault. When pressed to battle themselves, the raven-folk make frightening and unpredictable opponents, never hesitating to use their vast knowledge of their foes' weaknesses to their advantage.

Corax do not usually organize for longer than it takes to swap secrets and plan some broad strategies, but occasionally some purpose spurs several Corax to form a pack — called a "murder" by Garou who don't know ravens from crows — which lasts as long as it suits the needs of the Corax involved. Corax are also consummate Umbral explorers, second only to the Nuwisha, and leave many trails and markers there that can only be seen by another winged traveler.

In the wide lands of the Savage West, the Corax are faced with a cultural conflict within their own kin: many Corax come with the immigrants to fly through broad new skies and learn the secrets of this vast land, but many other Corax also have lived among the Pure Ones for centuries (especially along the Pacific Northwest). As Garou on both sides of the frontier do battle and wrestle for territory, they call on their Corax allies to scout out enemy positions, often pitting Corax against each other. Most of the raven-folk have made a secret pact to try to get their Garou allies to see eye-to-eye, preferably by using trickery and withholding information, but some Corax are unable to forgive the atrocities around them. These dissenters are dangerous free agents, selling their secrets to any interested ears and igniting the already explosive situation as they see fit, and many of their brethren have made it their duty to hunt down these renegades and bring them back to the flock (as it were).

As if that weren't trouble enough, the Corax have their talons full digging out the agents of the Wyrm, and the emerging dominance of the Storm Eater is provoking worried speculation along the frontier. Several intrepid Corax are also on the verge of discovering true scope of the Enlightened Society of the Weeping Moon (see "Hunters and Humans," above); if successful, this could force a showdown between Gaia's Chosen and the Society that would make the O.K. Corral look like toddlers playing with pop-guns....

For more on Corax, see **Frontier Secrets** and **Changing Breed book: Corax**.

**Tribal Totem:** Raven (Many take Helios as well)

**Initial Willpower:** 2

**Initial Gnosis:** 4 (Regardless of breed)

**Initial Rage:** 1

**Backgrounds:** No restrictions

**Special Quirks:** Corax have two breeds: homid (same as Garou) and corvid (born of raven parents). There are no metis Corax, due to their specialized breeding rites. Corax also have no auspices; all of them have the same purpose under Helios. Corax are *not* affected by silver, but suffer the same consequences from gold; in homid form, they may handle it, but are quite uncomfortable doing so, and in any form they suffer aggravated damage from it as Garou do from silver. Corvid Corax have the same Ability restrictions as lupus Garou do during character creation.

In addition, Corax may drink from the eyes of corpses, gaining a view of either the best or worst aspects of the last moments of a body's life. This is part of their natural role, retaining stories that would otherwise be lost and helping to honor the dead, and Corax take the responsibility very seriously. The Corax must get the permission of the body before taking an eye; this requires no special Gift, just a simple spoken request. Most bodies agree, as it may help put their spirit to rest, but politeness is definitely a plus — after all, the body has nothing to lose by refusing a request, either. Once permission is granted, the Corax must enter Corvid form and make a Static Mental Challenge against five Traits; if successful, they may drink one eye and gain a vision of the last moments of a corpse's life. The left eye provides a vision of the worst part of death, the right eye shows the best part of death, but only *one* eye per corpse may be taken in this fashion except by the rarest of Corax. This means that most of the time the Corax has a lopsided view of the events leading up to death and must puzzle it out as best she can. (At the Storyteller's discretion, the ability to drink from both eyes may be purchased as the *Double Draught* Merit, at the cost of two Traits.)

**Special Renown:** Corax honor the same Renown as the Garou do, although two of their initial three Renown Traits must be Wisdom Renown; the final initial Trait may be of any of the categories they choose. Though they have no auspices, Corax advance in Rank as Theurges; that is, they need the same Renown Trait totals to advance in Rank as a Theurge would.

**Tribal Advantage:** Raven's Special Presents

Raven doesn't raise fools, and even the youngest Corax has the basic tools to start uncovering secrets. At character creation, each Corax receives a free level of *Enigmas* and *Subterfuge* as well as the Physical Trait: *Nimble*. In addition, once per story a Corax may call for a free retest directly pertaining to uncovering a secret, as their keen nose (beak?) for sensing the truth guides them in the right direction.

**Tribal Drawback:** Sparklies!

Ravens are attracted to all manner of shiny objects, and for the Corax this fascination even extends to things that might be dangerous for them to handle (like gold). While they do not blindly pick up baubles in the middle of bear traps, Corax are suckers for beautiful jewelry, lost keys and even just oddly shaped pieces of metal. Whenever a Corax is confronted by a particularly shiny, large, or interesting-looking object, she must make a Static Willpower Challenge against six Traits or spend a Willpower Trait to avoid giving the object at least a cursory visible examination. (Most Corax will pick up the item if they can and give it a once-over that way.) This is a minor but constant annoyance to the Corax, and should be roleplayed accordingly; a player needn't agonize and test over every bauble, but should simply roleplay their character's interest as often as possible and save the real tests for important items and dramatic moments. Due to their light skeletons, all Corax receive the Negative Physical Trait: *Delicate*.

## Forms:

### Homid

**Trait Adjustments:** None.

**Change Description:** Same as any other person, except most Corax are almost painfully thin, with powerful muscles lacing their lean frames. A Corax's bones, while not hollow, are lighter than normal, allowing her to generate excellent lift in her other forms. (After all, not many people built like John Henry can get themselves off the ground!)

**Roleplaying:** No change.

### Crinos/Rara Avis (Bird-Man)

**Trait Adjustments:** The Corax gains the following Traits: *Attentive, Discerning, Nimble, Observant, Tireless, Wiry*. (Corax gain Mental Traits to simulate the keen perception of their raven senses.) They also incur the following penalty: *Bestial x 2* and *Tactless*.

**Change Description:** Unlike the Garou, very few Corax prefer this form for anything but intimidation and desperate combat, as they consider it ungainly. A crude amalgam of bird and man, in Crinos form a Corax gains feathers instead of hair, her face elongates into something resembling a beak, and her fingers and feet curve into wicked talons. The Crinos form is capable of flight, although it is considered far less maneuverable than the corvid form.

**Roleplaying:** While most Corax are mortified to be seen using this form, especially by other Corax, they suffer no personality change from the transformation. Their beak-mouth prevents complicated human speech, however, and combined with their dislike of this form tends to make them clipped conversationalists (for Corax) when in this form. Raven speech is unaffected.

### Corvid (Raven)

**Trait Adjustments:** The Corax gains the following Traits: *Nimble, Observant, Attentive, Discerning, Alert*. However, the Corax also suffers the following penalty: *Bestial x2, Puny*.

**Change Description:** A normal-seeming raven, although many Corax are somewhat larger than their regular cousins, even up to twice their size. The Corax's sense of vision is greatly enhanced in this form, and most of them can easily rival their eagle cousins for visual acuity.

**Roleplaying:** Corax have no personality change in this form, though the ease of spying this form provides often sets their natural curiosity even more ablaze than normal. Corax may communicate with ravens easily in this form; after all, now they're just another member of the flock.

## Gifts

Corax begin play with three Basic Gifts, all of which must be selected from the assortment below. While both breeds of Corax differ in their philosophies, which usually leads to them selecting different beginning Gifts, any combination may be selected by either breed. Many Corax pick up a Garou Gift or two here and there as they get older, especially if they choose to run with a pack, but outside of what secrets they learn from others the following Gifts are the only ones Corax may learn; learning the Gifts of any other group costs an additional experience point.

**Note:** Many Corax Gifts deal with prophecy and uncovering hidden lore, both of which can be problematic to an unprepared Narrator. When dealing with future omens and visions, the Narrator should provide future information based on what they believe might occur later in the session or chronicle, but players should know that not all visions come to pass and that later events or unexpected decisions can drastically alter what might have seemed to be a safe prediction earlier. (Always in motion is the future!) As for hidden lore, make sure to balance the needs of the story with the nature of the Gift — if uncovering a particular piece of information would ruin a story, you are within your rights to deny the character. However, don't shortchange the Corax on their traditional role by often denying them information; instead, if a piece of lore might ruin the story, give it to the Corax anyway but wrap it in layers of riddles and clues, decipherable but still a daunting enigma. If the players know you're not doing this just to "screw them over," and they are playing a Corax well, more than likely they'll jump at a chance to unravel such an elaborate puzzle.

## Basic

**Enemy Ways** — A Corax with this Gift is a fine-tuned danger detector, capable of determining exactly what type of foes are nearby and how many there are. The Corax must make a Static Mental Challenge against seven Traits; success tells if there is indeed danger within 10 steps of the Corax, and if so the she may spend a variable number of Mental Traits to learn more about it. For two Mental Traits, the Corax may learn how many enemies are within the Gift's range; for two more Mental Traits, the Corax may determine what type of creature each foe is (werewolf, human, vampire, etc.). In no instance does this Gift have a range beyond ten steps. If player characters are subjected to this Gift, either the Corax or a Narrator must ask them out of character if they intend to do put the Corax in danger (see below); they must answer honestly. This Gift functions in regard to enemies on the other side of the Gauntlet, but the Corax may only learn their number, not their composition. Characters do not necessarily know when this Gift is used on them unless they have a means of detecting supernatural scrying, but are not likely to be amused if it is somehow brought to their attention — it's not a great vote of confidence for a friend to assess you as possible threat!

**Note:** "Danger" is defined for this Gift as "someone or something which imminently threatens to harm the Corax." Thus a vampire plotting to bring out the eventual death of the Corax is not detectable by this Gift until he actively begins hunting her, but a tunnel about to collapse, a rival who seeks to kill the Corax later that night, or a posse out gunning for feathers are all certainly detected. Note also that the Corax cannot use this Gift to determine what type of creature a being is *unless* they are considered a "danger" to the Corax; the Corax cannot simply walk around using this Gift as a random supernatural detector.

**Morse** — Corax are never out of touch with each other for very long, and this Gift ensures that a Corax can always pass on a message to her fellows. The Corax must simply spend a Gnosis Trait and tap out her message in Morse code on some hard surface, and the nearest Corax will hear it clear as day, no matter how far away that might be. If the nearest Corax is a player character, the sender may seek her out and deliver the message in private (it cannot be overheard); if not, a Narrator should take on the role of nearest Corax and respond accordingly. Of course, if the nearest Corax doesn't know Morse, this Gift may not be quite so useful, but that's the risk one takes with this Gift. Benevolent Narrators may allow a Static Mental Challenge against eight Traits for characters who don't understand Morse code to try to figure out the gist of messages more complex than a simple "S.O.S.!"

**Omens and Signs** — Most Corax are skilled at picking out the threads of the intangible in mundane events, but this Gift renders that talent second nature. The Corax must make a Static Mental Challenge against six Traits to activate this Gift, and due to the nature of omens a Narrator should be present to deliver the prophecy. The signs received this way are often very vague and require the Corax to decipher them on her own; after all, Raven doesn't want his children to get complacent in their efforts to find the truth! Truly momentous events might be felt a long way off at the Narrator's discretion. Corax tend to use this Gift sparingly, as overuse tends to evoke false omens.

**Razor Feathers** — Corax have very few combat talents, but this Gift helps even the odds a bit in battle. The Corax must spend a Physical Trait and a Gnosis Trait to activate this Gift, but once it is activated the feathers along the edge of the Corax's wings take on the strength and sharpness of steel, making them useful tools and lethal weapons. Damage from the feathers is aggravated, but after any successful attacking Physical Challenge involving her wings, the Corax may immediately call for a Simple Test; on a win or a tie, she inflicts an additional non-aggravated wound. This Gift lasts for as many turns as half the Corax's Physical Traits (round down), but may be used as many times per scene as the Corax is willing to pay the activation cost. This Gift may only be used in Rara Avis form.

**Truth of Gaia** — As the Philodox Gift.

**Voice of the Mimic** — With this Gift, the Corax may imitate any noise she's ever heard, from voices and accents to the sounds of rifles and train whistles. One Mental Trait must be spent to activate this Gift, but it remains in effect for the duration of the scene. Only one Trait needs to be spent, no matter how many different sounds the Corax wishes to imitate during the scene. These imitations sound exactly like the original, and cannot be determined as "false" by *Heightened Senses* or other supernatural means. A *Subterfuge* or *Performance* Social Challenge might be called for in the case of *truly* outlandish impressions, but only to convince a listener of veracity — the sound is still perfect, the challenge is just to see if the Corax is noticed as the source or otherwise gives the ruse away.

**Word Beyond** — The Corax may use this Gift to use available materials to make a marker in the Umbra decipherable only by other Corax. The Corax must spend a Mental Trait to use this Trait, but may then either leave a secret message for any other Corax who pass by the area. The player may write it down and put it in an envelope marked for Corax only, leave it with a Narrator, or otherwise encode it, but regardless no one other than a Corax may decipher the message. Of course, the marker may be destroyed, but only at the Narrator's discretion — most Corax markings are designed to be noticeable only from the air (of course), or are otherwise quite inconspicuous. After all, what's the point of a secret message if everyone else knows where it is?

## Intermediate

**Dark Truths** — As the Uktena Gift: *Sharing Raven's Supper*, except the difficulty of the Static Mental Challenge is only seven for the Corax. (Hey, how do you think the Garou learned that neat little trick?)

**Dead Talk** — Corax have long held truck with the dead, learning their secrets and preserving their stories as part of Gaia's plan. This Gift allows the Corax to have a conversation with a body no more than a day dead; the Corax must spend a Gnosis Trait and make a Static Mental Challenge against six Traits. If successful, the Corax may ask the corpse questions for roughly a 10-minute period before the Gift fades, which it will answer honestly (although those who die unpleasantly may answer in curt phrases). Note that most of the time it is the body itself answering the questions, for chances are the corpse's ghost is long gone. (If the wraith does happen to be nearby, it may converse freely with the Corax for the duration of the Gift, but is under no compunction to answer questions.)

**Eyes of the Eagle** — Corax have good eyesight as it is, but this Gift makes their vision superhumanly clear and accurate. This Gift requires a Gnosis Trait and a Mental Trait be spent, but remains in effect for the remainder of the scene. The Corax is two traits up on and automatically wins all ties on challenges involving vision, has eyesight roughly twice as good as an eagle for the purposes of range and clarity, and most of all becomes able to see through visual obstructions such as darkness or fog as if it were high noon. Nothing short of a solid object blocks the Corax's vision. This Gift can be used in conjunction with Gifts that require line of sight, making it a potent Gift indeed in the right hands.

**Hummingbird Dart** — Another Gift to balance the odds in battle, this Gift allows the Corax to pluck one of her own feathers and toss it like a dart, essentially assuring her a supply of ranged weapons even if she's apparently unarmed. The Corax must spend a Rage Trait and make a Static Physical Challenge against five Traits for each dart she wishes to create, but once created the dart flies straight and true, in defiance of physics and aerodynamics. The dart inflicts a single non-aggravated wound, unless used in conjunction with *Razor Feathers*, in which case the dart's damage becomes aggravated.

**Tongues** — As the Homid Gift.

## Advanced

**Airt Sense —** As the spirit Charm of the same name, except the Corax must spend one Gnosis Trait and make a Static Mental Challenge against seven Traits to use it. If successful, the knowledge of the Umbra granted by this Gift halves all travel times in the Storm Umbra.

**Gauntlet Runner —** This Gift allows the Corax to lower the level of the local Gauntlet, allowing her and others to step sideways more easily, but also potentially allowing nasty things on the other side to cross over, and so it is used sparingly. The Corax must make an Extended Static Mental Challenge against eight Traits; each win or tie lowers the local Gauntlet level by one. This Gift affects roughly a 20-foot area, but no matter how successfully it is used, the Corax must still use a reflective surface to step sideways. The Spirit Keeper should be notified when this Gift is used.

**Portents —** This Gift allows a Corax to sneak a peek at the important events of the near future, in a much broader way than previous Gifts. The Corax must spend two Gnosis Traits and remain undisturbed for at least 10 minutes; she may just want a general omen, or she may name an area of interest (say, the future of the local whorehouse or the president of Covington Railroads) and hope that Raven provides. The visions provided are vivid and accurate as prophecy can get, which is not to say that they aren't sometimes wrapped in riddles or symbolism — the meaning is still clear and accurate enough, if you can puzzle it out. And the riddles are a small price (by Corax standards) for the view of the future this Gift offers. Obviously, the Storyteller should be contacted when this Gift is used to ensure that the prophecy is as true as possible.

**Theft of Stars —** Raven brought the sun, moon and the stars, and what Raven brought Raven can take back. This bizarre but effective Gift allows the Corax to steal the light of these celestial bodies from her target, making him unable to see any light derived from a natural source. Hence the target as blind at high noon as he is under a full moon, and gains the disadvantages of the *Blind* Flaw for the duration of the Gift as long as he remains in natural light only. Of course, artificial light sources such as campfires or lanterns allow him to see, but who in the Savage West burns precious candles or lamps during the day? Not to mention that someone wandering around with their lantern lit in the middle of the morning is bound to attract less than favorable comments from his neighbors. This Gift lasts for one hour, and requires that the Corax spend a Rage Trait and a Willpower Trait in addition to besting her target in a challenge of her permanent Willpower Traits versus his permanent Willpower Traits.

**Thieving Talons —** As the Ragabash Gift. (Not that the Garou admit who taught it to them these days, naturally.)

## Rites

Like the Nuwisha, the Corax use many Garou rites, and even claim to have taught the Garou a few (especially the *Rite of Talisman Dedication*); in any event, most Corax rites are designed to accommodate the solitary life of the raven-folk, and for protecting the precious knowledge that they uncover in their travels. Unlike Nuwisha, Corax have no special list of rites to choose from, as their years of traveling alongside Garou and spying on their ways have taught them any rite a Garou could teach and then some. However, Corax are very cautious about showing off their knowledge, as they know the Garou are very suspicious of those they see as having stolen their secrets. The Corax are in no hurry to start a second War of Rage over something as silly as a few purloined campfire rituals.

The rites unique to the Corax are as follows:

## Basic

**Rite of the Sun's Bright Ray (Mystic) —** This rite, which takes five minutes of chanting to perform, brings light to a darkened area, even underground. This light is considered to be true sunlight for all intents and purposes, and lights an area roughly 20 feet on each side (in case of debate, consult a Narrator and use common sense). This light lasts for one scene, although the rite may be renewed with another five-minute ritual if a longer duration is required. Once created, this light cannot be extinguished by the Corax — the rite must run its full course, so Corax are careful to use this rite only when bright light will not give them away. As indicated, this light causes damage to vampires as per actual sunlight, which makes this rite a deadly surprise indeed; however, players who attempt to crisp a convention's worth of Kindred by using this rite in the game's only play area risk the wrath of enraged Storytellers as well as fellow players, so care should be taken to ensure that this rite is not overused.

**Rite of the Fetish Egg (Mystic) —** This is one of the most sacred rites of the Corax, and never undertaken lightly, as it not only produces a new Corax if successful but also requires great care and sacrifice on the part of the rite's leader. It must be performed in the Storm Umbra, must be attended by another Corax of the opposite breed, and requires four hours to complete; three hours are taken to create the egg itself, and another hour to bind the new Corax spirit to it. The Corax must succeed at a Static Gnosis Challenge against four Traits before the rite begins, and three permanent Gnosis Traits must be expended during this ritual; if the rite is interrupted at any point it automatically fails and the three Gnosis Traits are still lost. Even if the rite is successfully completed, the hard part is not yet over; Corax eggs are prized as treats by many unsavory types, and while the parent Corax automatically senses if the egg is in danger, most eggs are carefully hidden and guarded to avoid the need to defend them in the first place. Furthermore, the cry of a new Corax as it breaks the spirit-egg (which coincides with the fledgling's First Change in the physical world) can be heard for miles by Corax and creatures in the spirit world. If someone with feathers doesn't arrive to help the kid through the change and guard the egg, it is usually snacked on by all sorts of unpleasant things.

Still, this rite is the *only* way new Corax come about, and so brave and elder Corax still attempt it despite the great risks and costs. The rarity of it only increases the need for Corax to be self-sufficient, after all, and helps bond Corax to each other with a tight sense of purpose and family.

## Advanced

**Rite of Battle Blessing (Mystic) —** This rite, which is only permitted to be known by three specially chosen elder Corax (called the Morrigan) at a time, allows the Corax to tip the tide of battle in favor of one side or another. All three Morrigan must be present for this rite to be used, which means it will seldom be seen in most games (much less learned by all but the most exceptional players), but when it is used its effects are devastating. Each Morrigan may spend Gnosis Traits up to the limit of her *Occult* Ability, and for each Gnosis Trait spent by the Morrigan victims of this rite are considered one Trait down on all Challenges while they remain on battlefield. Targets cannot be down more Traits than it would take to reduce them to zero. This rite should not be allowed to become a regular factor in a game, as it remains one of the most potent advantages Raven has given his Children and he does not like to see it used often or unwisely, as such usage robs it of its power and mystique.

**Rite of Memory Theft (Punishment)—** This rite is the most serious punishment Corax can levy on each other, and is bestowed on those found guilty of dangerous stupidity or who have spilled valuable secrets. Three Corax are required to perform this rite, including the Ritemaster, and they must surround the target (who is usually restrained or subdued by this point), bearing a vessel painted with pictures of the target's deeds. The vessel is opened as the target's deeds are recited, with the memory of each event vanishing into the box as it is named, until the target remembers absolutely nothing which occurred after her First Change (including the rite and who participated in it). This memory theft is an all-or-nothing process; memories cannot be selectively deleted. The Ritemaster then crushes the vessel, gaining all the target's memories as if they were her own. This is seldom a pleasant process — after all, the Corax must have committed some great trespass to be chosen for this rite, and having such intimate knowledge of that dark deed weighs heavily on the ritemaster's heart. At the Storyteller's discretion, the Ritemaster may gain/the target may lose Abilities as a result of this rite, and if so the exactly number of levels gained/lost are also up to the Narrator. Obviously, a Narrator should be present from the beginning of this rite, since it has a severe impact on both the target and the

Ritemaster, as well as to facilitate the relating of the target's memories to their new owner.

There is no game "system" to this rite, other than what may be necessary to subdue the target, but would-be memory raiders beware — the same restriction applies to Corax rites as does Garou; that is, if the rite is knowingly undertaken against an innocent Corax, those performing the rite lose their memories instead. If the rite is performed unknowingly on an innocent Corax, the target still loses her memory, but if her innocence can be satisfactorily proven to the Ritemaster the rite may be reversed by performing the whole ritual in reverse. There is no known method for returning the memories of a Corax who was rightfully found guilty and subjected to this rite.

**Quote:** *Well, I've only been in town a couple of days, but I heard that old man Humphries ain't been quite right lately: muttering to himself, drawin' hexes all over his barn, giving that pretty Ally Rae the evil eye, real spooky stuff. Now, I don't know about witchcraft, but I'd guess if your pack wanted to look for the Weeping Moon folks, he'd be a good place to start. How'd I know that? Let's just say I have this old beak of mine in all the right places in these parts.*

The Garou are not the only children of Gaia with the knowledge of the Changing Ways. There are a few others who can shift into animal forms; two of these others, the Nuwisha and the Corax, share the Savage West with the Garou and are detailed on page 278 and 287. In the ancient times, the Garou made their bid for clear dominance over the other shapeshifters, in a war that began between the Gurahl and the European Garou. The so-called War of Rage quickly escalated to include all of the Changing Breeds; it ended only when the Silver Fangs declared it over before the other races were totally wiped out. The other Bête have never recovered their number, and many have never forgiven the Garou.

The other skinchangers live on the periphery of the World of Darkness, keeping clear of their Garou "cousins" for reasons of safety and secrecy, but many of them have taken to visiting the frontier of the Savage West as conflicts heat up, seeking to throw their own unique influences and opinions into the mix.

The following breeds are the ones that the Garou know to exist, and are most likely to encounter. Other skinchangers are rumored to have survived the War of Rage, but these are discounted as rumor only.

## Ananasi (*Werespiders*)

**Totem:** Any

In the Beginning Times the Ananasi served the Weaver, but then the Weaver went mad. The queen of the Ananasi went to the Weaver to cure it, but the Weaver encased her in a dark opal and turned her over to the Wyrm. The Wyrm then used her as a hostage to force the Ananasi to serve its corruptive ways. Then the queen commanded her subjects to leave the

Wyrm and serve the Wyld to free her. Most did, but in the end the Wyld's forces could not fully trust the Ananasi. Today, the werespiders protect Gaia and work toward freeing their queen. The Ananasi can live on blood (human or animal), have Blood Pools like vampires (instead of Rage), are nocturnal and are basically living vampires. Their forms are Homid, Lilian (eight-appendaged, spiderlike humanoid form), Pithus (giant spider) and Crawlerlings (an army of very small spiders). If Ananasi are needed as Storyteller characters, they should be designed with access to Weaver, Wyrm and Wyld Gifts.

## Bastet (*Werecats*)

**Totem:** Bastet have their own totems, ranging from Butterfly to Hatii the Thunderer and King-of-Beasts. Garou know little about these totem spirits, save that they are powerful.

The "Eyes of Gaia" have the grudging respect and eternal distrust of the Garou. The watchfulness, curiosity and graceful arrogance of the Bastet contrast them sharply with the Garou, whom they see as crude, uncouth, dirty and stupid. The Bastet regard themselves as the guardians of humanity, so the Impergium drove a tremendous wedge between the two Changing Breeds. Of all Bastet, Garou in the Savage West are most likely to encounter the werecougars, or Pumonca, who have deep roots among the Pure Ones. Taciturn loners who are at one with the land, as well as consummate warriors and survivors, the Pumonca often fight alongside native endangered native populations. This frequently makes them allies of the Wendigo and thus little loved by the European Garou as a whole. Pumonca Gifts can be represented well with a selection of Silent Strider, Red Talon and Lupus Gifts.

For more on the Pumonca in the Savage West, see **Frontier Secrets**.

### Tribes

There are nine distinct Bastet tribes:

| Tribe | Duty | Cat Type |
|---|---|---|
| Bagheera | the sages | Panthers |
| Balam | the defenders | Jaguars |
| Bubasti | the mages | Egyptian Abyssinians |
| Ceilican | the mad ones | Housecats |
| Khan | the berserkers | Tigers |
| Pumonca | the guardians | Cougars |
| Simba | the warrior kings | Lions |
| Swara | the messengers | Cheetahs |
| Qualmi | the shamans | Lynxes |

Storytellers working with another type of Bastet than the Pumonca should adjust a character's access to Gifts in order to reflect a Bastet's tribe accurately. For more on the Bastet in general, see **Changing Breed book: Bastet.**

## Gurahl (*Werebears*)

**Totem:** Bear and Ursa Major (the Great She-Bear)

The Gurahl are pacifiers, purifiers, protectors and healers. They claim mastery of death as well as life, and can step through the Dark Veil into the lands of the Lower Umbra. The bear cults spread throughout the world are testament to Gurahl influences and interaction.

It was a failure of the Gurahl, allowing the Wyrm to gain a foothold in the world in ancient times, which led directly to the creation of the Garou. Conversely the Gurahl decision not to teach the Garou how to defeat death was one of the causes of the War of Rage. Gurahl can spend Rage at a one-to-one ratio to increase the number of Health Levels they inflict in Physical Challenges. In the Savage West, the great bears have been driven from the contested areas and are only seen very rarely, usually during a time of great stress or, conversely, a time when great spiritual advice is needed. Most Garou, even the Pure Ones, have never seen a Gurahl in person, and react to them with a kind of stunned fascination at first. Gurahl have access to Philodox and Children of Gaia Gifts, and any other Gifts or Rites related to healing or peace.

## Mokole (*Werelizards*)

**Totem:** Dragon

The Mokole call themselves the "Memory of Gaia," and can recall tales from the time of the Dinosaur Kings and beyond. They have fought the Garou since those first times, and since they were wiped out in every region but the Congo and Amazon Basin, they still hate the Garou about as much as they hate the humans. Extremely rare in the Savage West, as they were chased out of this region long ago by the Pure Ones, they nonetheless are occasionally found in marshes or swampland in the southern or southeastern United States, where small enclaves of them and their Kinfolk dwell to this day.

The Mokole still practice the Impergium to this day. If needed as Storyteller characters, they should be designed with access to Ahroun, Black Fury and Get of Fenris Gifts. A Mokole's full animal form can be of any one reptile type except snake (alligator, komodo dragon, cayman). Their monstrous form is always a 20' dinosaur of one sort or another.

## Ratkin (*Wererats*)

**Totem:** Rat, City Father/Mother, Thunder (rare)

Ratkin have always been the skulkers in the shadows, the outcasts and the unwanted. Originally it was their job to keep human population in check but when their ways of subtlety and natural selection did not work, the Garou stepped in and began the Impergium. The Ratkin and the Garou fought, and nearly all the Ratkin were destroyed. Those who remained retreated to the sewers, where they breed with the rats that dwell in the dark. Most Ratkin are of the rodens breed (equivalent of lupus, born of rats), as many humans find them offensive to be around.

Ratkin are the ugliest of Gaia's Children, and they seethe with Rage against those who vanquished them. Unsurprisingly, Ratkin and Bastet *hate* each other. Recently, with the coming of the Industrial Revolution the Ratkin have seen something of a rise in their fortunes, as the cities of humanity are developing ever more hiding places and back-alley markets, which is just to their liking. Some Garou even whisper that the Bone Gnawers are aware of this and allow it due to their tribal allegiance to Rat, but most dismiss that claim as being too much of an insult even for a Bone Gnawer. Ratkin have access to some Shadow Lord, Ragabash and Bone Gnawer Gifts, specifically those dealing with information, obscurement, movement and survival.

### Rokea (*Weresharks*)

**Totem:** Unknown

If the Garou are considered the most deadly predators on the land, the Rokea hold that title for the waters of the planet. Little is known about the Rokea; they have little connection to Gaia (preferring a mysteriously Wyrmlike totem, the Kraken), cannot travel into the Umbra, and do not have any vulnerability to silver. They are mystically connected to the sea, and deal with any intrusion into their territory with a simple diplomacy tactic: (sounds of flesh tearing). Rokea have access to Ahroun and Lupus Breed Gifts (adjusted for underwater use).

## Kinfolk

*In love there is always one who kisses, and one who offers the cheek.*

— French proverb

Those who are born of Garou ancestry but who do not become Garou themselves are called Kinfolk, and they occupy an unique niche in Garou society (if they become involved with it at all). The most direct definition of the role that Kinfolk take among the Garou is that of second-class citizens; Kinfolk cannot earn rank as Garou, cannot change forms, are noticeably less combat efficient, and cannot sidestep into the Umbra. As such, full Garou often look down upon their less able cousins.

On the other hand, Kinfolk, both human and lupine, bear (and often raise) Garou children to their First Change, act as go-betweens, couriers, spies and sometimes cannon fodder for the embattled Garou. Werewolves regard Kinfolk as gifted, precious and valuable, but not as equals. They may be friends, but they are rarely partners.

Kinfolk are the buffers between Garou and human society. The vast majority are content with not having "bred true." They revere their secret pedigree, and will do almost anything to aid the Garou's fight to save Gaia. Only a few actually grow to resent not being Garou. However, the Wyrm finds its way into the hearts of such Kinfolk and uses them to devastating affect against the Garou.

There are certain advantages to being Kinfolk. While Kinfolk are not Garou, they do draw certain gifts from their heritage. Kinfolk can have Numina (see **Laws of the Hunt** for **Mind's Eye Theatre**): True Faith, Sorcery and Psychic Phenomena. They can learn minor Gifts and rites, and some even Awaken enough to become mages. Kinfolk are immune to the effects of silver and the Delirium, and they do not panic animals by their presence. Garou law still applies to Kinfolk, but they can get away with a lot more than Garou can because, after all, they're only Kinfolk.

For more information on Kinfolk, see **Kinfolk: Unsung Heroes**.

## The Tribal Roles of Kinfolk

• **Black Furies**: Their Kinfolk work in politics, business and property ownership, protecting the wilderness and fighting for suffrage and other causes. In general, the women run the show, but in male-dominated cultures male Kinfolk are more visible (out of necessity). One European network, the Sisterhood, dates back to the days of medieval witch-hunters, and still works to protect and aid the oppressed, gather occult artifacts and guide worthy Garou through the group's homelands. Many of these Kinfolk wield political power and magical abilities. American Kinfolk are often quite headstrong and independent, becoming land owners or local politicians of note. Lupine Kinfolk guard the Furies' lands and caerns.

• **Bone Gnawers**: Members of this tribe have perhaps the closest relationship with their Kinfolk. They form close adoptive families, and help each other to survive. Bone Gnawers don't look down on their Kinfolk nearly as much as other Garou, possibly because of the way the other Garou look down on them. After all, they've sweated at the same manual labor and swigged the same ale with these folk for centuries, so who's to say who's better than whom?

The Barking Chain is an important gossip network of Bone Gnawer Kinfolk. Members bark and yelp information across cities, and homids often find jobs doing the "distasteful" chores of the rich and powerful in their home cities, where they often have opportunities to scrounge up useful gossip.

• **Children of Gaia**: These Kinfolk often reflect what is best in both wolf and man. Humans work endlessly for peace and understanding through social change and lupines stand sentinel over the caerns and tracts of pristine wilderness. Both display greater tolerance than many "normal" members of their species.

• **Fianna**: Boon companions, drinking partners and links in the mystic chain that spans centuries, these Kinfolk tend to be the bards, artists and rabble rousers of their towns or packs. Unfortunately, the hatreds between many people of the Old Country also divide the Fianna and their Kinfolk, as Irish Fianna side with Irish Kinfolk, British Fianna with British Kinfolk, etc.

• **Get of Fenris**: Inspired by their cousins' ruthless nobility, the Get's Kinfolk strive for greatness in all things. The savage Get are as harsh on their Kinfolk as they are on themselves, producing strong warrior lines and some of the most powerful wolves and greatest warrior-heroes of history. Few tribes foster such fierce loyalty — or such rabid hatred — among their Kinfolk. Many of the soldiers guarding frontier towns have Get blood in their veins, as do some of the more honorable hired guns that roam the prairie.

• **Iron Rider**: The savvy Kinfolk have a great nose for business, and are frequently among the best connected families in town, helping their Garou cousins in business and doing what they can to keep humans ignorant of the whole affair. Iron Riders and their kin tend to get along very well, as they share a common love of their cities and many other traits most Garou do not understand about their human relatives. Ambitious to a fault, though, these Kinfolk can become hostile to their cousins if they feel they have been exploited or underappreciated. The lupine Kinfolk of this tribe, growing fewer all the time, are now mostly used as guards for family businesses. Those Iron Rider Kinfolk who travel outside their beloved cities are found as rail men, engineers and entrepreneurs of all kinds.

• **Red Talons**: Red Talon Kinfolk are wolves. Period. These protect and are in turn fiercely protected by their Garou cousins. Red Talon Kinfolk watch and report to the Talons, but rarely play a direct role in their cousins' affairs.

• **Shadow Lords**: This tribe exacts the highest toll from its Kinfolk. It is beaten into their heads that in this Wyrm-ridden world they must think like the Wyrm, fight like the Wyrm and sometimes act like the Wyrm. Nothing less than total ruthlessness is respected, and nothing less than perfection is accepted. The constant trials, threats and discipline imposed by these Garou have made their loyal Kinfolk something to be reckoned with, but have also driven many into the coils of the Wyrm. A mayor with his eye on the state house or a sheriff who keeps order at all costs often have more than a little Shadow Lord blood in them.

• **Silent Striders**: All too few of these Kinfolk ever learn of their heritage, but those who do become the most welcome of allies, ready with a warm bed, cash and a safe refuge. Most are also wanderers — Gypsies, drifters, hired hands, migrant workers and lone wolves. Few other tribes inspire such loyalty and friendship from their Kinfolk. In return, the Striders respect and cherish their Kinfolk, and never willingly place them in danger, believing their lives are dangerous enough as it is.

• **Silver Fangs**: Leaving the Iron Riders and Shadow Lords far behind (and often scoffing at them both as mere upstarts), the Kinfolk of the First Tribe are the real movers and the shakers of human society, the nobility, gentry and old money. The Fangs' lupine Kinfolk range across huge protectorates, lording over vast tracts of land. Throughout history the Silver Fangs have wielded power through their human cousins. While the days of hereditary nobility are gone, Kinfolk of the Fangs have risen to the challenge of a new world and excelled in business and politics — fields where ability is often more important than breeding.

• **Stargazers**: The mentor-student relationship that is the norm among the Stargazers extends to the way they treat their Kinfolk. It is said that their lupine Kinfolk think more abstractly than humans do, and far more wisely. Some Kinfolk guard and maintain the monasteries of their cousins, while all tend to reach for the mystical paths and spiritual awakenings that they believe will save the world.

• **Uktena**: These Kinfolk come from all native peoples of all lands. They are brought together and given purpose through their kinship. Uktena Kinfolk scour the globe to learn new secrets to bring to their Garou cousins, and walk the places that most never even dream exist.

• **Wendigo**: These Kinfolk practice and cherish the ways of their ancestors, and work hard to keep the Wyrmcomers from gaining a foothold in their lands, however they have to do it. Ordered by the Wendigo to avoid all intimate contact with the Wyrmcomers, they have an isolationist attitude that has given rise to extremism among the remaining tribes. Lupine Kinfolk of the Wendigo roam the deep northwest forests.

• **Black Spiral Dancers**: These make up a sorry and dangerous lot, taught to accept their place or die slowly. They are the stalkers, the inbred mountain clans, the worthless bandits and the other scum that continuously bubbles to the top of the human gene pool. Lupine Dancer Kinfolk are clearly both mentally and physically sick, and they pass their illnesses on to those whom they attack.

## Creating Kinfolk

Kinfolk can be made as player characters using the rules for humans in the **Laws of the Hunt** book, or by following the same basic steps as Garou characters, with these exceptions:

Instead of Gifts, a Kinfolk character gets nine points which he can spend in the following ways:

Basic Gift that does not require Gnosis or Rage to activate — 3 Traits
Basic Rite that does not require Gnosis or Rage to activate — 3 Traits
Numina (as per **Laws of the Hunt**) — Varies
Merits and/or Flaws — Varies

See also "Kinfolk Background," pp. 83.

# Do's and Don'ts

The Savage West will put you in contact with a lot of different people, some of whom are likely to be wired on adrenaline and consumed by the danger and mystery of the story. Under such circumstances, intensity can lead to disagreement and arguments, and neither of these things is conducive to having a good time. Listed below are some important extra guidelines to help keep tempers in check and the story flowing smoothly. Do your part to make everything work.

• **Don't go wild** — The idea here is not to get carried away and hurt yourself. You should never pretend to attack anyone physically, and you should never do anything remotely dangerous. Describe and mimic any action that could be considered even slightly dangerous.

• **Be a teacher** — Achieving victory by taking advantage of someone's lack of knowledge is completely without class. Teach the sucker every trick and nuance beforehand, and then beat him anyway. Now *that's* a triumph worth bragging about.

• **Don't use weapons** — We've said it before, we'll say it again. Don't even carry representations of weapons. Not even in this wildest of Wests.

• **Protect the Veil** — Don't perform illegal-seeming activities in public places, and make sure you use prop cards for any unusual or dangerous items that your character possesses.

• **Don't overact** — Don't act out strong emotions unless everyone present is aware of what's going on, and always be ready to simmer down if someone asks to take a breather from a particularly intense scene. It may be wonderful to be immersed in the passion of an exchange with another character, but always remember that the real person behind that character has to be comfortable for it to be really great, and unnerving them or tiring them out just doesn't do that.

• **Stay in character** — Step out of character only if you have to. Respect others' needs to step out of character, for whatever reason. Never abuse this courtesy by saying you are out of character just to avoid an encounter.

Experienced players learn to weave the system of challenges into their conversations and can be rather sly about it; they can avoid alerting the "mundanes" that anything is happening. This is the linchpin of **Mind's Eye Theatre**. Real people try to solve things calmly and collectively, not by pulling six-guns every five seconds. Characters should follow their example.

• **Don't debate the rules** — Nobody likes a rules lawyer. Don't start rules arguments during the game. Call for a Narrator. If you have a problem with a Narrator's call, wait until after the game to argue your case. In the meantime, don't hold up the rest of the plot.

• **Foster intrigue** — Don't ever limit yourself to the goals and motivations that a Narrator gives you at the start of a session — take control. Get involved! After all, it's your story.

• **Create your own plots** — Create your own story and work other characters into it one by one. Characters are made to act, not to react.

• **Watch out for other players** — Keep an eye out for players who look bored; a bored player is the perfect assistant Narrator. Remember that some players who get really bored tend to have their characters start killing other characters for no other reason than to have something to do.

• **Respect the Narrators** — Remember that the Narrators have gone to a huge effort to create the story. Be nice to them. Request their help only when you really need it, and thank them whenever they do come to the rescue.

• **Roleplay, roleplay, roleplay** — Not everything has to come down to a challenge. Avoid "rulesmongering" and roleplay things out instead. A challenge should be a last resort, when players cannot agree upon what should happen. It's much easier and more fun to agree and storytell than it is to play Rock-Paper-Scissors. If you use the rules only as a contingency to fall back on, you emphasize storytelling.

• **Enjoy the surprises** — Be ready for surprises and learn to enjoy them. Don't throw a fit because the sheriff happened to show up right when you were about to make your move; the world your character occupies is full of mysteries; you shouldn't know how everything is going to work. Treat each situation as a puzzle, and attempt to deduce a solution. That's what your Narrator hopes you will do.

Don't bring out-of-game knowledge to your character. Just because you've read every **Werewolf** supplement cover to cover doesn't mean that your new cub character has any idea of what's happening to her. Bringing outside knowledge in game is called "metagaming," which is a polite name for "cheating."

• **Be patient with changes** — Be patient when things change in midstream. Tell the Narrator about your plot ideas before the game starts, so she has time to prepare for your plot's effects. If your ideas are good, the Narrator will probably thank you and write your plot into the next story.

# FAQ

*Which vampiric Disciplines work against Garou in the Umbra?*

None. Spirit Thaumaturgy (see **Laws of Elysium**) can detect a Garou in the Umbra, but that's it.

*Can Garou Gifts that heighten senses or reveal truth, such as Truth of Gaia, and Sense Wyrm and be used against vampires who employ Disciplines such as Mask of 1000 Faces, Illusion or Soul Mask?*

Yep. These Gifts allow a Mental Challenge against the vampire. A success sees through the Discipline, while a tie or loss still indicates that something is amiss — sort of that anxious feeling animals often exhibit before a big storm.

This sort of power is rife with possibilities for abuse ("*Well, I failed the test but I still know something's wrong so I blast the entire area with my shotgun and then jump on the bits.*"), so Storytellers need to watch its application carefully.

*Can a Garou be sensed and/or attacked when she "peeks" from the Umbra?*

No, nor can Disciplines be used against the Garou so long as he remains in the Umbra.

*How big does a reflective surface have to be for a Garou to use it to step sideways, and can it be in the Umbra?*

The "mirror" must be shiny enough for light to glint off of it; pools of quicksilver, actual mirrors and knife blades all work, and it can be in either the Realm (physical reality) or the Umbra. The size of the object used as a mirror does not matter, but small objects are more difficult for Garou to concentrate on.

*What is the highest possible level of the Gauntlet?*

Nine.

*Does a Garou have the breed of his father or mother?*

A Garou takes the breed of his mother.

*Don't Black Furies have to help female Black Spiral Dancers?*

No, a Fury can kill any female who is "of the Wyrm."

Tribal Advantages or Drawbacks never require a character to do anything obviously stupid or suicidal. They are meant to enhance roleplaying, not to provide cheap ways to kill off characters. On the other hand, players should be held to their Advantages and Drawbacks as much as possible. Use some common sense either way.

*Can a Garou's tribe, breed or auspice modifiers allow him to have more Traits than might normally be allowed for his Rank?*

Yes.

*When does a vampire become Wyrm-tainted and when does he become a Servant of the Wyrm?*

A vampire is designated as being Wyrm-tainted when he has three or more Beast Traits. A vampire becomes a Servant of the Wyrm when he has five Beast Traits. All Sabbat vampires are by definition Wyrm-tainted, and a Sabbat vampire becomes a Servant of the Wyrm when she acquires her third Path Trait.

*Can a Garou attempt to track someone who is using Unseen Presence?*

Yes, but only when in Lupus form or while using some form of heightened senses.

*Can two Garou with the Gift: Spirit Speech use the spirits' language to speak to one other?*

Yes. Just make certain that any characters eavesdropping on the conversation are aware that the discussion is taking place in *Spirit Speech*.

*What is the maximum number of times a character can have a particular Influence?*

Vampires, Garou, ghouls, and so on can only have an Influences up to the number listed in **Laws of the Wild** (pp. 29-37). What those specific Traits are is irrelevant.

*How often can a Garou burn a Rage Trait to move from Mortally Wounded to Incapacitated?*

She can do so until she runs out of Rage Traits.

*Does every Garou have a Tribal Advantage and Drawback?*

Tribal Advantages and Drawbacks are optional, but a character cannot have one without the other. The character must take both or neither.

*In* ***MET: Masquerade*** *and* ***Laws of the Night*** *it says that Gangrel vampires (known in the Savage West as the Dark Prowlers) do not show a taint of the Wyrm when dealing with the Garou. Only Gangrel with three or more Beast Traits bear the scent of the Wyrm. Is this true?*

Gangrel are the exception to the rule of *Sense Wyrm/Beast Traits*. They "smell" different to Garou because of their "beastly" nature between them, and thus don't hold to the standard rules vis-a-vis Wyrmitude. Use the ruling from **Laws of the Night**.

Incidentally, there is only one other exception: vampires who have achieved Golconda, or a spiritual balance of their vampiric and human natures. These Leeches never show any Wyrm Taint, but they are *exceedingly* rare.

*Are Kindred immune to possession by Banes?*

Nope.

*Are the Banes attracted by negative emotions that surround most Kindred dangerous to Garou?*

No. They're minor Gafflings, using the Kindred to find "food" for them. If they were strong enough to be a threat, they'd be able to hunt on their own.

*What's the maximum number of Influence Traits a character can have in one influence?*

The highest number listed on the chart is the highest degree of control possible by one person.

*Can a Garou go through a Ward in the Tellurian by stepping through the Umbra, or teleport into one?*

Yes. Garou are in the Penumbra, and unless the Ward was created there as well, it only applies to the Tellurian.

# Index

# Laws of the Night 1999

FINAL

# More Than Human

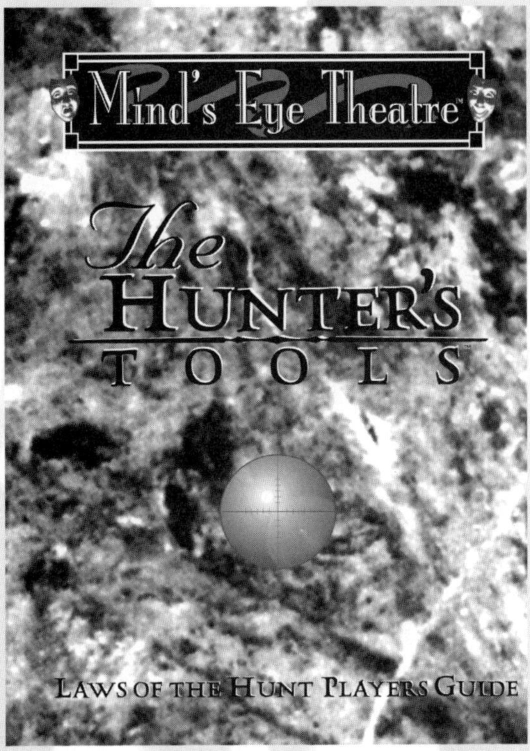


## More Than a Match for the Denizens of the Night

The secrets of the elusive Gypsies revealed.
The complete rules for hedge magic, with Master-class sorcery.
Additional psychic powers, merits and mortal organizations.

## May 1999

Mind's Eye Theatre